DALE BROWN'S DREAMLAND

Dale Brown's Dreamland: Satan's Tail is the seventh in a series of novels written by Dale Brown and Jim DeFelice, centred on 'Dreamland', a high-tech aerospace-weapons testing facility in Nevada. The previous volumes are *Dale Brown's Dreamland*, *Dale Brown's Dreamland: Nerve Centre*, *Dale Brown's Dreamland: Razor's Edge*, *Dale Brown's Dreamland: Piranha*, *Dale Brown's Dreamland: Strike Zone* and *Dale Brown's Dreamland: Armageddon*. Dale Brown is a former US Air Force captain and is the author of sixteen acclaimed *New York Times*-bestselling thrillers, all of which are available from HarperCollins.

'When a former pilot with years of experience in America's Strategic Air Command turns his hand to writing thrillers you can take their authenticity for granted. His writing is exceptional and the dialogue, plots and characters are first-class . . . far too good to be missed.'   *Sunday Mirror*

'You have to hug the seat when reading Dale Brown. The one-time US Air Force captain navigates his way at such a fearsome pace it is impossible to take your eyes off the page.'   *Oxford Times*

'A master at creating a sweeping epic and making it seem real.'   CLIVE CUSSLER

DALE BROWN'S
DREAMLAND

Satan's Tail

WRITTEN BY DALE BROWN
AND JIM DEFELICE

HarperCollins*Publishers*

HarperCollins*Publishers*
77–85 Fulham Palace Road,
Hammersmith, London W6 8JB

www.harpercollins.co.uk

This paperback edition 2005
1

First published in the USA by
HarperCollins 2005

A catalogue record for this book
is available from the British Library

ISBN 0 00 718254 6

Typeset in Times by
Palimpsest Book Production Limited,
Polmont, Stirlingshire

Printed and bound in Great Britain by
Clays Limited, St Ives plc

DREAMLAND
DUTY ROSTER

LIEUTENANT COLONEL TECUMSEH 'DOG' BASTIAN
The master of Dreamland, his 'bark' and 'bite' have won him many powerful Pentagon friends . . . and enemies.

CAPTAIN BREANNA BASTIAN STOCKARD
A woman in a man's Top Gun world, she will stay on the attack and keep her cool when the fighting spins out of control.

CAPTAIN HAROLD 'STORM' GALE, USN
Commander of Xray Pop, a cutting-edge naval squadron, his 'shoot first' attitude puts him on a dangerous collision course with Washington and Dog Bastian.

CAPTAIN DANNY FREAH
War hero and potential future political star, Dreamland needs his bravery and his brilliance more than ever before.

JED BARCLAY
Barely old enough to shave – a science 'whizz kid' and deputy to the National Security Advisor – he is Dreamland's link to the President and will be called upon to take the ultimate risk in the midst of crisis.

MAJOR MACK 'THE KNIFE' SMITH
An ace with more MiG kills than any flier since Vietnam, he was taken out of the game by a terrorist in Brunei . . . but nothing will keep him out of the fight.

Prelude:

Lost Comrades

The shock of light from the rising sun stopped Jennifer Gleason as she rounded the mountain. She raised her arm to ward off the glare, standing at the edge of the trail as her companion, Lt Colonel Tecumseh 'Dog' Bastian, continued to the pile of rocks. Dreamland – the United States Air Force High Technology Aerospace Weapons Center – stretched out before them on the floor of an ancient lake, its desert surface glowing as the pink fingers of the sun brushed back the shadows of the night. It was an awe-inspiring moment, the sort of thing that made you appreciate the enormity of creation and man's small place in God's scheme. Jennifer shuddered, humbled by the view.

The past few months had been a struggle for her, personally and professionally; they had shaken everyone at Dreamland. But standing here as the new day dawned, the scientist felt her hope and faith in the future renewed. She had come through a difficult storm, and if she was not the same person she had been before her troubles began, she was wiser and stronger in many ways.

She glanced upward, watching Dog scramble the last twenty feet to the monument they'd come to visit. It was a simple, polished stone, etched with the names of those who had died while serving at Dreamland. All were friends of hers.

Dog reached into his pocket for a small stone he'd taken from in front of his hut before they started their hike – a token, he said, of remembrance, not a fancy or formal thing, just a sign to the dead that he remembered their sacrifice. Important to him, which was what mattered.

Not a fancy or formal thing: That was Dog.

Jennifer watched as he placed the small stone in the pile at the base of the monument. His eyes had welled up, and she saw something she thought no one else in the world was privileged to see: a single tear slipping down his cheek.

Jennifer turned back to look at the base in case he glanced around and caught her staring. After a while he came over and put his arm around her waist.

'Beautiful view,' he said softly.

Jennifer went to the monument and paid her own respects, tracing each name with her finger. As they started down, they talked about breakfast and how hungry they were, but soon fell silent again. The long spells of quiet walking, both of them scrambling in the same direction, apart and yet together, were her favorite part of the trips they took.

When they rounded a curve about two-thirds of the way down, a pair of robot helicopter gunships undergoing tests at one of the test ranges a mile away roared into view. The small aircraft had stubby wings and counterrotating rotors; at rest, they looked like miniaturized Russian-made Kamov Ka-50 Hokums, with wing-mounted small jet engines and a stabilizer a good distance forward of the rear tail. In flight, however, they looked like spiders with bird-shaped beaks, flitting over the desert. Because of their similarity to the Russian gunship, the aircraft had been dubbed Werewolves, the English translation of Hokum.

Dog pulled up behind her, scanning the horizon before realizing what she was watching. The aircraft began unleashing a coordinated attack on an enemy 'tank' – a plywood box in a dugout ravine. Rockets spit from the pods under their forward wings – 'arms,' as the designers called them. The tank disappeared in a cloud of smoke.

'Good shots,' muttered Dog.

'Decent,' said Jennifer, whose team had helped develop the attack programs. 'I could have done better.'

'You're telling me you can beat the computer?'

'As if that were an accomplishment,' she said. 'I wrote most of the program.'

'Ray Rubeo says no human can beat it.'

'That's just Ray. I kind of like flying the Werewolf, to be honest,' she said. 'Maybe I should quit being a scientist and become a pilot full-time.'

He folded his arms and smirked. 'Take real flying lessons first. Then we'll talk about it.'

'I may. Then that smirk will be on the other side of your face.'

His smile grew wider. He leaned forward and kissed her, then started walking again.

'Good aircraft,' he said. 'Would've been useful in Brunei.'

Jennifer turned and followed him down the trail. She could tell he was brooding on the men he had lost, in Brunei and elsewhere.

'You want to strangle the people who killed them, don't you?' said Jennifer when they paused for a rest.

'Wouldn't we all?'

'Seriously, don't you want to?'

'Of course,' said Dog. He swung his upper body left, then right, loosening up his back and shoulder muscles. 'But I can't. I don't have the luxury of revenge.'

'It's a luxury?'

'Maybe that's not the right word,' he said.

'Would you if you could? Take revenge?'

'I don't know what I'd do if I could,' he said. He stared in the distance, gazing at the Werewolves; but probably not seeing them, she thought. 'I've taken revenge at times,' he added. 'I've pulled the trigger on people. As a pilot. You go after someone who shot at your friend, your wingmate. That's revenge.'

'Is it?'

'It's not enough, that's the problem,' said Dog. 'I could strangle each of the terrorists who fired the mortar that killed Kick, and it wouldn't be enough. You can't get enough. That's the problem, Jen. You can strangle them and pummel them and blast them to bits. It's not enough. That's the thing that gets you in the end. It's just not *even* – it's still lopsided.'

He started walking again. Jennifer watched him, wanting to know more but sensing she couldn't, or at least that she wasn't going to learn anything more by asking questions. When they came to the ledge above the road where they'd parked, she waited as he climbed down ahead of her, watching as he found the foot- and hand-holds. He stared at the rocks intently, but his hands seemed to move independently, the fingers nudging into the proper spots by touch.

'I love you,' she whispered, before descending on her own.

I

Gimp Boy

Dreamland
3 November 1997
0801

'Hey, gimp boy!'

Major Mack Smith stared straight ahead at Dreamland's administrative building, known as the 'Taj Mahal,' ignoring the razzing. He'd expected this sort of greeting, and after considerable thought decided there was only one thing to do: ignore it. Still, it wasn't easy.

Worse, though, was the indignity of being wheeled into the Taj by an airman who'd been detailed euphemistically as his bodyguard.

'Can't even push yourself up the ramp, huh? A wimp as well as a gimp.'

The concrete ramp to the entrance of the low-slung Taj had been poured in several sections, and there was about a three-quarter-inch rise between the first and second. It wasn't the sort of thing someone walking would notice, but for someone in a wheelchair – especially if, like Mack, they weren't used to it – three-quarters of an inch rattled the teeth. He grimaced as the wheels cleared the curb.

'Sorry, sir,' said the airman, so flustered he stopped dead on the ramp.

Mack curled his fingers around the armrests of the chair, pressing out his anger. 'Not a problem.'

'Sorry,' said the poor kid, pushing again.

Mack's tormentor, sitting by the door to the building, laughed. 'Bumpy ride, gimp boy?' he said as Mack neared.

'Good morning, Zen,' said Mack.

'How's it feel?'

'It feels good to be back at Dreamland,' said Mack.

'How's the wheelchair feel?' said Zen.

The automatic doors flew open, but Mack's airman, thinking that Mack wanted to talk to Major Jeff 'Zen' Stockard, remained stationary. Mack glanced back at the airman. Pimples and all, the kid was looking at him with *pity*.

He felt sorry for him.

Sorry for Major Mack 'the Knife' Smith, holder of not one, but *two* stinking Air Force crosses. Mack Smith, who had shot down more stinking MiGs than any man since the Vietnam War. Mack Smith, who had run a small country's air force and saved Las Vegas from nuclear catastrophe.

Mack stinking Smith, now in a wheelchair because of some maniac crazy terrorist in Brunei.

A wheelchair that the doctors agreed he'd be getting out of any day now . . .

The kid felt sorry for him.

Sorry!

Well the *hell* with that.

'I can take it from here, airman. Thank you for your time,' said Mack. He put his hands on the wheels of his chair and pushed himself forward.

Just as he did, the doors started to close. For a moment Mack thought he was going to crash into them, which would perhaps have been the ultimate embarrassment. Fortunately, they slid back and he made it inside without a crash.

'Don't tire yourself out,' called Zen after him. 'I want to race you later.'

'That was a bit over the top.'

Zen whirled his head around, surprised by his wife's voice. Breanna had come out from the building while he was watching Mack make his maiden progression in a wheelchair.

Zen shifted his wheelchair around to face her. 'Somebody's got to put him in his place.'

'You're being way too cruel, Zen.'

'Turnaround is fair play.'

'He never tormented you like that.'

'No, he just made me a cripple.'

Zen, controlling two robot aircraft as well as his own, had been engaged in a mock dogfight with Mack nearly two years before, when one of the robots clipped his wing at very low altitude. The ensuing crash had cost Zen the use of his legs. Technically, Mack had not caused the crash – but in every other way, he had, egging him on, doing much the same thing that Zen had just done to him, and cheating on the accepted rules for the engagement.

'I never thought there would be a day when Mack Smith outclassed Zen Stockard,' said Bree.

'You going for breakfast?' Zen asked, changing the subject.

Breanna frowned at him, but then said, 'I have an hour to kill before prepping for my test flight. I thought I'd get some breakfast over at the Red Room. I haven't had a good omelet since Brunei.'

'I'll walk with you. No, wait.' He put his hands on the wheels and pulled back for a launch. 'I'll race you.'

Aboard DD(L) 01 *Abner Read,*
off the Horn of Africa
3 November 1997
1902

Captain Harold 'Storm' Gale put the binoculars down and folded his arms across his chest. The sea ahead of *Abner Read* was mottled and gray; the sun had just set, and an unusually thick storm front sent a light mist across his bow, obscuring not just his sailor's vision, but the long-range infrared sensors that were looking for telltale signs of ships in the distance.

Perfect conditions for pirates. And perfect conditions for hunting them.

'Two boats,' said the *Abner Read*'s captain, Commander Robert Marcum. He was looking over the shoulder of the petty officer manning the integrated imaging system on the bridge to Storm's left. The screen synthesized

14

data from several different sensors, presenting them in an easy-to-read format. 'Just closing to five thousand meters.'

'Adjust our course,' said Storm. He walked from the window at the front of the bridge to the holographic display, where data from the Tactical Warfare Center – his ship's version of a combat information center – was projected, showing the *Abner Read*'s position and that of the oil tanker they had been shadowing. The holographic display presented a real-time view of the ocean created from ship's sensors, complete with a computerized version of the surrounding geographic features and a rundown of threats within sensor range. The display could show everything from standard chart data to the range and likelihood of one of the *Abner Read*'s Harpoon missiles hitting a target; it was one of three aboard the ship, allowing the group commander to choose whether to be in the Tactical Warfare Center or on the bridge during the engagement. (It also allowed the Navy to designate a ship's captain as overall group commander, a plan contemplated for the future.) Storm spent most of his time in Tac, which would have been the 'traditional' place for a group warfare commander to station himself; tonight, the lure of the hunt had drawn him here so he might actually see his prey.

Storm studied the three-dimensional image, gauging his location and that of the other ships. The contacts were identified by the sensors as fast patrol boats – small, light ships equipped with a deck gun, grenade launchers, and possibly torpedoes. They were the modern-day equivalent of the PT boats that America had used to help turn the tide in Guadalcanal and other fierce, shallow-water conflicts in the Pacific during World War II.

The question was: Whose boats were they? One of Oman's or Egypt's accompanying local merchants, in which case they were friendly? One of four known to be operated by Somalian fanatics turned pirates, in which case they were hostile? Or one of the half dozen belonging to Yemen, in which case they were somewhere in the middle?

The three other vessels in Littoral Surface Action Group XP One were several nautical miles to the south, too far away to help if these turned out to be the pirates he was hunting. This was the *Abner Read*'s fight to win or lose.

Storm reached to his belt and keyed his mike to talk to Lt Commander Jack 'Eyes' Eisenberg, who was in the Tactical Warfare Center one deck below the bridge. His wireless headset and its controller were linked to a ship-board fiber-optics network that could instantly connect him not only with all the sailors on the *Abner Read*, but the commanders of the vessels in the rest of his task group. With the touch of a button, he could click into one of several preset conferenced channels, allowing all of his war fighters to speak to each other and with him in battle.

'Eyes, what do we have?'

'Two boats. Roughly the size of Super Dvoras. They should be our pirates.'

'If they are, there'll be at least two more.'

16

'We're looking. Should we go to active radar?'

'No, let's hold off. No sense telling them we're here.'

Past experience told them that the small boats could detect radar; more than likely they would run away, as they had several times before.

The contacts had been found by a towed array equipped with a passive sonar system to listen to the sea around it. Designed for use in the comparatively shallow waters, the system compiled data on surface as well as submarine vessels. Like devices such as the AN/SQR-18A (V) Sonar Tactical Towed Array System – used on the Knox-class frigates from the late 1970s on – the Littoral Towed Array System, or LITAS, was built around a series of hydrophones that listened for different sounds in the water. These were then interpreted and translated into ship contacts.

In theory, LITAS could hear anything within a twelve-mile radius of the ship, even in littoral waters where sounds were plentiful and easily altered by the shallow floor of the ocean. But like much else aboard the *Abner Read* and its companion vessels, the new technology still needed some adjustments; five miles had proven the average effective range thus far on the voyage, and the presence of a very loud vessel such as the oil tanker tended to mask noises very close to it. The approaching storm would also limit the range.

The four-ship war group Storm headed was as much about testing new technology as she was about catching the pirates. And the *Abner Read* was the centerpiece of both the task group and the tests. Named for a World War

II destroyer that fought bravely in the Pacific until being sunk by kamikazes, the new ship had all the spirit of her predecessor but looked nothing like her. In fact, though she was called a destroyer, she bore little resemblance to other destroyers in the U.S. Navy – or any other navy.

It had often been said that the U.S. Navy's Arleigh Burke destroyers represented the culmination of nearly one hundred years of warship design. Truly, the Arleigh Burkes were the head of the class, in many ways as powerful as World War II battleships and as self-sufficient. The *Abner Read* showed what the next one hundred years would bring. Indeed, there were many who hadn't wanted to call her a destroyer at all; proposals had ranged from 'littoral warfare ship' to 'coastal cruiser.' The Navy might be ready for a radical new weapon, but a new name seemed too much of a break with tradition, and so she was designated a 'destroyer, littoral' – or DD(L) – the first and so far only member of her class.

At 110 meters, she was a good deal shorter than the Arleigh Burke class, closer in size to a frigate or even a corvette. Where the Arleigh Burkes had a bulky silhouette dominated by a massive radar bulkhead, a large mast, and thick stacks, the *Abner Read* looked like a pyramid on a jackknife. A pair of angled pillboxes sat on the forward section of the deck, which was so low to the water, the gun housings were generally wet. Her stern looked like a flat deck; the section over what would have held the rudder on another ship was open to the ocean, as if the sea wanted to keep a finger on her back. The ship didn't have one rudder – it had several, located in strategic spots along the tumbleform hull. The rudder and hull design made the *Abner Read* extremely maneuverable at low and high speed. And while the exotically shaped underside and wet deck took a bit of getting used to, the *Abner Read* had remarkably good sea-keeping abilities for a small ship. It didn't so much float across the waves as blow right through them. Stormy ocean crossings were *almost* comfortable, certainly more so than in a conventional ship of the same size, even though the vessel had been designed primarily for shallow coastal waters.

The screws that propelled the ship were located almost amidships, recessed in a faceted structure that helped reduce their sound. They were powered by gas turbines whose exhausts were cooled before being released through the baffled and radar-protected funnel. The engines could propel the *Abner Read* to about forty knots in calm water. More important, she could sustain that speed for forty-eight hours without noticeable strain.

The three smaller craft that had accompanied the *Abner Read* to the Gulf of Aden looked a bit like miniature versions of her. Officially called Littoral Warfare Craft, or LWCs, they were designed from the keel up to work with the DD(L). Not only did their captains receive orders from a commander in the DD(L)'s tactical center, but the ship received sensor data as well – each had an integrated imaging system on her bridge identical to the one on the *Abner Read*. The vessels were crewed by only fifteen men, and in fact could be taken into combat by as few as five, though the mission had shown that a somewhat larger complement would be more comfortable. About 40 meters long, they were roughly the size of a coastal patrol boat and needed only twelve feet of draft at full load displacement. The vessels had a 25mm gun on the forward deck, a pair of multipurpose missile launchers – loaded, in this case, with Harpoon antiship missiles – toward the stern, and below-waterline torpedo and mine dispensers. Smaller than the *Abner Read*, they had a correspondingly smaller radar signature. Their long, knifelike bows and finlike superstructures had led inevitably to a warlike nickname: Shark Boats.

XP Group 1 – better known as Xray Pop – was one of twelve proposed integrated littoral warfare combat groups that would eventually combine surface warfare ships with unmanned helicopters and aerial vehicles, small submarines, and Marine combat teams. But like Xray Pop, the littoral warfare concept was still very much a work in progress. The Navy had said 'XP' stood for 'extended patrol.' The sailors who manned the ships knew it actually meant 'expect problems.'

Storm firmly believed littoral warfare was the Navy's future. The teething pains he suffered on this maiden mission would help shape warfare for the next fifty years. He'd freed Xray Pop from the engineering spaces and Pentagon offices and dragged littoral warfare out into the real world, and he meant to show it would work.

Which meant sinking the bastards in the little boats.

'One of the unidentified patrol craft is heading in our direction,' said Eyes.

'Do they see us?'

'Not sure.'

Storm moved back to the window of the bridge. The UAVs designed to operate off the ship's fantail were running nearly eighteen months behind schedule. Without them, the *Abner Read* had no beyond-the-horizon capability and in fact had a very limited weapons range. Storm hadn't intended on operating completely without airborne cover – a pair of P-3 Orions from the Seventh Fleet had been moved up to Kuwait to provide reconnaissance during his operation. But the P-3s had been pulled out for higher priority missions in the Philippines, and the promised replacements had not materialized. And while he had been offered helicopters, these were still back in Pearl Harbor, as near as he could determine.

Not that he would have wanted them anyway. They were too big for the *Abner Read*'s low-slung hangar area, which had been designed for the UAVs. They'd have had to be lashed to the helipad.

'More contacts,' said Eyes. 'Two more patrol boats. I think these are the Somalians, Captain.'

'They're a bit far from home,' said Storm, feeling his heart beginning to pound. 'Are you sure these are not Yemen craft?'

'We're working on it.'

Storm could hear the voices of the others in the background, ringing out as more information flooded the sensors. The Tactical Warfare Center was a Combat Information Center on steroids. A holographic display similar to the smaller one on the bridge dominated the compartment. Synthesized from all of the available sensor inputs on the ship, as well as external ones piped in over the shared Littoral Warfare Network, the display showed the commander everything in the battle area. It also could provide scenarios for confronting an enemy, which made it useful for planning. Tac also held the *Abner Read*'s radar, sonar, and weapons stations.

Two more contacts were made, then a third: Storm felt the adrenaline rising throughout the ship, the scent of blood filtering through the environmental system – the *Abner Read* was on the hunt.

'Two more boats. Small coastal craft.'

'No markings.'

'Deck guns on one.'

'Another contact. Something bigger.'

'Storm, we have an Osa II,' said Eyes. 'Definitely a Yemen boat – what's he doing out?'

The Osa II was a Russian-made missile boat that carried Soviet-era SSN-2A/B 'Styx' surface-to-surface missiles. A potent craft when first designed, the Osas were now long in the tooth but packed a reasonable wallop if well-skippered and in good repair. The Yemen ships were neither.

Storm studied the tactical display. The Osa II flickered at the far end of the hologram, about five miles away.

'Looks like they're getting ready to attack the tanker,' said Commander Marcum.

'Good,' Storm told the ship's captain.

'Gunfire! They're shooting across the tanker's bow!' Eyes paused for only a second, gathering information from one of the crewmen manning the high-tech systems below. 'The oil tanker is radioing for assistance. They are under attack.'

'Weapons,' said Storm.

'Weapons!' repeated the captain, addressing his weapons officer.

'Weapons,' bellowed the officer on duty in the weapons center, Ensign Hacienda. The ensign's voice was so loud Storm might have been able to hear it without the communications gear.

'Prepare to fire the gun,' said Marcum.

'Ready, sir.'

'At your order, Storm.'

The gun was a 155mm Advanced Gun System, housed in the sleek box on the forward deck. The weapon fired a variety of different shells, including one with a range of nearly one hundred miles that could correct its flight path while on course for its target. At the moment, the *Abner Read* carried only unguided or 'ballistic' ammunition, which had a range of roughly twenty-two miles – more than enough to pound one of the boats firing on the tanker.

'Eyes, give them fair warning,' said Storm.

'Aye, Captain.' The disdain for the rules of engagement was evident in his voice. Storm shared the sentiment, though he did not voice his opinion.

'No acknowledgment. Attack is continuing. We –'

Eyes was nearly drowned out by a stream of curses from one of the men on duty in the Tactical Center. Storm knew exactly what had happened – the computer had gone off-line again, probably as they attempted to transmit a fresh warning in Arabic using the computer system's prerecorded message capability. It was one of the more problematic modules in the integrated computing system. It would take at least a full minute to bring it back.

The tanker's running lights were visible in the distance. Storm picked up his glasses and scanned the horizon. They were still too far from the small patrol boats to see them, even with the infrared.

'Missile in the air!'

The warning came not from one of the men on the bridge or the Tactical Center, but from the computer system, which used a real-language module for important warnings. Talking wasn't the only thing it did: In the time it took Storm to glance down at the threat screen on the *Abner Read*'s 'dashboard' at the center of the bridge, the computer had managed to identify the weapon and predict its course.

A Styx antiship missile.

'Well, we know which side he's on,' said Storm sarcastically. 'Countermeasures. Target the Osa II.'

The ship's captain moved to implement the instructions. He didn't need Storm to tell him what to do – and in fact he wouldn't have been ship's captain of the *Abner Read* if he weren't among the most competent commanders in the Navy – but he also knew Storm well enough to realize the captain wouldn't sit in the background, especially in combat.

'Computer IDs the missile as a type P-20M with an MS-2A seeker,' said Eyes.

The MS-2A was a solid-state radar that featured the ability to home in on the electronic countermeasures – or ECMs – being used to jam it.

'Is he locked on us?' asked Commander Marcum.

'Negative. Trajectory makes it appear as if he fired without radar, maybe hoping we'd go to the ECMs and he'd get a lock.'

Or it was fired ineptly, which Storm thought more likely. Nonetheless, they had to act as if it were the former.

The holographic information system projected the missile's path – a clean miss. As Eyes said, the missile was aimed well wide of them; it would hit the ocean about a half mile to the south.

'Belay ECMs,' said Marcum. 'Repeat: no counter-measures. Target the missile boat with our gun.'

Storm nodded. Marcum *really* understood how to fight these guys. He'd make a good group commander down the road.

'Missile is on terminal attack,' warned the computer.

The Styx missile slid downward, riding just a few feet above the waves, where it was extremely difficult to stop. One of the Phalanx 20mm Gatling guns that provided close-in antiair coverage rotated at the rear of the ship, tracking the antiship missile as it passed. A yellow cone glowed in the holographic display, and the gun engaged, obliterating the missile at long range, even though it wasn't a threat.

A problem with the program of the automated defensive weapons system, Storm noted. It tended to be some-what overprotective – not necessarily a bad thing, but something that could stand a little tweaking.

'Torpedoes!' sang the computer.

'Toward us or the tanker?' Storm demanded.

'Not sure,' said Eyes, who was scrambling to make sense of what was going on.

'Who fired the torpedoes? The missile boat?' said Marcum.

'Negative – they must have come from the patrol craft. That's a new development.'

The patrol craft were relatively small, and until now had not been seen with torpedo tubes on their decks. Storm decided this was a compliment, in a way – after a week of running off, they'd decided to change their tactics.

The tanker was about three miles off their port bow, with the attacking pirates slightly to starboard. This was not the usual pattern of attacks – ordinarily four or five fast patrol boats and a few small speedboats would charge a slow-moving, heavily laden ship, fire a few dozen slugs to get its attention, and then send a heavily armed boarding party aboard. The ship's captain would be persuaded to phone his company headquarters and have a transfer made to an offshore account specially set up for the night. Once the transfer was made – the amount would be about ten thousand dollars, relatively small considering the value of the cargo – the tanker would be allowed to go on its way. The small 'fee' charged helped guarantee that the pirates would get it; most multinational companies considered it a pittance, cheaper than a port tax – or trying to prosecute the perpetrators.

'Those torpedoes are definitely headed in our direction,' said Eyes. 'We don't have guidance data.'

Marcum ordered evasive action. As the helmsman put

26

the *Abner Read* into a sharp turn, the ship's forward torpedo tubes opened, expelling a pair of small torpedo-like devices. They swam about a quarter of a mile; at that point, the skin peeled away from their bellies and they began emitting a thick fog of bubbles. The air in the water created a sonic fog in the water similar to the noise made by the ship. The destroyer, meanwhile, swung onto a new course designed to minimize its profile to the enemy.

'They must have guessed we'd be nearby,' said Marcum. 'I think they homed in on our radio signal when we tried to warn the oiler and threw everything they had at us. Rules of engagement, Captain. They make no sense.'

'Noted for the record,' said Storm.

And wholeheartedly agreed with.

'Tanker captain says he's been fired on,' reported communications. 'Asking for assistance.'

'Inform him we intend to help him,' said Storm.

The ship took a hard turn to port, still working to duck the rapidly approaching torpedoes.

'Steady, now, Jones,' Marcum told the man at the helm as the ship leaned hard toward the water. The helmsman had put a little too much into the maneuver; the *Abner Read*'s bow tucked well below the waves as she spun. The ship forgave him, picking her bow up and stabilizing in the proper direction.

'Torpedo one has passed. Torpedo two has self-destructed,' said the computer.

'They're running for it,' said Eyes.

'They can't run fast enough,' answered Storm. 'Full active radar. Target the missile ship. I want him for dinner.'

Dog looked up at the familiar knock. Chief Master Sergeant Terrence 'Ax' Gibbs appeared in the doorway, head cocked in a way that indicated the chief wanted to talk to the colonel in confidence for a few moments. Bastian might be the commander of Dreamland – the Air Force's secret high-tech development facility in the Nevada desert – but Ax Gibbs was the oil that made the vast and complicated engine run smoothly.

'Chief?'

'Couple of things, couple of things,' said Ax, sliding into the office.

Dog knew from the tone in the chief's voice that he was going to once again bring up their chronic personnel shortages. He reached to his coffee cup for reinforcement.

'Need a refresher?' asked Ax.

'No thanks.'

'I've been looking at head counts . . .' Ax began, introducing a brief lecture that compared Dreamland's overall workforce to a number of other Air Force commands and facilities, as well as DARPA – the Department of Defense Advanced Research Program Agency – and a number of private industry think tanks. The study was impressive for both its breadth and depth. Ax's numbers not only compared overall positions, but broke them down to real-life instances, such as the number of people sweeping the floors. (Dreamland had exactly two people doing this,

28

both airmen with a long list of other duties. The men had been drafted – to put it euphemistically – into the service when budget cuts eliminated the contract civilian cleaners.)

'. . . and we're not even considering the fact that a good portion of the head count here is also involved in Whiplash,' added Ax. He was referring to Dreamland's 'action' component, which included a ground special operations team, headed by Danny Freah, as well as whatever aircraft were needed for the mission.

'Preaching to the converted,' said Dog.

'Yes, but I do have an idea,' said Ax. 'Congresswoman Kelly.'

'Congresswoman Kelly?'

'Congresswoman due in next week on the VIP tour,' said Ax. 'She has a staffer who has a brother in the Air Force. If a nonclassified version of the report were to find its way into the staffer's hands . . .'

'No thank you,' said Dog curtly. He reached for some of the papers Ax had brought in.

'Colonel –'

'I don't want to play Washington games.'

'With respect, sir.'

Dog put down the papers and looked up at the chief. Ax's lips were pressed together so firmly that his jowls bulged.

'Ax, you know you can speak freely to me any time,' said Dog. 'Hell, I expect it. None of this "with respect" shit. You want to call me a jackass, go for it. You've earned it.'

'Colonel . . . Dog.' The chief pulled over the nearby chair and sat down, leaning forward with his elbows on the desk. 'Your people are really busting. Really, really busting.'

'I know that.'

'We *have* to get more people here. And that's true every-where. Dr Rubeo was saying –'

'Ray could find a cloud over the desert, and does so regularly.'

'Even the scientists are overworked. Jennifer has what, five different projects going? She's been the main test pilot on the Werewolves after Sandy Culver and Zen. Did you know that?'

'Did I?' Dog laughed. 'She brags about it all the time.'

'Well, now I like her a lot, but she has other things she's gotta do. And the rest of the people here, hell, they're as bad or worse. Civilian scientists, military officers, and enlisted – they're all overworked workaholics. Problem is, Colonel, sooner or later the people who can leave *will* leave. Sooner or later, when you haven't had a chance to sleep in a week, it catches up to you.'

'Who hasn't slept in a week?'

Ax rose from the chair.

'I'll do what I can, Ax,' said Dog. 'But I'm not sneaking through the back corridors of Congress to get what we need.'

'Yes, sir. Major Smith is outside, reporting for duty.'

Ax opened the door before Dog could say anything else. Mack Smith was sitting in the outer office, flirting with the secretary.

'Mack,' said Dog, getting up. 'I thought you were in rehab.'

'I am,' said Smith. He turned awkwardly in his wheelchair and rolled toward the doorway. Even though the door had been widened after Zen returned to active duty, it was a tight squeeze. It took Mack a few seconds to maneuver through the doorway.

'Major Mack Smith, formerly of the Brunei Royal Air Force, reporting for active duty,' said Smith.

'I thought we agreed you would use the facilities here but wait to get back to work until the doctors gave you a clean bill of health.'

'Ah, the doctors say I'm fine.'

'The doctors said there's no reason you won't get your legs back. That's not quite fine.'

'What do the doctors know? Besides, Zen didn't wait.'

'Zen's circumstances were different,' said Dog.

'Sure. He had a high-powered lawyer read the Air Force and the DoD the riot act,' said Mack. 'And he was related to the base commander.'

Dog bristled. Zen was his son-in-law, but he had had nothing to do with his reinstatement.

'Zen was posted here before I arrived,' said Dog.

'Look, Colonel, the thing is – I'm bored out of my skull, right? I'm going through rehab. I have to come onto the base every day. Might as well put me to work, right?'

'It's not that I don't want to put you to work, Mack.'

'I can get a high-priced lawyer if I have to,' said Mack. 'I hear Zen's is available. Us gimps have to hang together.'

Dog felt his face flush at the word 'gimps.'

'You're worried that I won't do the crap work, right?' added Mack. 'You're looking at a new man, Colonel. Brunei taught me a lot.'

'One of the things it taught you is that you don't like administrative crap work,' said Dog. 'You told me that yourself. Several times.'

'I don't like it, but I'll do it. Same as you. We're not that different, you and me, Colonel. We like to have our sleeves rolled up,' he added.

God help me, thought Dog, if I have *anything* in common with Mack Smith. 'All right,' he said. 'There are a lot of things that need to be done. None of them involve flying.'

'Who's flying? Bring them on.'

'The Piranha program needs a liaison. Someone who can work with the Navy people to help them move it to the next phase.'

'Right up my alley,' said Mack. 'A big part of my job in Brunei was interfacing with Navy people.'

He was referring to his position as head of the Brunei air force, which had in fact required him to work with members of the country's other military services. From all reports – including Mack's – it had not gone well.

Piranha was one of several Navy projects being developed under contract at Dreamland. An underwater robot probe, it could be controlled by ship, submarine, or aircraft and operate for several weeks without needing to be refueled. The technology that guided it was similar to the technology used in the Flighthawks, which was one of several reasons it was being developed here. Dreamland had used Piranha to halt a nuclear war between India and China.

'What else do you want me to do?' asked Mack.

'Let's start there. Remember, you're a liaison, *not* the program director.'

'I'm the idea guy,' said Mack. 'Got it.'

'Not exactly.'

'Don't worry, Colonel. I have it. Listen, I really appreciate this. I won't forget it, believe me. I'm happy to be back. Like I said, Brunei taught me a lot. This is a new Mack Smith you're looking at.'

As the major rolled out of the office, Dog struggled to keep his opinion of how long the new Mack Smith would last to himself.

Aboard the *Abner Read*
3 November 1997
1942

'We have a lock on the Osa missile boat,' reported Weapons.

'Marcum, he's yours to sink,' said Storm.

'One of the patrol boats is turning toward us,' warned Eyes.

'Torpedo in the water,' warned the computer.

'Fire,' said Commander Marcum.

A deep-throated rap from the front of the ship drowned out the acknowledgment as the number one gun began spitting out shells, one every five seconds. The holographic display did not delineate every hit – the designers thought this would be too distracting – but the target flashed red as the barrage continued.

'Direct hit,' reported Eyes. 'Target demolished.'

'Evasive action,' said Marcum. 'Evade the torpedoes.'

The crew sprang to comply. One of the torpedoes stayed on target with the *Abner Read* despite the countermeasures, and the lithe vessel swayed as the helmsman initiated a fresh set of maneuvers. The torpedo finally passed a hundred yards off their port side, detonating a few seconds later.

'Close the distance on the patrol boat that fired at us,' Marcum told the man at the wheel.

The helmsman pushed at the large lever that worked the computer governing the ship's engines. They were already at full speed.

'UI-1 is about a minute from Yemen waters,' reported Eyes. 'Outside of visual range. The others are well beyond him.'

'I have a lock on target designated as UI-1,' said the weapons officer.

'Captain, it's my responsibility to report that the target ship is approaching Yemen territorial waters,' said Commander Marcum. 'Our rules of engagement prohibit sinking a vessel outside of neutral waters.'

'Are you giving me advice?' Storm asked.

'Sir, I'm operating under your orders. I was to notify you of our status prior to engagement . . .' Commander Marcum paused. 'I want to sink the son of a bitch myself.'

'Noted. Sink him.'

'Weapons: fire!'

'Firing.'

Both guns rumbled. Within thirty seconds the patrol craft had been obliterated.

The three other pirate vessels had disappeared. Relatively small contacts, they were easily lost in the clutter near the irregular coast. The computer generated approximate positions from their last known citing, rendering them yellow clouds in the holographic projection. They were well inside Yemen territorial waters – out of bounds.

Storm turned his attention to the three Shark Boats. He directed *One* and *Two* to sail westward, hoping to catch the patrol boats if they went in that direction. The third would remain to the east, in case they went that way. The *Abner Read,* meanwhile, would search for survivors from one of the two vessels they had just sunk; if recovered, he might be persuaded to share what he knew.

Storm clicked his communications channel into a public address mode that allowed him to communicate not just with all personnel aboard the *Abner Read*, but with everyone in the combat group.

'All hands, this is Captain Gale,' said Storm. 'The DD (L) 01 *Abner Read* has sunk its first enemy combatants in action this November 3, 1997. I was privileged to witness the finest crew in the U.S. Navy undertake this historic mission, and I commend everyone, from Commander Robert Marcum to Seaman Bob Anthony – Bobby, I think you're our youngest crewman,' he added. Storm turned and saw Marcum grinning and nodding. 'It was a hell of a job all around. Xray Pop has been christened, ladies and gentlemen. Now look sharp; there's still a great deal to be done tonight.'

**Humboldt County,
northwestern California
3 November 1997
1205**

Lieutenant Kirk 'Starship' Andrews got out of the car he
had rented in Los Angeles and walked across the gravel
parking lot toward the church. He could hear the strains
of an organ as he approached; he was late for his friend's
memorial service.

He was thankful, actually. He felt he owed it to Kick
to be here, but didn't particularly want to talk to anyone,
Kick's parents especially. He just didn't know what to
say.

The music stopped just as Starship came in through the
back door. He moved quickly toward the last pew in the
small church, eyes cast toward the floor. The minister
began reading from the Second Book of Chronicles, a
selection from the Old Testament of the Bible concerning
the bond between Solomon and God: ' "Give me now
wisdom and knowledge, that I may go out and come in
before this people." '

The passage spoke of wisdom and riches; the minister
used it as a starting point as he asked God for the
wisdom needed to accept a young man's death. The
reverend spoke frankly of the difficulty of comprehending the loss. 'Lieutenant James Colby was a hero,'
he said. 'But that does not make his loss any easier for
us to take.'

Was Kick a hero? wondered Starship. He was a decent

pilot and a hard worker; he'd been brave and seen combat. But was he a *hero?*

Kick had died in the line of duty, caught in a Megafortress when it crashed during an aborted takeoff in Malaysia after guerrillas had seized the kingdom of Brunei. Starship had been on the aircraft himself, strapped in next to Kick on the control deck for the Flighthawks. The fact that he was here and Kick wasn't, he thought, was just a matter of dumb, stupid luck. Bad luck.

If he had died, would *he* be a hero?

Starship listened as the service continued with different friends recounting their memories of Kick. He'd gotten his nickname not from the high school football team – which was the story Kick had told – but from peewee soccer. It came during his first game as a six-year-old, when he scored a goal. The nickname had stuck from there, becoming widespread in high school, where he'd switched to football and set a county scoring record booting extra points and field goals.

Starship's mind drifted as the service continued. If the luck had run differently – if he had been the one who got the freak piece of shrapnel, and the sudden shock that combined to do Kick in – what would people be saying about him?

Smart kid – number three in his high school class and in the top five percent at the Academy.

Should have chosen a few more gut classes and got top honors.

Won an assignment to Dreamland on the cutting edge of aviation.

A mistake. He was flying robot aircraft, glorified UAVs. The computer did most of the work. It was like sitting at a desk all day.

'I'll bet you're Starship.'

Starship turned and saw that a woman had come into his pew from the side. Maybe five-two, with dark hair and green eyes, she looked a lot like Kick.

'Alice,' she whispered. 'Kick's sister.'

'Hi.' He stuck his hand out.

'We're glad you could come.'

'Yeah, um, I'm sorry.'

'I know.' Distress flickered across her face, but then cleared. 'We're having – my parents are inviting people over later. You should stop by.'

'I kinda gotta get back,' Starship lied.

'Well, OK. But say hello to them on the way out.' She smiled – this time with visible effort – and then slipped out of the pew. Starship watched as she slid into another pew farther up. Somehow this made him feel better, as if he hadn't been singled out, and when Kick's parents asked him at the end of the service if he would stop by 'just for coffee,' he agreed and got directions.

Dreamland
1231

Mack felt the muscles in his shoulders tense into hard rocks as he lowered himself into the pool. He had to relax if he was going to do the exercise, but relaxing on command was just about the most difficult thing in the world to do. He lowered his gaze to the surface of the pool and concentrated on breathing slowly, very slowly, as slowly as he possibly could, taking long, deep breaths, as one of the physical therapists at the hospital had recommended.

'All right now, Major, you want to start with a nice, easy breaststroke,' said Penny Hartung, treading water next to him.

'Yeah, that's what I'm going to do,' he said. But he didn't let go of the rail, afraid that he would sink into the water like a stone.

Which was impossible, since he was wearing a life preserver. But fear wasn't necessarily rational.

'You all right?' asked Frank DeLia, the other therapist. Frank was kneeling above him at the poolside.

'Oh yeah, I'm good,' said Mack, finally pushing away. He fought against the impulse to paddle madly, moving his arms out slowly as he'd been told.

'Legs now. Legs,' said Penny, hovering beside him.

Yup, legs, Mack thought. *Legs, legs, legs.*

The large beam that had fallen across his back and legs after the terrorist blew himself up had temporarily shocked his backbone. The medical explanation was somewhat longer and more complicated, but the bottom line was that he had temporarily lost the use of his legs. The thing was, no one could say how long 'temporarily' was supposed to be. He'd already seen several specialists; he got the impression they all thought he should be walking by now.

Not that he didn't agree.

Mack pushed his arms out and willed his legs to kick. He didn't feel them move. He thought his hips wiggled a little.

'Legs,' repeated Penny. 'Legs.'

He got a mouthful of water as he started to lose momentum. He had his whole upper body working, and thought his legs must be working as well.

'Push, push,' said Penny.

'Doing it.' Mack checked his position against the far side of the pool. He'd gone maybe five feet. 'Legs,' he said himself, deciding he might do better if he gave himself a pep talk. 'Legs. Let's do it.'

There was a tremendous splash on the other side of the pool: Zen, who worked out here regularly.

'Come on, gimp boy. That the best you can do?'

Mack ignored Zen, keeping his head toward the other side of the pool room. He sensed Zen swimming toward him. Determined to ignore him, he concentrated on doing a sidestroke, or at least as much of a sidestroke as he could manage.

'Your arms are punier than Olive Oyl's,' said Zen.

Legs, Mack thought. *Legs*.

'Use your damn legs,' said Zen.

'I'm trying,' said Mack between his teeth.

'Not hard enough.'

'Yeah. I am.' The burn in Mack's arms was too much; he stopped and took a breather.

'Don't be such a damn wimp,' said Zen. He plunged beneath the water, stroking away.

40

It occurred to Mack that swimming underwater when you couldn't use your legs to help must be – *was* – extremely difficult. But then, just about *everything* you did when you couldn't use your legs was extremely difficult. And Zen didn't complain or ask for help – hell, he got mad when people tried to help him.

Which Mack understood. He'd thought after Zen's crash that Zen got mad only with him, because he held a grudge. Now he realized Zen got mad with everyone. The reason was simple. Most of the people who wanted to help you – not necessarily all, but most – were thinking, *You poor little baby, you. Let me help you.*

For someone like Zen or Mack, being treated like a baby, being pitied – *well the hell with that!*

But you needed help sometimes. That was the worst part of it. Sometimes you just couldn't drag yourself up a full flight of stairs, not and bring your wheelchair with you.

'Ready to start again, Major?' asked Penny.

'Oh yeah. Starting,' said Mack, pushing.

'Ten laps, gimp boy!' yelled Zen from the other side of the pool. 'You owe me ten laps.'

'Right,' muttered Mack.

'I'm going to do twenty in the time it takes you to do one.'

'It's not a race,' said Penny.

The others liked Zen, so they wouldn't tell him to shut up, Mack thought. And he wasn't going to tell him to shut up either, because that would be like saying Zen had won. No way. Let him be the world's biggest jerk. Great. Fine. Just because you couldn't walk didn't make you a stinking hero or a great human being. Zen was a jerk before his accident, and he was a jerk now.

A bigger jerk.

'Legs,' said Penny.

'Yeah, legs,' grunted Mack.

Humboldt County, northwestern California
1235

Kick's family lived on a cul-de-sac not far from the town center in McKinleyville, California, the sort of location a real estate agent would call 'convenient to everything.' Starship parked at the far end of the circle. As he walked up the cement driveway, he started to regret his decision to come. He paused at the bottom of the steps, but it was too late; someone came up the drive behind him, and as he glanced back, the front door opened.

'You're his friend. How do you do?' said Kick's father at the door. 'Have a drink, please. Make yourself at home.'

'Maybe just a beer, I think,' said Starship, stepping inside.

'Bud's in the fridge. Help yourself.'

Starship moved inside. As he reached the kitchen he saw Kick's sister bending into the refrigerator – and noticed that she had a large engagement ring on her finger.

'Oh, Lieutenant Andrews,' she said. 'I'm glad you changed your mind.'

'I can only stay for a few minutes.'

'Want something to drink?'

'A beer maybe.'

'Just like my brother.' She reached in and got him a Bud Lite, then introduced him to some of the other people in the small kitchen. Two were friends of Kick's and about his age; Starship thought the men shrank back a bit as he shook their hands, maybe put off by his uniform. There was an aunt, the sister's fiancé, a cousin, and the minister, who proved to be much younger up close than from the back of the church. Starship took his beer and moved toward the side of the kitchen. The others were talking about something that had happened at the local school.

'It was an unfortunate situation,' said the minister as Starship slid to the side.

'Yeah, really bad,' said Starship.

'He died a hero.'

'Do you think that matters?'

The minister blanched. Starship hadn't meant it as a challenge – hadn't meant anything, really. The question simply bubbled out of his private thoughts.

'Don't you?' said one of Kick's friends.

Starship felt a moment of hesitation, a catch in his throat as if his breath had been knocked from him.

'I don't think he's not – wasn't brave, I mean. I think it sucks that he died,' he said. 'I think it's really terrible. And he was – he volunteered. We all did, and it's important what we do.' He knew he was babbling but he couldn't stop. 'He was a brave guy, I mean, as brave as most people, I think, but it wasn't like – it's not like a movie thing, you know, where the guy charges out and people are shooting at him. We do have guys like that. They just march right through anything. And to be a pilot, I mean, you do face death, you know. But, you don't think about it like – it's not a movie thing. It didn't happen like you'd think it would happen in a movie. We were there and then he was dead.'

Finally he stopped talking. He felt thankful, as if someone else had been making his mouth work and he had no control.

'The Lord does have a plan for us all,' said the minister.

Starship wanted to ask him how he knew, and more important, how someone could find out what the plan was. But he was afraid of opening his mouth again. He didn't want the others to misunderstand him, and he didn't want to insult the minister. Starship knew he wasn't the most religious person in the world; he believed in God, certainly, but if he found himself in church more than twice a year, it was a lot.

No one else in the kitchen spoke. Starship thought everyone was staring at him.

'That was a nice passage from the Bible,' the cousin told the minister.

'There's a lot of solace in the Old Testament,' said the minister.

Starship realized that the reverend was struggling to find the right words to say. Which surprised him. Weren't ministers supposed to have this stuff down cold?

'Did you know Kick well, Lieutenant?' asked the cousin.

'Uh, we were in the same unit. We were together –'
Starship stopped short of telling them how Kick had died.
Partly it was for official reasons: Details of the mission
remained classified. But mostly he didn't want to talk
about it – didn't want to describe how he'd pulled his
friend from the wreck, only to discover he was dead.

Everyone stared.

'He was a heck of a pilot,' said Starship finally. He
could talk about this – this was easy, nothing but facts
and no interpretation; easy, straightforward facts. 'I'll tell
you, I saw him fly an A-10A once. We, uh, we had one
at the base.' He checked himself again, knowing he
couldn't mention Dreamland, much less what aircraft
were there. 'Had that A-10A turning on a dime. Ugly
plane.'

One of the friends mumbled something in agreement,
then ventured that Kick had always liked to fix cars when
he was in high school. Starship downed the rest of the
beer, then slipped out as quickly as he could.

**Aboard the *Abner Read*,
off the Horn of Africa
3 November 1997
2042**

Storm adjusted the loop at his belt, easing the brake on
the safety rope system so he could move more freely on
the deck of the ship. Angled and faceted to lessen its
radar profile, the ship's topside was not particularly easy

to walk on, even in relatively calm seas, and with no railing along the sides of the ship, the safety rope was an absolute necessity. He walked forward along the starboard side, steadying himself on the gun housing.

The *Abner Read* had sent its two rigid-hulled inflatable boats from the stern to search through the floating debris to the northwest. The two men on deck had seen something near the ship and, with bad weather approaching and the boats a good distance away, had worked together to pick it up before it was lost. One of the men had actually gone over the side, using his safety gear to climb down the knifelike bow area, perching on the side and fishing for the debris with a long pole.

Another commander would have probably considered this a foolhardy move, and very possibly had their captain discipline the men – if he didn't do so himself. But Storm wasn't another commander. While the man who had gotten down on the side of the ship had been dashed against the hull rather severely by the waves, in Storm's opinion he had shown precisely the sort of can-do attitude the Navy ought to encourage.

'A jacket, sir,' said one of the sailors, handing him the dark blue cloth that had been retrieved.

More precisely, it was half a jacket. There was something in one of the pockets – a folded *rial*.

Yemeni currency. Hard proof that the Yemenis were involved, just in case anyone doubted him.

'Damn good work,' said Storm. He put the jacket under his arm. 'Damn good work.'

'Thank you, sir,' shouted the men.

'Carry on,' said Storm. He paused. 'And don't drown.'

The sailors laughed. 'Yes, sir.'

Storm turned to go back. This was the Navy at its best – filled with sailors who weren't afraid to show initiative, and whose voices carried the proper tone of respect even in casual conversation. He'd selected the best men and women for Xray Pop, knowing the plank owners of the littoral warfare ships would be the seed of the new Navy. They were what the entire Navy ought to be, and it damn well would be when he ran the fleet.

'Captain, you have an eyes-only message waiting, sir,' said the seaman who met him at the hatchway. Storm followed the man to the communications department, where the crew snapped to as he came in.

'Gentlemen. Where's my message?'

'Right here, sir,' said the ensign in charge. He stepped back to let Storm sit at the computer terminal. The message had been transmitted through a secure text system. The ensign made a point of going to the radioman at the other station as Storm typed in his password and brought the message onto the screen.

REQUEST FOR RULES CHANGE DENIED. YOU ARE TO
   PROCEED AS DIRECTED.
I EXPECT A FULL BRIEFING SOONEST.
                       ADMIRAL WOODS

Hardly worth the effort of encoding, thought Storm. But then, his opinion of Admiral Woods was hardly a high one. Admiral Woods – CINCPACFLT, or Commander of the Pacific Fleet – had made such a mash of the so-called Piranha episode that the Air Force – *the U.S. Air Force!* – had to step in and save the day.

Not that a war between India and China was worth heading off. Like ninety percent of the Navy, Storm would have preferred to watch the two powers slug it out in the Pacific and Indian Oceans until all they had left between them were a pair of rubber dinghies. Still, if it had to be broken up, it would have been much better if the Navy had done the job.

Woods was currently aboard the *John C. Stennis*, which was steaming with her battle group in the eastern Indian Ocean, where the U.S. had recently prevented a war between India and China. The situation remained tense, and the only thing keeping the two countries from launching nukes at each other were two U.S. carrier groups: the *Stennis* and its Carrier Group Seven, and the *Carl Vinson* and Carrier Group Three, off the Chinese coast. A number of other Pacific Fleet assets were near Taiwan, encouraging new peace talks that would result in a permanent free China – just so long as the words 'free' and 'permanent' weren't used anywhere in the treaty.

Storm had asked Woods to change his rules of engagement to allow him to attack the pirates in their home waters and on land. Woods was his second strike – he'd already received a no from the head of the Fifth Fleet, Admiral P. T. 'Barnum' Keelor. Technically, Keelor was his boss – but only technically. Based at Manama in Bahrain, the admiral had the unenviable position of trying to run a fleet with no ships, or at least no permanently assigned warships. Aside from a mine countermeasure vessel and some support craft, all of his assets were rotated in and out from the Atlantic and Pacific fleets. Most of his main force – two Arleigh Burke destroyers from the Seventh Fleet – had been sent to the waters off Yugoslavia to assist the Sixth Fleet as it tried to stop a war there. The other had its hands full in the Persian Gulf.

Though Xray Pop operated in his territory, Storm's orders had come directly from the Pentagon via Woods. He hadn't even met Keelor, and wouldn't before the end of his mission. Keelor was too busy trying to keep the Persian Gulf clear of Iranian mines to deal with him, which was just fine with Storm.

Woods ought to be twice as busy, Storm thought, but he seemed to relish harassing him.

'Arrange a secure video conference with the admiral for tomorrow some time, at his convenience,' Storm told his communications specialist. He checked some routine matters, then made his way back to Tac. In the meantime, the rigid-hull inflatable boat they had sent to look for survivors from the missile gunboat had returned empty-handed. The gunboat had sunk without a trace. The Shark Boats had reported no further contacts.

'We'll let the *Abner Read* recover her boats and spend the night here, ride out the storm,' he told Eyes. 'Then we'll go south as planned. Let's see if these bastards have the balls to take another shot at us.'

'I'd like to see them try,' blurted one of the men nearby.

'Did you have a comment, mister?' said Storm, looking over.

'No, sir,' said the man, eyes now pasted on the display screen in front of him.

Storm smiled and winked at Eyes. He had the best damn ships and the best damn crews in the whole Navy.

Dreamland
3 November 1997
1331

The session in the pool had done enough of a number on his ego that Mack Smith decided he would eat lunch by himself, resorting to one of Dreamland's vending machines. This was a challenge in itself – it was impossible to reach the coin slot without dramatic contortions. Fortunately, one of the civilian workers happened by as Mack was just about to give up; she took his change and even punched the buttons for him, and her perfume softened a bit of the sting.

Mack had been offered the option of using a motorized wheelchair but had declined, largely because Zen didn't use one. The advantages were obvious now as he struggled to build momentum up the ramp to the office he'd been assigned. Working a wheelchair efficiently required a certain rhythm as well as upper-body strength, and he hadn't acquired either yet.

He hoped he never did. He wanted more than anything to get the hell out of this damn thing.

Ray Rubeo was waiting for him inside the office. The scientist stood staring at an empty computer screen on the worktable at the side of the room, a deep frown on his face. Mack couldn't recall a time when the scientist hadn't worn the frown; Dreamland's senior scientist seemed to think scowling was part of his job description.

'You were looking to talk to me, Major?'

'Pull up a chair, Doc. I'm already sitting.'

'I'm fine.'

One thing in Rubeo's favor, thought Mack as he pushed around to the large table that was supposed to serve as his work area: He didn't give him a look of sympathy.

The table was about two inches too high to be comfortable to work at. Mack leaned forward and unwrapped his sandwich, which was some sort of processed ham and mayo on whole wheat.

'So?' asked Rubeo.

'So what, Doc?'

'You wanted to talk to me. In person. I am here.'

'Yeah, I do. I'm taking over Piranha.'

'Taking over Piranha? How? That's a Navy project.'

'I don't mean taking it over, exactly. I'm, you know, liaisoning. So I'm getting up to speed.'

Rubeo's frown deepened. Mack ignored it.

'I was looking at the reports and it seems to me there's one constant. You need more people.'

'I would say that is a constant, yes.'

'So the first thing we have to do is get you more people.'

'And?'

This was not exactly the response Mack had anticipated. While he knew that the scientist didn't have it in him to jump up and down in thanks, he had hoped that by acknowledging that the staff was overworked he might show from the start that he was on the team's side. This, of course, would pay dividends down the line, when he had to pressure them for more results.

'And I'm going to try to get you more people.'

'Thank you, Major,' said Rubeo, in a tone that suggested thanks was the last thing he had on his mind. The scientist started to walk from the room.

'Hey, Doc, where are you going?'

'Was there something else?'

'I thought maybe you could run down where we were with some of the related programs. It seems to me that the real potential here –'

'You haven't been given the reports?'

'What're these tactical UAV things, the Littoral Combat Intrinsic Air Multiplier Systems? Now those are pretty interesting.'

'Piffle,' said Rubeo.

'Piffle?'

'A worthless Navy project. We're not involved. They want to run the tests here – assuming they ever get the project out of their CAD programs.' Rubeo wrinkled his nose, as if he'd caught a whiff of sulfur. 'You might try informing them that there's very little water in the middle of the Nevada desert.'

'I thought they were just adaptations of the unmanned helicopter system,' said Mack. 'I thought the project only got bagged because of the budget.'

'UHS was a Dreamland project, that is correct,' said

the scientist, referring to the program by its initials. 'This is different. If the Navy would deign to use a design that was originally done for the Army – as UHS was – then there would be no problem.'

'They won't use it?'

Rubeo rolled his eyes.

'These Navy things look like the Werewolves,' said Mack.

'Hardly. The Werewolf *works*.'

Rubeo started away. Mack wheeled forward and grabbed his shirtsleeve.

'What about the Integrated Warfare Computing System?' asked Mack. 'It's already installed in their littoral combat ships. We have some interfaces for it.'

The scientist snorted.

'Problems?' asked Mack.

'The Navy's computer code reminds me of the programs that were part of the TRS-80,' said Rubeo. 'Without the benefit of being compact.'

'I assume that's some sort of put-down, right?'

'The TRS-80 was a Radio Shack computer dating from the 1970s. Yes, Major, it was a put-down. We have interfaces, though to be honest, why anyone would want to use them is beyond me. Their systems crash every eighteen to twenty-four hours.'

'So why don't they just bag the crappy computer and use one of ours? Or even something off-the-shelf?'

'You haven't dealt with the Navy much, have you?'

'I'll just straighten them out, then.'

A faint glimmer of a smile came to Rubeo's lips. 'I hope you do, Major. Can I go now?'

'Sure,' said Mack. 'We should have lunch sometime. I really want to get to know you better.'

'Yes,' said Rubeo, leaving.

McCarran International Airport,
Las Vegas
1630

Captain Danny Freah walked past the row of video slot machines and turned left into the large baggage claim area. The flight from New York had landed a few minutes ago, and passengers were just starting to filter in. As Danny walked toward the carousel, a short man in a gray suit approached him from the side.

'You're Captain Freah, I'll bet,' said the man.

'Danny Freah, yes,' said Freah. 'Lee?'

'That's me,' said the man, Lee Rosenstein, pumping Danny's hand. 'I thought you'd be in uniform.'

'I'm off-duty,' Danny told him.

'Well, good. You deserve some time off after all you've been through,' said Rosenstein. 'Let me just grab my suiter. I see it coming around the bend.'

Rosenstein darted toward an opening in the crowd and grabbed a black suitcase with a multicolored twist of yarn around the handle.

'Clever,' said Danny, pointing at the identifier as they walked toward the exit.

'Until it falls off,' said Rosenstein. 'Usually I get to carry it on, but the gate person couldn't be bribed.'

He smiled, which Danny figured meant he was kidding about the bribe. Without breaking stride, Rosenstein reached to the outer pocket of the suitcase, zipped it open, and retrieved a Mets cap, plopping it on his head. It clashed a bit with the black suit.

'Been a while since I was in Vegas,' added Rosenstein as they reached the hallway. 'Not since March or April.'

'I took a taxi. They're this way,' said Danny. Rosenstein had already started to the right, where a line snaked around a set of ribbons on the sidewalk.

'Man, it's beautiful weather. Was raining and about thirty-six when I left New York this afternoon.'

'It's a little warm for this time of year,' said Danny.

'Let's go right to Venezia,' suggested Rosenstein. 'I'll check in, then we'll catch some dinner.'

'Sounds good.'

'I was thinking of Delaman's to eat. Supposed to be the best restaurant between San Francisco and New York,' said Rosenstein. 'I don't know if that's true, but the last time I was there it was pretty good. Hey, don't worry about paying, Captain – this is on my dime.'

'I wasn't worried,' said Danny. He wouldn't have known Delaman's from a diner, but now felt embarrassed at the other man's suggestion that he would pay. 'We'll go fifty-fifty.'

'First thing you have to learn as a candidate for Congress,' said Rosenstein, 'is when to let other people pay for your dinner and when not. This is a time you let other people pay. Enjoy it while it lasts.'

'I don't know that I'm running for Congress,' said Danny.

'Everybody says that.' Rosenstein smiled. 'All the more reason to let me pay.'

Dreamland
1713

Zen hunched over the control panel, watching the computer simulation of the small aircraft's maneuvers as it ran through a mock bombing run. Flown entirely by the computer, the aircraft managed to duck two antiair laser shots as well as an old-fashioned but still deadly flak barrage as it approached the enemy radar station. It then took a very hard cut right – the angle looked to be nearly forty-five degrees – as it tossed the five hundred pound bomb. The bomb, loosened from the underside of the robot aircraft just at the start of the maneuver, skipped through the air and landed about two meters from its target, the radar van that had been controlling the antiaircraft installation. As the simulation continued, the robot aircraft spun back down toward the ground, recording the damage its bomb had done.

'The concept definitely works,' said Zen, pushing back from the panel. 'In the computer, at least.'

'If it works on the computer, it'll work in real life,' said Jennifer Gleason.

'I'm not debating that,' said Zen. 'I just don't see how it's worth it moneywise to turn the U/MFs into bombers. A guidance kit on a dumb bomb is a heck of a lot cheaper.

And having a real airplane gives you a heck of a lot more flexibility.'

'I don't do philosophy,' said Jennifer. 'Just computers.'

Zen was in charge of the Flighthawk U/MF-3 project, a responsibility that included not only the present generation of high-speed robot interceptors but also the next generation U/MF-4, which had just flown the simulation. The U/MF-4 was a small, slightly faster aircraft that incorporated everything they'd learned from using the Flighthawk in combat over the past two years. It could remain airborne at least twice as long without refueling, and would be able to operate approximately fifty miles from its mother plane. Its autonomous mode – the developers' fancy word for flying on its own – was much improved, thanks largely to the refined onboard tactics library developed from the battles Zen had flown with the U/MF-3s. It could also carry a heavier payload, a capacity intended not for bombs but rather a lightweight though powerful chemical laser, which so far had not made it past the conceptual stage.

All in all, the U/MF-4 was a better aircraft than the U/MF-3. But was it better *enough* to justify the billions of dollars it would take to field a fleet of them?

If it could be used as an attack aircraft as well as an interceptor, maybe – at least that was the thinking at the Pentagon, which had urged the bomb trial.

Urged as in ordered, with a bit of politeness and necessary decorum thrown in. Zen hated Washington politics, but it was a necessary part of life here.

And not just his. Of the three men and two women

currently assigned to the sketch phase of the project, at least two would be let go if the U/MF-4 project were put completely on hold. They were all highly skilled workers, engineers who at least in theory ought to have no problem finding another job. But theory and reality didn't always match. And the stakes would be a hundred times greater at the next stage.

'I can have the simulation transferred to video for you by tomorrow morning,' said Jennifer.

'Thanks.' With everything squared away, Zen went up the ramp to the elevators and then out through the large Megafortress hangar that had been cut into the Nevada desert like an oversized curbstone. The warm air – it was a balmy eighty degrees – felt good after the filtered and AC'd bunker air he'd been breathing the last few hours.

'Hey, Major, how's it going?' asked Captain Michael Latrec as Zen rolled toward the Taj. Latrec was a flight surgeon – an Air Force doctor whose specialty was dealing with flight crews and the sometimes peculiar effects of air travel. He probably spent as much time dealing with the common cold as anything else, but then again, a runny nose at Mach 3 and 65,000 feet could hardly be called common. 'You believe this weather?'

'Love it,' said Zen.

'It'll snow tomorrow, watch.'

'Probably.'

'How's Mack?'

'I busted his chops pretty bad,' said Zen.

'You did? You busted on him?'

'Nah. I just pushed him, like I said I would.'

'You don't have to ride him,' said Latrec. 'More like encourage him. Get him to work out, keep at it, that kind of thing.'

'That's what I'm doing. You sure it's all in his head?'

'No. I didn't say it was all in his head. He definitely sustained injuries. It's just – he may need encouragement to keep going. You were encouraged, and I thought you could give him the same motivation. Been there, done that, that sort of thing.'

'I'm working on it, Doc.'

'Mack probably appreciates it.'

'That's not going to happen,' said Zen. 'Unless he gets a brain transplant.'

'I think you'll be surprised,' said Latrec. 'Going through something like this . . .'

Latrec's voice trailed off, obviously because he realized he was talking to an expert on the effects of 'something like this.'

'Don't sweat it, Doc. And by the way, you owe me a case of Anchor Steam from the World Series. I haven't forgotten.'

'Oh yeah. Stinking Marlins.' Latrec was from Cleveland, and, after the Yankees, hated the Florida Marlins with a passion. Zen didn't particularly care, but he knew a good bet when he saw one – the Marlins were underdogs and he was able to leverage a six-pack against a case.

'I've been thinking about changing the beer,' said Zen. 'I've been drinking these British beers since Brunei. Samuel Smith. Maybe the Oatmeal Stout.'

'Jeez, where am I going to find British beer around here?'

'Plenty of places in Vegas,' said Zen. 'And if not, schedule a house call to an air base in London.'

Dog waited impatiently for the last techie to finish adjusting the in-flight diagnostic monitor – a fancy name for a black box flight recorder – on the right side of his aircraft so he could start the engine on the XF-16Z, the tester he was scheduled to have gotten off the ground forty-five minutes ago.

Last minute technical glitches and engineering fussiness were part of a test pilot's routine, and Dog was only too happy to put off the pile of pressing bureaucratic details awaiting him over at his office. Technically, taking a turn as a pilot in the heavy test schedule wasn't part of Dog's job at Dreamland, and it had been pointed out several times that spending too much time in the cockpit might keep him from the admittedly more important job of running the base and its Whiplash component. But from Dog's point of view, what was the sense of being a pilot if you didn't fly? Why had the government spent something approaching a million dollars training him and keeping his skills sharp if not to strap Combat Edge flight gear onto his body on a regular basis? And besides, putting his posterior against an ACES II ejection seat every few days or so made the fact that it spent so much time against a cushioned leather seat almost bearable.

Almost.

But the delay was threatening his plans to have dinner with Jennifer. The two hadn't had much time to see each other since the end of the so-called 'Armageddon' mission. Their deployment to the kingdom of Brunei and Malaysia had interrupted his campaign to more actively 'woo' Jennifer, a campaign that he had undertaken with the planning and precision a top pilot would put into a bombing mission.

Not that bombing was like wooing. Not at all. He had to remind himself *not* to make that comparison to her, at all costs.

'Wooing.' Was that even a word people used anymore? Was the word 'dating' more appropriate? But dating women seemed like something he had done a million years before. And besides, dating didn't really cover what he wanted to do. He wanted her to understand, to feel, that he loved her. And was 'wooing.' Not bombing.

'Just another minute, Colonel,' yelled the engineer, disappearing back over the side of the heavily modified F-16.

The Z, as the XF-16Z was called, had started life as an F-16D, a two-seat version of the versatile fighter-bomber manufactured by General Dynamics. The Dreamland wizards had lengthened the fuselage and completely altered the wing and tail, which looked as if they belonged on a stretched version of the F-22 fighter. The slim body of the Fighting Falcon had been bulked up as well, so that the airplane looked more rectangular than round. This was partly to accommodate the larger engine, which was a Pratt & Whitney power plant originally proposed for the Joint Strike Fighter; the engine was capable of sustained cruising at Mach 1.2 while consuming a little less fuel than an F-16C would have at subsonic cruise. That there was much more room for fuel in the Dreamland version increased its operating range, giving it a typical combat radius well in excess of a thousand miles, depending on its mission and load.

The XF-16Z had been authorized shortly before Dog got to Dreamland. It originally had been intended as a test bed for a variety of technologies, including the wing construction (considered but rejected for the Joint Strike Fighter) and electronics suite (which would probably form the basis of the next generation of Wild Weasel upgrades). But it also showed how older airframes might be given new life; the Z could do for the F-16 what the Megafortress had done for the B-52 – remake a venerable, solidly designed twentieth century aircraft into a twenty-first century cutting-edge warplane. The Z was a cheaper-to-operate alternative to the strike version of the F-22; it could also be employed as a very capable Wild Weasel and – assuming the weapons people continued to make the progress they'd shown over the last twelve months – a likely platform for the lightweight attack version of the Razor antiair laser currently under development. The chemical laser was scheduled to be strapped to the belly of the Z for tests by early January.

Today's test was rather prosaic – Dog was merely helping the techies shake out some bugs in the radar unit that helped the aircraft track other airplanes around it. A pair of UAV drones – early model Pioneers – would be launched as soon as he was airborne; Dog would fly a few circuits and wait for the radar to pick up the craft and track them.

An easy gig, if the techies would just clear out so he could spool up the engine. The engineer reappeared at the side of the cockpit with a small meter, apologizing for some sort of glitch in the circuitry.

'How long is this going to take?' asked Dog.

'Uh, depends. I get a green here and you can go.'

Dog couldn't help noticing that the needle on the engineer's testing device swung into the red zone and stayed there. The engineer mumbled a curse under his breath, then looked up at the colonel and turned red.

'Sorry.'

'I've heard those words before,' said Dog. 'Is this going to scrub the mission or what?'

'Um, maybe.' The techie reached down and reseated his tester's clips. This time when he turned the switch dial, the needle pegged the green post on the meter. 'Eureka,' said the engineer. 'Good to go, sir.'

But as the technician disappeared down the side and the crew with the power cart got ready to 'puff' the XF-16Z's engine to life, a black SUV with a blue flashing light raced toward the aircraft. A sergeant from the Whiplash ground action team, Lee Liu, got out and trotted toward the aircraft.

'Urgent Eyes-Only communication for you, Colonel,' shouted Liu.

Dog undid his restraints and climbed over the side. 'Di-Tullo, you're going to have to scratch unless you can find the backup pilot,' he yelled. 'Somedays you can never win.'

* * *

Forty minutes later Dog watched the tussled hair and tired face of Jed Barclay pop onto the screen at the front of the Dreamland Command Center.

'Colonel, how are you?' he asked. Jed was the National Security Council assistant for technology, and the Martindale administration's de facto liaison with Dreamland.

'I'm fine, Jed. You look a little tired.'

Jed smiled. 'Stand by for Mr Freeman.'

The screen blinked. The feed indicated that the transmission was being made from the White House situation room, which had recently been upgraded, partly to accommodate secure communications with Dreamland.

'Colonel Bastian, good evening,' said Philip Freeman, the National Security Advisor. 'The President has issued a Whiplash Order. Hopefully, this mission won't be as intense as some of your others. I'm afraid I have an appointment upstairs. Before I go, I wanted to mention personally that I appreciate the effort you and your people made in Brunei. Good work, Colonel.'

'Thank you,' said Dog.

Freeman turned away from the screen.

Jed Barclay stepped back into view. 'Roughly three weeks ago, one of Libya's Russian-made submarines left its port on the Mediterranean,' he said. 'Ordinarily, they go out a few miles, dive, circle, and go home. This one didn't. I have some graphics for you, but the illustrations are pretty, uh, basic.'

A blurry black and white photo of a submarine replaced Jed's face. Dog listened as the NSC assistant described the submarine, an old but still potent diesel-powered member of the Project 641 class, code named 'Foxtrots' in the west. Roughly three hundred feet long, the Libyan submarine had a snorkel and improved batteries, which allowed it to travel for several days while submerged. Capable of carrying over twenty torpedoes and possibly submarine-launched cruise missiles, the vessel posed a serious enough threat to shipping that NATO had sent additional forces to track it down. An Italian destroyer succeeded in locating it west of Sicily and trailed it as it traveled toward Gibraltar. But the submarine eventually gave it the slip.

Two days later a British antisubmarine warfare group off the Moroccan coast in the Atlantic recorded sounds of a submarine under distress. It failed to surface, and all contact was lost. The boat had not been positively identified, but was thought to have been a Foxtrot. Given the Libyans' dismal history with the Russian submarines, it seemed likely that the sub had broken up and sunk. An extensive search operation failed to turn up anything.

That closed the matter – until five days ago, when an American submarine in the Indian Ocean off the African coast reported a series of very distant contacts with a submarine it had never encountered before. The American sub was trailing a Russian cruiser at the time and couldn't do much more than listen passively as the other submarine passed a good distance away. The crew had originally identified the craft as a Kilo Project 636, a very potent diesel-powered submarine manufactured and exported by Russia. Subsequent analysis, however, indicated that was wrong. The analysts were pegging it as a Foxtrot or perhaps a member of the somewhat more refined and larger Tango class.

'The same sub?' Dog asked Jed.

Jed said it certainly seemed to be. If so, it was a potentially ominous development. A loose association of pirates were currently operating in the Gulf of Aden. They had patrol boats of various sizes and configurations; they were using them to rob and extort money from ships headed from and toward the Red Sea and the Suez Canal. They were also running guns and ammunition to rebel movements in Eritrea, Somalia, Sudan, and Ethiopia.

The pirates had been active for several months, their status with the legitimate governments in the region unclear. The Arab League claimed that both Somalia, Yemen, and Ethiopia were working against the pirates, but none of the other countries would agree to work with the UN or NATO to combat them. This was no surprise in Somalia – the government wasn't much more than a fiction. Sudan and Yemen had their own share of conflicts and troubles, but Ethiopia's reluctance to cooperate was difficult to explain; they were inland and historically not allied with either country. The only possible explanation had to do with Islamic terror organizations and secret government alliances – a possibility that implied the Libyan submarine might be the first of many.

Things had gotten so bad that two weeks earlier a small contingent of U.S. ships had entered the Gulf of Aden and begun combating them. They were under orders to remain in international waters and attack only with 'hard evidence' or if called by a ship under direct attack. Thus far their successes had been limited.

'A submarine would take the conflict to a whole different level,' said Jed. 'It's a pretty bad time for us – most of the Pacific Fleet is near Taiwan, and what's not there is spread out around North Korea and India. Meanwhile, the Atlantic Fleet is trying to deal with Yugoslavia and the Russian buildup in the Baltic.'

'Which is why the pirates are so active,' suggested Dog.

'Probably. This is where they've been.'

A map of the Gulf of Aden came on the screen. Roughly 550 miles long, the arm of the Indian Ocean sat below the Arabian peninsula, sandwiched between the peninsula and the Horn of Africa. Somalia lay at the bottom, on the horn shape; Yemen was at the top, on the Arabian peninsula. To the left was the entrance to the Red Sea, which led to the Suez Canal at the far north.

Jed had shaded the areas along the coasts of Somalia and Yemen to show where the pirates had been most active – a swath roughly five hundred miles long.

'The attacks have been mostly in international waters, where the ships try to stay. The pirates then go into the coastal zones where they know they'll be safe,' said Jed. 'If the submarine is going to join them, it'll come up from this direction here.'

He pointed at the right side of the map, on the horn, where Somalia butted into the Indian Ocean.

'You don't think it's heading for the Persian Gulf?' asked Dog. The Persian Gulf, which bordered Saudi Arabia, Kuwait, Iraq, and Iran, lay farther east, just off

Jed's map. 'The Libyans have worked with the Iranians before, and the Iranians are the ones to watch in the Middle East, if you ask me.'

'Um, yes, but they've been pretty quiet since Razor's Edge,' said Jed, referring to the code name for an operation in Iran concluded some months before. Whiplash had destroyed an Iranian laser similar in design to the American antiair weapon known as Razor. 'Besides, a NATO squadron is already operating there,' he added. 'There's an American destroyer and two French ships guarding the Strait of Hormuz, and an Italian vessel farther north in the Persian Gulf. If the sub does try to get into the gulf, those ships will find it at Hormuz. The Gulf of Aden is much more problematic. If the submarine is in territorial waters, we can't touch it, and may even have trouble just tracking it.'

Though Jed didn't explain, Dog realized that the administration was reluctant to push the territorial waters issue, not so much because it feared foreign reaction, but because of congressional criticism of the Martindale administration for acting unilaterally over the past six or seven months. Even though the administration had twice prevented wars between China and Taiwan and once between China and India, the politicos used the international criticism to bash Martindale. Senate Majority Leader Barbara Finegold had as much as said so in an interview on CNN a few days before, when she promised to hold hearings on President Martindale's 'hidden foreign agenda.'

'Why would the Libyans get involved with pirates?'

Dog asked. 'Are they getting a cut of the booty or what?'

'The pirates aren't just thieves,' Jed explained. 'They're part of a network of Islamic militants. They're attacking shipping partly for money and partly to help fund an Islamic revolt in North Africa. Sudan, Eritrea, Somalia, maybe even Ethiopia and Yemen – they're all in play. There are organizations in each country, and they're each affiliated with Al Qaeda, the people who are operating in Afghanistan.'

'And who funded the takeover in Brunei.'

'Same people. The Brunei movement probably used some of the money the pirates raised. We don't have any evidence that they're involved with the Libyans, or this submarine,' added Jed. 'But there have been efforts to get Ethiopia and Yemen as well as Egypt and even Oman to join the conflict. Ethiopia and Yemen both scrambled planes a few days ago.'

'To attack the pirates?'

'More like to protect them. But they deny that.'

'What happens if we find the sub?' asked Dog.

'It depends on exactly what you find. If there's evidence of it working with the pirates, the Secretary of State will take it to the UN. He's pushing for a resolution that will authorize action against them no matter where they are.'

The Dreamland Command Center was set up like a theater, with benches of computer displays arranged in a semicircle down toward the front screen. The displays could be tied to different systems during an operation, or used to tap into various databases. Dog stooped down to the one near him and tapped in the address for a mapping system, bringing up a detailed view of the Somalian coast. There were literally thousands of places a submarine might go along the coast of Africa.

'Where do the pirates operate out of?' he asked, looking at his map.

'We're not sure, exactly,' said Jed. 'They move from place to place, all along the coast. They hide among the local population, use old military bases, even civilian areas.'

'In order to check some of these places out,' Dog said, 'we're going to have to put Piranha right into them. And I mean right into them.'

'You're authorized to put Piranha as close as you have to. It's understood that the probe may go into territorial waters. That's why we want Piranha. As long as the controlling aircraft stays in international airspace.'

'That's easy, if nothing goes wrong. What happens if the probe gets hung up in the mud?'

In theory, the probes were expendable; the idea was to use them in a situation like this, where exposing men could be dangerous and politically inconvenient. But at the moment, they were also very expensive – each one cost roughly a million dollars. And there were only four.

'They've passed all the trials with flying colors,' said Jed. 'And we used them in the Pacific. They're funded in the next fiscal year for regular procurement.'

'You've been in Washington too long, Jed. That's not an answer.'

'Um, sorry. It would depend on the circumstances. The, uh, political situation is pretty sensitive right now.'

'So's the technology.'

'Not my call, Colonel.'

'What if I find the pirates while I'm searching for the submarine?' Dog asked. 'Do I tell this Navy operation?'

'Not unless it's threatening them.'

'Shouldn't we be working with them?'

'Mr Freeman – and the President – intended this to be separate,' said Jed. 'They're pretty busy doing what they're doing. They've been informed of the sub, and that we'll be looking for it, but that's the extent of it at the moment,' he added. 'Um, I didn't think you and the Navy exactly got along.'

That was an understatement. The last time Dog had worked with the Navy, he'd nearly decked an admiral.

'I get along with everybody,' he replied. 'Should I make contact with the Navy people or what?'

'If it becomes "operationally necessary," you can contact them. That's in the Whiplash directive. So, you know, it's kind of your call there. I think Mr Freeman and the President thought you'd want to keep your distance. I should mention that the Navy doesn't put much stock in the reports of the submarine getting that far. Not at all, actually. They're pretty much against wasting any resources to find it. That's the word they use – *waste*.'

'We can definitely get a mission package with Piranha prepared within twelve hours,' Dog said. 'But we need a base in the area to work out of.'

'What about Diego Garcia?'

Located in the Indian Ocean south of India, the island

atoll in the Chagos Archipelago had a long runway and secure if primitive facilities. It was the perfect staging area for an operation – except for the fact that it was a few thousand miles from the Gulf of Aden.

'It's a heck of a hike,' Dog told Jed. 'It'd be bad enough to make a bombing run up to the gulf from there. You're talking about patrols that have to last several hours to be effective, eight or twelve ideally. You put a four- to six-hour flight each way on top of that and you're going to have exhausted flight crews pretty quick. How about somewhere in Saudi Arabia?'

'The Saudis are pretty touchy about American military people on their soil these days,' said Jed. 'I don't know.'

'During the Gulf War, we used an airport at Khamis Mushait for some Stealth fighters,' said Dog. 'It's close to the Gulf of Aden. We can scoot down to the Red Sea and get over the Gulf of Aden without crossing Yemen territory.'

'I can check,' said Jed. 'I'll have to get back to you. There's like a thirteen-hour difference between here and there. It's past eight in the evening here in D.C., five in the afternoon where you are, and, um, like past four A.M. there.' Jed glanced at his watch, working out the differences. 'Tomorrow. Four A.M. tomorrow.'

'I can figure it out.'

'If it took twelve hours to get Piranha ready, could you like, be there when? Tomorrow?'

'I have to talk to some of my people first,' said the colonel. 'I would guess we could arrive sometime tomorrow night our time at the very earliest. I don't know what sort of shape we'd be in to launch a mission. I'll have to get this all mapped out.'

'OK, Colonel. Anything else?'

'How about tripling my budget and sending me a thousand more people?'

'Afraid I don't have that kind of pull,' said Jed.

'Neither do I,' said Dog. 'Dreamland out.'

Las Vegas
1715

Danny Freah waited as the server rearranged their forks. To call the restaurant fancy was to underestimate it by half; the entrées cost twice what Danny had paid for his watch.

'You're sure no drink?' said Rosenstein as the server set down a single malt scotch.

'Nothing for me. Thanks.'

'Good. Very good,' said Rosenstein, taking a sip. 'I noticed you're an NOE.'

'What's that?'

'Not Otherwise Enrolled,' said Rosenstein. 'Your party registration. You're not enrolled in a political party.'

'I haven't been involved in politics.'

'Unlike your wife.'

'Jemma's always been pretty political.'

'Nonpolitical is hot. The thing is, in that district, I'm pretty sure you could get both Democratic and Republican nominations. Conservative party as well. Not Liberal, but you're not going to want that anyway, right?'

'I don't know that I want anything.'

'Still playing hard to get, Captain?'

'I'm not playing anything.'

Rosenstein took a long sip of his scotch, savoring it. 'I'm not here to sell you on running for office. I'll just lay out the time schedule for you. But . . .' He paused, obviously for effect. 'War hero, young, black, well-spoken – Congress can use someone like you.'

'You had me until you said well-spoken,' said Danny. 'You've never heard me speak.'

'We can work on that. Game plan: Form a committee January 2. Make the rounds until early February. Parties meet. Get the endorsements in March. Circulate petitions. This is New York, so there will be primaries. That's not going to be the problem, as long as we've taken care of business in January and February. It'll be in your favor, actually; help get your name around. The primaries are the real action in the city anyway. Money's the only hiccup, and I think we can handle that without a problem. We usually break the donor lists down three ways to start. In your case we'll add two more – veterans and military contractors, and black professionals. Obviously, you'll do pretty well with those groups, and we want them to see you as their candidate right off. They don't translate into many votes in your district, but they'll ante up.'

'Ante up?'

'I'm sorry, it's Vegas, you know? Look, I do this for a living, so sometimes I get to sounding pretty cynical. Don't be put off. You won't have to worry about any of that. That's why we get a good financial chair. It's his problem. Or hers. You'll bring a different perspective to Congress, Captain. And I'm not blowing smoke in your ear. You can make a difference in Washington. Congress will be just a start. Mark my words.'

Danny had hoped that meeting Rosenstein would end his ambivalence about running for political office, one way or the other. But right now he only felt more confused. He'd expected the political operative to be cynical, so he wasn't shocked that he spoke about people in terms of how much money they might be able to contribute. And by now so many people had told him that he ought to run that he was almost used to being called a 'hero,' even if from his point of view he was only a hardworking guy who did his job.

What confused him was his duty. Day by day in the military, in his experience, it was usually obvious: You followed orders, you accomplished your mission, you looked out for your people.

But there were higher responsibilities as well. If you had the potential to be a leader, then you should lead. That was one of the reasons he'd become an officer, and why he'd gone to college on an ROTC scholarship. Or to put it in the terms his mom would have used, 'If you have the brains, don't sit on them.'

So if he had a chance to be a congressman – to shape the country's laws and maybe make a difference – should he take it? Was it his responsibility to become a congressman because he could?

'Heads up, Captain. Here come our appetizers,' said Rosenstein as the waiter approached.

As Danny started to sit back, the beeper on his belt went off. He glanced down at the face and saw the call was from Dreamland.

'I have to go make a phone call,' he told Rosenstein, getting up.

'Colonel needs you,' said Ax when he reached the base. 'Said it might be a case of whiplash.'

'On my way,' Danny snapped.

Dreamland
1930

'I don't see the point of you deploying with us, Mack,' said Dog. 'There's not going to be much for you to do.'

'Piranha's my project, Colonel. You put me in the slot, right? I have to liaison. Let me liaison.'

'There's nothing to liaison with, Mack. You're needed here.'

'I'm just twiddling my thumbs here.'

'You're supposed to be doing a lot more than twiddling your thumbs.'

'You know what I mean, Colonel. I want to be where the action is. Hey – I'll learn to drive the Piranha. We're short on operators, right?'

'I'm not going to train you on the fly. We have Delaford and Ensign English. Zen and Starship are already checked out as backups; that gives us four operators. We can do the mission like that for a while.'

'Is it because of the wheelchair?' asked Mack.

'It's not because of the wheelchair,' said Dog. 'But since you bring that up, I think frankly that you would be better served by continuing your rehab here.'

'Ah, I'm doing fine with it.'

'All the more reason to keep up with it. If you'll excuse me, I have some packing to do.'

Near Karin, Somalia, on the Gulf of Aden 4 November 1997 0431

Ali Qaed Abu Al-Harthi stood on the bow of the small boat as it approached the rocky cut. It had been a long day and night, and while not without success, Ali focused now on the loss of his crew. The dozen Yemenis aboard the missile boat had abandoned ship as soon as the missile had been fired, and then were picked up promptly, but seven good men had been in the patrol craft the Americans had blown out of the water.

One was his son, Abu Qaed.

Surely Abu was at God's bosom now, enjoying the promise of Paradise. But this was of small consolation to a father, even one so devout and committed to the cause of Islamic justice as Ali.

He remembered teaching the boy math when he was only three; he recalled bringing him to the mosque for the first time; he saw him now with the proud smile on his face as they made the Hajj, the great pilgrimage to

Mecca that all devout Muslims must undertake once in their lives.

Was that not the proudest day of Ali's life? To toss the stone at the Satan pillar with his strapping son at his side? He had thrown his stone and turned to watch Abu throw his.

There could be no prouder moment. There had been no moment more perfect in his life.

They had made the pilgrimage together only a year ago. Ali had gone twice before; the third was like a special gift from God.

He would trade it to have Abu. Surely he would trade his own life.

Ali gazed to the west. An ancient fishing village sat on the port side as he came toward shore. Just to the right of it a group of rocky crags leaned over the water. A weathered cement platform, now three-quarters covered by rubble, gave the only clue that the rocks had not been put there by nature. Italian and German engineers had begun establishing a large base here during the early part of World War II. Though abandoned before it could become operational, their work provided several good hiding places, most important of which was a cave that had been intended as a submarine pen. Most of Ali's smaller craft could squeeze under the opening, making it possible to hide them completely from overhead satellites and aircraft.

A second facility sat a half mile to the west – just on the starboard side of the prow as Ali had the helmsman adjust his heading. This was a dredged mooring area of more recent vintage, though it too had been abandoned to the elements. Several rusting tankers and small merchant ships sat at permanent anchorage, everything useful long ago stripped from the hulks. Some rode high in the water, empty; others rested just below the surface, the elements having won their relentless onslaught against the metal hulls. In the early 1970s the facility had been a metal and materials salvage operation owned by a group of Somalis with connections to the government. A Marxist revolution led to a government takeover of the operation, which had more to do with the failure of the principals to pay bribes than political philosophy. The men were slaughtered and the ships soon forgotten, left to stare at the rocks. The buildings beyond had been abandoned, until Ali had set up shop here a year before. He rarely visited – the key to his success was to move constantly – but tonight he had returned to examine his prize: the dark shadow on his right, sitting well above his vessel.

So at least Abu and the others had not died in vain, Ali thought, even if it was not a trade he would have freely made.

The helmsman turned the boat to port, bringing it around toward its berth. Ali waited stoically, thinking of his son one last time. The scent of the midnight storm that had helped them escape the Americans hung in the air, a reminder of God's beneficence in the midst of struggle. The rain had been fierce but lasted only an hour; long enough, however, to confuse their enemy.

'Captain!' said the man on the pier as he jumped off the boat. 'I have brought the ship in.'

'Saed?' Ali asked.

'Yes, sir!'

'Why is the vessel not being camouflaged?'

'They only just arrived,' said Saed. 'The captain wanted food for his crew.'

'Find him and tell him that if the ship is not properly fitted so that it looks like the other wrecks before the Russian satellite passes overhead at ten, I shall cut him into a dozen pieces with my knife. It is to take the place of the one that was destroyed yesterday. It must be as close as possible. The Russians may miss it, but the Americans will not.'

The pilot nodded, then ran off.

Zeid, Ali's second-in-command, was waiting on shore. 'All of the American ships are near the Yemen coast,' he said. 'Our people have been quite active – they make not a move without us seeing.'

'Yes.' Ali did not pause, but walked directly toward the building he used as both command post and personal quarters.

'The torpedoes nearly struck the American ship,' said Zeid, catching up. 'That would have been quite a blow.'

Ali didn't answer.

'I would like to be the one to sink Satan's Tail,' said Zeid, using the nickname they had given to the shadowy warship that had hunted them for the past two weeks. 'It would be a moment of glory for all time.'

'Yes,' said Ali softly.

The American ship and its three smaller brethren had surprised him the first night it appeared, and only God had managed to save him – God and a timely distress call from the ship they'd tried to attack, saying that a man had gone overboard. Ali watched from Yemen waters as the American vessel, roughly the size of a frigate but much lower in the water, turned its daggerlike bow toward the tanker. For a moment the moonlight framed it against the waves. It had two wedge-shaped gun turrets on the forward deck; behind the superstructure, its topside looked like a piece of wood planed flat. The stern had a slot, as if it were a barracuda's tail, flapping against the waves.

Satan's Tail.

And like the devil, it slipped into the shadows and was gone.

Ali almost believed it had been an apparition, but the next day the ship and one of its smaller cousins chased the patrol boat he had taken to transport some of the Egyptian brothers to Djibouti, where they could help the movement there. Satan's Tail made the journey almost impossible, and Ali nearly had to confront a Djibouti gunboat before finding a way to slip past and take his passengers to an alternative landing point north of the capital. This stretched his fuel reserves, and he was forced to appropriate some at a marina. He did not regret taking it, but it was a troublesome complication.

Since that time, Ali had worked with the knowledge that the American ships might be just over the horizon. He had mobilized his army of spies – mostly fishermen and coast watchers – to help, but reports were difficult once they were far from shore. Simple detectors in his fleet could detect the powerful radars American ships usually used, giving an hour of warning, if not more, of their approach. But these ships did not use those radars. In fact, the only radar they seemed to use was an older Italian-made radar that Ali had learned of many years before, during a long apprenticeship as a junior officer with the Italian navy. It was clearly not their only means of searching for him, but he had not been able to detect any aircraft operating with them, let alone the radars that such craft would field. It was possible that they were using a very sophisticated acoustical device, though if so, it was far superior to any he had seen in the NATO or Egyptian navies. The heavy traffic of the channel and shallow waters of the coast gave them some amount of protection, but Satan's Tail was a difficult adversary. He had found out tonight its guns were even more dangerous than he had feared, their salvos unlike anything he had ever seen at sea before. Like all demons, the American vessel would not be easily exorcized.

The answer, he hoped, had arrived that evening, sneaking into port during his diversionary action two hundred miles away. In itself, the vessel wasn't much. A member of the Russian Polnocny class, she had been built many years before in Poland to support landings by amphibious forces. Her upturned bow could be beached and the doors opened, allowing vehicles to roll off the large tank deck that ran through the center of the ship. But Ali wasn't interested in its ability as an amphibious warfare vessel; he had no tanks and no desire to fight on land. Indeed, the work he had spoken of to his man included modifying the deck to make the ship appear from the air as much as possible like an old junker, a local merchant ship a few months from the scrap heap.

Once the Russian and American satellites passed on their predictable schedules overhead, the real modifications would begin: the addition of advanced SS-N-2D Styx ship-to-ship missile launchers. Vastly improved over the early model fired from the Yemen missile boat, the missiles had a forty-six-mile range and included an infrared backup, allowing them to find their targets even if jammed by an electronic countermeasure system. The missiles would allow Ali to attack Satan's Tail from a distance without having a good 'lock' from the radar, which he suspected would be impossible. While the odds on a single or even double shot succeeding were high, Ali believed from his training that a barrage firing in two or more waves of missiles would succeed. An anti-ECM unit built by the Indians to update the missile confused NATO close-in ship protection systems, such as those that typically used a Phalanx gun to shoot down cruise missiles. Whether the units – or even the missiles, which had been purchased from North Korea – worked would only be determined in combat. But Ali intended to find out as soon as possible.

The missiles would be camouflaged as crates on the ship's deck. The 30mm cannons and a large 140mm gun designed for land bombardment had been stripped years before, something Ali thought would now be in his favor, since even if the vessel were properly identified, she would appear toothless.

The two men guarding the door to Ali's headquarters snapped to attention as the commander approached. One had been a lifelong friend of his son's; Ali remembered carrying both boys on his back when they were five. He paused, placing his hand on the young man's shoulder. 'My son has gone tonight to Paradise,' he told the young man.

The guard's face remained blank, not comprehending.

Inside the office, Ali knelt to the floor and bent his head in silent prayer, as was his custom. But his body shook and the words wouldn't come. He began to sob, wracked by grief.

'It is a terrible thing to lose a son.'

Ali looked across the darkened room. Sitting in the corner was the Saudi. It had been months since they had spoken in person; Osama bin Laden's beard seemed whiter even in the darkness.

'How did you know?' asked Ali.

'If you were a superstitious man I would tell you a lie, and you would believe, wouldn't you, because your emotion is so great?' The Saudi rose from the chair and came toward him. He seemed much thinner than the last time they had met, more worn by the weight of his mission to free the faithful from their chains. But there was strong energy in his walk, and when he touched Ali on the shoulder, it was as if that energy sparked into his body. The pain of losing his son retreated, and Ali rose and clasped the older man's hand.

'Thank you for your comfort,' he told him.

'My comfort is nothing. Allah's comfort is all. We will

84

have much need of it before our war is over.' He stepped back and looked at Ali, nodding. 'You have done well with your fleet. The large vessel has arrived without being detected.'

'With God's help.'

'You intend it to attack the Americans?'

'Yes.'

The Saudi nodded. It was clear that he had reservations, though it was not his way to interfere directly. He ruled largely by persuasion and was, in Ali's experience, a very logical man, as well as a religious one.

'The Yemenis were able to contribute the vessel with their missile,' said the Saudi.

'A rotting tub with a single missile that could not be aimed properly,' said Ali. 'But we made use of it. We drew the American toward us as a diversion, and nearly succeeded in striking them. They are angry.' He smiled faintly.

'Does their anger frighten you?'

'No. I welcome it.'

'You wish to avenge your son?'

'I do.'

'You should not.'

The words surprised him.

'Your son has found his place in heaven,' the Saudi explained. 'You have no need for revenge in jihad. You must fight for God's agenda, not your own. Only when you are truly pure will you succeed.'

The Saudi was prone to long speeches extolling the virtues of the righteous war and the need for God's soldiers to be pure. Ali was not in the mood for such a speech. He lived not in the world of ideals, but in the real world, and he had just lost his son.

'I fight as I am,' he said, sitting in his chair.

'And we are all the better for it. Tell me, if you had your wish, what would it be?'

'What would I wish for? My son back beside me.'

'And?'

'Many things. More weapons, fuel for my ships. Better communications. Missiles that can be fired at long range. More ships.'

'Airplanes?'

Ali frowned. The Ethiopians had promised several times to send aircraft to his aid, as had Yemen and Sudan. Supposedly they had taken off on missions several times in the past week, but if so, Ali hadn't seen the proof.

'I don't need airplanes,' he said.

'Not even against the American ship?'

'They shouldn't even attempt that. It could easily shoot them down. However –' Ali pitched his body forward. 'The American Navy sometimes uses unarmed radar and electronics aircraft called Orions. Those would be easy targets for a fighter. There must be one operating somewhere in the Gulf of Aden, perhaps disguised as a civilian. If that were shot down, that would help me.'

The Saudi nodded thoughtfully.

'I can tell them the sort of radar signals to look for,' said Ali. 'I will have a message delivered to the embassy.'

'Deliver it to Yemen as well.'

The air force in his native land was staffed entirely by

cowards who would never act, but Ali told the Saudi he would do so before his first meal.

'Other ships will join you within a few days. Large, powerful ships that you can use. A vessel from Oman,' added the Saudi.

'Oman? From the corrupted government?'

'Brothers there are active. Details will be provided in the usual way.'

'A missile boat would be very useful.' Ali ran his hand over his chin. He needed fuel, food – those were the problems of a commander, more difficult to solve than the tactics of warfare.

'If you had everything you wished for,' said the Saudi, 'what would you do?'

'I would sink the enemy's ships.'

'The one that killed your son?'

'Yes.'

'Is that the limit of your ambition?'

'I would sink every ship that I could find,' said Ali. 'I would continue to obtain the tribute that is God's so we could fight the only war. I would show the West that they are not the rulers of the world.'

The Saudi stared at him. His eyes were the eyes of a viper, black diamonds that missed nothing.

'What would you do with a submarine?' said Osama.

'A submarine?' Had anyone else made this suggestion, Ali would have thought it a joke – but the Saudi did not joke. 'A submarine would be very useful.'

'Friends in Libya who agree with our aim have volunteered to join you. The vessel has been sailing for many days. It had to go around Africa. We have been trying to get word to you in a way that the Americans and Jews could not intercept. Finally, I decided I must come myself.'

The Saudi told Ali that the submarine would arrive at a point ten miles due north of Boosaaso and surface at ten minutes past midnight on the morning of November 8. If no contact was made, he would surface the next night, and the next.

'They will surface every night to look for you. They will do so until they run out of fuel and food. If you do not come, they will destroy the first American warship they see. And then the next, and so on, until they have no more weapons to fire. Then they will crash their ship into the enemy, and commit their souls to Allah.'

'We will meet him,' said Ali. He was somewhat skeptical at the mention of Libya. The Libyan Navy had several submarines, all Russian vessels that the Italian navy had tracked when they came out of port. These were Project 641 and 641B ships, members of the Foxtrot and Tango class, large, oceangoing submarines. Not quite as quiet as the Kilo class of diesel-powered export submarines, they were still potent ships – but only if properly maintained and manned. In his experience, the Libyan vessels were neither.

'There is one other matter of interest,' said the Saudi.

Ali understood that this was meant to be the condition for the largesse Osama had brought. He listened without emotion as the Saudi told him that God's plans were immense, and the war against Satan immeasurable from a human perspective. Personal feelings could have no place in it. Only after this lengthy preface did he get to the heart of the matter:

'Friends of ours have learned that a British aircraft carrier named the *Ark Royal* is due to sail through the Suez Canal at the beginning of next week. Have you heard of it?'

'Of course. It's the pride of their fleet.'

'If the ship were to be sunk, it would be a major blow to the West. The British could not afford to replace her. Others would see what happens to those who work closely with the devil. The blow would be much mightier than any attack on a smaller ship, however great the lesser strike would be.'

'There will be many protections in place,' said Ali. It was clear that the Saudi knew nothing about sea matters; suggesting an attack on an aircraft carrier was foolhardy, even by a submarine. 'Aircraft carriers sail with several other vessels and are watched constantly.'

'According to our Egyptian friends, the carrier is on a journey to India. Perhaps they will not be on their guard the entire distance.'

'Perhaps,' said Ali.

'The Egyptians will make much information available. Some I do not entirely understand, I confess. They speak of three escorts, and an air arm at half strength.'

Three escorts would be standard – two optimized for air defense, one for submarine warfare. They were good ships, though certainly not unbeatable. The air arm probably referred to the carrier's complement of Harrier jump jets; half strength *might* mean as few as four planes were aboard the carrier. Ali would have to find out; such a low number would limit patrols severely. The ship would also have helicopters for radar and antisubmarine work – potentially more of a problem than the Harriers.

Was he thinking of attacking? Against such strong odds?

It would be suicidal.

He did not care for his own life now. Death would be welcome. And wouldn't God see to it that he succeeded?

The answer was obvious. This was an order from God; the Saudi was only a messenger.

During his time with the Italian destroyer *Audace*, one of their regular exercises had called for an attack on the flagship of the Italian fleet, the *Giuseppe Garibaldi*. The *Garibaldi* was somewhat smaller than the *Ark Royal*, displacing only about half the tonnage. In some ways it was much more capable, however – unlike the *Ark Royal*, it carried potent surface-to-surface missiles and torpedo launchers; even during the exercises when it was stripped of its escorts it held off Ali's ship. In fact, it usually did better without escorts: There were never enough to properly screen against a surface attack if it was launched properly, but the carrier crews saw the other ships and believed they were well-protected. They were less than vigilant.

The attack would have to be orchestrated very carefully.

The surprising thing he had seen during the exercises was the ineptness of the flight crews when locating attacking ships. They trained almost exclusively to bombard land targets or combat submarines. The captain of Ali's ship had dodged one patrol merely by identifying the ship as one of the carrier's screening vessels. The vessel had been permitted to get close enough to launch its surface-to-surface missiles unscathed.

The commander had been reprimanded for his trickery; Ali thought he should have been commended. It was the pilot's fault, after all; truly he should have been able to tell the difference.

If he could sink it – if he did sink it – wouldn't that send a message that anyone who was friends with the Americans could be targeted? Wouldn't the nations of the Middle East – the small ones especially, like Djibouti and Bahrain, but also the bigger ones, Egypt, Saudi Arabia – realize they weren't safe?

Ali looked over at his visitor and found him smiling.

'You understand how truly majestic it would be,' said Osama. 'I can see it in your face.'

'Yes, I do understand,' said Ali. 'But – it would not be an easy task. I would need much information – considerable information.'

'You will have it.'

'The Iranians?'

'The Iranians will not be cooperative. We will work to get you other resources,' said the Saudi. 'And God will be with you. Come. It is almost dawn. Let us prepare to pray. It will be a glorious day.'

II

Xray Pop

Aboard the *Abner Read*
4 November 1997
0800

Storm sipped the cold coffee, its acid bitterness biting his lips. Admiral Johnson had been called away from the camera in the secure communications center aboard the *Vinson*. The pause gave Storm a chance to regroup and reconsider his approach. By the time Johnson's face flashed back on the screen, Storm was more deferential.

'As you were saying, Captain?' said Johnson.

'We have reviewed the data, and the weapons were definitely aimed at us,' said Storm.

'You still disobeyed your orders of engagement. You were not within visual range and therefore could not positively identify the craft.'

'Admiral, I believe that United States warships are permitted – excuse me, *directed* – to take any and all prudent actions to protect themselves.'

'You were not supposed to pursue any warships into territorial waters,' said Johnson, who wasn't about to let go of this. He continued over the same territory he had covered earlier, speaking of the delicacy of diplomatic negotiations and the political situation in the Middle East.

Storm took another sip of his coffee. No other commander would get this lecture; on the contrary, they would be commended for forceful and prudent action and the sinking of two pirate vessels, wherever their rusty tubs had gone down. Storm was only getting blasted because Tex Johnson hated his guts.

'Talk to the intelligence people. I have other things to do,' said the admiral finally.

Storm leaned back in his seat, waiting for Commander Megan Gunther and her assistants to come on line. But instead the screen flashed with the chief of staff, Captain Patrick 'Red' McGowan.

'You son of a bitch you – congratulations on sinking those bastards!' said Red.

'Thank you, Captain.'

'Don't give me that Captain bullshit, you dog. Tell me – did those idiots you were chasing blow themselves up or what?'

'Just about,' said Storm.

'So you sunk them with the gun, huh?'

'Didn't seem worth a missile,' said Storm. 'Of course, a tactical decision like that would be made by the ship's captain.'

'Bullshit. I'm surprised you didn't go down and load the damn gun yourself.'

'Computer does all the hard work.' Storm smiled. He might be a micromanager and a pain in the butt and all that – but he also knew that he took care of his people when the shit hit the fan. And they knew it too.

'They're mighty pleased back at the Pentagon. Everybody's lining up to buy you some champagne.'

'Everybody except your boss.'

'Ah, don't worry about Tex. He's just pissed that you're getting most of the credit. He'll come around. By tomorrow he'll be reminding people Xray Pop was his idea.'

Red meant that as a joke – Tex had opposed the idea as premature, and Storm had only prevailed by calling in favors owed to him at the Pentagon. It didn't hurt that he'd had several assignments under the present Chief of Staff, Admiral Balboa, when Balboa headed CentCom. Balboa was a bit too pansy-assed for Storm, but connections were connections.

'I'm telling you, Tex is warming up to you,' added Red. 'He has the commendation all written out.'

'The only reason that might be true is if you wrote it.'

Red smiled. 'So how many of the little suckers are left?'

'No idea,' said Storm. 'There were at least three other boats last night, all of them patrol-boat-sized. And we've seen others. It's a motley assortment.'

'One of your little Shark Boats couldn't take care of them?'

'I have to tell you, Red, not having over-the-horizon systems is hurting us quite a bit. If we had those Orions we'd be doing much better. Listen – give me the *Belleau Wood* and I guarantee we'll wipe these guys off the face of the earth.'

Red laughed, but Storm wasn't joking. The *Belleau Wood* – LHA-3 – was an assault ship capable of carrying Harriers and AH-1W SuperCobras as well as nearly two thousand Marines. The ship looked like a downsized aircraft carrier, which she essentially was. When Storm had originally drawn up the proposal for Xray Pop and the mission here, he had wanted *Belleau Wood* or one of her sister ships involved, intending to use the airpower to provide reconnaissance and air cover. He also would have used the Marines to strike the pirate bases.

'What happened to your Sea Sprite helicopters?' asked Red when he noticed Storm wasn't laughing.

'Still back at Pearl. It's a sore subject, Red. Those helos weren't designed to operate from the *Abner Read*, let alone the Shark Boats. I need the UAVs.'

'Not going to happen.' Red shrugged; weapons development wasn't his area. 'Any other news? You find that lost Libyan submarine?'

'Give me a break, huh? The Libyans can't even get out of port, for cryin' out loud. They're not going to sail around Africa.'

'National Security Council thinks it's real. Rumor has it Phil Freeman is sending a detachment out of Dreamland to look for it.'

'Dreamland? Out here?'

'Strictly to find the submarine.'

'As long as they stay out of my way,' said Storm. He'd heard of Lieutenant Colonel Tecumseh 'Dog' Bastian: He'd gotten his nickname because it was 'God' spelled backward. Bastian was so full of himself he could have been in the Army, Storm thought. 'That Yemen missile boat we sunk – does that mean we can go into Yemen waters now?'

'You heard that the Yemen government claims it was stolen, I assume.'

Storm snorted in derision. 'Sounds like the story we told the night we stole the Army's mule for the game.'

Red smiled. As students at Annapolis, Red, Storm, and four other midshipmen had conducted an elaborate operation to procure the Army mascot prior to the Army-Navy game. The operation had involved considerable daring, skulduggery, and not a little deceit – but its success had guaranteed that the six would live forever in Academy lore. It also hadn't hurt their careers.

'Untie my hands, Red. Let me go after these bastards where they live. They don't respect the law. Why should we? Let my ships go into territorial waters.'

'Talk to the politicians,' said Red. 'Even Tex'll back you on that.'

'Untie my hands. That's all I ask.'

'That and an assault ship and half of the Navy's Marines.'

'I'll take two platoons of Marines. With or without the ship.'

'Where will you put them?'

'Marines? I'll give 'em a rubber raft and tell them that's all they get until they take over one of the patrol boats. I'll have the whole damn pirate fleet by nightfall.'

Near Karin, Somalia,
on the Gulf of Aden
4 November 1997
1731

Fatigue stung Ali's eyes as he walked up the gangplank to the large ship. He had not slept since the battle. It was not simply a matter of restlessness, or even the demands of his position. He feared that he would dream of his son the same way he had dreamed of his wife after her death. The dreams had been vivid and heart-wrenching; he could not face such an ordeal now.

The ship was nearly twice as long as his boats. Once part of the Russian navy, it had fallen into great disrepair after being delivered to Somalia as part of a deal the communists used to sway the corrupt government years before. The ship had fallen under the control of a warlord in Mogadishu, who had agreed to donate it to the Islamic cause in exchange for weapons and cash.

Rust stained the hull and the odor of rot hung heavy over the ship. Netting and fake spars had been strategically placed ahead of the forecastle to make the vessel look more like a merchant trawler from the air. Ali had no illusion that this would fool a discerning eye intent on discovering the ship; he merely wanted to make it easier to overlook.

'Admiral Ali,' said the ship's captain, greeting him as he came aboard. 'It is a pleasure, sir.'

'I am not an admiral,' Ali told him.

'Yes, sir,' said the captain. He led the way around the deck of the ship, showing Ali to the bridge.

'I wish to see the engines,' said Ali.

'The engine room,' said the captain doubtfully. When Ali did not respond, the captain dutifully led him to a ladder and they descended into the bowels of the ship. The stench of rot increased as they went down; the way was dark and the passages narrow. Ali noticed several sets of pipes and wires that were broken, and there were bits of the decking that seemed as if a shark had bitten through.

In truth, the engine room was not as bad as he expected when he saw the captain's frown. Water slopped along the floor, but it was less than an inch. The massive 40 DM diesels seemed clean enough, and while the space smelled of diesel oil, Ali had been on several ships in the Egyptian navy that were much worse. There were two men on duty, one of whom did not speak Arabic – a Polish engineer familiar with the engines whom the captain had somehow found and managed to hire.

'He is, unfortunately, a drinker,' said the captain as they went back topside. 'But he knows the engines.'

'You have done very well getting the ship here,' said Ali. 'But you have much more work to do.'

'I understand, Captain.'

'We will obtain the missiles in a few days. How long will it take you to install them?'

Ali listened as the ship's commander told him that he had two men trained by the Russians to work with the

101

systems, and several others willing to work with them. This neither answered the question nor impressed Ali.

'Two brothers from Egypt will join you tomorrow and help with the work,' Ali told the captain. 'They will help you determine how much additional laborers are needed. One of my men will install a radio system with an encryption system.'

'Thank you, Captain.'

Ali nodded. 'We need a name.' The vessel looked the opposite of a warship, and giving it a warlike name would be an affront, he thought. It needed something nobler. '*Sharia.*'

The word meant 'Islamic law' in Arabic. It was the only true law, the law that would be restored when the *jihad* was won.

'It is a good name. Fitting.'

'Make sure your crew does not embarrass it,' said Ali, turning to go back to the dock.

Approaching Khamis Mushait Air Base, southwestern Saudi Arabia
6 November 1997
1331

Breanna put the aircraft into a wide turn over the desert to the east of Khamis Mushait, waiting for the ground controllers to decide that she was cleared to land. The other Megafortress, *Wisconsin*, had landed ten minutes ago. It wasn't clear what the hang-up was, since there were no other aircraft visible on the ramps or anywhere near the runway.

The city looked like a clump of dirty sugar cubes and miniature plastic trees stuck in a child's sandbox. Yellowish brown sand stretched toward the horizon, as if the desert were marching toward the city and not the other way around. This was actually a relatively populous area of the country, with highways that had existed for centuries as trade routes and cities that had been shady oases before the Pharaohs built the pyramids. But from the air the land looked sparse and even imaginary.

'What do we do if we don't get cleared in?' asked Lieutenant Mark 'Spiderman' Hennemann, her copilot.

'Then we launch our Flighthawk, have Zen take out the tower, and settle down right behind him,' she said.

The copilot didn't laugh. 'Bree?'

'I'm kidding,' she told him. 'If you're going to fly with me, Spiderman, you better get a sense of humor.'

'I'm working on it,' he said, as serious as if she had told him to review a flight plan or procedure.

Breanna began to laugh.

'Did I miss another joke?' asked Spiderman.

'Never mind. See if you can get a hold of Colonel Bastian on the ground and find out what *i* hasn't been dotted.'

'Will do.' Spiderman punched the flat-panel touch-screen at the right side of his dashboard. 'We have about fifteen minutes of fuel left.'

'Looks like that's how long they have to decide whether we're allowed to land or not.'

The Saudis took nearly all of them before not one but two officers came on offering their 'most sincere and humble apologies' and directing the Megafortress to land. Breanna brought the plane in quickly, setting the big jet down on the ample runway. She found a powder-blue Saudi Royal Air Force car waiting as she approached the far end of the runway; the car led them past a group of Saudi F-15s to the far end of the base. Well-armed Saudi soldiers were clustered around a pair of trucks parked at the side of the ramp. An Air Force advance security team had been sent down from Europe and was waiting near the revetment where they were led.

'Ah, home sweet home,' said Breanna as she and her copilot began shutting down the aircraft after parking.

Dog took another slug from the bottle of mineral water. He felt as dry as the desert outside, even though he'd already finished two liter bottles since landing. Commander Delaford, meanwhile, poked at the large map they had mounted on the wall of the command center the Saudis had loaned them. The facilities – built less than a year before and never used – combined living and work quarters and could have fit at least two squadrons if not more. And they weren't little rooms either – this one was about three times the size of Dog's entire office suite. His small team was clustered around a table that could have accommodated the entire Joint Chiefs of Staff and their assistants.

'The problem is,' continued Delaford, 'the best place to launch the Piranha probe to guarantee that it won't be spotted going in is in this area here, well off the Somalian coast and a good distance from the shipping lanes. But that puts it six hundred miles from the most likely places for the submarine to be. At forty knots, that's fifteen hours of swim time before the probe starts doing anything worthwhile.'

'Let's just deploy the probe at the same place where we put the sentinel buoy,' suggested Zen. 'If we have to be close to land and the water anyway, let's take the risk at one place and at one time.'

'You'd have to go a little farther south, but not that much,' said Delaford.

'If *Baker-Baker* takes both drops, it can't carry a Flighthawk,' said Breanna. 'But I think limiting ourselves to one aircraft in the target area makes it less risky that we'll be seen visually. The moon will be nearly full.'

They discussed the trade-offs. The Somalian, Sudanese, and Ethiopian air forces were all equipped with modernized versions of the MiG-21, relatively short-ranged but potent fighters. The radar in the Megafortress would make the large plane 'visible' to them from no less than one hundred miles, possibly as many as 150 or 200, depending on the equipment they carried and the training the pilots received. On the other hand, the ground intercept radars that were used in the countries were limited, and it would be difficult for them to vector the airplanes close enough to the area.

'Don't kid yourself,' said Dog. 'This is probably like Bosnia – there'll be spies all over the place. They'll know when we take off.'

'It'll still be hard to track us,' said Breanna.

'Why don't we fly *Wisconsin* with a Flighthawk over the area first, doing reconnaissance,' said Zen. 'Then head south over the general area where Piranha will head. We come back and hand off the Flighthawk to *Baker-Baker*, land, replenish, and take off for another mission in the morning.'

'Stretching the crew,' said Dog.

'Just me. Ensign English can drive the Piranha on the second shift, and you can have the backup flight crew take the aircraft. 'We can get back to twelve hours on, twelve hours off. One Flighthawk per mission.'

'I think it'll work,' said Breanna.

'Still, the turnaround on the mission times will be ridiculously tight,' said Spiderman, who was acting as maintenance officer as well as copilot of *Baker-Baker Two*. 'We're really stretched out here. We have the backup crews, but we're pushing the aircraft and systems. We need more maintainers and technical people, Colonel.'

'Our MC-17 should be here with the full load in two hours,' said Dog. 'We'll bring more people and equipment in as needed.'

As usual, the most difficult part of the mission wasn't actually the objective itself, but getting the people and material into position to do the job in the first place. The so-called 'little people' – the guys and gals who fueled the aircraft, humped the supplies, tightened the screws – were in many ways the ones the mission actually hinged on. And Dog knew that the hardest part of his job wasn't dodging bullets or Pentagon bullshit – it was finding a way to get his support people to the places they were needed the most.

'All right, let's all take a break and get a feel for our

quarters,' said Dog as the outlines of their tasks were finally settled. He glanced at his watch. 'I'll brief the *Wisconsin* flight and mission in an hour. Breanna, you and *Baker-Baker* should be ready to launch two hours after we do.'

'When are we going to come up with a better name for the plane?' Breanna asked. 'It has to have a real name.'

'Let's deal with that later,' said Dog.

'Yeah,' said Zen. 'We're going to need an hour just to find our rooms in this place. The building's bigger than half the cities in Saudi Arabia.'

'One other thing,' said Dog. 'The Saudis have opened their cafeteria on the other side of the base; Danny's making the arrangements. Listen, I know I don't have to remind any of you that we're in a Muslim country, and a very sensitive one at that. Please, pass the word – best behavior. We're ambassadors of goodwill here. Frankly, the lower the profile we have the better.'

'We're going to be too busy to have much of a profile,' said Delaford.

'Hopefully,' said Dog.

**Near Boosaaso, Somalia,
on the Gulf of Aden
6 November 1997
1731**

Ali steadied himself on the open bridge of the patrol boat as it cut across the shadows below the Somalian coast. Their target sat about a mile away, still steaming lazily

107

for Boosaaso, a port on the Somalian coast. The ship was a freighter carrying crates of packaged food from the Mediterranean. Once the vessel was secured, they would offload as much of the supplies as they could. Ali's men would also scour the ship for anything useful; he was especially interested in batteries and items such as electrical wires that could be used in the repair of the *Sharia*, the Somalian amphibious ship that they were working on. Finally, several hundred pounds of explosive would be packed into the hull, a timer set, and the ship directed toward the open channel: payback to the Greeks who owned her for trying to renege on an earlier arrangement.

'Boarding party is ready, Captain,' said Bari, the dark first mate.

'Signal the other vessels,' said Ali.

'Yes, Captain.'

The merchant ship, the *Adak*, lumbered along at eight knots. It was likely her small crew hadn't even spotted the three fast patrol boats and four smaller runabouts charging toward her stern.

Ali's crew moved to the 40mm gun on the forward deck. He picked up the microphone as they drew alongside the ship.

'Brothers, I speak to you today as a member of the Gulf Cooperation Council,' Ali declared, his voice booming over the loudspeaker. 'Your cargo is required in the struggle against the great enemy. Surrender without resistance and you will be accorded safe passage home. Any who wish to join our cause will be welcomed with eager arms.'

A figure appeared at the rail. Ali repeated his message.

'They're sending an SOS!' said the radioman from below.

'Fire!' Ali told his crew over the loudspeaker. 'Boarding parties, attack.'

Aboard the *Abner Read*,
Gulf of Aden
6 November 1997
1734

Storm had just stepped into the head when Commander Marcum beeped him on the communicator system. Grumbling, he secured his pants and hit the switch at his belt.

'What is it?'

'Storm, we have an SOS from a merchant ship about ten miles from Boosaaso on the Somalian coast,' said the ship's captain. 'They said they were under attack. The radio seems to have gone dead. Seaman who monitored the call couldn't tell if it was real or not. I suspect a trap. Eyes isn't sure. He's working on it.'

'What's the ship?'

'The *Adak*. It's out of Greece. This wouldn't fit with the normal pattern of attacks. It's back to the south a bit quicker than they normally move.'

Which, to Storm's way of thinking, made it all the more likely to be exactly that: an attack.

Boosaaso was a tiny port at the north of Somalia; there

was a small airport near the city. They were a good two hours away from the area.

'I'll be in the Tactical Center in a minute,' Storm said. 'Have Eyes rally one of the Shark Boats; keep the others in reserve in case it's a decoy. If the *Adak* sends another SOS, don't radio back. I don't want to tip off anyone who's listening that we're on our way.'

'Aye aye, Cap.'

Near Boosaaso, Somalia,
on the Gulf of Aden
6 November 1997
1738

The mortar at the rear of the boat made a thick thump as it fired the projectile toward the superstructure of the merchant vessel. The rope whistled behind it as two of Ali's sailors waited for the device it had fired to land. The mortar's payload looked like a folded grappling hook, designed to open as it landed. As soon as the ropes stopped flying through the air, the men grabbed and pulled them taut, securing a connection with the ship. In a matter of seconds they had thrown themselves into the air, swinging across the space and climbing up the side of the vessel. This was the most dangerous moment for Ali's teams as they boarded. Anyone on the other ship with a hatchet and an ounce of courage could sever the line, sending the heavily armed men into the water. To help lessen the chance of this, two of Ali's team peppered

110

the top rail with their machine guns. Ali himself had unfolded the metal stock of his AK-47, though he did not believe in wasting bullets without a target.

Smoke curled from the superstructure of the merchant ship. The fools! They'd gained nothing by calling for help.

Ali saw the first member of his team clamber over the deck, then the second and third. The other boats drew close; more men followed. There were shouts, gunfire. A swell pitched his small craft toward the merchant vessel. At the last second God intervened, pushing the boats apart.

A ladder, two ladders, were dropped off the side. His men were now firmly in control of the deck.

'We monitored a message from some of our brothers in Yemen, Captain,' said Bari, coming up from the radio area. 'I thought it best to bring it to your attention.'

'What?'

'Two large American aircraft landed in southern Saudi Arabia this afternoon,' said the mate, his black face blending into the growing darkness of the evening. 'Perhaps they were the Orions you spoke of. The alert is being spread through Yemen and across the gulf to our other friends.'

A green flare shot from the deck of the merchant ship. His men had taken it over.

'Thank you, Bari,' he told his mate. 'Keep me informed. In the meantime, take command here while I go aboard our new vessel.'

'As you wish, Captain.'

Mack slid into the water and began paddling slowly. A lifeguard watched from the other end, but otherwise he was alone, and would be for the rest of the session. The rehab specialists were off-duty today, and more important, Zen was halfway across the world and couldn't barge in to harass him.

He knew that should have made him relax, but Mack felt even more stressed and tired as he pushed toward the other side. How the hell did Stockard do this every day, anyway? The guy had been in decent shape before his accident, but he was no athlete, not by a mile.

Mack, on the other hand, had gotten letters in high school football and baseball. He had worked out semiregularly, not so much in the past few months maybe, but still, he could be considered in at least reasonably good shape. Yet here he was, struggling to reach the far side of the pool.

He tried pushing his legs – this was supposed to. be about his legs, not his arms. But they wouldn't respond. They were never going to respond, he thought, despite what the doctors said.

He'd known that the moment he opened his eyes in the hotel in Brunei. Breanna was there, looking over him. He'd seen that look in her face, and he knew. If anyone was an expert on whether people would walk or not, it was Breanna.

He had to give Zen one thing – he'd sure as hell picked the right wife.

Mack had met a pretty decent woman in Brunei, as a matter of fact: Cat McKenna, a contract pilot who was now the de facto head of the air force there.

McKenna was more than decent, actually – she was probably the most competent woman pilot and officer he'd ever met. She was also, without doubt, one of the ugliest-looking women he'd ever met. Reasonable enough body, but her nose alone would have stopped a truck. And her chin . . .

But he missed her.

God, thought Mack as he finally reached the edge of the pool, the stinking paralysis is affecting my brain.

**Aboard the *Wisconsin*,
over the Gulf of Aden
6 November 1997
1908**

Zen took over from the computer as the Flighthawk U/MF-3 dropped off the aircraft's wing, ramping up the engine and banking toward the waves below. The aircraft's vital signs flashed in the lower left-hand quadrant of his screen: airspeed pushing through four hundred knots, altitude going down through twenty thousand feet. He had a full tank of gas and all systems were in the green.

'Successful launch, *Wisconsin*,' he told Dog, who was piloting the Flighthawk's mother plane.

'Roger that, Flighthawk leader. We're proceeding on course as planned. The only thing we have on the water in the immediate vicinity is that barge we told you about earlier.'

'Copy. Should have a visual in thirty seconds.'

Zen checked his position on the sitrep screen. This was essentially a God's eye view of the world, with the Flight-hawk marked out as a green arrow at the center of the screen. Using data from the *Wisconsin*'s powerful radar, the computer could detect ships as well as aircraft. The barge that Dog had mentioned appeared as a black rectangle marked SV1 – surface vessel contact 1 – in the right-hand corner of the screen. Zen could get informa-tion about it by asking the computer. If SV1 were a warship, the computer would have checked it against an identification library and provided details on its arma-ment. An operator on the flightdeck – one handled surface contacts, one air contacts – had a database of commer-cial shipping in the area that identified most, though not all, of the major traffic through the Gulf of Aden.

'Full visual on the barge,' said Zen. The computer focused the camera in the Flighthawk's nose on the craft. 'You getting that, Dish?' Zen added, speaking to the oper-ator handling the surface radar.

'Roger that, Flighthawk leader,' Sergeant Peter 'Dish' Mallack replied. 'We copy. Looks like an oil equipment barge. Definitely benign.'

Zen started a turn, taking the Flighthawk around the rear of the craft. The computer kept the camera trained on it, providing a detailed view to the crewman upstairs. Dish used a 'de-dappler' program to analyze the image, strip-ping away and manipulating possible camouflage to make educated guesses about what was aboard the craft. It wasn't foolproof, and relied on close-up video to work well, but it beat staring at shadows with a magnifying glass for hours.

'Confirmed. That is definitely an equipment barge,' said Dish. 'Can we get an infrared image? I'll just double-check the number of people.'

'On this run,' said Zen. He brought the Flighthawk down below three thousand feet and eased off on the slider at the back of his joystick controller. The slider was actually the throttle; the Flighthawk controls had been designed to allow the aircraft to be flown with only one hand. The idea had been that the pilot would control a second Flighthawk with his other hand. In real life, however, switching hands had proven cumbersome and confusing in combat. Typically, the pilot would control one Flighthawk at a time, while letting the computer take the other. Zen routinely flew two but had handled four in exercises.

'Five people aboard,' said Dish as Zen climbed away from the barge. 'Looking good, Major.'

'Let's see how we do a little closer to shore,' he said, continuing on their survey.

Near Boosaaso, Somalia,
on the Gulf of Aden
6 November 1997
2008

The cannon had destroyed a good portion of the bridge, but the ship itself was in decent shape. Ali had no trouble from the surviving crew; they were all good

Muslims, willing to follow his commands – at least while his men were aboard.

Ali's men quickly fell into their routine, bringing over the material for the bombs while removing everything they could find that would be of use.

The captain had had the good sense to die when the first shells raked the superstructure of his ship. This made it unnecessary for Ali to execute him. But as it was necessary to demonstrate that his orders were to be followed without question, when the ship had been secured and most of what they wanted moved off it, Ali had the merchant vessel's crew brought before him on the deck. He asked for the radioman, who after some hesitation stepped forward.

'Why did you make the distress call?' Ali asked.

'My captain directed me to.'

'Do you believe in God?'

'I believe in God, yes.'

'Make your peace with him.'

The man flinched, but bowed his head and began to pray. Ali, who was not without compassion, waited until he finished before executing him, firing a single bullet into the center of his skull.

He had just signaled to his men to throw the man overboard when one of the lookouts ran to him.

'A ship in the distance,' said the man, out of breath. 'It may be Satan's Tail.'

**Aboard *Baker-Baker Two*,
over the Gulf of Aden
6 November 1997
2112**

'Ten seconds to target point,' said Spiderman.

'Roger that,' said Breanna. 'Bay.'

'Bay,' said the copilot. The large doors at the rear of the fuselage swung open. A green light flashed in the heads-up display in front of Breanna; the sentinel buoy was ready to go.

She leaned on her stick, nudging the big aircraft onto her mark. Breanna had the option of letting the computer fly the Megafortress to the release point, but what was the point of that?

'Deploy,' she told the copilot as they hit their mark.

'Sentinel buoy is away,' said Spiderman as the bomb bay dispenser ejected the large cylinder.

Breanna snapped the *Wisconsin* upward and began a hard bank to the southeast, getting into position to launch Phoenix.

'You're up, Commander,' she told Delaford.

'Piranha team is ready,' he said over the interphone.

'Thirty seconds to Piranha release point,' said Spiderman.

'Radar contact!' said Jackson Christian, who was operating *Baker-Baker*'s AWACS-style radar, monitoring other aircraft. 'Bogie at 322, one hundred miles. Identified now as a Chendu F-7M Fishbed, export Chinese fighter aircraft. Might be Sudanese.'

117

'Pretty far from home if it is,' said Breanna.

'Can't match it up otherwise,' said the sergeant. 'Radar is definitely that type, which rules out one of the Ethiopian MiGs.'

'If it is from Sudan, he's at the edge of his combat radius, if not beyond it,' said Breanna. 'Keep tabs on him. Alert Colonel Bastian. Tell him we're proceeding with launch. Commander Delaford?'

'Ready.'

'Spiderman?'

'Counting down. We are at eleven seconds, ten . . .'

The Megafortress hit a turbulent layer of air as it came down closer to the water. The big aircraft shuddered, then responded sluggishly to the control inputs, her right wing fighting against Breanna's stick. She leaned in the seat, as if her body might somehow transfer a bit of spin to the controls and the probe as they ejected it. This may actually have worked, for despite the buffeting, the computer recorded a bull's-eye as Piranha hit the water. The probe shot beneath the waves, preprogrammed to dive to fifty feet. Breanna leveled off and Spiderman initiated their third countdown – the launch of a guidance buoy to control the Piranha.

Downstairs on the Flighthawk control deck, Starship watched Commander Delaford completing the diagnostic series on the sentry buoy. The first buoy they had dropped was basically an automated listening post, transmitting the same data sets as the Piranha probe. It sank itself twelve feet below the surface, using a thin filament antenna to send its data. Shaped more like a tangled ball of yarn, the antenna sent its signals through the Dreamland dedicated satellite system at regular intervals; it could also be tapped directly by the Megafortresses. The signal could be detected, which was one of its few disadvantages, but none of the countries in the region were believed to have equipment sophisticated enough to do so.

'We're two miles south of Barim Island,' said Delaford. 'Looking good.'

'Guidance buoy is in the water,' reported Spiderman over the Megafortress's interphone, or intercom system. The buoy was used to control Piranha from the Megafortress; it had to be roughly fifty miles from the probe and no more than fifty from the aircraft.

'Roger that, thank you,' said Delaford.

Starship shifted around in his seat, trying to get comfortable. For the time being, his job was to back Delaford up, continuing to learn how to operate Piranha. They'd run the simulations on the flight over, and except for the fact that the Megafortress was moving, he couldn't have told the difference.

'Initiating equipment calibration,' said Delaford. 'Bree, we're going to need you to stay close to the buoy until we're ready.'

'Roger that,' said the Megafortress pilot. 'Be advised we now have two aircraft ID'd as Sudanese F-7Ms that are on an intercept. They'll be in our face in about two minutes.'

'I need five,' said Delaford.

'Acknowledged,' said Breanna. 'You'll have them.'

**Aboard the *Abner Read*,
Gulf of Aden
6 November 1997
2115**

'Looks dead in the water, Cap,' said Commander Marcum, handing back the starlight binoculars. 'No sign of the pirates around anywhere.'

Storm took the glasses but didn't answer. The *Abner Read* had a pair of small decks that could be folded out of the superstructure on either side of the bridge – almost literally flying bridges, which were generally kept inside to prevent disturbing the radar profile. They were small and narrow, and weren't high enough to afford much of a view – one of the drawbacks of the ship's stealthy design.

'There's only one way to find out what's going on over there. We have to board her,' said Marcum.

Storm scanned the vessel one more time from bow to stern. The ship had clearly been fired on; there were cannon holes in the superstructure and the bridge appeared to have been gutted.

'I volunteer to lead the boarding party,' said Marcum. 'Only way we're going to find out, Storm. The only way.'

'There's no question we have to board the ship. But you can't go.'

'I'd like to. You would if you were me.'

'No I wouldn't,' said Storm. He shrugged, because it was an obvious lie. 'Send Gordie to lead the team.'

'Yeah, I know,' said Marcum.

'Sudanese F-7Ms on a direct intercept, at our altitude,' said Spiderman. 'Twenty miles and closing. What do you think, Captain?'

'I think they're going to run out of fuel halfway home,' said Bree. 'Obviously someone told them we were here. The other Megafortress is well south.'

The EB-52 design was not as stealthy as the F-117 or B-2, but it nonetheless presented a small radar profile to conventional radars such as those used by the F-7M. Opening the bomb bay doors increased it exponentially, but still, the F-7Ms had help from somewhere.

'About sixty seconds to intercept,' Spiderman said. 'Should I hail them?'

'No. They want to play chicken. Be ready with the ECMs and Stinger just in case.'

She altered her course slightly and rearranged her orbit so the Megafortress's tail was in their face as they approached. This wasn't meant just as an insult: She wanted the Stinger defensive weapon ready in case the other pilots did something stupid.

'Going over our wings,' said Spiderman. His voice had gone up two octaves. 'Ten seconds.'

'Boys will be boys,' said Breanna. She flicked on the interphone, talking to the rest of the crew. 'Preparing evasive maneuvers. Check your restraints, and please keep your hands in the car at all times.'

'Twenty feet over us, both of them.'

'Assholes,' said Bree, pushing her stick to increase the separation.

Aboard the *Wisconsin*,
over the Gulf of Aden
2119

'We're over you, *Baker-Baker*,' said Dog. '*Hawk One* has the MiGs in sight. No weapons radar at this point.'

'Affirmative. I think they just want to play tag.'

'Any hostile acts?' he asked.

'Negative, unless you want to call aggressive stupidity hostile.'

'Depends on the circumstances,' said Dog.

'Question in my mind is who told them we're out here,' said Breanna. 'They had to be vectored toward us from a good distance away. They're breaking off.'

They were – and headed toward the *Wisconsin*.

'I'm on them, Colonel,' said Zen, flying the Flighthawk. 'Looks like they want to check us out. No missiles.'

The Sudanese aircraft were roughly ten miles away from the *Wisconsin*, which was now a few miles north of *Baker-Baker*. Zen flew the Flighthawk between a mile and two miles behind them; it was probable that they couldn't even see him.

'Coming at you,' said Zen.

'Let them come,' said Dog. 'Just keep an eye on them.'

The air surveillance radar on Dog's plane showed the

Sudanese aircraft nearly merging as they approached. Close encounters at high speed were always reckless, but in this case the Sudanese pilots were being particularly foolish. Not only was it dark, but they had no way of knowing what the Megafortress was or would do. It was a large aircraft, one they'd surely never encountered before. That demanded caution, not hotdogging – and these bozos looked like they were going to knock each other out of the sky the way they were going.

He spun the Megafortress through its orbit as the planes passed. They rounded south and headed back toward land.

'All right, looks like they're heading home,' said Breanna. 'I have a mind to go and spank them.'

'Are you sure they're from Sudan?' asked Dog.

'We'll keep tabs on them and see. As I was saying, I still wonder who told them we were out here. I wonder if somebody at Khamis Mushait tipped them off.'

'Very possibly.' Dog checked his position. '*Baker-Baker*, I'd like to resume our patrol south closer to Somalia, get some idea of the area.'

'Go for it. We can take it from here.'

'Roger that.'

He tacked south and then eastward, riding over the gulf toward the coast. When they were about thirty miles from land, he banked gently and began running parallel to Somalia, gradually fine-tuning his position until he was about fifteen miles from the craggy shore. The African continent lay roughly thirty thousand feet below, part of the dull blackness out the copilot's side window. Zen's Flighthawk slipped along below them at 2,500 feet, providing a close-up view of the shoreline and nearby ship traffic. The night seemed quiet, with a few empty tankers heading toward the Persian Gulf and a cluster of fishing boats tied up near a settlement on the shore.

Within an hour they were coming up toward Laasgoray, a tiny hamlet on the coast.

'Colonel, we have a couple of surface contacts moving at pretty high speed here,' said Dish Mallack from his radar station upstairs. 'Uh, two, hold – three patrol boats. They're being ID'd by the computer as members of the Super Dvora Mk II class. That's an Israeli ship, patrol boat, so the computer is just making a match to the closest type.'

'Flighthawk leader, see if you can get a close-up view,' said Dog. He checked the sitrep map. The *Abner Read* – just barely visible on the radar – was about fifty miles farther east and just to the north, next to a much larger ship. Here was his chance to say hello to the task group's commander, and maybe give him an assist at the same time.

'I think these may be the pirates Xray Pop has been hunting,' Dog told Zen. 'Track them while we make contact.'

'I'm on it,' said Zen.

**Near Laasgoray, Somalia,
on the Gulf of Aden
6 November 1997
2220**

Ali strained in the direction the helmsman was pointing, but he saw nothing in the sky.

124

'It came from that direction,' insisted the man. 'It flew toward us, then banked in the gulf.'

A figment of the man's imagination? Or an aircraft hunting for them?

'Stop the boats. Lie dead in the water,' said Ali. He took the signal lamp and flashed the message to the other boats personally as their speed slackened and the boat's prow lowered into the water. 'Man the forward gun and the SA-7,' he told the crew.

Two of the crewmen went to the stern and opened a waterproof locker where the antiaircraft missile was kept. The SA-7 was an old weapon dating to the Cold War, but properly handled, it could be effective against low flying aircraft, helicopters especially.

'Any word on the *Adak*?' he asked Bari, inquiring about the merchant ship they had left behind when Satan's Tail approached.

'No sir. The timer has another five minutes to run.'

'There!' shouted one of the men at the bow. They swung the cannon in the direction of a shadow looming out of the dusky coast to their south.

'Hold your fire!' ordered Ali. 'No one is to fire until I give the order. Bari, signal the others.'

Ali watched as the black triangle approached. It was low, no higher than fifteen hundred feet above. At first it seemed to be a great distance away; then Ali realized it was close but smaller than he had thought. For a moment he feared it was a missile, homing in on them. Despair fluttered in his stomach – he thought of the moment he realized his son was gone – then he realized that the craft was passing overhead.

'A radar is tracking us, Captain,' said Bari. 'It may be an aircraft. It seems to be at long range, but it may be the way the signal is sent, a mechanism designed to be difficult to detect.'

'The docks at Laasgoray, quickly!' said Ali, spinning around and taking the wheel of the boat himself.

**Aboard the *Abner Read*,
Gulf of Aden
6 November 1997
2223**

'We've found three bodies so far,' said Gordie, who was heading the boarding team. 'The bridge is a mess. Auxiliary controls look OK, though. We probably could get her into port with a skeleton crew. We'll know better in the morning.'

'Storm, we have a report coming in from an Air Force unit,' said Eyes, who was standing next to him in the Tactical Center. 'I assume it's the Dreamland group you mentioned, though they won't specifically identify themselves. They have a location on three fast patrol boats about fifty miles from here. They're on Com Line External Two.'

'Hold on, Gordie. Let me deal with this.' Storm went to his station in the Tactical Center. He punched the communications panel at the left. 'Is this Colonel Bastian?'

'This is Technical Sergeant Mallack,' said the man on the other line.

'This is Captain Gale. Give me your boss.'

'Uh –'

'*Now*, mister.'

There was a slight pause, but no click or discernible static on the line.

'This is Colonel Bastian.'

'Colonel, you have surface contacts?'

'We have three fast patrol boats that are similar to Israeli Dvora II class. My radar operator has the specific locations. They're about fifty miles from your location, about seventeen miles offshore but heading toward coastal waters. I haven't had a chance –'

'Sink the bastards.'

'Excuse me?'

'You're ordered to sink them.'

There was a pause. 'You're giving me an order?'

'Colonel, I'm sitting in the water next to a merchant whose crew they slaughtered. Sink them.'

'You know these are the ships?'

'What do you want? Pictures? If I'd been close enough to see them, I would have sunk them.'

'Sorry, Captain, but my orders don't allow me to sink unidentified boats, or any boat for that matter,' said Dog. 'I can track them for you; that's the best I can offer.'

'That's not good enough,' said Storm. 'They'll be in forbidden territory in a second. Sink them.'

'Thanks for the advice.' The line snapped dead.

**Aboard the *Wisconsin*,
over the Gulf of Aden
6 November 1997
2223**

Dog shook his head, wondering why every Navy officer he ever dealt with had an ego larger than an aircraft carrier.

'Patrol craft are starting to move again,' said Sergeant Mallack. He'd gotten his nickname, 'Dish,' not because he worked a radar, but because he always went back for seconds, and sometimes thirds and fourths, in the mess hall.

'Any hostile action?' Dog asked Zen.

'Negative. They manned their guns and got a missile ready, but didn't attack.'

'Follow them at a distance.'

'Flighthawk leader.'

**Aboard *Baker-Baker Two*,
over the Gulf of Aden
2224**

'So what do you figure the Sudanese F-7Ms were up to?' asked Spiderman as they got ready to drop their second control buoy.

'Just a macho thing to show us that they're here,' replied Breanna. 'And to see what we were.'

'They didn't go slow enough to see anything.'

128

'Maybe they were too scared to slow down,' said Breanna. 'Piranha, how are we doing?'

'Probe's just humming along,' said Commander Delaford. 'We have control from the second buoy. Proceeding on course as planned.'

'All right. We're going to swing south and drop our next control buoy, then climb and take a look around.'

'Roger that,' acknowledged Delaford.

'You sleeping yet?' Breanna asked Starship.

'No ma'am,' said the lieutenant. 'Just wishing I'd had a Flighthawk to kick those two ragheads in the rear.'

'All right, let's all just relax,' said Breanna. 'We're going to be out here for quite a while tonight. No sense using up all our adrenaline in one shot.'

'Contacts, hot, Fishbeds!' said the radar operator. 'From the southwest – Ethiopians. Just crossing Somalian territory.'

Aboard the *Abner Read*,
Gulf of Aden
6 November 1997
2225

Storm pounded the ledge at the base of the control console twice before he was able to corral his anger.

'Captain?'

Storm looked up at Eyes.

'Flyboys have found our bad guys. But they don't want to get their hands dirty.' He went over to the display, dialing the range out so he could see the area where Bastian had located the pirates.

'We can get a Shark Boat over in a little more than an hour,' said Eyes.

'They'll be gone,' Storm said. He contemplated going into Somalian territory after them but knew he couldn't – Johnson would jump on it as an excuse to block his career forever.

He could, however, wait for them offshore. Spread a net and catch them when they tried to run.

'Maybe we can have *Boat Three* pick up the boarding party while we go up there,' said Storm. 'Have the two other Shark Boats come as well.'

'Marcum's not going to like that,' said Eyes.

'I wouldn't either. But I think it's our best bet here.'

'*Boat One* is closest.'

Storm reached to his belt and hit the preset, connecting him with the commander of Shark Boat. '*Boat One,* this is Captain Gale. I have a target for you. We'll get the position but you're to stay in international waters and wait until he gets there.'

'Shit.'

Storm punched the button to connect with the boarding party. 'Still there, Gordie?'

'Aye, Cap. What's going on?'

'Looks like the flyboys have found our bad guys. We may arrange for you to have another taxi pick you up. Can you handle that?'

'I can handle anything.'

'Stand by. Commander Marcum will contact you directly.'

130

'Aye.'

Storm took another look at the hologram, then decided to tell the ship's captain personally what he had in mind. He found Marcum out on the folding bridge, looking at the tanker alongside.

'Killed them all?' asked the ship's commander. The other ship was less than twenty feet away, a brooding hulk on the water.

'Looks like it,' said Storm. 'We have a possible location on our pirates. Very close to Laasgoray. They have a fifty-mile head start. I have *Boat One* heading there. I want *Abner Read* to help.'

'What about the boarding party?'

'I'd prefer to have *Boat Three* stand by and pick them up if they need assistance. This way we can leave right away.'

Storm could tell from the look in Marcum's eye that he didn't want to leave his men behind. It was a natural objection, and even though Xray Pop had been configured for exactly that sort of flexibility, Storm couldn't blame him.

'All right,' said Marcum. 'Tell me one thing, though.'

'Yeah.'

'Can we get these bastards?'

'I want to. But not if they're close to shore.'

'Which they will be by the time we get there.'

'Very likely.'

Marcum frowned. Storm turned to go back inside the ship. As he did, the world lit with a red glow and Storm felt himself flying through the air, propelled by a massive explosion.

III

Territorial Waters

Aboard the *Abner Read*,
Gulf of Aden
2234

Storm smashed head first into the side of the captain's chair at the center of the bridge, rolling to the side as the force of explosion pummeled the *Abner Read*. He tried to stand but fell back against the helmsman. Acrid smoke filled the small space, and for a moment he feared the ship was on fire. That fear helped him find his balance, and as alarms began to sound around him, he gave his first orders, calling a fire control party to the bridge.

Scrambling on his hands and knees to the flying bridge, he found Marcum clinging to the damaged decking. He grabbed the lieutenant commander's arms and yelled at him to pull himself up, but Marcum didn't respond. A sailor ran over, leaping down across the deck to help pull the ship's captain inside; it was only then that Storm realized Marcum's grip had tightened around the deck piece in death. A thick piece of metal had buried itself in the back of Marcum's skull. If that hadn't killed him, he would have bled to death from the wounds caused by the shards of steel in his chest and side.

'God, protect him,' said Storm, and then he turned to the business of helping the living.

**Aboard the *Wisconsin*,
over the Gulf of Aden
6 November 1997
2235**

Dog listened as the chaotic conversation between the American ships continued on the radio channels they were monitoring. His reaction mixed outrage with impotence and shock.

'Should I contact them and ask if they need assistance?' said his copilot, Captain Kevin McNamara.

'Give them a minute to sort things out,' said Dog. 'We'll continue our patrol in their direction so we can respond if they do require our help.'

The task force's position was marked at the left-hand side of Dog's control panel screen. The Megafortress was already flying in their direction. It would take a little more than ten minutes to get there.

'Zen, there's been some sort of explosion on the ship Xray Pop boarded,' Dog told the Flighthawk pilot over the interphone. 'It's not clear exactly what's going on. I want to be prepared to assist if necessary. I'm taking us east in their direction until we have confirmation that we're not needed.'

'What do you want to do about these patrol boats?' Zen asked. 'They're splitting up.'

'They're pretty clearly in Somalian waters.'

'Yeah.'

'According to our orders, we can't touch them.'

'Copy that.'

'And, frankly, we have no clear evidence that they're connected to that ship. We have their locations marked. We'll continue tracking them by radar as long as we can, but helping Xray Pop is going to be a priority. We may need the Flighthawk for search and rescue.'

'Flighthawk leader,' said Zen, acknowledging.

Dog nudged the throttle bar, bringing up his thrust to full military power. The weapons dispenser in the Megafortress's bomb bay included a pair of Harpoon missiles capable of obliterating the patrol craft. Hitting them would feel good, and it might even be justified. But he wasn't here to feel good, or even to avenge the death of American servicemen. He was here to accomplish a mission which, technically at least, had nothing to do with Xray Pop.

'I have Xray Pop,' said the copilot.

'This is Colonel Bastian. What's your situation? Are you under fire?'

'Negative,' said the voice on the other end of the radio. 'There's been an explosion on a nearby ship. We're standing by to recover the wounded.'

'I understand,' said Dog. 'Do you require assistance? We're about ten minutes flying time to your location. We can aid in search and rescue.'

'I require you to sink those bastard patrol boats,' said Storm, breaking into the line. 'Sink them, damn it.'

Dog took a second before responding. He'd been in

the other commander's position; losing your people was a gut-wrenching experience.

'I'd like to sink them, Captain,' said Dog. 'But my orders are not to engage the enemy if at all possible, especially in Somalian waters. Do you require assistance?'

'Sink the bastards!'

'We can help with search and rescue. It'll take us a little under ten minutes to get there.'

'If you show up, we'll shoot you down.' Storm, or someone on his ship, killed the transmission.

'Wow,' said McNamara, turning toward Dog.

That about sums it up, thought Dog, though he didn't say anything else.

Aboard the *Abner Read*,
Gulf of Aden
2245

Fortunately, the bridge hadn't actually caught fire – the smoke was from the nearby freighter, which had. While some of the computer systems had been knocked off line, the automated damage control system presented in the holographic display when Storm tapped the controls showed that the ship was in good shape. Her engineering spaces had not been harmed, nor had the structural integrity of the hull been threatened. None of the 'zebra' fittings – closures in overheads, decks, and bulkhead, as well as fittings such as valves, caps, and plugs normally secured during general quarters – had been damaged, and

138

all of the ship's systems had green lights, indicating they were functioning properly. While the damage control teams and different departments of the ship began verifying the automated system's findings, Storm turned his attention to getting the boarding team rescued. The crew had already begun playing searchlights across the water, and manned the second boat for the effort. *Shark Boat Three* was contacted, and pulled out the stops to respond. Anyone without more pressing duties turned to topside, adding their eyes to the watchmen's to scour the water.

The merchant ship had reeled over onto her side, the stern sliding low in the water. Flames shot from part of the hull. The bastards had put a decent-sized bomb on it, and they knew a thing or two about maximizing their efforts.

Storm went out onto the deck over the helo hangar, scanning the waves with his infrared glasses. The wind and sea combined to form an angry howl in his ears – the sound of hell calling, an officer had told him once, on an equally dark and grim night years ago. A seaman had gone overboard during an Atlantic crossing. They never found the poor bastard, and the captain of the ship was never the same, haunted by the memory.

'Man in the water!' called a lookout.

Storm turned to the left, training his infrared glasses in that direction as the watchman yelled to a rescue party along the port side of the *Abner Read*. For a moment he felt the urge to leap over the side himself, and in fact he might have if he'd spotted the man. But he mastered his impulse, and in any event by the time he saw the man, one of the boats from the other ships was bearing down on him.

Back inside, Storm checked with the bridge crew and Tac, then headed down to the launching area at the stern of the ship, where the boat would be recovered. The medical team scrambled ahead of him as he came down the ladder to the landing deck – the U-shaped enclosure at the fantail of the destroyer where the rigid-hulled boats were brought in and out. He heard some of the crewmen shouting and quickened his pace, arriving just as the corpsmen were carrying the recovered man into the dry landing deck, then watched as the two men worked over the victim. Finally, one of the corpsmen looked up and shook his head.

The dead man was Gordie, the officer who'd led the boarding party. His head and chest had been gashed by shrapnel. More than likely he had died before he hit the water.

The other corpsman leaned back, paralyzed, staring into space.

'You did your best,' said Storm. 'Come on now. Let's get ready for the next.'

Aboard *Baker-Baker Two*,
over the Gulf of Aden
2245

'Four aircraft now, and they are on afterburners,' said Spiderman. 'Computer has them ID'd as MF-type, upgraded radar of Elta type. They are within twenty miles. Inside visual range within sixty seconds.'

Breanna needed eighty seconds to get to the next drop point.

'Our friends are going to get fairly close,' she told Delaford. 'I'd prefer to hold off releasing the next buoy until they're past.'

'There's no hurry, Captain,' answered Delaford. 'What are they up to?'

'Probably more intimidation,' said Breanna. 'These are Russian-made MiG-21s with updated avionics. No indication yet if these aircraft have air-to-air missiles, but in theory these are slightly more potent. We'll keep you advised.'

'Still coming,' said Spiderman.

'*Wisconsin*, this is *Baker-Baker Two*,' Breanna said over the Dreamland radio circuit. 'We have four aircraft approaching from Somalian territory. We peg them for Ethiopians.'

'Copy that, *Baker-Baker*,' Dog replied. 'We see them.'

'How do you want us to handle them? Should we hail them?'

'Negative. Maintain radio silence. We're changing course.'

'Thought you were assisting Xray Pop.'

'They don't want our help. We'll be in your neighborhood in about twelve minutes.'

'MiGs have activated their weapons radars!' shouted Spiderman before Breanna could acknowledge.

Mack leaned back in the wheelchair, exasperated. Major Natalie Catsman, Dreamland's second-in-command, shrugged.

'I can't help you, Major. The Werewolves are not your program. And even if they were your program, we don't have resources for that work. Or the funding.'

'What funding do you need?' said Mack. 'You just heard Gleason say that the computer program is exactly the same. You could use the Werewolf to deploy Piranha.'

'I didn't say that exactly,' said Jennifer. 'I said –'

'That's not the point,' said Catsman, raising her hand. 'The point is, it's not your program. And even if it were, the units we have are already allocated. Two Werewolves are joining Captain Freah in Saudi Arabia for base security as well as additional testing. They're gone, as are their technical teams. That eliminates any possibility of testing the naval components this week, or next. Sorry.'

'So we send the Navy modules over to Saudi Arabia, with me, and we test them there,' said Mack. 'Jennifer can come – she's the only decent pilot anyway.'

'Sandy Culver is the lead pilot,' said Jennifer.

'If you're angling to go to the Middle East, Major, it's not going to work,' said Catsman. 'Colonel Bastian wanted you here. That's good enough for me.'

'He didn't say that specifically.'

'Yes, he did. Don't you have a rehab or something to go to?'

Exasperated, Mack pushed his wheels and attempted to sweep out of the office. His off-balance attempt nearly sent him into the doorjamb. He recovered at the last second, swiveling to the left and just barely clearing. He swore he heard snickering, but wouldn't give Catsman the satisfaction of turning around.

He was waiting at the elevator a minute or two later when Jennifer Gleason appeared.

'I made a shot to get you along, Jen,' said Mack.

'Thanks.'

'Catsman's a pain. I could do a better job than she could.'

Gleason didn't say anything.

Women always stuck together, Mack thought. But it was true – he was more qualified than Catsman to run the base.

Not that he wanted to run the base. He would, if it didn't mean sitting behind a desk in a chair all day.

Which, come to think of it, was what he was doing these days. God, he hated the wheelchair.

Aboard *Baker-Baker Two*,
over the Gulf of Aden
2250

The Ethiopian pilot repeated his warning: The aircraft must identify itself or be considered hostile and be shot down.

Breanna bristled. *Baker-Baker Two*'s belly was loaded

143

with Piranha guidance buoys; she had no offensive weapons. If the Ethiopian MiG fired, all she would be able to do was duck.

'Computer has weapons ID'd as AA-12 Adders,' said Spiderman, referring to the NATO designation of the antiair missiles the lead aircraft was packing. Known in Russia as the R-77, the missile was commonly referred to as the 'AMRAAMski.' It had an effective range of perhaps one hundred kilometers; when it came within twenty kilometers of its target, it turned on an active radar guidance system that was difficult to break. The aircraft probably also carried R-73s, known in the West as AA-11s. These were shorter range heat-seeking weapons, mean suckers in a knife fight.

'Radar is locked,' warned the copilot. 'They're firing at us!'

'Countermeasures. Hold on everyone – this may get ugly.'

Aboard the *Wisconsin*,
over the Gulf of Aden
2252

'They're firing at them!' warned McNamara.

Dog already had the throttle at the last stop, but leaned on the slider anyway.

'They're taking evasive action,' said McNamara, monitoring the radar at the copilot station. 'ECMs, ducking away. The Ethiopians split into twos, Colonel – looks like they're trying to get them from both sides.'

144

'Prepare our Scorpions,' he told him. 'Zen, the Ethiopians have opened fire. Two AA-12 Adders have been launched.'

'Flighthawk leader,' said Zen. 'Still zero-five from intercept on the southernmost group.'

Aboard *Baker-Baker Two*,
over the Gulf of Aden
2253

The Megafortress rolled on her left wing, pirouetting in the air as a cloud of metal chaff blossomed above her, an enticing target for the Russian-made air-to-air missile. Between the decoy and the electronic fuzz broadcast by *Baker-Baker Two*'s electronic countermeasures, Breanna had no doubt she would avoid the enemy missile. She was concerned about the follow-up attack. The lead MiG had swung sharply east and then cut north, undoubtedly hoping to swing back around while her attention was on his wingman's missiles. At the same time, he dove closer to the waves, hoping to go so low that her radar couldn't find him. If his maneuvers succeeded, he'd end up behind her, in perfect position to fire his closer-range heat seekers. Meanwhile, the second element of MiGs would close from the south, preventing her from running away.

The tactics would have been effective against another aircraft, but the Megafortress's radar had no trouble keeping track of the enemy plane's position, and unlike other aircraft, it had a stinger in its tail – literally.

As the first AMRAAMski sucked the decoy and exploded a mile and a half away, the MiG began accelerating, trying to close the gap between them.

'Stinger air mines,' Breanna told her copilot.

'Stinger is up,' said Spiderman.

'He's closing. Firing two heat seekers!'

'Relax, Spiderman, I've done this before,' said Breanna. The Russian-made missiles had been fired from roughly five miles away, too far to guarantee a hit against any aircraft, let alone the Megafortress. Breanna waited a beat, then tossed flares out as decoys and tucked hard right. But rather than cutting into a sharp zigzag and losing her pursuer, she stayed with the turn, inviting the MiG to close and take another shot. A cue in her heads-up display warned her that he had switched to his gun radar, but he was not yet in range. Breanna started a cut back, again just enough to keep her quarry thinking that he was the hunter.

'Firing,' warned Spiderman.

'Boy, he *is* a slow learner,' said Breanna. The MiG was roughly three and a half miles off, too far for his bullets to strike the Megafortress.

'Two more contacts closing,' warned Spiderman.

'Hang in there,' said Breanna. She nudged left, lining her adversary up. 'Stinger ready?'

'Uh-huh.'

'Now!' she told the copilot, slamming the throttles and using the Megafortress's control surfaces as air brakes to dramatically lower her airspeed. The Stinger air mines exploded practically in the face of the following MiG pilot. By the time he realized what was going on, his Tumansky turbojet had sucked in enough tungsten to open a salvage yard – which was about all his jet was useful for.

'He's down! He's ejecting!' shouted Spiderman. 'Way to go, Captain!'

Breanna's answer was to sleek her wings and mash the throttle back to military power, then tuck the Megafortress into a roll – two more radar-guided missiles were headed their way.

Aboard the *Wisconsin*,
over the Gulf of Aden
2255

Zen cursed as the missile flared beneath the wing of the MiG-21 closest to the Flighthawk – he hadn't quite made it in time.

'*Weapon is an AA-12,*' said the computer. '*Target is* Baker-Baker Two. Hawk One *remains undetected. Time to target engagement, thirty seconds.*'

Zen leaned forward as he flew, keeping an even pressure on the joystick controlling the Flighthawk, referred to as *Hawk One* by the computer. He couldn't worry about the missile now, even though it had been aimed at an aircraft flown by his wife; he had to concentrate on the MiG, three miles dead ahead of him.

Or rather, dead ahead of the Flighthawk. He was nearly twenty miles to the southeast. But when he flew the robot, it was as if he were sitting in its nose, rushing toward the enemy plane.

The rectangular aiming cue in his main screen began blinking yellow, indicating that he was approaching firing range. He nudged left slightly, putting the MiG's tailpipe in the middle of the screen, which was actually a holographic projection in the visor of his helmet. The aiming cue turned solid red; Zen waited another second, then pressed the trigger. A dotted black line appeared in front of the Flighthawk. Zen nudged the stick left, pushing the line through the rear tail plane and then up through the wing of his target. The MiG's right wing flipped upward, then pushed hard down. Black smoke appeared at the center of the Ethiopian plane, and then the aircraft veered right.

Zen didn't bother to follow. He tucked left, hunting for a second target.

Aboard *Baker-Baker Two*,
over the Gulf of Aden
2256

Breanna had no trouble ducking the first air-to-air missile; she could actually see it in the enhanced view screen. But the second AA-12 managed to get almost under the Megafortress's wings and exploded close enough for her to feel the rumble. The emergency light panel lit immediately; even without checking, she could tell she'd taken a hit in engine three.

'Three's losing oil!' said Spiderman.

'Roger that. Let's shut her down. Compensate.'

Breanna checked her position as the copilot took the

engine offline. They were seventy-five miles north of the Somalian coast, at only three thousand feet. The closest MiG was five miles to the south, running away.

'Trimming,' said Spiderman.

The two pilots worked together for several minutes, adjusting the power settings in the remaining engines and fine-tuning the flight-control surfaces to compensate for the loss of the engine. The computer actually did most of the work, computing the complex forces acting on the airplane and suggesting solutions that would allow it to function nearly as well as if it had all four power plants – or as the flight control computer calculated, *'eighty-five percent efficiency.'*

'MiGs have broken off and are heading back toward their base,' said the radar operator.

'Acknowledged,' said Breanna. 'Commander Delaford?'

'We're here.'

'How's Piranha?'

'On course and on schedule.'

'We'll drop the second control buoy in zero-five minutes,' said Breanna. 'Everybody catch your breath.'

Aboard the *Wisconsin*,
over the Gulf of Aden
2256

Zen pressed the throttle slider to maximum power, closing on the Ethiopian MiG. The other aircraft had fired its last missile and cut south toward home, inadvertently turning in the direction of the Flighthawk, which apparently had not been picked up by its radar.

Zen's screen flashed yellow.

'Flighthawk leader, the MiGs have broken off contact and are returning to base,' said Dog. 'They're no longer a threat.'

Zen's finger jammed against the throttle, urging the robot plane closer. His screen went to red, but he knew he didn't have a perfect shot yet, despite what the computer said. He nudged slightly to the right, willing the enemy tailpipe into the cue.

'Flighthawk leader, break contact,' said Dog.

He could squeeze the trigger now and splash the bastard. Zen wanted to – there was no reason, in his opinion, to let any of the Ethiopians escape.

'Zen?'

'Flighthawk leader,' said Zen, pulling off.

Dog nudged *Wisconsin* closer to the other Megafortress. The starlight video camera – it worked by magnifying the available light, which in this case was primarily from the moon rather than the stars – showed some nicks in the rear housing of engine three. The wing, however, looked undamaged, which jibed with what Breanna had said.

'I think your damage is confined to that wing,' he told her. 'What's your assessment?'

'I continue with my mission as directed. I have another buoy ready to go. I've already talked to Greasy Hands back at Dreamland. They'll have a replacement engine tuned and waiting at Khamis Mushait when we land.'

'Where did the chief steal that?' asked Dog. Greasy Hands was the top NCO and unofficial godfather of the Dreamland technical crew, or 'maintainers,' the men and women who kept the aircraft aloft. He knew more about the planes than the people who designed them.

'He had two shipped in from Dreamland with the ground crew,' said Breanna. 'Depending on the damage to the skin, he claims the plane will be ready for its next flight. I tend to agree with him. We've flown with much worse. I can deal with it.'

'All right,' said Dog. 'Launch the control buoy. We'll continue to monitor. Did you track the Ethiopian pilots who bailed out?'

'We have global positioning coordinates on one, and an approximate location on the other chute,' said Breanna. 'What do you want to do?'

If the MV-22 had been in Saudi Arabia, Dog would have ordered Danny Freah to recover them so they could be questioned. Since that wasn't possible, his options were limited. He could alert Xray Pop, but the squadron already had its hands full and was unlikely to be in a position to mount a rescue much before dawn, if then. As a humanitarian gesture, Dog probably ought to alert the authorities in Djibouti, which was about fifty miles from the crash site.

Should he show mercy to a man who had tried to kill his people?

'Give me the location,' said Dog. 'We'll see if we can reach someone to pick them up.'

IV

My Way or No Way

Aboard the *Abner Read*,
Gulf of Aden
7 November 1997
0800

Storm watched the rigid hull inflatable boat pull into the landing area at the stern of *Abner Read*. Two more bodies had been recovered from the destroyed freighter, which had sunk during the night. Three men had not yet been recovered.

He would get the bastards for this. He would get them and he would see personally that they paid.

As for Bastian . . .

'Captain?'

Storm ignored the seaman who had approached him, snapping to attention and bringing his hand up in a stiff salute as one of his dead sailors was lifted from the boat. A light rain made the work all the more grim; several members of the party helping recover the remains slipped on the wet deck as they carried their fallen comrades about the destroyer. They struggled to hold the dead bodies up off the deck until they reached the litters that had been laid out for them, determined to spare them one final indignity. Only when the last body was laid down did Storm turn and give the seaman his attention.

'Sorry, sir,' said the sailor.

Storm noted that the man's eyes were welled with tears.

'They'll be avenged,' Storm told him. 'We'll have justice.'

The young man nodded.

'What did you want to tell me?'

'Commander Eisenberg sent me to tell you that Communications has that transmission you needed,' said the young man. 'He also said to mention that your communications unit has given out, sir. He can hear you but apparently you can't hear him.'

Storm looked down at his belt. Somewhere during the long night he had pulled the wires of the unit out and broken part of the connection. The sailor was holding a replacement unit.

'Thanks,' said Storm. 'I'll take the transmission in my cabin.'

As he walked to his quarters, he pulled the old com unit off his head. Some of his blood had scabbed under the unit, and he winced as he pulled it off. Not much pain, he thought; just enough to remind him he was alive.

Admiral Johnson's face filled the screen when he flipped on the secure communications line. Storm told him what had happened; for once the admiral listened without comment.

'There were three patrol boats that fled the scene,' Storm told him. 'The Dreamland team tracked them to a

156

harbor in Somalia, then lost them when a group of Ethiopians showed up. They had time to shoot down two planes, but they couldn't lift a finger to help us.'

'Did the Dreamland people understand what was at stake here?' asked Johnson.

'Admiral, I can't begin to understand or speak for what was going on in their minds. I requested that they engage the boats and they refused. As for the Ethiopians – I think if we don't put our foot down, things are going to get a lot worse over here.'

'Bastian thinks he's the Lone Ranger,' said Johnson. 'He's not used to being part of a team.'

Finally, thought Storm, he and Admiral Johnson actually agreed on something.

'Have you recovered your dead?' asked Johnson.

'We're working on it. We will accomplish that. I've taken temporary command as captain of the ship as well as the task group. It seemed the most expedient and efficient way to proceed.'

Johnson didn't argue, and Storm didn't give him the chance, pushing on quickly.

'We will accomplish the rest of the mission, sir.'

'You damn well better.'

'I intend to, Admiral.'

The screen blanked. Storm reached to turn it off, but the voice of a communications specialist aboard the admiral's flagship stopped him.

'Captain Gale, Captain McGowan requests to speak to you, sir.'

'Put him on.'

The screen flashed. Captain Red McGowan, his face tired and drawn, appeared on the screen.

'Sorry for your troubles,' said Red. 'Sorry to hear your men were lost.'

'Thanks, Red.'

'Marcum too?'

'I'm sorry to say, yes.'

'Bastards.'

'I hate those mothers.'

Storm released a string of curses. His friend nodded as he continued, making no effort to calm him as he vented.

'I'll get them,' Storm said softly when his breath, but not his anger, had finally drained.

'What happened with the Dreamland aircraft? They were fired on?'

'Apparently, Bastian claims to have shot down two MiGs. They couldn't lift a finger against the patrol boats that were killing my people, but they could go out of their way to take out the Ethiopians. Ethiopians – I question whether they were even armed. The country doesn't have an air force worthy of the name.'

'You're going overboard, Storm.'

'In the two weeks plus that we've been here, they haven't attacked us once. Dreamland comes out here and all of a sudden the Ethiopians are flying miles away from their air bases and, bang bang, splashing into the gulf. I wish I could get away with that.'

'Bastian's not going to get away with anything,' answered Red.

'Do I get the *Belleau Wood* or what?'

'That's not going to happen, Storm. There's just no way.'

'Then untie my hands! I have the assets I need – let me use them.'

Red winced. 'If it were up to me.'

'Yeah, all right. Later.' Storm punched the button on the panel, ending the transmission. He went and washed some of the dirt and dried blood off his face, then changed into a fresh uniform. Calmer, he dialed into Communications.

'See if you can find Admiral Balboa for me,' Storm told the officer. 'Call the Joint Chiefs personnel office and ask them where Pinkie is – he's a lieutenant commander who owes me a favor. Better yet, call the Pentagon, OK? And Joint Chiefs, ask for Lou Milelo. He's a chief petty officer. Be respectful, very respectful, and tell him I need a personal favor. Then get me on the line. I'll be on the bridge.'

Near Boosaaso, Somalia, on the Gulf of Aden 0810

Ali folded the paper carefully in half, then took the lighter from his pocket and set it on fire. He watched intently as the flames consumed it, waiting until his fingers were singed to drop it into the nearby surf.

The message it contained had been disappointing. The

Ethiopian Air Force had attacked an American warplane with predictable results: Two of their pilots had been shot down. They were hoping he could look for the men in the gulf.

The Ethiopians might be brave, but they were also foolhardy. It wasn't clear from the message what sort of plane it had been, though Ali doubted it was an Orion or any similar radar or surveillance craft; such planes were typically unequipped for air-to-air combat. And any single American warplane was more than a match for the entire Ethiopian Air Force. Brave men foolishly led to their deaths by misguided leaders – this was not God's wish.

There was slim hope of finding the pilots, but he had been called on as a brother in religion, and could not turn down such a request. In exchange, perhaps the Ethiopians would have to help him. He needed a diversion so he could get the last of his patrol boats out of the port near Laasgoray, where it had spent the night being repaired. He needed it to join him in an attack on a fuel carrier tonight; if the attack went well, they would have more than enough diesel fuel for the *Sharia*, and the boats as well.

He took a pen from his pocket and wrote down a time and place.

'Take this message back,' he told the man who had come from town. 'Tell them we will do what they wish. But they must also try to have airplanes at this place and time. It would be very useful as a diversion. Let them use their courage to its best effect.'

160

Starship brought the Flighthawk onto the runway after the Megafortress had turned onto the ramp, taxiing around so the U/MF-3 trailed the big airplane like a dog following its master. He had definitely drawn the short stick on the mission. After the excitement with the Ethiopians, *Baker-Baker Two* hadn't been challenged. He'd spent most of the six hours since Zen handed off the Flighthawk flying crazy eights at twenty thousand feet, and hadn't so much as buzzed a dhow during the entire time.

Dreamland's MC-17 sat near the ramp area, along with an MV-22 Osprey. A pack of maintainers met *Baker-Baker Two* as she trundled to a stop. They were already working on the damaged engine when Starship came down the ladder.

Starship got out of his flight gear and debriefed the mission. Too keyed-up to hit the sack, he decided to get a late breakfast. The Saudis had a cafeteria-style grill on their side of the base; a whiteboard at the door welcomed U.S. FLIERS and announced a special of hamburgers and fries in their honor, the words presented in both Arabic and English.

Starship wasn't sure why burgers were being presented as breakfast fare, but wasn't about to argue. He took his to a table near a group of Saudis who were dressed in flight suits. One of the men smiled at him as he sat down, then came over and introduced himself as Major Bandar, inviting Starship to join him and the others. Well into their thirties, the men were all F-15 jocks who'd spent time in the States and had flown during the Gulf War. When they asked Starship what he flew, he answered by saying he used to fly F-15s himself.

'And now what do you fly?' asked Bandar. 'Mega-fortress?'

Starship held out his hands. 'Can't say.'

The others jeered good-naturedly.

'Oh, oh, top secret,' laughed Bandar.

'You fly the robot,' guessed one of the others. 'The midget with wings.'

'He doesn't look small enough.'

'What is it like? Is it difficult?'

Starship tried changing the subject, and finally got them to talk about the F-15s and their own routine. Bandar lamented that they were restricted to a flight a week, and that the missions were little more than hops north and back, barely enough to get the turbines spinning.

'Maybe we can work an exercise out with you some-time,' said Starship as the Saudis got up for a meeting. 'A little dissimilar aircraft tactics.'

'That would be very good,' said Bandar.

'I'd like to shoot down a Megafortress,' said the officer across from Bandar.

Starship started to smile but the pilot's expression made it clear he wasn't joking.

Now it was Bandar's turn to change the subject. 'If you are interested in seeing the town,' he said, 'let me know. I will be your guide.'

162

'Yeah? I wouldn't mind a tour,' said Starship.

'Meet me at the gate at 1400,' said Bandar. 'Two P.M.'

Starship hesitated. He was supposed to fly tonight and had been planning on sleeping.

'Two P.M.,' repeated Bandar. 'You'll be there?'

'Sure,' said Starship.

White House
0600

The Chairman of the Joint Chiefs of Staff, Admiral George Balboa, spent much of his time at the White House angry, but Jed Barclay had never heard him quite *this* angry.

Then again, he'd never heard his boss this angry either. The walls of the Executive Office Building were practically shaking as the two men shouted at each other. Fortunately, because of the early hour, there were few people in the West Wing to hear them – though given how loud they were shouting, Jed wouldn't have been surprised to find that they woke half the city.

'You're trying to create your own private army, Freeman. That's what Dreamland is – a private army.'

'That's baloney and you know it. It's slander.'

'You tell me what to call a deployment of military units that ignores the normal chain of command. And ignores international law.'

'I'd like to see proof of that. That aircraft was attacked. They have proof.'

'Manufactured by them, no doubt.'

'You're way out of line, Balboa. And for the record, Whiplash has always operated at the President's specific command – legally, per the law. It's the President's prerogative as commander in chief to direct units and set their missions.'

'Does the President know about it?'

'Ask him yourself.'

'I damn well will,' said Balboa.

Jed literally threw himself back against the wall as Balboa stormed from the office. Balboa's face was red, and the admiral's stubby legs and arms pumped like the rods in an overworked V-8 car motor. Jed held his breath as the admiral passed. Just as he exhaled, Balboa swung around.

'And you,' he shouted at Jed. 'You better wake up and smell the coffee here, kid. I thought you had a brain in your head.'

'I have a brain,' snapped Jed.

'You're a dupe. You better watch yourself, Barclay, or you're going to end up like Ollie North – if you're lucky. More like Dean and Erlichmann.'

He stomped away, disappearing around the corner. Jed walked into Freeman's suite, where he found his boss picking up files from the floor.

'Sorry about that, Jed,' said Freeman. 'The Chairman is a little upset.'

Jed nodded and began to help. 'Who's Dean and Erlichmann?'

'John Dean and John Erlichmann. They were in the

Nixon administration. They went to prison because they lied for the President.'

'Oh,' said Jed, sitting in the chair in the corner.

'That's just Balboa being Balboa. Don't worry about it.'

'Why would I be like one of those guys?'

'You're not. Balboa is throwing his usual smoke. He's still angry about the strike on China by Brad Elliott and company,' said Freeman. 'He'd love to prove that Dreamland was behind it.'

'Dreamland had nothing to do with it,' said Jed.

They were referring to the so-called Fatal Terrain episode, which had been pulled off by a semiprivate group operating on behalf of the Taiwan government – or at least that was the public version. Even Jed wasn't privy to all the details. But he did know that the Dreamland people weren't involved. Or at least he thought he did.

'Balboa apparently thinks that Dreamland and Whiplash should be placed back in the military chain of command,' said Freeman. 'Or I should say, under his chain of command.'

There had been various plans to bring Dreamland back 'online' as a regular command, but the President was ambivalent about doing so. Jed had always believed this was because, as the President had said, he didn't want to stifle the creativity there. But in light of what Balboa had just said, he had to admit there might be other reasons as well. Lieutenant General Terill Samson had been tapped to head nearby Brad Elliott Air Force Base, which on paper was supposed to have included Dreamland. But Dreamland's funding line was specifically excluded from the command, and no one in the Air Force – not even the formidable General Samson – had direct authority over Colonel Bastian and his people. Once a Whiplash order designated a mission, Bastian answered only to the President.

Usually through Jed. Which put him in the middle . . . maybe in the same place Erlichmann and the others had been.

'Among his other goals,' continued Freeman, 'Admiral Balboa is angling to have the Dreamland team in the Gulf of Aden placed under Captain Gale. Xray Pop could use help. There's no question about that.'

'But that would change their focus from the submarine to the pirates,' said Jed.

'They may end up being the same mission. Balboa is claiming the Dreamland people provoked the attack on their aircraft.'

'I heard, but that's ridiculous. Colonel Bastian wouldn't do that. Besides, Ethiopia has scrambled planes before.'

'Mmmm.'

Jed could tell that Freeman wasn't entirely sure. 'I can get the mission tapes,' he said.

'No, that's all right. Like I said, it's just Balboa being Balboa.' Freeman rose. 'It may make sense to have the Megafortresses work with Xray Pop. The only problem is that Gale and Bastian will spend so much time spitting at each other they'll forget who the enemy is.'

They were exactly fifteen miles offshore, directly north of the port where the Dreamland people had tracked the Somalian pirates. Storm had ordered the radars turned on so they knew the *Abner Read* was there, hoping that would provoke a response. Thus far it hadn't.

If he wanted to, he could unleash a barrage from his gun and obliterate the town just above the tiny port where the pirates had taken refuge. A dozen shells would erase it.

Two or three hundred years ago, when sails ruled the sea, that's what they would have done. There'd be no political niceties, no worry about a peace process or the UN.

'Captain, we have two unidentified aircraft approaching from the south at high speed,' said Eyes. 'Just popped up over the mountains, coming toward the coast.'

'Very good,' Storm said. 'Weapons, track them and prepare to fire.'

Zen tapped the command to share the video feed with Ensign Gloria English, who was operating the Piranha at the other Flighthawk station.

'What's that?' he asked.

'That, Major, is the future of the Navy. The DD(L)-01 *Abner Read*. A littoral warfare destroyer. It's the naval equivalent of a Megafortress, in terms of cutting-edge equipment. That's Captain Storm Gale's flagship.'

'Looks like a Popsicle with a couple of sugar cubes on it.'

'Be interesting to see what it could do in a tangle.'

'Zen, those Ethiopian MiG-23s are continuing north,' warned Dish, who had been tracking them on radar. 'They have activated their attack radars. Looks to me like they're going to attack the *Abner Read*.'

'Better warn them. I'm on it,' said Zen, plunging the Flighthawk in their direction.

Aboard the *Abner Read*,
Gulf of Aden
1416

The excited shouts over the ship's battle circuits revved Storm's heart as he glanced at the graphic rendering of the approaching MiGs in his hologram. The two aircraft were just crossing from the land to the water fifteen miles away, sweeping in their general direction.

'We have them targeted.'

'Stand by,' said Storm. The *Abner Read* had SM-2 missiles in its Vertical Launching System; the missiles could knock out a target at roughly ninety miles.

The MiGs weren't coming on an exact intercept,

but they were well within range to launch antiship missiles. Neither, however, had turned on a targeting radar, and thus had not committed a hostile act – which his orders required before he was allowed to shoot them down.

Orders he didn't particularly care for, orders that put him and his ships in danger – but orders which, if disobeyed, would be used by his enemies to derail his career.

'Communication from a Dreamland aircraft, warning us that two MiGs are approaching.'

'About time,' scoffed Storm. 'Connect me.'

'It's not easy cutting that circuit in, sir. There's a technical glitch on our side that –'

'Connect me.'

Aboard the *Wisconsin*,
over the Gulf of Aden
1417

'They're both MiG-23BNs,' Zen told the Navy captain. 'Computer says they don't have antiship missiles. Repeat, no missiles.'

'Bombs?'

'Appear to have no weapons of any kind,' said Zen. 'I think they're just up for their jollies. They're not reacting to your ship. I don't think they know you're there.'

'They must be up to something. The Ethiopians typically don't come over Somalian territory.'

'They did last night.'

The two Ethiopian warplanes were now ten miles off the Flighthawk's nose. Zen began a turn to the east, planning to bring the Flighthawk in an arc behind the MiGs. *Wisconsin*, meanwhile, had already begun tacking in that direction to stay close to the Piranha probe.

'Have a small patrol craft moving out of the port,' said Ensign English, who was commanding the probe.

'Feed me the location,' said Zen. The plot merged into the sitrep screen in Zen's helmet. The MiG fighter-bombers, meanwhile, continued northward.

'It's a sucker play,' said Zen. 'They sent the MiGs out to get everyone's attention while the patrol boat sneaks off in broad daylight.'

Aboard the *Abner Read*,
Gulf of Aden
1426

'MiGs see us,' Eyes told Storm. 'Changing course. Heading toward us.'

'Do we have a lock?'

'Having some trouble,' said Eyes.

The missiles themselves were dependable weapons, but were designed to work with a different targeting system. Sometimes they were locked even though the weapons panel indicated they weren't – and vice versa. The experts promised a fix . . . but by the time that happened, the new system would probably be ready.

'Weapons, can you target those planes?' Storm asked.

'Ready to fire at your command,' said the weapons officer. 'I can't guarantee a hit, because of the glitch.'

'I'm not asking you to, son.'

'Dreamland aircraft is back on the line,' said the communications officer. 'They say it's urgent.'

'Tell them to take a ticket,' said Storm. 'Have the Ethiopian aircraft been warned?'

'Affirmative.'

'Eyes, are those aircraft in Somalian territory?'

'Negative, sir. They have crossed into international airspace. They have not answered hails. I believe they show hostile intent. They are a bombing run, and we're in their crosshairs.'

'Noted. Engage the enemy.'

Aboard the *Wisconsin*,
over the Gulf of Aden
1428

Zen saw the first missile flash from the deck of the *Abner Read* and shook his head.

'Missile in the air!' warned Dish. 'RIM-67, Navy Standard Missile Two in ship-to-antiaircraft mode, targeted at the Ethiopian MiG.'

'He's a dead pony,' said Zen. He pushed the Flighthawk closer to the water. The patrol boat had her throttle open full bore and was kicking over the waves at close to fifty knots. It was crossing out of Somalian waters, heading for the open sea.

'Dish, have you advised Xray Pop? The patrol boat's getting away.'

'Told me to hold on,' said Dish. 'Second missile launched. Same deal, targeting the second MiG.'

'Flighthawk leader, we have to get into position to make another buoy drop,' said the *Wisconsin*'s pilot.

'I copy. I'm coming back,' said Zen. He changed the display from the optical camera to the sitrep, and was surprised to see that the two MiGs were still in the air, hightailing it back over the Somalian coast. 'Don't tell me Navy missed,' said Zen.

'Shanked to the right,' said Dish. 'My guess is there's a problem with the *Abner Read*'s radar – their signal is very degraded. Looks like the MiGs selected afterburners before the *Abner Read* got her first shot off,' added the radar operator.

'Storm's not going to be happy about that,' said English.

'You know him?' asked Zen.

'Only from what Commander Delaford has told me. They served together. Storm's a hothead.'

'And not a very good shot either,' said Zen. 'But at least he scared the pants off those Ethiopians. Idiots are still in afterburner. Probably run out of fuel halfway home.'

White House
0706

Admiral Balboa had calmed down considerably in the few hours since Jed had seen him, but that was only relative; he was still frowning and clearly irritable as they waited upstairs in the White House residence for the President. It was just after seven A.M. The President was supposed to leave no later than seven-thirty from the back lawn for a round of visits to the Midwest. The early morning session had been called primarily to update him on the situation in China, where a U.S. plane had been forced down by hostile action, but the Gulf of Aden was nearly as volatile. The Ethiopian Air Force claimed that two of their aircraft had been shot down without provocation, and had filed a protest with the UN. Meanwhile, the Navy was demanding more resources for Xray Pop, which had lost several men after boarding a pirated ship.

Jed realized that if the last administration hadn't cut the funding for weapons development, the task group would have had a much easier time of things; at the very least, it would have had more Shark Boats, working UAVs, and competent radar. But no one wanted to hear that, least of all Admiral Balboa, who seemed to think the last President walked on water, with an aircraft carrier to guide him.

'Young Jed, good to see you this morning,' said President Martindale, springing into the Treaty Room at the center of the upstairs floor of the presidential mansion. The President liked to have small, intimate sessions in the residence; he thought they were much more informal and likely to yield 'real' advice than sessions in the West Wing. Jed, though, thought that the history of the place intimidated some people – you were sitting where Abraham Lincoln walked his sick son to

173

sleep, where FDR poured cocktails and shared off-color gossip, where Kennedy sized up his conquests.

'Admiral, Mr Freeman, Jeffrey, Jerrod – everyone have coffee except me?' The President went to the large urn that had been wheeled into the room and helped himself. 'Let's hear what the Seventh Fleet's story is,' he said as he poured.

'I think we should talk about the Gulf of Aden first,' said Freeman. 'And get that out of the way.'

'Xray Pop lost twelve men last night,' said Balboa, launching into a short summary of what had happened.

Martindale nodded solemnly, and Jed guessed that he already knew everything Balboa was telling him. The White House military liaison would most likely have woken him with the news.

'There was also an attack on a Dreamland aircraft by Ethiopia,' Balboa went on. 'Provoked by the Dreamland aircraft.'

'That's not true,' blurted Jed.

Everyone looked at him. Jed felt his face shade red. He glanced at Freeman, who was frowning.

'Go ahead, Jed,' said the President. 'What happened?'

'First of all, there were two encounters, one early in the evening with the Sudanese, and then several hours later with the Ethiopians. The Sudanese did a fly-by; it's not clear how they knew that the Megafortresses were in the area, or even if they were military aircraft as opposed to, say, uh, civilians. They went away without incident. Several hours later the Ethiopians approached. They demanded that the Megafortresses identify themselves or be fired on. Since their mission was covert, they maintained radio silence. Four MiGs then engaged the Megafortress that was commanding the Piranha probe. Two were shot down, one by the Megafortress and the other by a Flighthawk.'

'They could have identified themselves as a civilian aircraft if they wanted to avoid trouble,' said Balboa.

'Well, no, because no civilian aircraft is supposed to be in that area,' said Jed.

'I thought the Megafortresses are invisible to radar,' said Jerrod Hale, the President's Chief of Staff.

'They're not completely invisible,' said Jed. He explained that the low-radar profile simply made the aircraft 'look' smaller to the radar, which meant it couldn't be detected at long range. But that profile grew exponentially when the bomb bay doors were opened, which would have happened when the Piranha buoys were dropped. In addition, the other Megafortress was using its radars to scan the surface and air; these could be detected and even used as a beacon by approaching hostiles.

'The, uh, the question is . . .' Jed couldn't get his tongue untangled and stopped speaking for a moment. His stuttering had become an increasing problem over the past several months, growing in tandem with his responsibilities. 'Who – Who told the Sudanese planes they were there in the first place? Because they'd flown pretty far from their bases. Once they see the Megafortress, they might tell the Ethiopians, but who told them? C-C-Colonel Bastian thinks there may be a spy at the Saudi air base. Someone who's passing information along. The same thing is probably happening with the pirates.'

'It's definitely happening with the pirates,' said Balboa. 'They see all these small boats watching them from territorial waters. Every move they make is observed. What's the use of a stealth design when there are spies everywhere?'

'Why are the Ethiopians and Sudanese cooperating with pirates?' the President asked Secretary of State Jeffrey Hartman. His tone suggested that the Secretary had ordered the countries to interfere.

'They claim they were on routine patrols,' said Hartman.

'That's not good enough,' said Martindale.

'I didn't say it was. Internal problems may be leading them to try and appease some of the more radical elements in their countries. That's why we have to work with the UN.'

'The hell with that,' said Secretary of Defense Chastain. 'We should have sank these bastards a week ago.'

'Xray Pop needs more resources,' said Balboa. 'And orders that allow them into the coastal areas.'

'What resources?' asked Chastain. Though in theory he was Balboa's boss, the two men didn't get along and hardly spoke.

'Give them the Dreamland people,' said Balboa, 'and some Marines to work as boarding parties.'

'What good are the Marines going to do against pirates?' Chastain asked.

'Board their ships. And attack their bases.'

'Wait now, let's not put the cart before the horse,' said Hartman. 'We need a UN resolution to operate and attack in territorial waters. Let's be very clear about that. This is a small part of a larger picture. If we don't work with the UN here, we'll never get the China issue settled. Or Korea. And that's where the real problems are.'

'Your big picture is killing our people,' said Balboa.

'The issues at stake here are immense,' said Hartman. 'We have to handle this delicately. Which I have to say is not being done.'

'Then you shouldn't have sent I-Take-Orders-from-No-Man Bastian out there,' said Balboa.

'Colonel Bastian takes orders from me,' said President Martindale, looking up from his coffee cup. 'I think we have to cut him some slack here. I doubt he instigated the attack.'

'It's important to get UN backing before we go into coastal waters,' Hartman told the President. 'If we don't, everything else will fall apart. And Congress will be all over you.'

'Congress is all over me already.' Martindale smiled faintly.

'We won't be able to count on getting a UN peace-keeping force in Taiwan,' said Hartman.

'We can't count on that now,' said Freeman. 'China won't accept it.'

'The hell with peacekeeping,' said Chastain. 'I say blow the bastards up and let's be done with it. We should have wiped the Chinese military out completely when we had the chance. With all due respect to the late General Elliott and his sacrifice –'

'Let's focus on the Gulf of Aden, shall we?' said Martindale. It wasn't a question. 'I have to agree with the Secretary of State. I want the UN resolution if at all possible before we act. That was the idea behind sending the Dreamland team to look for the submarine. They are doing that, aren't they, Jed?'

'They've started. They haven't found it yet. It may take quite a while.'

'It won't be found, because it doesn't exist,' said Balboa. 'It sank somewhere in the Atlantic off the coast of Africa.'

'The evidence was pretty persuasive that it was the same sub that was heard in the Indian Ocean,' said Jed.

'You're not going to start lecturing me on submarines now, are you, son?' asked Balboa.

'No, sir.'

'Philip, what do you think of Dreamland working with Xray Pop?' the President asked National Security Advisor Freeman.

'It might work. It would give them an over-the-horizon capability and air support that they don't have. It would make it easier to deal with the pirates, even in international waters. But I don't know if they could do both missions at once. Finding the sub, I mean.'

'There is no sub,' said Balboa.

'It would be useful to find the submarine,' said Hartman. 'The more evidence that we can gather to convince the Security Council –'

'The fact that the terrorists killed a civilian crew and blew up their ship won't do it?' asked Martindale.

'Similar incidents haven't in the past,' said Hartman.

'Jed, can Dreamland support Xray Pop and look for the submarine at the same time?' asked the President.

'I don't know. I'd have to check with Colonel Bastian.'

'The support mission has to be given priority,' said Balboa. 'That task has to be rolled into Xray Pop's mission, and the commander at the scene should make the final call on which resources go where.'

'I don't think that's a good idea,' said Freeman.

'What's the alternative? Put Bastian in charge of Xray Pop?' asked Balboa. 'That won't work – Captain Gale outranks him.'

'Knowing the Dreamland people, my guess is that they can find a way to do both jobs,' said Martindale. 'The Whiplash team is just providing service, along the same lines as it did in Iraq and Iran when Razor was raising such havoc,' said the President. 'Supporting Xray Pop will take top priority if push comes to shove.'

'And Captain Gale will be in charge,' said Balboa.

Martindale took a sip from his coffee cup and seemed surprised to find that it was empty. He went back over to the urn.

'Let's talk about China,' said Freeman.

'Is Gale in charge or not?' said Balboa.

'Yes,' said the President, pouring his coffee. 'And now on to other disagreeable matters.'

Khamis Mushait Air Base, southwestern Saudi Arabia 1610

Danny Freah watched the C-17 roll toward the Dreamland side of the base. It had circled above for over forty-five minutes, ostensibly waiting for an inbound Saudi aircraft that had declared an engine emergency. The Saudi airplane failed to materialize, and it wasn't because it had crashed – the pilots in the C-17 told the tower several times that there were no other aircraft anywhere in the vicinity. Danny had heard the entire exchange over the Dreamland circuit. It hadn't exactly filled him with confidence about base security.

As allies, the Saudis were a very ambivalent group. Most of the pilots were friendly enough, and the head of base security couldn't have been more helpful. But a few officers – obviously including people in the control tower – were openly hostile. The enlisted people were at best split down the middle, and the contracted workers, most of whom were either Palestinians or Pakistani, refused to go anywhere near the Americans. Which was just as well.

Dog had just sat down at the communications console in the Command trailer to get an update from Dreamland Command when the screen flashed with an incoming communication marked EYES ONLY, DREAM COMMANDER.

'Bastian,' he said after clearing the security procedures to allow the connection.

'Uh, Colonel, didn't expect to get you so quick,' said Jed Barclay. 'I, uh, just came out of a marathon National Security session. President and Admiral Balboa and Mr Freeman, Defense Secretary Chastain –'

'I don't need the roll call,' said Dog. 'Give me the bad news.'

'How do you know it's bad news?'

'Because you always beat around the bush when it's bad news.'

'They want to beef up Xray Pop,' said Jed. 'Under ideal circumstances –'

'We're being assigned to work with Xray Pop?'

'That would be it, Colonel. Under Captain Storm's command.'

Dog didn't respond.

'The orders will be cut I'd say pretty quickly. Um, they'll come through –'

'It's all right. We'll figure it out.'

'I, um, I know it's going to be kind of a – not a good situation,' said Jed. 'But –'

'Thanks.'

He killed the connection.

Dog leaned back from the console. The last time he'd been under a Navy commander, he'd been sent home within twenty-four hours. He'd probably beat that this time around.

'Hey!'

Dog turned around, surprised to see Jennifer standing in the trailer. She'd come in with the technical teams to work on the Werewolf and LADS lighter than air detection systems.

'Hey, yourself,' he said, getting up. She hugged him, and he gave her a kiss, trying not to seem *too* distracted.

Not that it worked.

'I thought you'd be happy to see me,' she said.

'I am, Jennifer, I am,' Dog told her. 'But right now I have a dozen different things to sort through, and then I have to brief a mission.'

'I was just looking for a kiss,' she said, pressing against him.

'I did kiss you.'

'My grandma gives better kisses.'

Dog clasped her in his arms and gave her a 'regulation' kiss, melting his lips into hers. It was long and it was delicious and it was dangerously tempting.

'I do have to get to work,' he told her finally, pulling back.

'I know,' she said.

Somehow the tone of her voice made him want her even more. But before he could suggest that they leave the trailer and find a place where he could give in to temptation, two members of the Whiplash security team who'd been checking on the C-17 and its gear came inside. Sergeant Lee 'Nurse' Liu, the senior NCO on the Whiplash team, gave him an update on the security situation, along with the prediction that the Werewolves would be operational within an hour.

'There's only one problem – Sandy Culver, the Werewolf pilot, is sick,' said Liu.

'How?' Dog turned to Jennifer, who had been on the flight with Culver.

'He has the flu or something,' said Jennifer. 'He didn't look too good when he got on the plane. And he started throwing up about an hour before he landed.'

'Captain Freah is checked out on the aircraft,' said Liu.

'So am I,' said Jennifer. 'That's why I'm here.'

'I understood you were here to work on their systems, not to fly them,' said Dog.

'I can do both.'

'We're going to need you on the LADS system,' said Dog. 'You can't do everything.'

'I can if I have to.'

'Danny can fly them,' said Dog. 'Or Zen in an emergency. When you're finished with everything else, we'll talk about it.'

'Colonel, you have a call on the satellite telephone system,' said Sergeant Jack 'Pretty Boy' Floyd, who had taken over the communications station. 'It's from the Navy.'

'That'll be the new boss, wondering when we're going to genuflect,' said Dog. 'Excuse me.'

He walked to the back of the trailer and waited until Pretty Boy stepped aside before clearing the communication in.

'Bastian.'

'This is Captain Gale.'

'Captain, good afternoon,' Dog said evenly. 'I'm sorry for the loss of your men.'

'Yes. That won't happen again. I understand you've been looking for a submarine with a Piranha probe.'

'That's right, Captain.'

'I'll tell you what, Colonel. Let's cut the bullshit here.'

'Gladly.'

'I've heard about you. You have a reputation for getting things done. I appreciate that.'

'Thank you.'

'I also have heard that you're a cowboy. You don't take orders from anyone.'

'On the contrary, I take orders very seriously,' said Dog.

'As long as you follow mine, we'll have no trouble. You can call me Storm.'

Is that supposed to make me feel warm and fuzzy inside? Dog wondered.

'What areas have you searched?' Storm asked.

'The Somalian coast from the Eritrean border east about fifty miles. We've only just started.'

'Well, the search has secondary priority now,' said Storm. 'You're working for me now and we're going after the pirates.'

'Understood.'

'When I give you an order to sink someone, I want them sunk.'

Dog said nothing.

'The pirates work both sides of the Gulf,' the Navy captain continued. 'They use hit and run tactics and then retreat. Because of our rules of engagement, they know they're safe near the coast. So I have to catch them in international waters. You spot them, vector me toward them, and I'll attack.'

'It would be just as easy for me to attack them myself, then,' said Dog.

'You didn't last night.'

'I was following my orders.'

'Well, you have new orders now. You spot the pirates, and I'll take care of them.'

Dog thought Storm was a jerk, but that didn't mean his frustration wasn't justified. He'd been given a difficult job to do, then had his hands tied behind his back.

'Listen, Storm,' said Dog, deciding to offer an olive branch. 'We can do a lot more for you than just fly around the ocean spotting patrol boats. For one thing, the sort of surveillance you're asking for can be conducted by lighter-than-air blimps. I can have a dozen flown in from Dreamland; we can post them around the gulf and give the control units to your ships. You'll have around-the-clock coverage of the entire gulf. And we can get you some better communications systems. I understand that you had a lot of difficulty communicating with my aircraft earlier. I know there was some sort of foul-up with your antiair missiles and you missed a MiG you were aiming at; one of my specialists believed it had to do with the radar link to the guidance system. Maybe I can get some of my radar people –'

'Just get your aircraft working with my intelligence officers by 2000 hours, Bastian. I'm in charge. Not you.'

The line went dead.

Khamis Mushait
1621

Bandar's tour of Khamis Mushait started with what seemed to be an old fort, but according to the Saudi pilot was just an old building at the edge of the original city. Khamis Mushait had once been a popular trading and rest spot for desert caravans. It still had an impressive market, as Starship saw when he and his guide walked through an open-air bazaar that appeared to stretch for acres and acres. Among the displays were elaborately decorated china and furniture. Bandar found a vendor and bought some fruit juice for them, refusing to let Starship pay. Then he pointed in the distance at the large white castle, relating a ghost story about Bedouins who had roamed the desert a thousand years ago. One of the band had been killed out of jealousy and his body left to rot; as punishment, the men were turned into eternal ghosts and forced to wander until the man's body was given its rightful honors. Since this could never happen – it had been devoured by beasts and birds of prey – they wandered to this very day. Bandar finished the story by claiming that he had heard their camels thundering across the plains several times.

Starship laughed and asked if Bandar truly believed in ghosts.

'You don't?' The Saudi laughed.

'Nah.'

'Nothing you can't see?'

'Something like that.'

The tour led back toward the mosque. Starship suddenly felt curious about the interior and asked if he might look inside. Bandar started to make a face, clearly uncomfortable.

'It's OK,' said Starship. 'I didn't mean to offend anyone.'

Before Bandar could answer, someone nearby began yelling at them in Arabic. Bandar spun around, and then began answering the man as he continued to yell.

'It's all right. Don't worry about it,' said Starship. He

took a step backward. Two or three other men who'd been nearby walked closer.

'No, he's wrong,' said Bandar. 'You are a guest in our country.'

'It's all right. I don't want any trouble or anything,' said Starship. 'I have to get back anyway.'

Bandar turned and said something to the other man, who unleashed another tirade. A few more people came up. Starship touched his guide's arm, trying to get him to come, but Bandar waved his hand dismissively.

'I'm sorry,' said Starship.

'Go home,' said one of the other men in English. 'Go away. We don't want you.'

'I didn't mean any offense,' said Starship. 'Really, I'm leaving.'

'Go away,' said another.

By the time Bandar stopped arguing, a thick crowd had gathered. They trailed Starship and the Saudi pilot back to the car. Most of the people simply looked curious, but they made it hard for Bandar to go without hitting them. Something or someone hit the back of the car as they cleared the crowd. Starship turned around; the road was cluttered with angry people, fists raised in the air.

'I really didn't mean any trouble,' said Starship.

'People forget their manners,' said Bandar.

'It's all right.'

As they drove back toward the airport, Starship tried to think of something to say. 'It's a really nice city,' he said finally. Bandar grunted something, and Starship thought it best to keep his mouth shut.

A large crowd had gathered near the gate of the airport. Surprised, Starship at first didn't realize that they were protesters, and it wasn't until a group began running toward the car that he realized what was going on.

'Troublemakers,' said Bandar.

Starship slid down in the seat, eyes pasted ahead as people surged against the side of the car. Saudi police ran toward them. Bandar managed to get inside the gate without hitting anyone.

'Wow,' said Starship.

'Troublemakers,' repeated Bandar. 'I'm sorry.'

'It's all right.'

'Ignorant troublemakers.'

V

Invaders

Gulf of Aden,
north of Xiis
1810

The wind bit at Ali's face, snapping at his eyes and nose as they sped toward the looming shadow of the tanker three miles away. Ali welcomed the bite; it took his mind off his son.

The Saudi had been as good as his word: Offers of help were pouring in from brothers throughout the Middle East. Two ships had joined him tonight: a large, Al Bushra-class patrol boat from Oman, liberated from unrighteous rulers by true believers, and a patrol boat from Eritrea roughly similar to the patrol craft he was already using. An additional thirty men had volunteered beyond the two dozen needed to crew both vessels; most were raw youths, but seemed willing to follow his orders without question.

Though classified as a patrol boat, the Al Bushra dwarfed his other ships, measuring nearly 180 feet. A pair of Exocet missile launchers had been installed on the deck behind the superstructure, giving the ship considerable firepower. Surface-to-air missiles had replaced the

76mm cannon on the forward deck. The ship could make only 24.5 knots, too slow to keep up with the faster boats, but she had room for a large boarding party. Most of Ali's new recruits were aboard her; they were unlikely to see real action but would learn a great deal from tonight's encounter.

She was running about a mile behind him, commanded by his cousin Mabrukah. The captain who had brought her bristled at being put under another man, and Ali knew he would have to alter the arrangement eventually, but tonight he had no time to devote to personalities, and needed someone who knew his ways without needing to question them.

God had brought him additional volunteers for a purpose. He had two difficult tasks to achieve tonight. Not only was he to meet the submarine at midnight, but his best chance for capturing a vessel that could fuel his fleet would occur a few hours before, as an old oiler now used as a fuel transport sailed through the gulf. Unfortunately, the oiler was more than 250 miles from the rendezvous point with the submarine. According to the spies, it had come down past Saudi Arabia already and would be passing near this spot sometime within the next few hours.

Ali had decided capturing the oiler was more critical, and thus decided to lead that mission personally. He had sent one of his patrol boats with a pilot to meet the submarine. If the takeover went well, he would head east and link up with the submarine.

Perhaps Allah intended that he accomplish both – a

gray shadow appeared on the horizon ahead: their target.

'Signal the others,' Ali told Bari, his second-in-command for the operation.

The flotilla of pirates spread out on the water, a pack of wolves stalking their prey. Ali set a course for his vessel that brought her toward the stern of the slow-moving target. He stood in the open wheelhouse of his patrol boat, staring at the shadow as it grew. The wind sucked the heat from his face, turning it to a mask of cold bones.

A light blinked at the oiler's fantail.

Ali turned to Bari. 'Our people aboard have secured the radio. Pass the signal – begin the attack.'

Khamis Mushait Air Base
1810

Dog bent down to look at the video display. Four or five hundred Saudis were gathered on the main road to the airport, fists raised, chanting in Arabic that the invaders must go home.

'Invaders!'

That was the term they used, translated by the translation software in the Dreamland Command trailer. And they said it loudly enough for the microphones in the video camera to pick up, even though the Osprey hovered overhead.

'Invaders!'

'This is relatively calm,' Danny told him. 'A half hour

ago I wasn't sure what was going to happen. At least now the Saudi police have the crowd cordoned off. The base itself is secure.'

'Until some jerk drives up in a truck full of explosives,' said Dog.

'He won't get past the gate. We've set up bullet panels on the approaches to our sector, along with tear-gas mortars. We have the Osprey overhead. I'm keeping the Werewolves in reserve. But if they get past the tear gas and bullet panels and we have to shoot, it'll get bloody. We can withstand an attack, but it won't be pretty.'

The bullet panels were large rectangles filled with 9mm rubber bullets. They were considered nonlethal deterrents for use against a stampeding crowd; when triggered, they fired a hail of hard rubber in the air. Combined with the tear gas, they would turn back all but the most determined protesters.

The Osprey's guns were loaded with live ammunition, as were the Werewolves. Danny's assessment was an understatement – they'd slaughter whoever was in their path.

'This couldn't have been spontaneous,' said Dog.

'No,' said Danny. 'But I wouldn't underestimate the emotions involved.'

'I'll talk to Washington. We have to relocate. Probably to Diego Garcia.'

'What about Captain Gale?'

'I'll talk to him too. Though frankly I'd rather get my teeth pulled.' Dog glanced at his watch. *Wisconsin* was scheduled to launch at 2000, and he was slated to lead the mission. He hadn't even started planning his brief for it.

'Starship is outside,' said Danny. 'I think he thinks it's all his fault.'

'Send him in.'

Dog got up from the video station and walked to the large common room at the front of the trailer. Starship flinched when he saw him.

'Colonel.'

'Lieutenant, I believe you forgot to ask if you had permission to go into town this afternoon,' said Dog.

'I thought it would be OK.'

'So what happened?'

'It didn't seem like that big a deal. I went with a Saudi pilot. We were in the town and, uh, there was a mosque, and I asked if I could take a look.'

'Why?'

'I wasn't trying to be disrespectful. I was just – if I went to church, I mean it was the same thing. You know? I was looking around. I just want to understand.'

'Understand what?'

'I want to understand why Kick died and I didn't.'

Starship's eyes widened momentarily, as if he'd seen something passing behind them in the room. They held Dog's for just a moment, then turned down, settling on the dark shadows at the base of the floor.

Dog wasn't the kind of officer who could play father figure or priest, which he knew was what Starship really needed. He did understand, however, what the young man was going through. He'd experienced it himself, or at least something like it, much earlier in his career when he'd lost a friend. But now he felt powerless to help the lieutenant, to do anything more than tell him the riot wasn't his fault, which it wasn't.

'All right, Starship. I understand that you meant no harm. The situation at the gate has nothing to do with you. You just happened to be in the wrong place at the wrong time. This was organized before you went near the mosque.'

'I don't think Bandar – the pilot – I don't think he set me up,' said Starship. 'I didn't go inside or anything. I was just looking around.'

'It's immaterial now. We're supposed to fly in two hours. Better get ready for your mission.'

Gulf of Aden
1830

Ali gripped the rope, pulling himself up the side of the ship. His AK47 clunked at his back as he clambered over the side of the tanker, helped by two of his men. The ship's captain stood a few feet away, frowning in the dim light.

'I thought we were not to be stopped again,' said the captain as Ali approached. 'You told me this yourself.'

'I am flattered that you remembered me, Captain,' said Ali. They had stopped the ship three months before, and Ali had, in fact, made that promise. 'It is regrettable that circumstances made it necessary to engage you again.'

Bari, Ali's second-in-command, approached from the

side. Bari had led the first team over. 'Plenty of fuel,' he told Ali. The tanker carried marine gas oil and marine diesel, the heavy grade of fuel oil commonly called 'bunker oil,' which was used by large ships.

'Set the course,' Ali told him.

'Should we wait for the Al Bushra to come alongside? The crew here seems compliant enough. They remember our last encounter, and most are Muslim brothers from Indonesia and Pakistan, with a Turk or two for discipline. There were no weapons.'

'Good. Have the Al Bushra come about and stand by to assist if necessary. But if you judge the situation acceptable, don't lose the time bringing more men aboard,' said Ali. 'Transmit the message telling the *Sharia* to sail. You should be able to meet them in six hours so they can fuel and return to the mooring before the Russian satellite passes. The boats will come with me. God has graced us and made things easy this evening.'

'What are you saying?' demanded the captain of the tanker.

Ali raised his rifle. 'Pray,' he told the captain. The man made no sign to comply, and so he shot him where he stood.

Aboard the *Wisconsin*, over the Gulf of Aden 2125

Starship checked his position on the sitrep map, trying to get a feel for the night's mission. Xray Pop was located about twenty miles north of Bandar Murcaayo in the Gulf of Aden; the Piranha unit was exploring an area of the Somalian coast near Bullaxaar. They were supposed to bring the probe eastward toward the task force; this would take between six and eight hours. The realignment would allow the Dreamland team to cover Xray Pop and run Piranha at the same time. Colonel Bastian had ordered two more Megafortresses and additional Flighthawks to join them; once they arrived, the search for the submarine and support of Xray Pop could proceed independently.

'Ready for Flighthawk launch,' said Dog.

'Flighthawk launch ready,' said Starship. He authorized the launch verbally for C^3, the Flighthawk control computer, then curled his fingers around the control stick. His heart pounded steadily as the Megafortress tipped forward and picked up momentum. The big aircraft lifted upward as the release point was reached, using the wind sheer off the wing as well as gravity to push the Flighthawk out of its nest beneath the wing. The computer had already ignited the robot plane's engine, and by the time Starship took over, he was zooming into a layer of clouds that seemed to last forever. The milky soup furled in all directions; he felt as if he were flying into someone's dream.

Unlike Zen, Starship preferred using the computer screens at the control station to guide the plane, instead of the command helmet. He found it easier to tap the screen to change views and get data. He had a standard pilot's helmet and mask, but often left them at the base of his ejection seat, resorting to them only during obvious combat situations. Zen argued that a 'normal' helmet made working the board difficult, but Starship disagreed; the weight of the control helmet tended to twist his neck and give him headaches if he wore it for more than an hour.

'*Hawk One* is launched and operating in the green,' he told Dog. 'Coming through fifteen thousand feet, going to five thousand. On programmed course.'

'Good work, Starship,' said Dog. 'Be advised we have a civilian merchant ship for you to check out, two miles due south of your present course.'

'On my way, Colonel.'

'Piranha control, we are in range for the handoff. *Baker-Baker* is standing by,' added Dog over the interphone.

'Piranha control is ready,' said Delaford, who was sitting next to Starship on the Flighthawk deck. 'Initiating transfer procedure.'

With the Flighthawk launched and the probe now under Delaford's control, Dog had a few moments to relax before lining up for a buoy drop about thirty miles to the east. He checked back in with Danny at Khamis Mushait via the Dreamland Command frequency.

'Peaceful at the moment,' said Danny. His voice came over the circuit a half second before his image appeared on the screen on the left-hand side of Dog's control panel. 'Base commander was over a little while ago, full of apologies and trying to be reassuring. He says this is being stirred up by bad elements.'

'That's nice,' said Dog sarcastically. 'Did they beef up security?'

'Claims it's at the max now. Has Washington gotten back to you, Colonel?'

'Negative. But I can't imagine that they're going to tell us to stay around,' added Dog.

'We can bug out as soon you give the order,' said Danny. 'And as soon as we know where we're going.'

'Probably Diego Garcia,' said Dog. 'Unless somebody comes up with an alternative. Did you get the blimp up?'

'Half hour ago. We're going to run a drill with the Werewolves around 2400, just to make sure the systems are all working together.'

'All right. But get some sleep at some point.'

'I will.'

'All right, Danny, I have to get into position to drop a buoy. Let me know if anything comes up.'

Starship pushed the Flighthawk over the stern of the merchant ship, riding slow and low across its topside. The low-light video image appeared gray on his main screen. Though slightly blurry, it was clear enough that there were no weapons aboard the ship.

'He's probably a smuggler,' said Commander Delaford. Starship was providing a video feed to one of the commander's auxiliary screens so the Navy expert could offer his opinions. The Piranha's onboard controls were more than adequate to take it to its new location on their own, and would alert Delaford automatically if it encountered anything suspicious or ran into a problem. The commander could easily divide his time between the probe and helping Starship.

'Why do you think he's a smuggler?'

'According to the database of area shipping we've compiled, he's headed for South Africa,' Delaford explained. 'But he's on a beeline for coastal waters, well out of the normal traffic area. If we follow him, my bet is we'll see him rendezvous with some smaller boats just inside territorial waters where he knows he can't be touched if Xray Pop comes calling.'

'Doesn't the Navy force know what's going on?'

'Absolutely.'

'So how can these guys get away with it?'

'Well, for one thing, you can't just stop any ship on the high seas. International law permits inspections only in certain circumstances. So even if the ship were carrying weapons, you'd have to prove that some law was being broken.'

'Like smuggling guns?'

'Unfortunately, you can't just stop and search a ship because you think it has guns,' said Delaford. 'There are countries that we have treaties with, where the terms of the treaty might allow a search. But even there, you would need at the very least probable cause and some sort of OK or at least notification. The administration has tried negotiating that, mostly to stop smuggling of weapons-grade plutonium or ballistic missiles. But what we're talking about here, pretty much the whole nature of the thing, we simply don't have the authority to stop the ship and search it against its captain's will. The UN and other international organizations are working on protocols to prevent certain types of smuggling and make it possible to take action, but they've been working on them for years. Most arrests are made in territorial waters where the local government is going to enforce its laws. At the moment, if you don't catch them in the act, or you don't find some very obvious problem with the ship manifest or something else, in the end you're going to have to give the weapons back. In theory,' added Delaford. 'Besides, Xray Pop can't be everywhere at once. Stopping and searching a ship can take considerable time if you do it right. The Navy has specially trained teams to handle it, and let me tell you, it's a dangerous job in a place like this. Thoroughly searching a vessel that size could take six, eight hours, even more.'

'What about the pirates?' said Starship. 'Why aren't we just blasting them? We know what they're up to. They're just terrorists.'

The same people who killed Kick, he thought, though he didn't say it.

'The thing that sets us apart from pirates is that we follow the law,' said Delaford. 'You have to remember that, Starship.'

'How does the law stop us? It shouldn't.'

'It doesn't, specifically. But what we can do depends on where they are,' said Delaford. 'If they're in international waters, we can defend anyone that they're attacking – or to put it in your terms, blast them. But outside of international waters, an attack on another ship isn't actually piracy. So an attack in coastal waters is subject to the laws of the country where it occurs.'

'Unless it's Somalia, where there is no law.'

'There are laws. Whether they are enforced or not is another question.'

'But these guys attack in international waters. How come they're free?'

'Again, because they're in the territory of another country. They can also claim that they're under the jurisdiction of Somalia or Yemen or wherever, and are entitled to the protection of their laws.'

'Sounds like bullshit to me.'

'Well, think of it this way. One of the things the War of 1812 was about was America's rights to its territorial waters and the rights of its seamen. Britain was stopping American ships and impressing seamen. America said it had no right to do that.'

'That doesn't sound like the same thing,' said Starship.

'It has to do with the law of the sea, and one country putting itself ahead of the law because it has the power to do so.'

'I don't think we're above the law,' said Starship. 'But I don't think these crazies should be shooting at us either.'

'Agreed. The fanatics don't care how many people die,' added Delaford. 'They know they're not going to win in the short term. This isn't about a single battle for them, or even a short war. They see this as a hundred year struggle. They want us to invade Somalia – they want us to invade all of Africa, all of the Middle East. They think if that happens, Islam will rise up and there will be a new golden age. Those people back in Saudi Arabia who were protesting outside the gates, the people who threw stones at you because you were curious about a mosque – what do you think their reaction would be to an invasion?'

'But we're not here to invade. We're just trying to protect shipping in the Gulf of Aden.'

'Absolutely,' said Delaford. 'That's what we have to remember. That and the fact that no one's going to thank us for it.'

Starship turned his full attention back to the Flighthawk, circling eastward to visually check the area where the control buoy would be dropped.

Whatever the law said, and whatever the geopolitical and religious implications were, Kick had been killed by fanatics. They didn't hate Kick specifically; they hated all westerners.

And Starship hated them.

Storm's voice exploded in Dog's ear as soon as he opened the circuit to the *Abner Read*. 'You went over my head!'

'I didn't go over your head, Captain. I informed the White House that we had a serious diplomatic situation. I need to relocate my people before things get uglier.'

'You went over my head! You instigated an incident –'

'Look, Storm, I don't particularly like you, and it's clear you don't like me. But neither I nor my people instigated anything in Saudi Arabia. There was clearly a well-thought-out plot to provoke a riot at the entrance to the base. I reported the incident to Washington as commander of Dreamland – *not* as part of the Whiplash team working under your command.'

'Stop the legal bullshit, Bastian. The fact is, you talked to the White House without talking to me.'

'Actually, Storm, I did try to talk to you. You wouldn't pick up the phone. Check with your communications officer.'

'I'm warning you, Bastian. Play by my rules.'

Dog checked his course on the navigation screen. They had to drop below three thousand feet to drop the buoy as configured, and they were still above the cloud cover at 25,000 feet.

'Are you there, Bastian?'

'I am here, Captain. As a matter of fact, I'm just double-checking where here is.'

'Is that supposed to be a joke?'

'Not that I know of.'

'Colonel, we have a surface contact coming out of the coast near Karin, about fifty miles due south of us,' said Dish, who was operating the surface radar aboard the *Wisconsin*. 'Thing is, I don't have that marked as a major port, and this is a pretty big ship. Nothing in the database about a tanker or anything either.'

'Run that by Commander Delaford and see what he thinks about it,' said Dog. 'Ask him if it's worth jogging down in that direction for a look-see.'

'Bastian?'

Dog clicked his talk button. 'Yes?'

'You're to move your operation to Diego Garcia as soon as possible. Note I said possible, not convenient.'

Gee thanks, thought Dog.

'We'll be there in twenty-four hours, if not sooner,' said Dog.

'When are you rendezvousing with my ship?'

'It'll take us a few hours to get the probe close enough to get overhead.'

'Make it here as quickly as you can.'

'Aye aye, Captain.'

Khamis Mushait Air Base
2130

With things outside the gate quiet for the moment, Danny Freah decided to do two things he'd been putting off since arriving in Saudi Arabia: call his wife, and take a shower.

He did the latter first, scalding the desert sand out of his pores. By the time he got out he felt like a lobster – but a relaxed one. He got dressed and returned to the Dreamland Command trailer. After checking to make sure that nothing had changed outside – it hadn't – he put through the call, trying her university office first.

'Dr Freah.'

'Hi, Doc. I was wondering if you could cure my sore throat,' said Danny. It was an old joke between them – her Ph.D. was in black studies.

'Well, hello, stranger. Where have you been?'

'You'd be surprised.'

'No, I wouldn't. Have you talked to Rosenstein?'

'I'm fine, how are you?'

'Don't duck the question.'

'I haven't had a chance,' said Danny.

'There's a party at the Guggenheim Museum two weeks

206

from today that would be fantastic for you to attend,' said Jemma Freah. 'All the important people are going to be there. It's a cocktail party, mixing art with politics. A lot of bucks. Definitely a good place to press the flesh.'

Politics was the last thing Danny wanted to talk about. He leaned back in the chair, stretching his legs under the console carefully to avoid the stack of black boxes controlling the communications functions.

'How are you, Jem?'

'Fine, but I have a class in two minutes. Can you make that party?'

Danny had no way of knowing how long the present deployment was going to last. It was conceivable that, if the Dreamland team moved to Diego Garcia, he'd be able to go home for a few days, maybe even an entire week, around Thanksgiving – Diego Garcia not only had its own security, it was at least arguably more secure than any base in the Continental United States because of its location. But about the last place in the world he wanted to even think about being was a political cocktail party.

Would he ever feel differently?

If not, then why run for office?

'I don't know what I'll be doing then,' said Danny.

'Why not?'

'You know I can't go into details, Jem.'

'Yeah, well, look, I have to go to class. Send me an e-mail.'

'Good idea,' he said, though he really didn't have anything to say. In fact, he wondered why he'd bothered to call at all.

Starship brought the Flighthawk south, dropping through two thousand feet as he approached the lumbering ship. There were two much smaller vessels moving in its wake, twenty-foot open boats. The infrared camera in the nose of the Flighthawk painted the ship a ghostly green in the display; the angle seemed odd – the bow looked as if it poked up out of the ocean. Starship thought there was something wrong with the camera or viewer, and hit the diagnostic section for a self-test.

The test showed no problem. The ship looked to Starship like an old oil tanker; it carried crates or something lashed to the deck.

'What do you have there?' asked Delaford.

'I don't know. I'm getting some distortion from my infrared viewer. Bow's kind of out of whack. I'm switching to the low light. Pretty dark, though.'

'Looks like an old amphibious vessel,' said Delaford. 'See how the bow sweeps up?'

'Yeah.'

'It's not in our database,' said Delaford. 'Can you get closer?'

'I can just about land on his deck if you want.'

Starship tucked the Flighthawk into a roll, knifing down through one thousand feet. He continued to accelerate as he dropped toward the water. As the altimeter ladder ramped down through five hundred, he started to level

208

off, getting a high g warning as he pushed the robot plane into an extremely sharp turn to take it over the ship. He leaned forward against his restraints, pushing the robot toward her limits. For the first time on the deployment, and for one of the first times since he had started flying the U/MFs, he felt as if he were on board the tiny aircraft. He sensed the rush of gravity as he bent the wings to complete his turn. The aircraft took over 9 g's; he could feel his body reacting, tensing and leaning against the forces the Flighthawk was encountering.

This is what Zen means, he thought to himself. This is what it's supposed to feel like.

'There used to be some sort of gun at the rear deck – at the forward area too,' said Delaford, somewhere far behind him.

Starship poured on the dinosaurs, accelerating back toward the Megafortress. He was still low, barely a hundred feet over the waves. He began another turn, banking much more gently, lining up for a run over the bow area for another angle.

Delaford was talking over the interphone, telling him about the ship: 'The Somalians had a large Russian vessel that was designed as an amphibious ship. It was supposed to be used to transport tanks and equipment. Hasn't been used in at least five years. This is probably it, patched up to be used as a freighter, or more likely being taken to a salvage operation. Stolen, maybe.'

This is how it's supposed to feel, Starship thought again. The ship grew in his screen, its upturned bow on the right side. He realized he should slow down for a more detailed view, but by now it was too late; he was already beyond it.

'One more pass, low and slow,' he said aloud. He nudged his throttle back and took a breath, reminding himself to stay in control. He could feel his pulse thumping in his throat.

Get too excited and you lose it.

That was Kick's saying, wasn't it?

You with me, Kick?

Get too excited and you lose it.

Yeah.

Starship exhaled very slowly as he took the Flighthawk into a turn, trying to stay calm. But just as he reached the far point of the turn, the computer warned that he was at the far end of his control range.

'Three seconds to disconnect,' it said in his ear.

'Colonel, I need you to come east.'

'It's unnecessary, Lieutenant. Get back to the *Wisconsin*.'

'I just need one more pass.'

'Back to the *Wisconsin*,' said Dog.

Starship opened his mouth to argue, then realized it was a moot point – the computer was counting down to disconnect on his screen. Reluctantly, he pulled it back toward its mothership.

'My bet would be it's on its way to the scrap heap,' said Delaford, examining the video scans of the ship again. 'A lot of metal.'

'What about the crates on deck?'

'Possibly more junk inside them,' said Delaford. 'Or else like I said, someone's trying to use it to bring cargo

210

back and forth. I kind of doubt that but you never know out here. People can be very resourceful.'

'Maybe they're going to invade someplace.'

'These warlords have enough trouble keeping control of their little spits of land,' said Delaford.

Starship reached for the steel coffee mug, draining the last bit of coffee. Flying circles around the sky for hours on end was bad enough, but doing it on such little sleep was sheer torture. He had some caffeine pills he could take – as well as stronger medicine if absolutely necessary – but he preferred to hold them in reserve.

'*Hawk One*, we have two ships approaching from the north,' said Dog. He gave him a heading and a GPS location about sixty-five miles ahead of the Megafortress.

'On my way, Colonel,' replied Starship. He nudged the Flighthawk's control stick forward, descending gradually toward the two ships.

'Big one in front looks like an oiler,' said Delaford as he got close, 'the sort of ship that carries diesel fuel for others.'

'Like a tanker?'

'More like a floating gas station. There are a few of these ships that were used by navies in the past, mostly the Russians, and then were sold off and used with very little conversion as transports. Database is working on it.'

The computer needed twenty points of reference to identify a ship and compare it to the database for identification. The points could range from size measurements to mast and stack configurations.

An ID flashed on the screen as Starship's Flighthawk closed to within two miles:

DUBNA CLASS, OIL

'Database is comparing it to a Finnish-built ship used by the Russians,' explained Delaford. 'Carries a couple thousand tons of bunker oil and about the same of light diesel, some other supplies. I have it in the registry – it's a Turkish ship, looks like it was bought from Ukraine two years ago.'

'What's the other one?' asked Starship.

Before Delaford could answer, the computer gave its opinion:

BUSHRA CLASS PATROL BOAT
OMAN NAV

'That's incredibly far from home. Couple of hundred miles,' said Delaford.

'Maybe they're protecting them from the pirates.'

'Maybe.'

Dog looked at the low-light video as it played in the panel on the Megafortress's 'dashboard.'

'The Oman ship doesn't look particularly hostile,' he told Delaford.

'Granted,' said the lieutenant commander. 'But there are a couple of things out of place. There's an Exocet missile launcher on the deck behind the smokestack. You can see it in the view of the starboard side. That's not standard equipment on those boats. Oman does have Exocets, but they're usually on their Dhofar missile boats, which are a little newer. There's also an antiair battery, a missile system on the forward deck.'

'Doesn't add up to pirates,' said Dog. 'So they've updated the ship, so what? It might be protecting the other ship.'

'Very possibly. Or perhaps pirates have taken over the Oman ship and have used it to capture the oiler. It's filled with fuel. It can fuel other ships at sea, or at least bring fuel supplies to ports.'

'But most of the patrol boats don't use the heavy fuel it has.'

'Good point,' said Delaford. 'I'm not saying I know what's going on. Quite the opposite.'

'All right. Let's try hailing them and find out what they're up to,' said Dog. He turned to his copilot. 'McNamara, ID us as a Navy flight on a routine patrol. See if you can hail the Oman ship.'

'On it, Colonel.'

'How's your fuel, Starship?'

'Going to need to tank in about twenty minutes,' said Starship.

'Get some close-ups of both of those ships,' said Dog. 'Then we'll set up for a refuel.'

'Roger that.'

'Not acknowledging us,' said McNamara.

'Try the oiler.'

'Yes, sir.'

'Delaford, the Oman ship isn't talking to us,' said Dog. 'Anything except the obvious occur to you?'

213

'No.'

'Radar,' said McNamara. The copilot was warning Dog that the Oman ship had just turned on an antiaircraft radar. 'Shouldn't be able to see us at this range. Not sure about the Flighthawk as it goes over, but they don't have a lock at the moment.'

Starship pushed the UM/F toward the Oman vessel, accelerating for a quick fly-by.

'People moving on the deck of the second boat,' he told Dog. 'Up near the, uh, front, the bow, near the gun.'

If they were fanatics, killers, he could erase them with a squeeze of his trigger. They deserved it – murderers. They'd killed Kick.

Would that bring him back?

Of course not.

Would it feel good?

Not really. Not in the way he wanted it to.

'What should I do, Colonel?'

'Just stand by,' said Dog. 'Let me talk to my friend, Captain Gale.'

Aboard the *Abner Read*,
Gulf of Aden
2150

Storm pressed the button on the communication control, connecting through the satellite phone.

'What is it, Bastian?'

214

'Hold on, sir,' said a voice he didn't recognize.

Bastian came on a second later.

'We have something that you may be interested in, Storm,' he said. 'Some sort of tanker being trailed by a gunboat that's supposed to belong to Oman. We're not sure if it's an escort or if it's joined the pirates.'

'Hail them.'

'We've tried that. No answer from either ship. I'm going to patch you over to Commander Delaford,' said Dog. 'He can fill you in on what the ships look like and what he thinks they may be up to. I'll stand by. Using the satellite phone to connect isn't working very well, Storm. Your voice blanks in and out.'

'And what do you propose instead?'

'As I tried to tell you earlier, we have mobile communications units that will let you tie into the Dreamland network. If you work with me instead of against me, we might actually get something done.'

'I'm getting plenty done, Bastian. Put Delaford on.'

The line descended into static for so long that Storm was about to call in his communications expert to get the Dreamland people back when Delaford came on.

'Storm, we have a gunboat out of Oman trailing what looks to be an old oiler converted for use as a civilian tanker,' Delaford explained. 'It's an Al Bushra, a large patrol boat originally built by France. They've mounted Exocets on it.'

'Exocets?'

'Absolutely. I can't tell whether they've taken them off one of their missile boats or what, but they're definitely there.'

'He's pretty far from where he belongs,' said Storm.

He hadn't encountered any Oman ships during their patrol; they usually stayed close to port, where the government could keep a close watch on them.

'He's escorting an oiler that's been converted to civilian use as a tanker,' said Delaford. 'We have the oiler in the database registered to a Cameroon company. It took on fuel in Turkey and does a regular route, mostly bunker oil, over to the East African coast, sometimes to Asia. Never to Oman.'

'And they're not answering radio calls?'

'No. They're headed in the direction of Somalia, though they're in international waters. It looks weird, but there's no proof of anything.'

'You sure Bastian's not making this up?'

There was a pause. 'I'm sorry, Captain, we have a bum connection I think. I'm not sure what you said.'

'You're sure this is for real?' said Storm.

'It's real. I'm looking at a video of it now.'

'All right. It's definitely worth checking into.'

Storm looked at the holographic display. The two ships were over two hundred nautical miles to the southwest. It would take six hours, at least, to get there. But the addition of an Oman ship to the pirate fleet would be a major development.

Eyes looked at him expectantly. Storm put up his forefinger, signaling that he would explain in a moment.

'It'll take us several hours to get out there,' Storm told Delaford. 'Do you think the Dreamland people can track him until then?'

'With their eyes closed.'

'Give me Bastian.'

'I'm here,' said Bastian.

Just like him to eavesdrop, thought Storm. 'Trail the ship. See where it goes. We're going to come east and board them.'

'I can do that, but I may have to put the Piranha into sleep mode,' said the Air Force flier.

'What does that mean?'

'I'm uncomfortable discussing it in detail,' said Dog.

'The satellite line is encrypted.'

'I'm still uncomfortable talking about details of the system. You're going to have to take my word for it.'

Everything with this guy is a struggle, thought Storm. Everything.

'Do what you have to do,' he told Bastian.

'I intend to.'

'Listen Bastian . . . Bastian? Are you still there?'

'Still here.'

'We're losing the stinking communications satellite around four o'clock in the morning. We're going to have to find another way to communicate. Get those Dreamland communications things en route to me ASAP.'

'I'll have an Osprey launch within the hour.'

Khamis Mushait Air Base
2200

'I can get three portable units out there right away, Colonel,' Danny told Dog. 'But that leaves me without the Osprey for over four hours.'

'You don't think the Werewolves are enough to keep you covered?'

'They can, but I can't use the Werewolves to bug out if I have to.'

'All right, let's rethink this,' said Dog.

'What if we send one of the Werewolves?'

'A round trip is over twelve hundred miles,' said Dog. 'It can't make it back without refueling.'

'Couldn't it refuel on the *Abner Read*?' asked Danny. 'If they have a helipad, maybe they have fuel.'

'We can check,' said Dog. 'Talk to the technical people first about what they'd have to do to carry radio units. Make sure it's feasible before you talk to Storm. Is Peterson still sick?'

'Afraid so. Fever of 102, last time I checked. I can fly it,' added Danny.

'No, you have too much to do. So does Jennifer. Is Zen around?'

'Zen's right here,' said Danny.

'Put him on.'

Danny got up and walked into the conference area of the command post. 'Boss wants to talk to you,' he told Zen, who was playing poker with Spiderman and two of the Whiplash sergeants. 'He's looking for a pilot for the Werewolf.'

'The Werewolf?'

'I can do it,' said Danny. 'Jen's over working on the LADS connection and –'

'Don't sweat it; I've flown them plenty of times,' said Zen, wheeling himself backward to the communications area. 'Piece of cake. Computer does all the work if you let it.'

The trailer rocked as Sergeant Ben 'Boston' Rockland burst through the door.

'Hey, Cap, we're being invaded, but I think they're friendly,' he said. 'The Marines have landed.'

Two burly Marine Corps sergeants followed Boston inside. They were followed by one of the slimmest Marines Danny had ever met.

And by far the prettiest.

'Lieutenant Emma Klacker, U.S. Marine Corps. No need to worry; you're secure now.'

Danny laughed. 'Oh are we? What'd you do, bring a division?'

'We don't need a division,' said the lieutenant. 'We're the Marines. Relax, Captain. Nobody's coming or going on this base without your approval.'

The Whiplash troopers sitting around the table smirked at each other.

'Raise is two bucks to you, Zen,' said Sergeant Kevin Bison. 'Now that we're safe, I feel I can open up my game and bet the limit.'

'You making a joke, soldier?' said Klacker.

'Oh, no, ma'am. I'm just feeling real warm and toasty now that the Marines are here to save my bacon.'

'Lieutenant, maybe you and I ought to discuss this outside,' said Danny.

Lieutenant Klacker glared at Bison, gave the evil eye to the rest of the trailer, then exited. As Danny passed the Marines, one of them said in a stage whisper, 'No disrespect, sir, but I'd watch out. She's got one hell of a temper. And if she volunteers to scrimmage you in tae kwon do, don't do it.'

'That's all right,' said Danny. 'I never scrimmage. Or fight fair.'

Klacker was waiting for him outside. 'Why are you letting your men disrespect the Corps?'

'They're not,' said Danny.

'Disrespect is *bullshit*, Captain.'

'Whoa, hold on, Lieutenant. I agree. None of my people are going to disrespect the Corps. Whiplash has worked with the Corps before. We have nothing but respect.'

'What do you mean, Whiplash?'

'That's who we are.'

The Marine officer looked at him suspiciously. 'Bullshit, you are. We were told there was an Air Force survey team down here that needed help with some local rioters.'

Danny laughed.

'What the hell's so funny, Captain?'

'That must be the cover they were using up at CentCom or something. We're surveying, all right – we're hunting around the gulf for a Libyan submarine.'

'You're the guys who went into Iran? Whiplash from Dreamland?'

'That's us.'

'You're Freah?'

'That's what it says on the uniform.'

'I heard of you.' She frowned, as if she still didn't believe him. 'You're younger than I heard.'

Danny laughed. 'I hope that's a compliment.'

'It is.' She stuck out her hand. 'My friends call me Dancer. Yes, Captain, I was one, in another lifetime. I have other nicknames, but I don't use them in polite company.'

'I'm Danny.' He held out his hand. Based on what the Marine inside had said, he almost expected to be tossed over her shoulder. But she only shook it, gripping it firmly but not trying to crush his fingers the way some women officers did, trying to prove they were as tough as men. 'I appreciate your coming down to help out,' Danny told her.

He explained that they had been ordered to leave, and were currently arranging to do just that. He covered a few administrative details, beginning with the fact that there was plenty of space in the building they'd been given if the Marines wanted to bunk out.

'Saudis have been letting us eat over at the cafeteria,' Danny added finally. 'Base commander said additional troops wouldn't be a problem. I didn't tell him they were Marines.'

Dancer smiled. 'Best to spring that on them at the last minute.'

Danny gave a brief overview of the defenses, showing her some of the nonlethal bullet panels and pointing out the general location of the blimp overhead. It couldn't be seen in the night sky, its skin of LEDs rendering it almost invisible.

'Details about a lot of our systems are classified,' Danny added. 'Obviously, we're going to be working with you, and we'll be sharing what you need to know. But I'd ask that you emphasize the fact that they are classified to your people.'

'They're not people, they're Marines.' Dancer smiled. 'Don't worry. They won't tell anybody the secrets to your success. But if I were you, I'd check on that poker game right away. My guys can be ruthless when the stakes are high.'

Aboard the *Wisconsin*,
over the Gulf of Aden
2350

'What's Piranha's status?' Dog asked Delaford.

'Still swimming merrily along,' he said. 'But we're going to have to drop another buoy soon.'

'You have a location for me?'

'Same as before,' said Delaford. 'Here.'

The computer took the plot from Delaford's system and integrated it into the sitrep map on Dog's cockpit panel. The Megafortress was about fifty miles due north of Mayhd on the Somalian coast. To reach the next drop point he'd have to swing eastward about thirty miles, which would mean taking the Flighthawk with him. They could watch the two ships by radar easily enough.

'We'll drop this buoy, but we may have to put the probe to sleep,' Dog told Delaford.

'I'd really prefer to avoid that if we can, Colonel,' said Delaford. 'We'd be better off putting it into autonomous mode and letting it go on its own to a rendezvous point.'

222

'Sleep mode' was just that – the probe turned most of its systems off and sat in the water until receiving a signal to reactivate. 'Autonomous mode' meant that it would use its internal system to take it to a specific point in the ocean. The discussion on what to do mixed tactical considerations with technical ones – the probes failed to wake up from sleep mode about twenty-five percent of the time. On the other hand, autonomous mode wasn't foolproof either – the internal navigation system was prone to small errors, which multiplied into tens if not hundreds of miles over time.

'All right, this is what we're going to do,' Dog said finally. 'We'll send Piranha west and rendezvous with it somewhere north of Butyallo or Caluula, small towns on the Somalian coast. In the meantime, we'll drop one last buoy.'

'Sounds good,' said Delaford.

'Starship, hang back near the Oman ship as long as you can, then come east with me for the duration of the buoy drop,' Dog told the Flighthawk pilot.

'On it, Colonel.'

'Let's do it.'

**Gulf of Aden
8 November 1997
0012**

Ali put down his glasses and checked his watch. They were more than a hundred miles from the rendezvous point for the submarine. They had made very poor progress for a number of reasons, including false reports on the radios that they monitored. Frustrated but resigned, Ali told the helmsman to slow the boat; there was no sense wasting their fuel or pushing their engines further. The other vessels in the flotilla slowed as well.

A container ship was heading westward in the direction of the Red Sea. On another night, it would be an inviting target.

'Captain, the radio,' said one of the men below.

Ali leaned down into the cabin, listening to the chatter over the shortwave radio. There had been talk of aircraft and ships all night, most of it false. Twice Ali had taken his boats toward hiding places because of radio reports of American destroyers; he'd had to use his satellite phone to call his own sources to see if these reports were true. He wondered if the Americans had realized that he used the radio calls as part of his intelligence network and decided to infiltrate it somehow. If so, they would have found people who spoke very good Arabic.

'Near Sury Point,' said one of the voices on the radio now. 'Three ships low to the water. One large, the others small. Moving quickly.'

Satan's Tail, Ali realized, less than forty miles from him, back to the west.

And within sixty of the Al Bushra gunboat the volunteers had taken from Oman.

If it was a true report. Could he trust it?

'Has Ghazala sent the signal that he met the submarine?' Ali asked the communications mate. Ghazala commanded the ship he had sent ahead to the rendezvous.

'Not yet, sir.'

If Ali turned the ships around and raced west, they could engage Satan's Tail before two hours passed. At the same time, the Al Bushra could launch her missiles against it. The American would be caught between the two forces.

If the American was where these reports said he was.

The oiler would have to sail on alone. And the *Sharia* would have to return to its mooring. She was not ready to do battle.

It was a gamble, based on possibly inaccurate information. But if he waited to verify it, the chance might slip through his fingers.

Had God given him the Al Bushra for this attempt? It had not been required for the oiler, and seemed to have no other role – surely it was intended to attack the devil ship.

'Signal the other boats,' said Ali. 'Satan's Tail awaits.'

Khamis Mushait Air Base
0020

'Where are you?'

'Fifty feet over Al Huwaymi, heading out toward the gulf,' Zen told his wife Breanna. The control unit for the Werewolves had been housed in the hangar behind the Megafortress parking area. Zen sat surrounded by the large black carrying cases used to ship the equipment, a tangle of wires forming a nest around his wheelchair.

The control unit had only two panels set up. Both were twenty-one-inch LCD flatscreens. The panel on the right showed a three-dimension simulation of where the Werewolf was, the area it flew over rendered as a wire model, with green and red lines delineating the topography. The Werewolf was a stubby yellow double cross that, if you squinted just right, looked a little like the aircraft itself. It reminded Zen of the first Flighthawk simulation – which wasn't coincidental, since the program was essentially the same one.

Give or take five million lines of code . . .

The panel on the left showed the video feed from the Werewolf's nose. The camera was not light-enhanced, and even though they were using the Dreamland satellite system, the transmission was choppy.

'Doesn't it feel weird to be sitting here in a hangar, five hundred miles away, guiding an aircraft over hostile territory?' asked Breanna as she handed Zen an ice cold cola.

'Four hundred and seventy-two miles away, and Yemen is not necessarily hostile territory,' said Zen. 'The computer is actually doing the flying. I just nudge the control stick every so often so it thinks I'm in control.'

'You know what I mean. I can see with the Flighthawks. I mean, you're in a plane. But this – it's like a computer game.'

'I guess,' said Zen, taking the cola.

'You used to say that.'

'I used to.' He took a long sip from the soda. 'I guess I've gotten used to it.'

226

'I guess.'

'Ten years from now, Bree, everything will be remote control.'

'I hope not.'

'Well, how did it feel flying the Unmanned Bomber?' he asked.

'Too weird. That's why I gave it up.'

'Temporarily. For the deployment in the Pacific.'

'Permanently.'

Zen glanced up at her. Breanna had gone through a lengthy debate several months before when she was offered command of the Unmanned Bomber project. It was an important project and a very important position, especially for an ambitious female captain. The Unmanned Bomber was a hypersonic aircraft designed to be fitted with either a laser or a high-energy discharge weapon. There was no guarantee that the UMB, as it was known at Dreamland, would go into production, but even if it didn't, the project was likely to be the touchstone for a dozen future systems, from engines to weapons. Taking command of the project would surely put Breanna on the fast track for a general's star, and beyond.

'You don't want the project?' Zen asked.

'I like to fly when I fly,' she said.

'Well, some of us can't.'

'I don't mean it like that,' she said, putting her hand on his shoulder.

'No harm, no foul,' he said. He'd have to save the discussion about her future for another time. 'I gotta do a cut here in thirty seconds,' he added. 'Then I have to contact Xray Pop and make sure the global positioning system is working properly. Okay?'

'Never interrupt a pilot on a mission, even when he's sitting in a hangar 472 miles away.'

'Four hundred and eighty-five. These things move pretty quick.'

Aboard the *Wisconsin*,
over the Gulf of Aden
0055

'The Oman ship is now heading northeast,' said Dish. 'Still moving ahead.'

'What about the tanker?' Dog asked.

'He's still more or less where he was. A little closer to the coast maybe. Definitely moving, just not very fast.'

'What do you think, Tommy?' Dog asked Delaford.

'The Oman patrol boat, the Al Bushra ship, she's headed in Xray Pop's direction. Beyond that, though, I'm just not sure. He's at twenty knots or so. That's close to his top speed, if not right at it.'

'Still doesn't answer any hails,' said McNamara.

Dog banked the Megafortress. They were at 35,000 feet, twenty miles off the coast of Somalia. None of the Ethiopian aircraft they'd tussled with the night before had come out. Several radars in Yemen had switched on and off during the night, but they were too far away to find them.

'Have a contact I think is the *Abner Read*,' said Dish.

'Just barely there. Very small radar return, now twenty miles to our east. Couple of other very small ships, very small, about ten miles farther east. The radar signature is so small we can't even ID the ship. Kind of like looking at a stealth bomber. I'd guess it's next to invisible to a surface radar until you're maybe inside five miles.'

'You sure about those locations?'

'Locations? Absolutely.'

'Commander Delaford – the Shark Boats that patrol with the *Abner Read* . . . Would they be trailing him by ten miles?'

'I'm not sure, Colonel. Why?'

'Just two of them,' said Dog.

'Actually we have four now, Colonel. They're moving fast – faster than he is. About fifty knots.'

Dog reached to the communications panel, punching into the Dreamland circuit.

'Zen, have you contacted the *Abner Read*?'

'I'm supposed to radio the ship when I'm five miles away, about forty-five seconds from now,' said Zen, piloting the Werewolf. 'We're about ten miles due north of the last calculated rendezvous point.'

'We have some contacts to your east. Can you see them?'

'Hang on.'

Dog watched the composite radar screen, which compiled the positions of both surface and ship contacts. The Werewolf was closer to the trailing ships than to the *Abner Read*.

'Can't see them,' said Zen. 'I can change course.'

'Don't do that,' said Dog. 'You say you're only five miles from the *Abner Read*?'

'Affirmative. They have to turn their lights on for me to land. The automated system can't interface with them, and they're a moving target.'

'All right. Contact them and arrange to drop those com units. I'm going to talk to Captain Gale and suggest you check out these contacts. How much fuel do you have aboard?'

'Another thirty minutes worth. I was told they had fuel on the ship.'

'They do. Stand by.'

Aboard the *Abner Read*,
Gulf of Aden
0100

Storm could hear the aircraft approaching in the distance.

'Lights,' he said into his microphone.

The landing deck of the destroyer glowed white. Storm looked upward, as much to shield his eyes as to look for the helicopter. The sound grew louder, the roar of a steam locomotive drowning out the sounds of the *Abner Read*; the hum of her engines and the high-pitched hiss of her lights.

'There, Captain, there she is.'

The aircraft buzzed across the fantail, ten feet off the deck. It circled to the right, buzzing to the end of the glow and coming back. It looked more like an alien space-ship than a helicopter. It took another pass, and then spun

230

smartly around, dropping into a hover and descending on the *Abner Read*'s helicopter landing pad.

Storm had never seen anything like it. The aircraft looked like a combination of an airplane and a helicopter. It was small, its body no bigger than a good-sized desk. And it had just executed a perfect landing on a destroyer moving at close to forty knots, all the while guided by someone hundreds of miles away.

He didn't like Bastian, but he had to give the devil his due – his techno toys worked pretty damn well.

Two of the *Abner Read* crewmen approached the helicopter as its rotors spun down. Because the Werewolf was so small, there was little clearance between the deck and the rotors, and they had to wait until the propellers stopped spinning. When they finally did, the men rushed forward, leaned in with big chain cutters, and snapped the wire restraints that held the case beneath the Werewolf's belly. The aircraft had landed on it; there was no way to retrieve it until the helo took off.

'Go!' yelled Storm. 'Go!'

The rotors spun in opposite directions, making an eerie whirling sound. The first revolution seemed lazy, almost against its will; the second was a little faster; with the third, the aircraft sprung upward in a fury and was gone.

'Lights!' yelled Storm.

As the lights were doused, the voice of one of the men in the Tactical Center below yelled over the combat intercom system: 'Here they come!'

'Hard right rudder!' said Storm. 'Weapons! Prepare to fire!'

231

A long streak of yellow flashed in the screen, morphing to white and then breaking back into yellow. Zen leaned on the control stick for the Werewolf, whipping the robot helicopter out of the line of fire. The computer opened a targeting window at the right side of his screen, boxing the cannon on the deck of the lead pirate ship. Zen reached forward and tapped the screen, manually designating the target and allowing the computer to fire as soon as it was locked. Unlike in the Flighthawk, he didn't have to line up head-on for a shot – the computer rotated the chain gun, firing to the right as the Werewolf flew nearly parallel to its target. The 30mm shells drew a thick line across the front of the small patrol craft, tearing through the gun, surrounding deck, and nearby superstructure. Zen banked sharply and took manual control of the gun to rake the rear of the patrol craft. The computer recorded the hits on a wire-model projection in the targeting screen, painting them as dark red flashes and estimating the damage: No critical systems had been hit, but the vessel's forward gun was out of action.

A barrage of bullets erupted from a second patrol boat a half mile away. The Werewolf pirouetted in the sky as Zen lined up the new target. The target box painted the enemy ship's bridge; Zen stabbed the screen and concentrated on ducking the sudden burst of bullets from the enemy ship. The Werewolf fired several times, recording hits on the bridge, but the patrol boat continued to fire and Zen had to pull off.

His control screen flashed red. FUEL STATE LOW, said a message in the middle of the screen.

'Is that all?' he said, relieved, but as if in answer, the computer flashed a fresh message:

DAMAGE TO REAR STABLIZER FIN. 25 PERCENT.

And then several others in rapid succession:

DAMAGE TO HYDRAULIC SYSTEM 1. OFFLINE.
DAMAGE TO HYDRAULIC SYSTEM 2. 24 PERCENT.
DAMAGE TO CONTROL SYSTEM 1, CPU UNIT. 20 PERCENT.

'Now's where it starts to get interesting,' said Zen, pushing the joystick to line up for another run at the pirate.

Aboard the *Abner Read,*
Gulf of Aden
0114

'Missile away!'

A Harpoon missile leapt from the vertical launcher on the forward deck. The flare from the lower stage of the rocket glared through the windscreen at the front of the bridge, painting the gear and crew an eerie yellow.

'Where are my guns!' Storm barked into his microphone.

At least three people answered, 'Firing!' as the destroyer started to rock with the beat of six 155mm shells fired in rapid succession from the forward weapon. The crew on the bridge and in the Tactical Center cheered as the weapon hit home.

'Target one is demolished!'

'Target one sunk!'

'We got the son of a bitch.'

'Take that for Commander Marcum, you bastards!'

'Take out the rest of the boats,' said Storm calmly. 'Steady, gentlemen. Executive officer, Eyes, everyone, steady, now. We have not yet begun to fight.'

Gulf of Aden
0115

The sea around them erupted as the American ship began spitting its shells. A helicopter zipped above, firing a cannon at the lead vessel in Ali's flotilla. One of the crewmen began firing the machine gun at it, the barrage so close and loud that Ali had to put his mouth directly to his helmsman's ear to make himself be heard.

'Continue the attack!' he shouted. 'We need more time. Torpedoes!' he added. 'Fire the torpedoes!'

One of the shells from Satan's Tail landed in the water ten or fifteen yards away, sending a spray of salt water over the boat. The small vessel rocked back and forth, slapped by the waves and explosions.

'Torpedoes! Fire!' yelled Ali. He reached down and picked up the flare gun. As the flare shot upward, he pulled the satellite phone from his pocket. 'Fire on these coordinates!' he told his cousin Mabrukah aboard the Oman missile boat. 'Fire! Fire! Fire!'

Aboard the *Wisconsin*,
over the Gulf of Aden
0115

'Missile in the air!' yelled Starship, his voice so loud Dog probably could have heard him without the benefit of the interphone system. 'Two missiles in the air!'

'Exocet antiship missiles,' said Dog's copilot, Kevin McNamara, much more calmly. 'Fired toward the *Abner Read*.'

'That's good enough for me,' said Dog. 'Target the Oman ship. Open bomb bay doors.'

'Bay,' repeated the copilot.

The Megafortress bucked as the large doors at the base of the rear fuselage swung open. Dog pushed his stick forward, nosing into a fifteen-degree angle toward the vessel that had just launched the missiles.

'Vessel targeted,' said McNamara.

'Fire Harpoon.'

The missile clunked off the rotating dispenser, already on a direct line to the enemy ship. Four hundred eighty-eight pounds of high explosives were locked into the fat target less than eight miles away.

Dog hit the preset button on the communications panel to open the radio channel to Storm. But the *Abner Read*'s

235

crew apparently had not been able to activate the communications unit yet.

'Broadcast a missile warning to *Abner Read*,' Dog told McNamara.

'Already have. Harpoon two is ready to fire.'

'Fire Harpoon two.'

'Launching.'

The turbojet engine at the rear of the missiles ignited, ramping their airspeed toward five hundred knots. They had one more of the antiship weapons left.

'Radar system on the missile boat is attempting to lock,' said the copilot.

'ECMs,' said Dog, ordering electronic countermeasures.

'They're firing surface-to-air missiles! Radar-guided! Harpoon one missed,' said McNamara, incredulous.

'Target them again.'

'Targeting. Missile in the air! Coming for us.'

Dog held to his course, waiting for the copilot to lock the Harpoon's guidance system on the target. The missile that had been launched was identified as an SA-S-4; the *Wisconsin* was flying at the outer edge of its range, though that was no guarantee of safety. With the bomb bay doors open, the Megafortress's radar cross section was more than ample for the missile's guidance system to see. They were high but moving relatively slow, and except for the ECMs, which confused the missile's guidance systems, they would be an easy target.

'We have a lock,' said the copilot.

'Fire Harpoon,' said Dog.

'Firing.'

'Crew, stand by for some jinking,' said Dog. 'Button us up, Kevin.'

As their last antiship missile dropped from the belly, the copilot closed the bomb bay, instantly making them less visible to radar. Dog pressed the chaff release button, sending bundles of metallic tinsel into the air. An old but still effective counterweapon, the chaff acted like a smoke screen, making it harder for the enemy to pick the Megafortress out of the sky. Dog jabbed the control stick to jerk the Megafortress in a new direction, a wide receiver giving the defensive backs an open-field fake.

Even so, it wasn't enough – a warning tone in Dog's headset told him the missile was closing in.

Starship pointed the Flighthawk toward the ship, leaning toward the screen as he nosed into a forty-five-degree dive, plunging at the rectangular bridge at the center of his screen. A puff of smoke flashed at the left side of his screen, and black lines began to rise on the right.

Starship felt the Megafortress lurch beneath him. He fought off the distraction. The targeting pipper danced left and right, the ship below seeming to slip back and forth as if it sensed he was coming. The screen blinked yellow and he pressed the trigger, even though he knew it was too early. The shells trailed downward and he let go, pulling up on the stick as the Flighthawk lost some of its momentum. He had no target now; he'd ruined his approach by firing too soon and was caught flatfooted in the air, flying toward a cloud of antiaircraft fire. Starship bit the side of his lip, angry but trying to control his emotions, knowing he wasn't that far off. He managed to duck right and pull around sharply enough to get a burst in, this time on target, but he was beyond the vessel before he could fire more than a handful of bullets.

Starship leveled off, took a breath, then pushed the plane into a long, almost lackadaisical bank low over the ocean, trying to convince himself that this was just another of the hundred or two hundred simulations he had run with Zen and Kick during training a few months before. Kick had been better at the attack missions – he'd flown an A-10A Warthog, a real stick and rudder aircraft, and was used to using the cannon on surface targets. Starship had learned a lot just by watching his laid-back, no rush approach; it was a different head than the balls-out fighter jock Starship was used to.

The Flighthawk had dropped below fifty feet, and the computer gave him a warning as he came out of the turn.

'Thanks, Mama,' he told it.

A message flashed on the Flighthawk control screen:

INDECIPHERABLE COMMAND. PLEASE REPEAT.

'Never mind,' Starship told the computer.

The warship filled his viewer, the superstructure looming in the right quadrant. The cursor flashed yellow, then red.

Starship pressed the trigger, watching as the bullets tore into the metal.

'Twenty seconds!' shouted the copilot as the enemy missile approached.

Dog counted off five more, then yanked the stick and fired off more chaff, trying to roll the Megafortress out of the way.

It worked – kind of. The missile sailed toward the spot the Megafortress had been, and then, sensing it had missed, ignited. The *Wisconsin* was far enough away to miss the main force of the explosion, though a ripple through the controls and a red warning light on the panel told Dog they hadn't escaped completely.

'Damage to the right stabilizer,' said McNamara, monitoring the system status screens at the copilot's station. 'Not critical.'

Dog had his hands full for the moment, steadying the big plane as a fresh volley of missiles were launched upward from the amphibious vessel.

'ECMs,' he told the copilot. 'Let's put a little more distance between us and them.'

'ECMs active. Harpoon one has its target – impact! We've got it.'

'Bastian, are you there?' asked Storm on the Dreamland circuit. His face appeared in the video screen; it was rounder than Dog had expected, younger as well, but the scowl seemed familiar.

'Missiles headed your way,' said Dog.

'Yes, we're taking evasive action. Where are you?'

'We've fired two Harpoon missiles at the Oman ship,' said Dog. 'He's fired surface-to-air missiles and we're taking evasive action.'

'Good,' said Storm.

He started to say something else but it was drowned

out by an explosion. The image shook; Storm fell to the side and then the screen blanked.

'We're flying east, Starship,' Dog announced over the interphone. 'Stay with me.'

'More missiles coming off the ship!' said Starship. 'A whole barrage! Looks like they're launching everything they've got! The front of the ship's on fire!'

'Exocets,' said the copilot.

'Better warn Storm,' said Dog.

Aboard the *Abner Read*,
Gulf of Aden
0121

As Storm felt himself falling backward he realized the close-in guns had somehow missed one of the Exocets. He hit the side of the holograph table before he could brace himself, and saw black as he fell to the deck of the bridge, floundering there for a moment before managing to roll over and get to his knees. He glanced across the bridge and saw that the helmsman had strapped himself into his seat and remained at his station.

'Damage control, report,' said Storm, pulling himself to his feet.

There was no answer, or at least none that he could sort out through the cacophony of voices over the open intercom. He punched the control pane on the holographic display for the ship's system report. The Phalanx close-in gun had actually struck the missile, but it had done so very close to the ship and the explosion had sprayed the *Abner Read* with shrapnel from the warhead. They had taken several hits amidships and there was a fire in the seamen's quarters belowdecks. Propulsion, Weapons, and Guidance were all operating normally.

'We're fighting a fire,' said a garbled voice, presumably one of the firefighters.

The damage wasn't that bad.

Storm pulled the headset off his ears, still partly dazed. He tapped the hologram's controls, bringing the image back to the bird's-eye view. One of the forward guns began firing outside.

There were three patrol boats, all running like hell toward the coast. The *Abner Read* was pointed in the other direction.

'Helm, come about,' said Storm. 'Pursue those ships.'

'Captain, there are missiles in the air,' said the ship's executive officer, who had come up from Tac to make sure Storm was all right.

'Pursue those pirates!'

'Aye, Captain. We're tracking incoming missiles.'

'Shoot them down, don't track them!' snapped Storm.

'Cap, the Dreamland aircraft pilot is trying to contact you,' said the communications officer. 'They want to know if we need assistance.'

Storm went over to the captain's chair, pulling up the handset. 'Bastian?'

'We're en route. They've barrage-fired several missiles at you, firing everything they have. We've hit them twice. They're on fire.'

241

'Help me pursue these patrol boats. There are three of them left. They're beyond our radar range.'

Outside, the Phalanx close-in antimissile gun began clattering, trying to ward off the missiles.

'We are en route. Be advised those patrol boats are in Somalian coastal waters.'

'You want me to call Washington and ask permission to sink them?'

'I just want to make sure you know where everything is. Bastian out.'

Gulf of Aden
8 November 1997
0121

Ali saw the shell land in the water a few hundred yards away. It streaked from over his shoulder, a ghost in the air.

'To port,' he told the helmsman. 'You're steering closer to their fire.'

The helmsman didn't answer. The boat continued to run in the general direction of the shells. Ali turned and reached to physically move his helmsman's hand. It was only then that he realized the man had been killed and was being held up only because he had strapped himself in place.

Ali took his knife and cut the belt, pushing the man aside so he could take the wheel himself. He angled toward the dark shadow of land to his right. Satan's Tail had never followed them this close to land before – but then, he'd never made such a bold attack before. They weren't going to give up now, territorial waters or no.

The missiles must have missed. Another failure.

He turned and shouted to his crewmen at the rear of the vessel. 'The mines. Unleash the mines. Then the smoke. We will hide beyond the Prophet's Rocks. Signal the others.'

Aboard the *Abner Read*,
Gulf of Aden
0123

Built by France, the Exocet gained fame as an air-launched missile, but it was originally designed as a ship-board weapon. The MM38 family – which included the versions launched at the *Abner Read* – had a range of sixty-five kilometers, or forty miles, and were designed to sink a good-sized warship. After launch, the missile entered what was called an inertial phase, flying in the general direction it had been aimed. A radar altimeter aboard the missile kept it at ten meters above the waves. The relatively low altitude made it difficult for some radars to detect and harder to intercept. As the Exocet neared its target, an active radar seeker in the head switched on, looking for the biggest bull's-eye it could find. At the same time, the missile tucked downward to about three meters above the waves, greatly increasing the difficulty of shooting it down. The MM38 had been superceded by newer designs, but the missile was still potent, especially when a number were used and programmed to attack from different directions.

As the missiles approached the *Abner Read*, the ship's Advanced Close-In Weapons System (ACIWS) prioritized each missile and directed its Phalanx guns at the threat, opening fire at a little over fifteen hundred yards. The *Abner Read*'s ACIWS succeeded the earlier Close-In Weapons System (CIWS) standard on most American vessels. Among other improvements, the ACIWS activated 'hot,' which meant that the system was ready to fire as soon as it was turned on, not needing the sixty-second activation time required by the CIWS. The ACIWS also did a better job identifying threats. Its guns, however, were exactly the same as those controlled by the older system – the venerable M61 Vulcan six-barrel Gatling design. The cannon had been used by American forces in one shape or another since 1958, when a pilot in an F-105 Thunderchief wrote his name on a test target with one. Despite a number of improvements in the associated systems and innovations like tungsten bullets, the gun itself had been virtually unchanged, a testimony to the hard work and solid engineering of its original inventors.

A stream of bullets spit into the air toward the first Exocet, hosing the missile down into the water. As a cannon rotated toward a second missile, the Exocet disappeared from the radar system, swallowed by the waves as its guidance system malfunctioned. The ACIWS interpreted this as some sort of electronic trick and rallied its weapons into the space it thought the missile was hiding in. The hiccup caused the system a second or two of hesitation before it could focus on the third and fourth missiles, which were skimming toward the destroyer's stern. One was destroyed at approximately five hundred meters from the ship; the last, however, was less than a hundred yards away when it detonated. This was of little consequence to the *Abner Read*, but it was very close to one of the Shark Boats, which had inadvertently maneuvered close to the mothership. Part of the missile smashed through the superstructure of the small vessel, destroying the embedded radio mast and a good portion of the baffling system that lowered the infrared heat signature coming from the smokestack. It also killed three of the Shark Boat's crew and sent one overboard, the ship stumbling in a spray of steam and smoke.

Storm couldn't see the strike from the bridge, but Eyes saw it on the board in the Tac Center, and immediately lost contact with the craft.

'*Three*'s been hit,' he told Storm.

Storm clicked into his preset. '*Boat Three*, this is Storm. Kelly, what's going on over there. Kelly?'

'Radio's out, Cap,' said Eyes.

'How bad are they hit?'

'System's still evaluating.'

Unsure what the damage was, Storm realized his people were his top priority. The pirates would get away once more.

He slammed the side of the holographic display in frustration.

'Bring us into position to help *Boat Three*,' he ordered. 'Eyes!'

'Yes, Captain.'

'Where are those pirates?'

'We've lost them close to shore, Cap.'

'Dreamland, I need you now,' Storm said, punching into the Dreamland line. 'Where are those patrol boats?'

'We can give you headings from the last-known GPS locations, but at the moment they're hidden in the clutter of the shoreline,' said McNamara, the copilot aboard the Megafortress.

'Give my weapons people whatever you have,' he said. 'Eyes – get with the flyboys and target these pirates. I want them sunk! Get *Boat One* into position to follow them. Have *Boat Two* stand by with us to render assistance to *Shark Boat Three*. We'll join *One* once we're sure of the situation here.'

'*Mines ahead*,' warned the computer, giving the helmsman a verbal warning as well as flashing it on his heads-up screen. Storm turned around and looked at the hologram, where the mines were popping up as small red triangles. The detection system could 'paint' the location of the mines in the HUD, but the *Abner Read* had to slow down for the system to work properly. And the Shark Boat could not proceed on its own through a minefield.

'Eyes! Some sort of minefield ahead. Warn the Shark Boat.'

'Sent a warning to them already, Cap.'

'Do you have the target data?' asked Storm.

'Working on it, sir.'

'Bastian, it's now or never,' Storm said, though he was not hooked into the Dreamland line. 'Now or never.'

Khamis Mushait Air Base
0128

Zen emptied his chain gun on the last of the patrol boats. He was now into his fuel reserves, and had to land or risk losing the Werewolf. He spun the aircraft back in the direction of the American ships, which were now nearly forty miles to the west.

'I'm out of fuel and out of lead,' he said over the Dreamland circuit, hoping the *Abner Read* had tied into the circuit by now. 'I have to land.'

'Who are you?' asked a voice.

'This is Major Stockard. I'm flying the Werewolf. It's the helo that brought the communications gear to the *Abner Read*. I've been shooting at your pirates for you but I'm running on fumes. I need to land.'

'What assistance do you need?'

Landing lights would be nice, thought Zen, but under the circumstances that was a bit much to ask.

'I don't need anything,' he said. 'I just want you to know. Don't fire on me. I don't want the hassle of trying to duck your Phalanx gun system.'

'OK, we understand. We understand. You're inbound. We see you on the radar. We're passing the word.'

The words FUEL EMERGENCY flashed on the screen.

Pass it quick, thought Zen, settling into a hover over the ship.

Aboard the *Wisconsin*
0133

Starship could see a light glowing in the distance as he approached, and realized it was the Werewolf Zen had been flying.

'*Hawk One* to Dreamland Werewolf,' he said. 'Hey, Zen, I'm approaching you from the northwest.'

'Werewolf,' acknowledged Zen. 'Starship, they have a Shark Boat that's been struck by a missile. They may have people in the water.'

'Roger that, Werewolf. I'll do a low and slow and turn with the infrared cameras.'

'Werewolf. Be advised, I'm into my fuel reserves.'

Dog broke into the circuit. 'Dreamland Werewolf, are you landing aboard the *Abner Read*?'

'That's my intention, Colonel.'

'All right. Starship, take the circuit around the stricken boat and assist with the rescue efforts. Then continue east and help us locate the pirates.'

'Roger that.'

Starship could see the robot helicopter veering to his left, skimming in an arc and landing on the nearby ship.

'Starship, do you have the location?' asked Zen.

'Roger that, Werewolf. I'm coming – Shit!'

The air in front of him erupted with 20mm shells.

Starship hit the throttle and pushed the Flighthawk's nose toward the water, but he'd been caught entirely by surprise. The left wing of the robot aircraft had been chewed severely by the Phalanx's 20mm cannon.

'Don't shoot! Don't shoot!' yelled Zen.

'Friendly fire! Friendly fire! I'm on your side! I'm on your side!' screamed Starship.

His systems screen lit, showing so many problems that the display looked like a solid splotch of red. Starship struggled to compensate for the mangled wing surface, leaning to the right with the joystick, as if his body might somehow help keep the tiny aircraft alive. He leveled off for a few seconds, but the Flighthawk's forward airspeed had dropped below one hundred knots and wouldn't come up. The computer began to push up the forward leading edge on the left wing for some bizarre reason. Starship had to override it with a direct voice command. He got an altitude warning but stayed with the aircraft, starting to build momentum. Then a second hail of bullets swarmed in front of him and the Flighthawk screen went dead.

He was so angry he smashed his fist in the middle of the control panel, breaking several of the keys.

Aboard the *Abner Read*,
Gulf of Aden
0134

'What the hell is going on!' demanded Storm. 'Where did that missile come from!'

'No missile – it was the Dreamland flight,' said Eyes.

'What? The Megafortress?'

'No, Storm, a Flighthawk. He was trying to locate our people in the water. The ACIWS read it as a missile.'

'Turn it off, damn it!'

'I did, sir, I did,' said the defensive weapons operator. 'I'm sorry. I'm sorry.'

'Rescue party, prepare to render assistance as needed,' Storm said.

'Cap, you're being hailed on the Dreamland channel by Colonel Bastian,' said the communications officer.

Storm switched over to the Dreamland circuit. 'Bastian?'

'You hit one of my planes.'

'I'm sorry. What the hell was it doing that low?'

'Taking a low level run to look for survivors from your boat damaged by the missile.'

'Do you need assistance?'

'It's an unmanned flight.'

'Right. Find those pirates.'

Aboard the *Wisconsin*
0145

Dog ran through the diagnostics again, reassessing the damage to the *Wisconsin*'s tail. According to the computer, shrapnel had ripped up the skin of about a fifth of the starboard stabilizer but its structural integrity had not been threatened. The damage did not appreciably limit the aircraft's maneuverability, though Dog knew he should be gentle until the plane was inspected on the ground.

Unlike a standard B-52, the Megafortresses had a V-shaped tail. The leading and trailing edges of the tail surface were adjusted by the flight computer automatically to improve the aircraft's flight characteristics. The adjustments were 'transparent,' or invisible to the pilot, with the computer interpreting what he wanted to do and adjusting all of the plane's control surfaces to do it. The flight control computer had no trouble compensating for the damage to the control surfaces on the tail; it also prepared an assessment of how much trouble it would have in more demanding circumstances, deciding that the Megafortress could perform at 'ninety-four percent efficiency.' Dog smiled at the assessment – computers, and the engineers who made them work, always wanted to put a number on things.

'We just can't find the patrol boats, Colonel,' said Dish. 'Faded into the coastline.'

'All right,' said Dog.

'We have to work on the systems recognizing those ships and filtering out the clutter from the coast,' added Dish. 'This system was adapted from the airborne system and optimized for large ships on the open sea. Coastlines bring all sorts of other problems. There are three or four dozen places they could be.'

'Agreed, Sergeant.'

'And no offense, sir, but, uh, if we coordinated better – working with Xray Pop instead of against them – we might have started with a better profile for the computer to use on its tracking. One of the difficulties of this all being automated.'

'Can't argue with you, Dish.'

One of these days, thought Dog, I'm going to sit down and write the collected common sense of Air Force sergeants. It'll be a best seller – though since it would come from sergeants, no officer would take it seriously.

Dog tracked out to the Indian Ocean, sweeping the gulf just in case the patrol craft had managed somehow to get this far. As he circled back he told Storm the pirates had slipped away.

'Figures,' snapped Storm.

'We should talk,' said Dog.

'I have my hands full right now, Bastian,' said the Navy captain, snapping the line dead.

Dog made a report to the lieutenant commander in the Tactical Center, who was considerably more cooperative, and even upbeat. The Oman ship they targeted had sunk soon after the battle, struck by two Harpoons from the *Wisconsin* and one from the *Abner Read.*

'We monitored a communication from a Liberian tanker a few miles away,' said Dog. 'They believed they saw some survivors.'

'Stay on top of that,' said the Tac commander, whose nickname was Eyes. 'What happened to that oiler?'

'We lost track of it. We'll look for it as soon as we swing back.'

'You probably saved their butts,' said Eyes.

'You figure the Oman government sent the ship to help the pirates?' asked Dog.

'Your guess is as good as mine out here, Colonel. It's the Wild West with speedboats.'

And Exocet missiles, thought Dog.

As they continued westward, he checked back in with the team at Khamis Mushait. Danny had gone off to bed; Sergeant Bison gave him the rundown. There were no protesters to be seen, and the Marines were now holding positions around the base. The technical teams were tearing things down and packing so they could relocate to Diego Garcia. The two Megafortresses Dog had ordered in from Dreamland were already en route there. Dog decided that he would have *Baker-Baker* take a short mission tomorrow, then head to the island directly, once they could work out the relief schedule. How long *Wisconsin* stayed in Saudi Arabia depended on the damage it had sustained; if it was minimal, he'd gas up and head out ASAP.

'Scientist wants to talk to you, Colonel,' said Bison.

'Put her on,' said Dog.

Bison moved away from the console. Jennifer's tired face came into view.

'You oughta be in bed, lady,' said Dog.

'Is that an offer?'

'I wish.'

'Me too.' She frowned. 'I have a bone to pick with you.'

'Take a number.'

'I could have flown the Werewolf.'

253

'Command decision.' Dog didn't feel like arguing with her.

'Because I'm a woman, or because I'm a civilian?'

'Because you've got a lot of other things to do, like make the LADS blimps work.'

'They're working.'

'And get ready to get over to Diego Garcia.'

'We're getting ready.'

'Zen's got more combat experience,' he told her.

'I can beat him in a Werewolf.'

'Be that as it may,' said Dog.

'Command decision?' She frowned, but then smiled. 'All right. Sorry to bust your chops.'

'At least you apologize,' Dog told her.

'I miss you.'

'Me too.'

'I'm going to bed now.'

Dog stared at the blank screen a few seconds, distracted in a way he knew he couldn't afford to be.

'We miss you back here, Colonel,' said Major Catsman at Dreamland when he checked in there. 'Mack Smith especially.'

'Mack?'

'He's telling everyone who'll listen and most of those who won't how he ought to be out there doing real work. He spends all day dreaming up schemes to get more projects under his control. Then he goes and harangues the people involved to try to get them to agree it's a good idea. Yesterday or the day before, it was naval warfare modules for the Werewolves. Today it was a ship-tracking system for the Unmanned Bomber. He may come up with a flying aircraft carrier tomorrow.'

Dog laughed.

'I'm serious, Colonel. He's driving everybody nuts. I see where he got his reputation.'

'Trust me, this is the new and improved Mack Smith,' said Dog. 'What naval warfare modules is he talking about?'

'I don't recall the specifics. He has studies and tests and things. I don't know if it's any actual programming. To be honest, I'm not paying much attention to most of what he's saying – there's too much to do here.'

'It occurs to me that Whiplash is currently interfacing with the Navy on a full-time basis,' Dog told Catsman. 'And the person designated to handle the interface is Mack Smith.'

'God bless you, Colonel.'

Dog laughed. 'Send him over to Diego Garcia. Clear it with the doctors first.'

'They'll carry him aboard the plane.'

Dog went over a few administrative things with Catsman, then signed off. With his copilot flying the plane, he got up and took a stroll around the flight deck, checking the radar operators and stretching – surely one of the pleasures of flying an aircraft whose basic design dated from another era. He went down the ladder to the Flighthawk deck, where Starship sat slumped back in his seat and Delaford reviewed the database of ship traffic.

'Wasn't your fault, Starship. Their system should have picked up on the identifier and it didn't,' Dog told the lieutenant.

'I know.'

There had been much worse accidents involving friendly fire; this involved only the loss of a robot, not a life. But Dog didn't think pointing that out would console his lieutenant. Instead he tried changing the subject.

'You ever been to Diego Garcia, Starship?' he asked.

'No, sir.'

'It's a pretty nice place.'

'We're relocating because of me?'

'No. Not because of you. Because some of the Saudis don't understand what it is we're about. Orders from the White House and our current mission commander.' Dog tried to hold his face neutral as he mentioned Storm. 'Nothing to do with you. Lighten up, Starship. Maybe you should try taking a nap.'

'I'm OK, Colonel,' said the pilot.

'Don't get morose. You did a good job with that ship back there. Watch the tape. You did a good job.'

Delaford looked over at him. 'Got a second, Colonel?'

'Plenty of them.'

'I was looking at our patrol route. I have a couple of places we can drop a buoy and recover the Piranha from automated mode ahead of schedule.'

'Sounds good. Transfer them to my station. We'll do it, assuming our tail holds up and Storm doesn't come up with something else for us to do.'

Khamis Mushait Air Base
0228

Zen pushed the door to the room open as quietly as possible, but it had a spring on the hinge and there was no way to keep it open and get inside without a sound. The light snapped on just as he stopped to let it close behind him.

'Hey,' said his wife from the bed.

'Hey back.'

The room was set up like an oversized hotel room, with the bathroom and a closet off a very narrow hall near the door to the outside. This made it hard to get into the bathroom with his wheelchair, and Zen's maneuvering was complicated by an inch-high piece of marble at the doorway. The marble looked real pretty, unless you had to roll over it.

'How'd it go?' asked Breanna, coming over in her robe.

'We ran into some trouble.' He slid the chair near the toilet seat and levered himself over. Tired, he nearly flopped into the space between his chair and the commode, but managed to lean forward just enough to plop onto the porcelain seat.

'Communications system didn't work?' asked Bree.

She stayed just outside the door, giving him privacy after a quick glance to make sure he was all right. It was one of the many dances they'd perfected since the accident.

'The communications worked. Dog spotted some fast patrol boats trying to sneak up on them from the east.

257

While Xray Pop was dealing with that, an Oman ship launched missiles.'

'Oman?'

'Yeah. Supposed to be friendly to the West. Haven't figured that one out yet. One of the Shark Boats got hit by a missile that the *Abner Read* was shooting down. They crossed too close because of the attack or something. Anyway, ship's still afloat but it's pretty badly beat up. They lost three guys. Then, just for good measure, *Abner Read* shot down Starship's Flighthawk.'

'You're kidding.'

'I wish. Their automated ship protection system thought it was a cruise missile. Starship thought he could get close to the ship because Werewolf was. Their system's more sophisticated than that, though. Lucky for him.'

'What happened to the pirates?'

'Dog got the missile ship. We got some hits in – Navy battered one of the little boats pretty well, and I know I hit two – but as far as I could tell, they all got away. They were moving pretty fast. You can't get much on the Werewolf radar beyond five or six miles, and the hook-in from the Megafortress isn't operational.'

Breanna put her hands on Zen's shoulders as he came out of the bathroom, kneading his muscles.

'Keep going,' he urged when she stopped. 'My neck is all whacked out. I had to stoop over the display.'

'Hop into bed and I'll give you a full body massage.'

It was more a dive than a hop. Zen pulled himself over the mattress, sinking in. His wife's hands felt fantastic.

'Admiral Storm still a jerk?' asked Breanna.

'Captain Storm. No worse than your dad.'

'My father isn't a jerk.'

'Demanding.'

'Oh, he is not. He has standards.'

'He can be a prick.'

Breanna smacked him, semiplayfully.

'I meant that in a good way,' said Zen. 'It's OK to be tough.'

'I doubt that Storm is anything like my father.'

'Probably not,' said Zen.

Breanna went back to giving him a massage. 'Maybe I should take this bathrobe off and you could give *me* a massage,' she suggested.

'Good idea,' said Zen. He felt his eyes closing.

'Jeff?'

'Good idea,' he mumbled, sliding into a dream.

Aboard the *Wisconsin*
0250

Starship looked at the main screen as the computer replayed his flyover of the Oman missile boat, watching it as if it were a training video, not his own engagement. He saw someone standing on the upper deck of the missile boat, aiming at the ship with a gun. The gun sparkled as the Flighthawk passed.

He hit pause and backed up to the beginning of the run, going through it in slow motion this time as he tried to gauge the impact of his 20mm cannon shells. The bullets were relatively small, designed primarily for use against other aircraft; in retrospect, he thought he should have been more selective in targeting the ship, looking for a vulnerable spot. He slowed the action down, watching the line of slugs slanting into the hull as the attack continued. The holes were nothing more than specks on the screen.

The man stood there again. What he'd thought was a gun turned out just to be a shadow.

Starship saw the flash again, and this time realized that the man on the deck hadn't been firing at him at all; he'd simply been running. The flash came from one of the Flighthawk's bullets as it struck the rail or perhaps the bulkhead behind him.

The man lay on the deck in the next pass. If his Flighthawk had done any other damage, it wasn't visible.

So I killed him, thought Starship. He leaned back in the seat.

Good. Revenge for Kick.

He leaned forward, hit the button to play the rest of the encounter. Midway through he backed up and again ran through the attack where he had shot the man.

'Good,' he whispered, but he didn't feel good at all.

Dog let McNamara handle the buoy launch, double-checking the plotted course and feeding him vital signs, but otherwise staying in the background as the copilot flew the plane. They slapped out the buoy and buttoned up, continuing their patrol. The Tac officer on the *Abner Read* gave them an update a short while later. A fleet ocean tug – basically an oceangoing tugboat large enough to pull an aircraft carrier by herself – had been dispatched from Bahrain to take the damaged Shark Boat under tow. The Navy was still undecided about where the Shark Boat would be taken for repairs.

'I'd like to have a word with Captain Gale,' said Dog when the update was done.

'All right,' said the Tac officer, with a tone that implied he was asking for trouble.

'What is it, Bastian?'

'We should rendezvous to discuss the situation tomorrow,' suggested Dog.

'Rendezvous?'

'I think we can do things better.'

'You'll have to come to me. I have no way of getting to you,' said Storm.

'Not a problem,' said Dog. 'I should be able to get there late in the afternoon, depending on what's going on in Saudi Arabia.'

'Good.'

'Good,' said Dog. He clicked off the circuit. Clearly the best time to talk to Storm was when he was too tired to argue.

On the other hand, the same was probably true of himself. He glanced at his watch. They had more than six hours scheduled on patrol. And by the time he got to the *Abner Read,* he'd be even more exhausted.

'Colonel,' said Delaford. 'I have contact with the Piranha. It's about a hundred miles south of us, just passing out of range of the buoy we dropped. It's headed west.'

'West? Didn't you point it east?'

'I put it in autonomous mode, which means it can change its mind if something comes up,' said Delaford. 'Looks like it found the sub.'

VI

Paradise

Gulf of Aden
8 November 1997
0301

Two of the patrol boats were damaged beyond repair. Ali took a last look around their decks, making sure his men had salvaged everything possible. He hated to lose the heavy guns, but they didn't have the wrenches needed to take the bolts from the decks. One of the men had tried to cut away the deck with a chain saw – a creative idea, thought Ali, until the chain snapped and the man got a slashing wound on his arm for it. They settled for the ammunition.

Ten men had died, and some of their blood stained Ali's hand and shirt. He saw it when he waded back to his own craft, noticing the stain on his hand.

He wished it were his enemy's blood.

He had lost the Oman ship, and with her, his cousin Mabrukah and several other men he knew very well. Satan's Tail had escaped. Ali knew because his spies had heard its radio transmissions, or at least some. One of the boats that accompanied it had been damaged, apparently by one of the missiles. A fisherman and his brother were making their way toward the area now in a small boat; he would know by morning how much damage they had done.

It wouldn't be enough. Nothing would be enough until he sank the large ship.

To do that, he had to return west. The *Sharia* and the others would have to be rallied. He would regroup, attack again.

The wind howled around his ears.

It sounded like Abu Qaed's voice, calling him.

'Quickly now,' he told his crew. 'Signal the others. We have a great distance to go.'

Aboard the *Abner Read*
0310

Following directions from the Dreamland technical team, Storm's communications specialists had managed to plug the portable communications system into the *Abner Read*'s own system, even allowing visuals. So when Colonel Bastian signaled that he had to speak to the captain immediately, the specialists called up to the bridge and told Storm he could see the man who'd become such a thorn in his side.

Storm told them to make the connection and stepped to the video screen.

An image snapped in. He saw the side of a helmet, and waited as the head turned toward the camera. The visor was up and the oxygen mask hung down, revealing a face softer than Storm had expected. The eyes were pensive, searching, and expressive.

The voice was as belligerent as ever.

'We found the submarine,' Bastian told Storm.

'What?'

'The Libyan submarine. About forty miles southwest of your present location, just barely in Somalian territorial waters. It's going west. Commander Delaford is on the circuit with the technical details. Tommy?'

'Hi, Storm. The submarine is definitely a Foxtrot, Project 641, Russian sub. May have been upgraded – the engines are quieter than the specs say they should be. It's definitely not a Kilo.'

'How do you know?' said Storm.

'Because we worked with a Kilo to develop Piranha,' snapped Bastian. 'And we sank one in the South China Sea.'

'Two,' said Delaford. 'This is the first time we've come across a Foxtrot. He's snorkeling right now, making about eight knots, a little slower. That's close to his best speed using the snorkel. He can go twice that fast on the surface, though he wouldn't be able to sustain it very long. If he goes deeper and just runs on his battery, he's not going to go much over two knots unless he really has to. If his batteries were in good shape he could probably do fifteen knots on them, but that would run them down pretty quickly.'

'Can you sink him?'

'We're not authorized to,' said Bastian. The eyes flashed. Then he added, 'I have one Harpoon left aboard. I can sink him on the surface, and maybe when he's snorkeling. As long as I have authorization.'

'I'll get permission,' said Storm. He'd been ready to bury the hatchet with the Air Force lieutenant colonel –

267

after all, his men had performed well – but the tone in his voice stoked Storm's resentment all over again.

'Permission or not, I think rather than sinking him, we should follow him, at least for a while,' said Dog. 'My guess is that he's going toward an important pirate base. If we follow him, he'll lead us right there.'

Storm realized that made sense, especially since the only weapon Bastian had was designed to strike a surface ship, not a submerged submarine.

On the other hand, the way Bastian suggested it – with a sneer in his voice for anyone who wasn't thinking as quickly as he was – nearly forced him to dismiss the idea out of hand.

Bastian is a real jerk, Storm thought, *but not a stupid jerk. He happens to be right.*

'Captain?' said Bastian.

A real jerk, though.

'All right, that's not a bad idea. Hold on.'

He went over to the holographic display. The damaged Shark Boat could not make it to the rendezvous without the *Abner Read*; the ship would be lost.

Which would have a greater impact on his career? Sinking the Libyan ship? Or losing a damaged ship to do so?

Probably the latter. In an ideal world – in an ideal *navy* – the objective would be the most important. But even the U.S. Navy was far from ideal.

At present. It would be better in the future.

'Storm?'

'Unlike you, Bastian, I try not to shoot from the hip. If we could slow him down, it would be an easier decision.'

268

'I have a way we might do that,' said Delaford. 'There's a patrol boat near him, a few miles away. It's possible he's trailing him, communicating somehow. If the Megafortress buzzed the surface boat, they might warn the submarine. If the sub dove deeper, he'd have to slow down, or least run on batteries for a while.'

'I think it's worth a try,' said Bastian.

'Yes. It is a good idea,' said Storm, glad that it had come from a Navy officer and not the insufferable flyboy.

Storm could order a Shark Boat to help trail the submarine at a distance; if it made an attack, the boat would be in a position to combat it. By the afternoon, the *Abner Read* and *Boat One* would meet the tug. He could have *Boat Two* escort the tug and head back.

A haul – he had three hundred miles to the tug rendezvous, another four hundred back, at least, even if they slowed it down. More than twelve hours, getting back and forth. But the Shark Boat could stay nearby, ready to strike if it looked like the sub was going to get away. It had lightweight torpedoes designed for undersea warfare. They'd be much more effective than lobbing a Harpoon and praying that the sub stayed near the surface.

'All right, Bastian, let's do it your way this time. I'll send a Shark Boat to shadow them, and have them stay just over the horizon.'

'I'm going to bring another Megafortress in to relieve me in a few hours. Not only do we have only one Harpoon aboard, we have no Flighthawks.'

A criticism of his ship?

Even Storm had to admit it would have been justified.

'Do it. Keep me posted,' said Storm. 'I'll expect a full report when you come to the ship tomorrow.'

'Out.'

The screen went dead.

Aboard the *Wisconsin*
0312

'Well, he was almost human that time,' Dog told Delaford.

'I think you're just being too hard on him, Colonel. He's lost a bunch of men, and one of his ships is pretty battered.'

'We'll see. I'll run ahead and make a buoy drop, then come back and harass the gunboat.'

'Ready whenever you are.'

The control setup for the Piranha allowed Starship to see the synthesized sensor view on his number two auxiliary screen. The submarine appeared as a reddish flicker at about nine o'clock on the rectangular screen; a row of yellow, orange, and blue flames made waves behind it, descending toward the bottom of the screen. Piranha swam about three hundred yards behind the Libyan submarine, a little less than a quarter mile. The sub didn't know it was there.

'We're going to say hello to the surface craft,' said Dog. 'We don't think the patrol boat has any antiair missiles, but there's only one way to find out. Hang on.'

Starship slapped against his seat restraints as the

270

EB-52 powered toward the waves. The aircraft tilted left, then right, taking a wide turn before climbing back out.

'Didn't shoot at us,' reported Dog.

'Sub is still moving forward,' said Delaford.

'Patrol craft has stopped,' said Dish, watching on the radar above. 'Maybe that's the signal.'

The submarine continued toward the patrol boat for another half mile or so, then began to submerge.

'We got their attention,' Delaford told Dog. 'He's going down.'

'How did he know?' asked Starship.

'Either they were listening as the engines cut out or they're using a light or something to communicate. At snorkel depth the submarine can use its periscope to watch the surface.'

'Are they blind when they go down?'

'No. They can use either passive or even active sonar to follow the patrol boat. He's probably going to dive for a bit, hang out there. When nothing happens, he'll come back up and proceed again. My guess is, the submarine captain is pretty cautious.'

'Why?'

'He could have made better time on the surface earlier. Rather than using his snorkel, he could have surfaced. It was night, and more than likely he wouldn't have been seen.'

'We would have seen him on radar.'

'True enough.'

'You try and psych him out so you know how he'll be when you fight him,' said Starship.

'You don't do that with the Flighthawks in air combat?'

'The situations are usually so fluid, you don't have time. It sounds good, but in real life it's just bang-bang-bang. For me, anyway.'

'Zen says he does it.'

'Zen's different. That's why he's Zen.'

Delaford laughed. Starship shrugged. It was true; Zen wasn't like most other pilots – he was Zen.

'He's stopped,' said Delaford, looking back at his screen. 'Hundred and fifty-five feet. I give him only a few minutes.'

Sure enough, the submarine began moving again ten minutes later, gliding upward. Within a half hour it had begun snorkeling again. They let it proceed for twenty minutes, then Dog brought the Megafortress in for another run – this one at five hundred feet and directly over the submarine's wake. The patrol boat veered hard toward the coastline.

'He's going down. Fast,' said Delaford. 'He's nervous.'

'Good for him,' said Dog.

'Fifty feet . . . seventy-five,' said Delaford. Excitement snuck into his voice. 'He's got his nose down. Angle is fifteen degrees. He's moving – he's in trouble here. Twenty degrees. Still growing. He may hit the bottom!'

The water the submarine was moving through was about 1,200 feet deep. But once the submarine built up downward momentum, it could be hard to stop. The pitch was important as well as its speed: The boat was designed to descend horizontally; if the nose of the sub pitched greater than thirty degrees, the vessel became virtually uncontrollable.

Starship watched the screen, which had become a frenzied mass of purple and red funneling lines – the computer's representation of the sound the submarine was making. The lines fluttered, breaking in the middle.

'Four hundred feet . . . four fifty,' said Delaford.

Starship watched the colors dancing on the screen. Was it this easy to kill your enemy? There were about seventy-five men aboard the average sub of this class – could you kill them by scaring them to death? Was war *really* that easy?

'Four seventy-five. He's slowing. Angle is less than fifteen. He's under control.' Delaford sounded disappointed. 'I may have misinterpreted his movement a bit.'

Starship wasn't entirely sure why, but he felt relieved.

White House
7 November 1910

'This is beyond piracy,' the President told the others gathered in his study next to the Oval Office. 'What does Oman say?'

'They claim the ship was stolen,' said Secretary of State Jeffrey Hartman.

'They're probably telling the truth,' said Robert Plank, the CIA director.

Jed's boss, Philip Freeman, looked at Jed, who nodded.

'I agree,' said Freeman. 'It may have been attempting to hijack a civilian ship, an old tanker type, when we came across it.'

273

'You're sure it's been sunk?' the President said, directing the question to Jed, who'd gotten data on the battle from Dreamland and supplied it to the others.

'Yes, sir. Another ship picked up some of its crew. They're holding them for Oman. They, uh, had to be subdued. So I think the story the Oman government is telling is probably true.'

'What happened to the tanker?'

'The owners haven't reported any trouble but we're still trying to get a definitive word.'

The President turned to Admiral Balboa. 'What was the latest on the submarine?'

Balboa looked at Jed. 'Mr Barclay seems to have the best information here.'

Jed felt his face flush. It was hard to tell whether Balboa was trying to put him on the spot or actually trying to be nice.

'Just that it's still under surveillance,' Jed said. 'It's definitely the Libyan boat. Some improvements. Last time I checked, just before coming here, it had moved closer to the coast, but was within a few miles of where it was originally spotted. It can't go very fast on battery power, and the thinking was that it might wait a few hours and then try to move again.'

'Xray Pop can sink it within an hour of getting the order,' said Balboa. 'Let's go in there and sink the submarine before this gets worse.'

'Wait until we get the vote in the UN,' said Secretary Hartman. 'We'll have it easily now. The session is Tuesday. It's only a few days.'

'What if they vote it down?' asked Chastain.

'They won't.'

'I think this new attack, with the Oman ship and the submarine, will cinch things,' said Freeman.

'Then let's push for an earlier vote,' said the President. 'That will emphasize how serious we think things are. We make the Oman ship the center of the presentation. The pirates are so bold they're stealing warships. No one's safe. It's a pretty strong argument. We can leave the submarine unmentioned for now. Frankly, if we can't convince them using the Oman ship, then we can't convince them at all.'

'The French will pull their usual bullshit,' said Chastain. 'They'll want pictures.'

'So we'll give them pictures,' said the President. 'Jed, can we use the photos you showed us?'

'Um, the security implications –'

'Everybody knows we were there,' said Hartman, suddenly warming to the idea. 'We could use some of the distance shots, just leave out details about the aircraft that took them. Call it a UAV.'

'I think that would work,' said Freeman.

Jed nodded. The President looked over at Balboa. The admiral nodded.

'Let's get moving. I'd like another update by midnight,' said the President. He turned to CIA Director Plank. 'Robert, Jed will run his material by you as well as Colonel Bastian's people to make sure nothing sensitive is released. All right, Jed? Nothing too sensitive, just what we need to show them we have the goods. I hope you didn't have any plans for the weekend,' he added.

'Um, just like, uh, water the plants.'

Everyone in the room laughed, though Jed hadn't meant it as a joke.

Khamis Mushait Air Base
0528

Breanna rolled over onto her side, pushing toward the weight of her husband.

Except he wasn't there.

'Jeff?' she murmured.

No answer.

She pushed deeper into the blankets, still swimming in the haze of fatigue.

'Where are you?' she said. When he still didn't answer, she put her hand out, then woke. 'Hey?'

His wheelchair was gone. She glanced at the clock – it wasn't quite five-thirty A.M.

'All right,' she said, more to herself than her absent husband. 'Where are you?'

Breanna pushed her legs out of bed and pulled on her clothes. Out in the hallway, the scent of fresh brewed coffee drew her toward the reception area, where Boston presided over a huge tray of doughnuts.

Dunkin' Donuts.

'Sergeant! Are these real, live Dunkin' Donuts?' exclaimed Breanna, the last vestiges of sleep whisked away by the scents. 'In Saudi Arabia?'

Boston beamed.

'You are going to be a chief master sergeant someday,' said Breanna, taking a strawberry jelly doughnut. 'Oh, Sergeant, you may be President of the United States if you keep this up.'

'Chiefs have more power,' growled Danny Freah, appearing from around the corner. 'Boston, where did you get these doughnuts?'

The Whiplash sergeant's smile widened, but he said nothing.

'You see Zen anywhere?' she asked Danny as she tried the coffee.

'Prepping for his next mission.'

'He is? Already?'

'Colonel Bastian wanted to move around the mission schedules because we're heading over to Diego Garcia. The maintainers have the plane fueled and ready to go. Loaded up with missiles and a Flighthawk.'

'He can't fly without a pilot,' said Breanna.

'I think Spiderman was going to command the mission and Dayton was going to take the copilot's slot.'

'That's my plane. And my mission.'

'Zen said something about you needing all the beauty rest you can get.'

'Oh, he did, did he?' said Breanna. 'Where are they?'

Zen had just finished reading the weather report – clear and dry, light wind – when the door of the trailer flew open. Breanna stormed in, a befuddled Marine behind her.

'Gentlemen,' she said, with a tone that was outlawed as a lethal weapon in twenty-eight states.

'Hey, Captain,' said Spiderman.

'Don't "Hey, Captain," me. What's the story here?'

'Um, we're getting ready for the mission?' said the pilot, backing away slightly.

Breanna leaned over the table and looked at Zen. 'Beauty rest? *Beauty* rest?'

Zen started laughing. The others backed away from the table.

'Um, sirs?' said the Marine.

'It's OK. She belongs to us,' said Zen.

'I will see all of you on the plane,' said Breanna, straightening. 'Dayton, you can come and spell Spiderman – the *copilot* – if you want. I expect you all on board and ready to go in ten minutes.'

She spun and left the trailer.

'Looks like this mission's briefed,' said Zen.

Approaching the *Abner Read*
1110

Dog had done many difficult things in his life, but on the trip out to meet with Storm, he accomplished the near impossible: He fell asleep on an Osprey.

The jolt as the tilt-rotor MV-22 veered into a landing pattern over the DD(L) shook him awake. Dog caught a glimpse of the ship as they descended. It didn't look like a ship, at least not one that sailed on the ocean. The angled gun enclosure and superstructure reminded Dog of something from the Star Wars series of movies. Low to the water and painted matte black, the ship looked a great deal more like a pirate vessel than the ones they'd fought the night before.

A whistle greeted Dog as he stepped down the ladder from the Osprey. A petty officer took a step forward and snapped a precise salute. Two sailors with M4s, shortened versions of M16s, stood a short distance away.

'Colonel Bastian, welcome aboard, sir.'

'Thank you,' said Bastian.

'Do you have a bag or aides, sir?'

'No, I'm it.'

'Captain Gale is this way, sir.'

Dog followed the petty officer through a door at the side of a large hangar opening. They walked through the empty hangar space to a set of metal steps. They walked down the steps – a 'ladder' in Navy terms – and across an enclosed gangway to another passage or hallway that opened onto a metal walkway across a large mechanical area. A huge network of pipes ran from below, connecting a series of what looked like large tanks to a thick, round aluminum tube. This was the heart of the ship's exhaust system, designed to lower the temperature of the exhaust as it left the gas turbines at the right. The low-heat signature of the exhaust made it more difficult for infrared detectors and missiles to 'see' it. The room itself, though, seemed no warmer or cooler than the hangar had been, at least to Dog.

'This way, Colonel,' said the petty officer, stepping through another hatchway. This led to a section of the ship filled by offices; with some slight adjustments for the location and decor, they might have been in an industrial park. 'Captain's quarters ahead, sir.'

A short, heavyset man stepped from the hatchway just as they approached.

'Bastian?'

'That's me.'

'I'm just going down to the Tactical Center. It's this ship's version of a CIC, or Combat Information Center,' said Storm. 'Come.'

Dog started to put out his hand, but Storm turned in the other direction. Dog followed down a ladder to a large room filled with computer work stations set into metal desks and cabinets. Most but not all of the stations were manned; a large, weary-eyed Navy lieutenant commander stood in the open area at one side, talking into a headset. This was 'Eyes,' Dog guessed; the man gave him a weary smile and went back to what he was doing.

A large glass table stood at the right side, slicing off part of the room from the rest. At first glance it looked like an area display, or re-creation one would find in a museum. It took Dog a few seconds of staring at it to realize it was a holographic computer display showing the *Abner Read*'s position and that of the other ships in the area.

'This is Peanut,' said Storm, introducing another officer. 'He's the executive officer of the ship. We lost our captain in battle. A very good man. That's Eyes. You've spoken to him. He's tactical officer and my second-in-command. He runs the show down here.'

Both men gave him grim smiles as they exchanged greetings.

'The *Abner Read* is designed to act as a coordinator as well as a combatant in littoral zones,' said Storm. 'Since combined action is still a new concept, we're working some of this out as we go.'

'I can relate to that,' said Dog. 'We do that ourselves.'

The other officers nodded, but Storm frowned. No one in the world could be as unique as he was.

'The Tactical Center is the brain of the task force, the next generation combat information center,' said Storm. 'All the systems are monitored here. That's Radar, Active Sonar, our Array, which you can think of as a very sophisticated listening device. In the future we'll integrate information from UAVs and underwater robot systems. We process the information and then deliver it to the other ships in the task group. It's not unlike what would happen in a task force built around an aircraft carrier and advanced cruisers and the rest. The holographic display shows the changing tactical situation around us. It can be used for everything from plotting an ocean crossing with computerized charts to working out the best method of attack. Our weapons center is on the other side here. Eventually we'll control robots as well as the ships' own weapons. Eyes, Peanut, we'll be in my quarters.'

Storm abruptly turned on his heel and went back the way he came. At the top of the ladder he turned left, walking onto the bridge.

Dog was surprised to find that there were only three men here. One sat in front of the wheel; a second had a large computer display. An ensign stood behind the captain's chair at the center of the bridge, as stiff as if this were a port inspection by the fleet admiral.

'This is the bridge,' said Storm.

Dog nodded at the men, trying to will them into something approaching ease. He feared they had been told he was the enemy.

Another holographic display stood at the right against the bulkhead; slightly smaller, this one currently showed a model of the ship and gave readings on the various engineering systems it used. Storm demonstrated that it had several different modes, including the ones he had seen in Tac.

'How much longer?' Storm asked the ensign.

'Another two and a half hours, sir.'

Storm nodded, but didn't explain to Dog what they were talking about.

'Are you in contact with my Megafortress?' Dog asked.

'Of course. The submarine is that way.' Storm gestured dismissively toward the ship's bow. 'We'll rendezvous with my Shark Boat and wait to see what happens. We have it under control, Bastian. Don't worry.'

Dog interpreted the conversation and Storm's comments to mean that the Shark Boat trailing the submarine was still about two and a half hours away. The submarine had remained submerged since their last pass; he didn't expect it to move now until nightfall.

'This way,' said Storm, walking to the other side. Dog followed through a hatchway to a cabin dominated by a large conference table. On the opposite side a hatch opened into the captain's personal quarters. With his bunk on one side and his desk on the other, it would have fit in a good-sized closet at Dreamland.

'We've had teething pains. Our biggest problem right now is radar coverage,' said Storm. He slid into a chair. 'It's nonexistent. You can sit.'

'Thanks,' said Dog.

Storm clearly didn't realize he'd meant it sarcastically. The only other seat in the cabin was piled high with charts and papers.

'We're designed to rely on radar inputs from other assets,' explained Storm. 'This way no one can use our radar to locate us. But like much of our gear, the data link isn't ready for deployment. Nor is the robot helo that's supposed to carry the radar. It's probably two years from being ready to fly. As a stopgap, a version of the SPY-3 multifunction radar is supposed to be adapted for our use. That's a joke – the customized version isn't even off the drawing board because of funding issues.'

Dog wasn't familiar with the SPY-3 system, though he guessed it was a follow-up to the present generation of sensors used by the fleet. The *Abner Read*'s unique design would surely complicate the radar's development, as would the need to integrate it with other systems.

All right, thought Dog; maybe some of Storm's attitude came from the fact that he'd been given a job without the tools to do it. Didn't make him any less of a jerk, though it at least might explain some of his behavior.

'In the meantime, our only radar is a poorly modified version of the SPS-63. It's an Italian design barely useful for navigating. According to the specifications, it's supposed to cover out to about forty nautical miles. It doesn't, not on our ship anyway. Has something to do with the antenna configuration and height. And contrary to advertising, the pirates have been able not only to spot it, but to use it to aim at us.'

'We may be able to figure out a way to pipe you our radar coverage,' said Dog. 'My technical people may have to modify some of the systems, but our airborne sensors were originally designed to interface with the combat information centers aboard aircraft carriers, so it ought to work. After some trial and error.'

'Hmmph.'

'Look, Storm: You and I don't have to get along at all. But we can work together to accomplish this mission. You have gaps –'

'What gaps?'

'Let me finish: You have gaps in your capabilities because the technology is still new or hasn't gotten out of the development stage. I'm used to dealing with that. That's what Dreamland's all about. We have some things that can help you. The Werewolves for starters. The communications system. We also have high-tech blimps that can carry radar –'

'Blimps?'

'They're lighter-than-air ships that can be positioned over the gulf and monitor traffic. You could use them for radar coverage and not give your position away.'

'Pirates will just shoot them down.'

'They use a technology that makes them blend into the surrounding sky. They're difficult to see. If the pirates

284

don't know they're there and aren't using radar, they probably would never see them. We used them in Brunei.'

'Yes.'

Dog recognized that particular 'yes.' It meant: I heard that you kicked butt there, but I'll be damned if I'm going to say anything that you might interpret as a compliment.

'If we're going to work together,' Dog said, 'then let me suggest –'

'You're going to work for me,' said Storm.

'If we're going to work together, there are some problems we have to fix,' said Dog. 'First of all is communications. I can get more portable communications units so you can tie your Shark Boats into the network. Everyone can get the same information immediately, no bottlenecks. I'd like to bring some of my technical people in to figure out if we can give you the radar information and anything else. Maybe we can download target coordinates, or supply targeting data to the Harpoons once they're launched. The Werewolves – running them from a base a few hundred miles away is doable, but it's not the best solution. I can airlift a mobile control unit in and put a pilot on board so you can fly them from here. And we have to do better about friendly fire.'

Storm scowled, but then nodded. 'Agreed.'

'The fact is, my Flighthawk pilot didn't understand about your defense system,' added Dog tactfully. 'He got the idea that because the Werewolf was close, he could get close. He thought it was an on-off thing. That's not going to happen again, but obviously we have to share procedures as well as information. Up and down the line.'

'I agree with you, Bastian. We don't have to be friends.'
Gee, thanks, you SOB, thought Dog.

Storm watched the Osprey circle away, taking Bastian back to his temporary base in Saudi Arabia. Bastian hadn't been the most polite officer – and looked a bit unkempt; he could have used a shave.

But he had at least said the right things. Whether he could deliver or not remained to be seen.

'How are we, Peanut?' Storm asked the exec, who was now on the bridge.

'Nothing yet, Cap. The Shark Boat is roughly forty miles dead ahead. We're sure the sub is still there?'

'Delaford knows what he's talking about. I trust him,' said Storm.

Tying the Dreamland people into his ships made a great deal of sense. The Werewolf gunships could help extend the task force's power well over the horizon. He wasn't necessarily convinced about the blimps – that seemed to him just a play to unhook the Megafortresses from the mission – but they might work down the road. Throw Piranha into the mix – the automated submarine probe was supposed to join the fleet within a year anyway – and the DD(L) warship and the Combined Action Group, or CAG, concept would begin to reach their potential.

From the way Bastian was talking, Dreamland had plenty of other projects – and maybe development money – that might help them. The trick would be prying them out of the flyboy's sticky fingers.

It was unfortunate Bastian was such a jerk to deal with.

Storm trusted Delaford to give him a straight story, at least, but clearly a Navy man wouldn't have much say under Bastian's command. If Bastian had trusted him at all, he would have brought him out to the ship with him.

He would have to find someone else at Dreamland to cultivate, someone overly ambitious who might be manipulated, or if not manipulated, at least influenced to cooperate for a higher cause: like his promotion.

Khamis Mushait Air Base
1238

Dog shouted a thank you to the Osprey crew as he hopped down and headed toward the Dreamland Command trailer. He was extremely hungry – Storm hadn't offered him lunch on the *Abner Read*, and he was damned if he was going to ask – but any thought of heading over to the cafeteria vanished when Danny Freah met him in front of the trailer.

'Our friends are back at the gate,' said Danny.

'I saw a dozen or so from the Osprey,' said Dog. 'A lot less than yesterday.'

'There are more on the way. In buses. Be here within an hour, according to the Saudis.'

'How many people?'

'There are twelve buses that the police saw coming from Mecca alone. Another ten or twelve from Jiddah, the city on the Red Sea. We seem to be a popular attraction. The, uh, base commander wants to talk to you about this.'

'I can imagine.'

Hands on hips, Dog surveyed the hangar area. The *Wisconsin* sat on the left, her Flighthawk mounted beneath her wing. The damage to the tail had been repaired; for once the computer had overestimated the extent of the injuries, and the maintainers confirmed there were no serious structural problems. The MC-17/W, her rear ramp open, sat to the right. Several large items had to be loaded into her: the LADS blimp, the Werewolves, the Dreamland Command trailer, and last but not least, the Osprey. It was a tight fit and would require at least two hours – much of it to get the Osprey in shape to be carried. Diego Garcia was too far for the tilt-rotor aircraft to travel without re-fueling, even if she were carrying just her crew.

'If we didn't pack the Osprey, how long would it take to get out of here?' Dog asked.

'Hour,' said Danny. 'Give or take.'

'Let me get with Washington and see if I can land the Osprey somewhere midway and have her refueled.'

'Aren't you supposed to check with Storm?' said Danny.

'I'm going to pretend I didn't hear that.'

Washington, D.C.
0450

The knock on the door of the condo came ten minutes before Jed was expecting it – and more important, before the coffee started pouring through the filter of Mr Coffee.

'Jed Barclay? Are you ready?' said a gruff voice outside the door.

'Um, almost,' said Jed.

'Lot of traffic on the road, sir. If we're going to make the airport we want to get moving.'

'Yeah, all right. Like, I'm coming.' Jed shut off the coffeepot. He swung his hand through the loop of his carry-on, grabbed his knapsack laptop bag, and opened the door. The driver was a Marine corporal assigned to the NSC; he wore a civilian suit and looked better dressed than Jed, whose tie didn't quite go with his wrinkled gray jacket.

'Mr Barclay?' said the corporal, glancing down at Jed's scuffed brown shoes.

'Yeah. Aren't you kind of early?'

'No, sir.' The corporal studied his face for a moment. 'Maybe we could grab some Joe on the way?'

'Definitely a good idea,' said Jed. 'There's an all-night 7-Eleven on the corner.'

As they got into the car, one of Jed's phones began ringing. He had three with him – a secure NSC satellite phone, an encrypted cell phone, and a personal cell phone.

It took a few moments for his caffeine-deprived brain to figure out that the call was on the encrypted line.

'Jed,' he said, popping it open somewhat hesitantly. 'Hello?'

'Jed, this is Colonel Bastian. Sorry to wake you.'

'Um, well, you're not waking me, Colonel. As it happens.'

'I need a favor. A pretty big one.'

'Um, uh – personal favor?'

'It is a personal favor to me, but it's not of a personal nature. I need a place for one of my Ospreys to land where it can be refueled.'

'Uh –'

'I know I'm not going through channels, but there isn't enough time,' said Dog.

'Yeah, OK,' Jed replied. 'What exactly do you need?'

'Basically, I need someplace between Saudi Arabia and Diego Garcia to refuel the Osprey. India would be best.'

'How soon?' Jed asked.

'Ten minutes ago would be great,' said Dog.

'Ten minutes ago I can't do. But I can work something out, I think. Can I call you back?'

'I'd kind of like to get this solved right now,' said Dog. 'What I'd like you to do is talk to my people back home and set it up with them. But I want to know whether it's doable or not.'

'Um, hang on,' said Jed as they pulled up in front of the convenience store.

'How do you want your coffee?' asked the driver.

'Plenty of milk and two sugars. Better make it the biggest they got – three sugars.'

The driver got out.

'I think it's probably doable,' Jed told Dog. 'I have to talk to State anyway.'

'Probably's not good enough for me, Jed. I need to count on you.'

'You can count on me, Colonel, soon as I get my coffee.'

It was not the worst flight Mack Smith had ever been on – but it had certainly been close. He spent the entire fifteen hours, twelve minutes, and thirteen seconds strapped into the stiff Flighthawk control seat on the lower deck of Megafortress *Charlie One*. He'd been so bored that he even took a few tries at the training simulations for Piranha that Lieutenant Cly Dai was flying at his station next to him. But you could only play computer games for so long.

It wasn't bad enough that he was a passenger on an airplane, instead of a pilot; he was an immobile one, strapped to his stinking ejection seat and unable to move without considerable help. The newly minted EB-52 had a temporary bunk area on the upper deck, along with a galley, restroom, and a VCR. But he'd have had to crawl up the steps to get to it, and the humiliation simply wasn't worth it. Getting down out of the aircraft was its own adventure. All of the EB-52s were equipped with an attachment on the ladder that allowed a wheelchair to be mechanically lowered by a pair of small electric motors. Though it doubled as a way to ease the loading and unloading of heavy computer gear, it had been designed specifically for Zen, and it certainly beat being carried down to the tarmac. But it involved a great deal of faith; the angle was precarious, and Mack was sure he would topple out of his seat the whole way down.

'I've got your bags, Major,' said Lieutenant Dai cheerfully as Mack wheeled away from the belly of the plane.

He paused to let Dai load the bags onto his lap. The extra weight and awkwardness made it difficult to work the wheels, and when Dai started pushing him, Mack didn't object.

Sergeant Lee Liu, a member of the Whiplash action team, stood in front of a battered pickup truck nearby, waiting for them.

'Major, welcome to Paradise,' said the sergeant. 'Hop aboard.'

'I'm not hopping anywhere,' said Mack. 'And I'm not getting in the back of that truck. I'll ride up front.'

'Just a figure of speech, Major,' said the sergeant.

Liu helped him into the cab and they drove to a small building overlooking the ocean. Two airmen met them there, members of a security team flown in to provide security until the rest of the Whiplash team arrived. In truth, Diego Garcia was probably as secure as any American base in the world, and the local Navy contingent could have done an adequate job guarding two or three full squadrons. Located on a small island atoll in the ocean below India, the only people here were either military or contract workers for the military. Completely isolated, the base was self-contained, an entire world unto itself. Depending on your perspective, it could be either Paradise, or hell – or maybe a little of both.

Mack tried to lower himself from the truck to the waiting wheelchair, but couldn't manage the maneuver; he finally gave in and asked for help. The airmen craned him upward and deposited him gently in the chair.

'Thanks, guys,' he said. 'I hope not to be in this sucker too long. Get my legs back any day now.'

'Yes, sir,' said one of the airmen.

The cement-block building wasn't much to look at, but Mack realized that it had two major assets: There was no step or curb to the front door, and the rooms were all on one level.

'This isn't the most comfortable facility,' said Liu, coming in behind him. 'But it's isolated from the rest of the base. There is a three-story structure on the other side of the tank farm. It's a little newer, but wouldn't be as easy to secure.'

'I think this one's fine,' said Mack, ignoring the musty odor as they continued down the hallway. There were small, simple offices and a large common room. As Mack surveyed the rooms, Liu told him that the Dreamland Command Trailer was due to arrive in a few hours; they would set it up outside. A secure communications system for the offices would be wired in, along with other gear as needed. Dog wasn't due to come in until nighttime at the earliest; he was meeting with Captain Gale aboard the *Abner Read*, the flagship of Xray Pop.

'We're three hours ahead of the base in Saudi Arabia and the Gulf of Aden, where the aircraft are patrolling,' added Liu, 'so if it's 1530 or three-thirty in the afternoon here, it's twelve-thirty there; 1600 is 1300, and like that. And just to really confuse you, when it's 1500 here and 1200 in the Gulf of Aden, it's 0100 in Dreamland. Got it?'

'Basically, it's party time somewhere in the world,' said Mack. 'As long as you can stay awake to enjoy it.'

They had just announced that the plane for New York was boarding when Jed's encrypted cell phone rang back with the message that a refueling stop had been cleared for the Osprey at Dabolin in the province of Goa, India. He pulled out the sat phone and hot-keyed the number for the Dreamland Command Center.

'Yes?' answered an unfamiliar voice.

'Um, who is this?' said Jed. He'd been expecting Major Catsman, whom he'd spoken to a few minutes before.

'Who is *this?*'

Jed, thinking that he had somehow gotten a wrong number and dialed a residence, hit the end transmission button.

It should have been *impossible* to get a residence, he thought. Jed looked at the buttons, and hit the combination again.

'Yes?' sneered the same voice.

'This is Jed Barclay.'

'Yes, of course it is.'

'This is Dr Ray, right?' said Jed, finally attaching the sneer to a face.

There was a pause, then Ray Rubeo cleared his throat very loudly. 'This is Dr Raymond Rubeo. What do you want, Mr Barclay?'

'I was just kind of thrown off there. Usually an operator answers or maybe an officer.'

'We are shorthanded and I am pitching in at the

Command Center,' said Rubeo, who sounded about as happy to be doing that as Jed was to be going to New York at five-thirty in the morning.

'Listen, pass the word that I got the approval. There's an Indian Navy aviation base at Dabolin in India. It's in Goa. So you can tell them they can take off.'

'They took off fifteen minutes ago.'

'They did?'

'Colonel Bastian apparently believes you when you say you'll take care of something,' said Rubeo. He cut the line on his end.

Aboard the *Abner Read*
1400

'Right there, Cap. It's three miles off the coast.'

Eyes pointed to the holographic display in the Tactical Warfare Center. Storm saw from the scale that they were fifteen miles from the submarine – a half hour's sail at most. The Libyan submarine sat almost at a complete standstill. The patrol boat that had been escorting the sub lay another mile or so farther east in very shallow water close to the shore.

Four torpedoes, fired from the vertical launch tubes, and the submarine and patrol boat would be history. No one would ever know.

That wasn't quite true. Bastian would know. The pirates would know. And eventually Johnson would find out and use it to scuttle his career.

He thought of his pledge to the sailor after his death that they would have justice.

Have it absolutely.

He stared at the image in the hologram, which had been synthesized by the computer from the sounds the array picked up – and the assumptions about those sounds that had been programmed into the system. The symbol of the sub flickered to the right, nudging northward.

Was he moving out from the protected waters?

God, let him come out to me. Let him come after someone. Just get close to international waters.

He could always say they had opened their torpedo tubes, clearly indicating that they were going to fire. That would justify attacking.

No one would buy that, not completely. But it would give the people who liked him enough cover to protect him.

Balboa would probably believe it. But Balboa was known to have little if any leverage with the President. And Johnson would work relentlessly against him.

Storm looked back at the display. The submarine wasn't moving northward at all. His eyes had seen what he wanted them to see – what his need for revenge dictated.

'We have a communication from the fleet about the approaching British carrier and her escorts, the *Ark Royal*,' said Eyes. 'They ran into some sort of delay at the Suez Canal. One of their ships is coming ahead and will be out into the gulf by early tomorrow morning.'

'Very good,' said Storm.

The *Ark Royal* was en route to Asia to help Americans

in the Philippines. It was more a gesture of allied solidarity – a useless one, in Storm's opinion, though he was thankful that he hadn't been told to work with the Brits.

He stared at the hologram. No, the submarine wasn't moving at all. It would, though. It had to.

'Watch the submarine carefully,' he said. 'If it starts moving toward the shipping lanes – if it starts moving at all – let me know.'

Aboard *Baker-Baker Two*,
approaching Diego Garcia
2232

'Almost there, Captain,' Spiderman told Breanna.

Relieved by *Charlie One* in the Gulf of Aden shortly before 1400, they had flown for just about six hours to get to the airstrip at Diego Garcia. Except for a few short breaks, Breanna had flown the whole mission herself. She'd die rather than admitting it, but she was starting to feel the strain of not having had a full night's sleep.

'I hear Diego Garcia is a pretty cool place,' continued the copilot. 'Lots of partying. "Gilligan's Island with guns" some of the guys call it.'

'Don't believe everything you hear,' said Breanna.

'It's not fun?'

'It's all right. To visit. You've never been there?'

'No, ma'am.'

'Interesting place,' said Breanna. 'Lots of sun and sand.'

'As long as there's a cot down there with my name on it, I'll be happy,' said Spiderman.

'Amen to that.'

Zen rolled onto the concrete in front of the hangar area, squinting from the glare of the nearby floodlights. There was a two and a half hour time difference between the Gulf of Aden and Diego Garcia, and it was now getting on towards eleven P.M. local time. But there were dozens of things to do before he could get to bed. He rolled over to the team that had swarmed around the Flighthawk to check on the aircraft's status, and was surprised when Chief Master Sergeant Clyde 'Greasy Hands' Parsons stepped away from the gaggle of maintainers and techies.

'Chief, what are you doing here?' said Zen.

'I wanted to personally kick the butt of the jerk who shot down my aircraft,' said Parsons. 'Then I'm going to work on my tan.'

'Go easy on Starship, Chief.'

'I'm not talking about the lieutenant. He didn't shoot it down. It's the Navy I'm mad at.' Parsons looked out toward the runway, where a C-5A was just landing, undoubtedly with more of their gear. 'Besides, he's only a lieutenant. Once you make chief, you let your under-lings chew out louies. They're too easy.'

Zen grinned.

'Although I may give you a good kick just to stay in practice, Major. You've been running this aircraft awful hard,' Greasy Hands added. 'Due for an overhaul. Oughta be grounded until we get a new engine in.'

'Can't afford the downtime,' said Zen.

'Take ten minutes, if I'm watchin' them.' Parsons smiled, a sure sign that he was going to make a joke. 'What do you think about a Chevy small block V-8? Bore that sucker out and watch her rip.'

'You going to tell me about your Chevelle SS again?'

'That was a hell of a car, Zen. I'll tell you, a hell of a car. They do not make cars like that anymore.'

'Thank God.'

'Well, that aircraft really ought to set a spell until we get it overhauled. I'm not talking about a rinse and wax either.'

'Colonel's not going to like that,' said Zen. 'And the Navy captain we're answering to isn't going to like it either.'

'Back in the day, the Air Force didn't take orders from the Navy,' said Greasy Hands. 'The Navy gave us grief, we flew low and slow over one of their aircraft carriers. Admiral got the message real quick.'

'They had aircraft carriers when you were young, Chief?'

'They were just coming in when I made sergeant.'

'Storm's not an admiral. And he's just as stubborn as the colonel.'

'That I'd like to see.'

'Hey, Jeff, how's it going?'

Zen turned around and saw Mack Smith wheeling toward him.

'What do you think of Paradise?' Mack asked.

'I think it's damn hot for November,' said Zen.

'I have some idea on integrating the Flighthawks with CAG Xray Pop. We could make coordinated attacks with the microbombs, get them right onto the pilot bridge of the patrol boats. At the same time, the Shark Boats and *Abner Read* could launch torpedoes at them. So while they're blinded, they're also sitting ducks.'

'Why don't we just nuke them and be done with it?' said Zen.

'I'm serious. You know, the chief was telling me that the replacement Flighthawk engine delivers more thrust, and I was playing with the numbers – I think we can get a lightweight torpedo on, as long as we were launching for a really short flight.'

'I'm going to go get something to eat,' said Zen. 'See you later, Chief.'

'Don't you think that's a good idea?' said Mack.

'I think it's so good you ought to join the Navy, gimp boy,' said Zen.

'Hey, give me a break, huh?'

'Which leg?'

'Ha, ha.'

'Where do we eat in Paradise, anyway?' said Zen. He saw one of the Whiplash troopers standing near a truck a short distance away and began rolling toward him. Breanna and the rest of the plane crew were walking in that direction as well.

'You don't think those are good ideas?' asked Mack. He was trying to follow but couldn't keep up with Zen.

'I told you, they're great, gimp boy. Now leave me alone.'

'Hey, lay off the gimp stuff, huh?'

Zen looked back. 'Maybe you ought to get a motorized chair. If you're planning on staying in that much longer.'

'Screw yourself, Zen.'

'You're as witty as ever, Mack.'

'And you're nastier than ever,' said Breanna, catching up.

Zen pushed his wheels toward the truck. All he wanted to do right now was get some food and go to sleep. For about three weeks.

UN Building,
New York City
1300

Jed looked at the graphics files again, making sure they were ordered properly. The Secretary of State wanted to go through the presentation at least once before meeting with the British and French ambassadors privately at two P.M. and the Saudi ambassador at four; the National Security Council's special session was due to start at six P.M. There'd be no chance to go through the presentation with him if he didn't get back soon.

Jed had arranged a dozen pictures and graphics in a PowerPoint program for the Security Council; they began with a map of the Gulf of Aden showing where the pirates had struck, documenting clearly that they were using coastal waters to hide. The last photo was a video capture from a Flighthawk; it showed the Oman gunship firing one of its missiles. The picture was shot from a distance and was grainy though provocative. Just as important, it didn't give anything about the Flighthawk away. Neither the robot plane nor the Megafortress would be mentioned in the presentation. From a security point of view, the only possibly dicey photo was a month-old satellite picture of a patrol boat tied up amid some civilian boats at a dock on the Somalian coast. The image had been taken by a KH-12 Improved Crystal satellite; Jed had reproduced it at a low resolution, but the image was still detailed enough to allow the identification of a goat in one of the yards. Three different people had already signed off on it, but Jed was still debating whether to blur it further.

'Here we are, Jed,' said Secretary of State Hartman, entering the room he'd been given to work in. 'You know Ambassador Ford.'

'Yes, sir.'

Stephen Ford was the U.S. ambassador to the UN. Jed had met him perhaps twice, but protocol insisted that they both act like longtime friends, or at least acquaintances, and they did so.

'Let's run through the slides, shall we? Then Stephen and I have to meet with the mayor of New York, Rudy Giuliani. Pretty colorful character.'

'Insufferable Yankee fan,' said Ford, who was from Boston. 'Thank God they lost this year.'

'Well, um, we begin with the area map and fade into a slide showing the pirates' strikes over time,' said Jed. He maneuvered the laptop so the others could see, hitting the buttons at regular intervals.

'I have more statistics – tonnage lost, number of ships. The numbers are conservative,' said Jed as he continued showing them the slides. 'I kicked out anything that might have been questionable.'

'Why?' asked Ford.

The question took Jed by surprise. 'I just thought, uh, that, you know, the Secretary wouldn't want to be questioned on something.'

'He'll always be questioned,' said Ford. 'You have to make the best case, Jed. Always lead with your best argument.'

Jed nodded – though there was no chance in hell he was going back for other numbers or changing the presentation if he didn't have to. These were pretty damning in themselves, with an average of nearly a ship a week stopped or attacked.

'This is a missile boat?' asked Ford, looking at the last image.

'Actually, a patrol boat that was being outfitted to be a missile ship. Or upgraded – refitted, I guess would be the right word.'

'Dreamland's involved in this?' Ford looked at the Secretary of State. 'That might be worth mentioning, because it would persuade China.'

'China has already agreed to remain neutral,' said Hartman.

'A yes vote is better.'

'There are, um, security issues,' said Jed.

'Well, there can't be too many issues,' said Ford cheerfully. 'There's a book coming out about the China incident called *Strike Zone*. I may write the preface.'

'Um, Dreamland still officially doesn't exist,' said Jed. 'It's not going to be in the book, is it?'

'Doesn't exist?' Ford laughed.

'I think we can get by without mentioning them,' said

the Secretary of State. 'And that book should be vetted before you do a preface.'

'Maybe I won't,' said Ford. 'But I can probably get an advanced copy, right?' He turned to Jed. 'Do you have any better pictures?'

'I dulled that satellite picture down because I was worried that it gave too much detail about –'

'No, I mean, more graphic. The presentation has to grab you,' said Ford. 'Real pictures. People dying. We need a storyline.'

Jed glanced at the Secretary of State. 'I don't have any pictures of people dying.'

'We have to sell this,' said Ford. 'That's what your slide show has to do.'

'This is all I have.'

'Put together a strong set, Jed. Work with what you have,' said the Secretary. 'I'll leave it to you.'

'Tell a good story,' said Ford, slapping Jed on the back as they left.

Diego Garcia
9 November
0030

The uncomfortable military-style 'cot' in *Wisconsin*'s upper Flighthawk deck left Dog's neck twisted all out of whack when he awoke shortly after landing. He tried stretching it but it remained knotted until Jennifer found him in the office Mack had set aside for him in their new headquarters building. She began kneading his muscles, and he leaned back, feeling some of the knots untangle.

'Ahh,' he said as the tension began to slip away.

'I can come back,' said Mack Smith at the door.

'That's OK, Major. Come on in. I twisted my neck,' said Dog.

'Sure,' said Mack, rolling forward. 'So, I have a list of ideas for you, Colonel. Thought you'd like to hear them.'

'Thanks, Mack, but hold that thought for about thirty-six hours. Your first order of business is to get with Xray Pop and communicate our new patrol schedule. Also find an update on getting the Werewolves out to them. We have two problems – our pilot is sick with the flu, and they don't have enough range on their own. Second one's easier to deal with. There's a base in India we can use to stage them out of – we can take them there via the M/C-17 and run the Osprey over to refuel them en route, since it's already set up to be used as a tanker. Chief Parsons can get the Werewolves adapted – they need their nozzle sets reworked. He said it wouldn't take too long to work out.'

'I can fly them,' said Jennifer.

'Thanks for volunteering, but you're going to be plenty busy over there as it is. I'm going to get Fred Rosenzwieg in from Dreamland.'

'That'll take a day at least,' said Jennifer.

'Quicker than waiting for Culver to get better.'

The Werewolves' lead pilot, Sandy Culver, had been evacked to Germany from Saudi Arabia because he'd lost so much fluids from the flu. It seemed to have been food poisoning – hopefully from something he'd eaten at home, not at Dreamland.

'Maybe I can fly them,' said Mack. 'They don't look that hard to learn.'

Dog reached back to stop Jennifer, who'd continued her massage as they were talking. 'This isn't a great time, Mack. I'm kind of tired. You must be too.'

'Nope. Want to hear some of my ideas?'

'Tomorrow's much better. How are your legs?'

'Getting there. I'll be walking any day.'

'Great. See you tomorrow.'

'One thing we ought to do is come up with real names for the aircraft, the Megafortresses especially,' said Mack.

'Tell you what – why don't you handle that?'

'Fine. I'll get right on it.'

'In the morning, Mack. People are tired.'

'Yes, sir.'

Dog watched him wheel out.

'I'll fly the Werewolves until the replacement pilot arrives,' said Jennifer. 'I have to be on the ship anyway. And I'd be testing the system.'

'You'll be too busy.'

'They're not likely to use them in the next twenty-four hours, are they?'

Dog shrugged. It was the obvious solution, yet still he resisted it. Not because she was a civilian, he thought, and still less because she was a woman.

Then why?

Because he didn't want her to get hurt.

'All right, if you can stand Storm, you can handle the

Werewolves until Rosenzwieg gets here,' he told her. 'Knowing Storm, he'll probably insist that you show him how to fly them so he can do it himself. Any chance of taking Mack with you?'

Jennifer rolled her eyes.

Dog took out the sheet he had used to write his air tasking order, which laid out the upcoming missions. Their four Megafortresses would be used on a straight rotation, one after the other, with only one over Xray Pop at a time. Because of the distances involved, each flight would spend roughly six hours going out to the gulf, six hours on patrol, and six hours returning. The arrangement called for three aircraft to be in the air at any given moment – one on patrol, one coming home, and one going to relieve the other. That gave the maintainers twelve hours to turn each one around; it sounded like a decent interval, but in practice it could end up very tight. Fortunately, they had more leeway with the Flighthawks, since they had six and were only planning on flying one per mission. But there were only four Flighthawk pilots, and only two – Zen and Starship – had combat experience. Dog had tried to arrange the missions so Zen and Starship would be flying on the night patrols, which was when the pirates were most active. Complicating this immensely was the fact that there were only three Piranha operators, counting Delaford and English. If anyone got hurt or sick, they were in trouble. Zen and Starship were the only backups at the moment.

He needed more planes, more crews, more support, but he'd settle for a closer base of operations. Northern or central Africa would be perfect; northern India would do in a pinch.

'Penny for your thoughts,' said Jennifer.

'They're worth a quarter at least,' said Dog. 'But they're not about you.'

'They *ought* to be.'

'What time is it in New York?' Dog asked, looking at his watch, which was still set to gulf time: 2216.

'About two-fifteen in the afternoon,' said Jennifer.

'Let me see if I can get a hold of Jed. Have you had a chance to look at those Navy systems?'

Jennifer leaned toward him and frowned. 'Didn't you just tell Mack it was getting late?'

'That was to get rid of Mack,' Dog said. 'I have a lot of work to do.'

Jennifer started to pout. Dog leaned up and gave her a kiss. 'I do have to work.'

'I know.'

'I love you.'

'Yeah.'

'Hey.' He pressed her arm gently. 'I do.'

'I know.' She smiled. 'Don't stay up all night.'

UN Building,
New York City
7 November 1997
1430

Jed stared at the picture of the Oman missile boat, replaying the conversation he'd had with Ford and the Secretary of State.

Tell a good story.

Put together a strong set of images.

Was he being told to lie? Or just do a good job?

He didn't have any pictures of people dying, as Ford had suggested. He did have a picture of the ship as it fired the missile – that looked pretty graphic. But beyond that?

A picture of the nearby oiler or tanker blowing up would be something.

Except that it hadn't blown up.

Jed brought up one of the photo editing programs on the computer and merged the shot with a blowup of the missile launch. At first it didn't look like much, but as he cropped it and played with the settings in the photo manipulation program, he got it to look pretty gruesome. He dappled and faded, played around some more – the ship appeared to be on fire in a shadowy image.

Was that what Ford wanted?

You couldn't fault the ambassador for wanting to make a strong message, thought Jed, and here it was, all in an easily disseminated jpg file: We have to stop these pirates. They're blowing up the world's oil supply.

And they were too. The message wasn't a lie. They were blowing up whatever they could, killing as many people as they could in the process.

Unfortunately, Jed Barclay didn't happen to have a picture of it.

Except for a phony one. Kind of artistic, though. And definitely dramatic.

His sat phone began to ring. He picked it up and turned it on.

309

'Mr Barclay, stand by for Colonel Bastian.'

Before he could say anything, Colonel Bastian's voice boomed onto the line.

'Thanks for helping us out on that situation today. What are the odds on us using that facility again?'

'Yeah, OK,' said Jed. 'The Navy, um, mentioned that you're supposed to work through them.'

'Did I get you in trouble?'

'Not yet.'

'We could use a base a lot closer to the gulf. Somewhere in Africa.'

'I've tried, Colonel. No go.'

'What about India?'

'Boss is opposed to that for a bunch of reasons,' Jed told Dog.

There was a knock on the door.

'Your lunch is here, sir,' said a voice in the hall.

'OK, cool,' said Jed. 'Just leave it. Uh, Colonel, I gotta run.'

'All right. If you can arrange for us to use that base again as a backup, though, I'd appreciate it.'

'I'll work on it.'

He ended the call, then pulled over the laptop. He slid his finger on the touchpad and moved the pointer to the X at the top of the corner of the program window.

DO YOU WANT TO SAVE? asked the computer.

He hesitated, then pressed YES.

Mack was too keyed-up and too time-lagged to sleep. He read some of the CD-ROM manuals on the Piranha and basic naval warfare tactics. By four A.M. he'd read his fill and was still restless. He pulled on a sweater and roamed out of the building. His wheels splashed through a deep puddle near the road.

'Hold on there,' said an authoritative voice behind him.

Mack turned around and recognized Boston, one of the Whiplash team members.

'Sergeant Rockland. Good morning.'

'Morning, Major. Out for a stroll?'

'A roll more like it.'

'Yeah.' Ben Rockland – Boston to those who knew him – pulled a cigarette out of his jacket pocket. He had an M4 rifle with him, a shortened version of the M16 preferred by airborne and some special operations troops. 'Want a butt?'

'No. I didn't know you smoked.'

'Out in the wilderness, there's nothing else to do.' Boston lit up and took a drag. 'How you doing with that thing?'

'Chair? Pain in the ass. Literally.'

'Yeah.' Boston took a pensive smoke. 'My brother is a paraplegic.'

'No shit. Sorry.'

'Yeah. Sucks big-time.'

'It does.'

311

'You're gonna be OK, though, right?'

He was. That's what everybody said. But he sure as hell didn't feel like he was going to be OK.

'Bet your ass,' said Mack. That was what people wanted to hear.

'Good.' Boston took a long puff on his cigarette. 'Well, don't get run over by a bike. That's the main means of travel around here.'

'I don't think there are too many people going to knock me over at this hour.'

'Probably not.'

'What happened to him?' asked Mack.

'My brother? Car accident.'

'No hope?'

'Nah. People, you know, they tell him to cheer up and shit, but, I mean some days he gives it a good show. He really does. But he ain't the same person. He played basketball in high school. Not like he was a star or nothing, but I mean, to go from that to this. Sucks.'

'Yeah.'

'You're going to get better, though.'

Am I, thought Mack. *When?*

'Hey, you need like a ride somewhere? We have two vehicles. We brought in a pair of gators, you know, the little ATV things.'

'I don't really know where I'd go this time of night.'

'Gym's open. Fitness center. It's over by the billeting office. Open 24/7. Come on. I'll just tell Nurse I'm taking you over.'

'Thanks, Sergeant. I appreciate that.'

'You can call me Boston. Everybody does.'

'Thanks, Boston.'

UN Building,
New York City
7 November 1997
1830

The corridor seemed to close in around Jed as he walked with the Secretary of State and the rest of the American entourage toward the chamber where the Security Council meeting was to be held. They were running late; the meeting should have started a half hour ago. But the delay was well worth it. The Secretary had spent the time convincing Russia to vote in favor of the proposal. Britain was strongly in favor. China had already agreed to abstain. That left only France among the permanent members that could veto the measure. The French had been presented a draft of the proposal, but the Secretary had not been able to schedule a meeting with them. According to Ford, that wasn't a bad sign. He predicted that Egypt, one of the rotating Security Council members and a key regional ally, would agree because of pressure from Oman as well as the U.S.

They reached the doorway. There were people ahead, murmuring. The Secretary paused, then swept right. Jed followed, and was suddenly inside the National Security Council hall. Along with the ambassador and Secretary of State, he moved to the U.S. spot at the table. Jed sat in one of the modernistic blue seats directly behind Ambassador Ford.

He'd seen the room on a tour as a kid and vaguely remembered it now – more for Rosie Crowe's hair than the awe he should have felt. He hadn't felt any awe at all then.

Now he did.

Security Council President Fernando Berrocal Soto of Costa Rica gaveled the session to order. The murmurs crescendoed and then there was silence.

Secretary of State Hartman leaned forward and began his speech.

'The international community cannot withstand the continued depredations of lawlessness in the Gulf of Aden, which escalate every day,' he read. The words had looked good on paper – they had sounded great when the Secretary tried them out on Jed and some of the staff – but they came off flat here, a little off-key and hurried.

Jed thought of what a nightmare it would be if he had to speak – how terrible his stutter would be.

The ambassador cited some statistics and then spoke of the 'horrible outrage' involved in the stealing of the Oman missile ship.

Jed saw the Kenyan representative frowning.

How could he frown? It was an outrage.

'Would someone dim the lights?' said the Secretary of State, moving to the final stage of the presentation, showing the evidence Jed had compiled.

There was a scramble at the side of the room as the lights were dimmed. They had given a CD-ROM with the presentation to one of the aides, who'd set up a projector and a screen. As the slide show began, Jed heard the ambassador reading the script he'd written, and cringed. He should have done a much better job, he thought, been more eloquent.

He glanced around and saw more frowns; mostly frowns. Ford was right: He should have gotten more narrative in. He *should* have used that slide of the ship exploding. No one would have frowned at that.

The lights came back on. The floor moved to the representative from Oman, who deplored the 'action of brazen, misguided thieves and radicals.' He called on the international community for action. Ford turned around and gave Jed a thumbs-up.

Then one by one the other permanent and rotating members of the Security Council took the floor. The Kenyan representative charged that the Americans had 'wantonly attacked a peaceful air patrol from the law-abiding country of Ethiopia' and 'murdered countless airmen aboard the planes.'

Secretary of State Hartman quickly countered that the aircraft had failed to answer hails and acted in support of the pirates. Even the Ethiopian government had denounced their interference with an American flight, he pointed out, claiming that the unit involved had mutinied.

Of course, Jed and the Secretary of State knew that the Ethiopian government actually authorized the mission, but the U.S. had indicated through back channels that it would go along with the lie, so long as no more Ethiopian forces materialized in the area.

Hartman made some points, but Jed saw that Ford had been far too optimistic. Kenya and France were clearly opposed to the measure. Egypt was on the fence. The objections being raised seemed ludicrous to Jed; the rule of law had to be preserved, international sovereignty had to be preserved, America was injecting itself where it didn't belong.

How about the fact that a hundred people had died since the attacks began? And a few hundred thousand dollars extorted? Money that was being used to kill innocent people, not only in Africa, but in faraway places like Brunei.

Do nothing? And let the attacks continue? Let more innocent people die?

Peace was attractive – but it wasn't the alternative here.

When the French ambassador said he had questions about the attack on the American ship, Ambassador Ford raised his hand and then whispered something to the Secretary of State.

'We can answer those questions,' said Ford when the president of the Security Council acknowledged him. 'We invite an open and frank discussion, Mr President. We will answer any questions about that incident.'

'Where was this attack exactly?' said the French ambassador.

The Secretary of State turned to Jed.

'Like, uh, about twenty miles west of Laasgoray and just outside territorial waters,' whispered Jed.

'Tell them.'

'Me?'

'Go ahead.'

Jed's throat constricted and he felt his fingers turn ice cold. He leaned forward to the microphone; Ford moved aside.

'The attack took place at approximately forty-seven degrees longitude and just short of thirteen miles from the coast in the Gulf of Aden. I have the GPS point.'

'Very smooth,' replied the Frenchman, smirking. He asked another question, this one about the U.S. forces, which Secretary Hartman took himself.

Ford tugged on Jed's sleeve and Jed moved back.

'Douceur,' the Frenchman had said. The translator had rendered it as 'smooth,' but Jed, who'd taken four years of French in high school and another two in college, realized that wasn't a precise translation.

Douceur. What did that mean? Sweetness.

A sweet-tongued lie, seemed to be the sense of the remark.

He listened as the session continued. The Russian representative took the floor and began peppering the Secretary of State with questions about pirate attacks that had been made over the previous months.

This is all BS, thought Jed. The Russian knows the answers to those questions because the Secretary of State gave him a background paper with all the information when they met.

The Secretary did not seem to mind, answering the questions patiently. The tone changed with the next speaker, the representative from the United Kingdom, who gave an impromptu speech on international law on piracy and the precedents for following the pirates into territorial waters when sovereignty was being abused by non-nationals.

As the tone of the remarks from the other countries gradually became more diplomatic – and harder to decipher – Jed's attention wandered. He saw Ford get up and go over to the French delegate; he came back smiling. A few minutes later a motion was made for a brief recess for dinner.

'Good work, Jed,' said Ford. 'Come on now, we're on to part two.'

'Part two?' Jed turned to the Secretary of State.

'Press conference,' said the Secretary. 'Replay for the Sunday papers and talk shows. Important part of the campaign.'

'Oh,' he mumbled.

'We'll get you some dinner when we're done. Don't worry,' said Ford.

Reporters had packed into the auditorium; TV lights were popping in the back as correspondents did brief pieces that could be used to introduce the small snippet or two they would take from the session. A large desk-like wooden table sat on the stage at the front. Jed hung back, but Ford prodded him to come sit at the table, where three chairs were set up.

'Time to face the music,' the ambassador joked in a stage whisper.

Jed forced a smile. His fingers were freezing again.

The Secretary repeated the highlights of his speech –

much more forcefully this time, Jed thought – then opened the floor to questions. The reporters were more skeptical than the French ambassador had been, one or two even suggesting that the pirates were 'liberators' rather than thieves.

Maniacs maybe, thought Jed.

'Jed, maybe you can talk about that Oman ship,' said the Secretary when the reporters pressed for details.

'Uh, sure. It was basically a patrol boat that was being refitted; you know, like updated. That included putting in missiles. That's where the Exocets came in. They're ship-to-ship missiles. These were early model missiles, which limited their effectiveness and –'

'I don't think we need the technical detail,' said Ford, good-naturedly. 'Don't want to get into classified areas.'

The specs were readily available in open source materials – not to mention company brochures – but Jed was only too glad to have a reason to stop talking.

'There's a rumor that Dreamland was involved,' said one of the reporters, an older man with an Indian accent.

Jed opened his mouth to speak but nothing came out.

'Cat got your tongue?' said the man.

'N-No,' he said. Feeling his tongue start to stutter, he stopped speaking. A weight pressed on his chest. He wanted to slide through the floor.

'We'd have no comment on that,' said the Secretary of State.

'What sort of Navy force was there?' asked a young Asian woman. 'The American force? What is it?'

Ford and Hartman looked at him to answer.

'It's a small-ship surface warfare force,' said Jed, forcing the words from his mouth.

'Which means what?' asked the reporter.

'Littoral warships.'

He turned and looked to the Secretary of State, hoping to be rescued, but the Secretary simply smiled at him.

'A littoral warship is what?' asked the woman.

The *Abner Read* had been acknowledged by the Navy several months before, and described as a 'frigate-sized vessel optimized for the littoral warfare role.' Jed wasn't worried about security – he just didn't want to stutter.

'That would be like – like a destroyer,' he managed. 'It's closer in size to a frigate. You could think of it as a small destroyer for, uh, coastal waters.'

'Like a Coast Guard cutter?'

Jed frowned. 'Well, not exactly.'

'Is it from Dreamland?' asked another woman.

'It's a Navy asset. I – I don't really know that much about it, to be honest.'

The questions turned back to the resolution, and Jed faded into the background again.

'We have to get back,' said Ambassador Ford finally. He rose, signaling the end of the press conference.

'Will there be copies of your presentation?' asked one of the press people, this one an American.

'Yes, of course,' said Secretary Hartman. 'The ambassador's staff will take care of that.'

Jed followed them out into the hallway.

'Good job, Jed,' said the Secretary. 'You ducked the Dreamland question masterfully. A very plausible denial that no doubt will help feed the rumors. Good work.'

'Um, did we want to feed the rumors?'

'The Dreamland people are incredibly popular behind the scenes for risking their lives to stop the war in China,' said Ford. 'Do we have those slides?'

'I didn't make copies or anything. I can copy the file onto a disk.'

'Let's do that – copy them off, I'll have Paul in my office make some copies for them. Here – we'll go upstairs, you download it or whatever you have to do, and then you go to dinner. I'll bet you're hungry.'

'Yes, sir. Is it OK to release it to the press?' Jed asked Secretary Hartman.

'Just copy the presentation and give it to Jake,' said Hartman. 'I'll go through it and release it myself.'

'You did good, kid,' said Ford, slapping him on the back. 'You're a real pro.'

Gulf of Aden
9 November 1997
0601

There was no surer sign that Allah was with them than this: They had managed to get across the Gulf of Aden and westward to Shaqrā on the northern, Yemen side of the gulf without being stopped by the Americans.

To cross more than two hundred miles of open water without being detected by Satan's Tail required more than skill or luck. Ducking between the traffic on the water, hiding near the coast, racing past places the Americans liked to check: all of this required a certain amount of experience and ability. But surely God's hand had led them across the water to safety. Surely God himself, the one true and only God, intended him for greater things.

And so, Ali told himself, he must avoid the easy temptation. A small British warship was moving through the gulf not twenty miles away, according to his spies. An air defense destroyer, it had been sent ahead of the screening force assigned to the British aircraft carrier *Ark Royal*. From the description, Ali had identified it as a Type 42 destroyer. He knew the type very well. It was designed primarily for antiaircraft defense, and its crew trained constantly to fight off aerial attacks. They were not nearly as good at dealing with thrusts from the surface, as the Italians he served with showed. Even a ship as large as a corvette could get close enough to launch torpedoes without being detected: 6.5 kilometers, or roughly four miles. Ali's boats had the same 12.5-inch torpedoes used in the Italian navy. He would not miss if he attacked.

But if he attacked, he would miss the aircraft carrier, traveling a day and a half behind.

To send the destroyer on ahead seemed to Ali typical of western egos. They were focused on the obvious danger – the Red Sea and the narrow passage at Bāb al Mandab. The destroyer was both an advance scout and a distant warning system – if aircraft came north from Ethiopia, it would see them long before the carrier.

Of course, sending the ship alone was also a matter of sheer hubris. The British were so full of themselves, so proud of their *Ark Royal*, that they couldn't conceive of a danger to the smaller ship. Who would want to strike a puny destroyer when the pride of their fleet was nearby?

He exaggerated. The British probably did not believe anyone would attack the carrier either. It was more likely that the destroyer captain was an arrogant know-it-all who had decided to race his superiors to the gulf. They were all egotists, untempered, unhumbled by the knowledge of God's superiority.

Allah would provide a plan to humble them. Hints of it were poking at the corners of his brain, but it had not revealed itself to him yet.

'We will rest here,' Ali told the crew. 'We will take shifts. As soon as dusk comes, we will cross back and rendezvous with our brothers. Then we will embark on our most glorious campaign.'

The men nodded solemnly.

'I am going below,' he added. 'Wake me if there is anything important.'

Diego Garcia
0900

The Navy ran Diego Garcia. While to the Air Force it was an emergency way-station for bombers operating in Asia and occasionally the Middle East, to the Navy it was an important telecommunications and support site for units operating in the southern Pacific. The Navy also hosted Defense Information System 'assets' there, top secret systems – mostly sophisticated antennas – that obtained data from a number of sources, including satellites and listening posts.

Though small, the base's amenities included a four-lane bowling alley, a ragged and coral-strewn golf course, and what was supposedly one of the best chief petty officers' clubs in the world. The Dreamland team was given access to the facilities, including the swimming pool, which opened at 0830 on Sundays. Zen managed to wangle his way in a few minutes early. The cement stairs were so steep, he got out of his chair and climbed up the grass hill while Breanna took the wheelchair up. It wasn't pretty, but it got the job done.

He swam his morning laps while Breanna sipped a coffee at poolside. They were just getting ready to leave when Mack arrived, pulled up the long flight of steps by a member of the security team who'd been traveling with him.

'You got a pool boy now?' laughed Zen as Mack was wheeled toward the water.

'Lay off,' said Mack.

'Why?'

'Come on, Zen. Time to go,' said Breanna.

Zen pulled himself from the pool, dragging himself across the cement to the wheelchair. 'Let's see you do some laps, gimp boy.'

'Zen, go easy,' said Breanna.

'I'm just encouraging him.'

'No, you're not.'

'He's a wimp gimp.'

'Screw yourself, Stockard. Asshole,' muttered Mack.

'What?' Zen pulled himself up into the chair. Mack looked like he was going to start bawling any minute. 'What'd you say, Smith?'

'Screw yourself.'

'You're lucky I don't come over there and give you a real workout.'

'That's enough, Stockard,' said Breanna, grabbing the back of his wheelchair.

'Why shouldn't I harass him? Why shouldn't I kill him?' said Zen as they wheeled back toward their quarters.

'I can't believe you're saying that.'

'Doctor's orders.'

'I doubt he wanted you to harass him.'

'Harass, encourage – he said help motivate. That's what I'm doing.'

'You're being damn cruel.'

'Like I don't have a right to be cruel?'

'No, you don't.'

'Fuck yourself, Bree.'

She grabbed his chair. 'Hey. Don't you ever say that to me again.'

For the first time in their relationship – for the *only* time in their relationship – Zen felt an almost overwhelming urge to punch her, to physically hurt his wife. The emotion was so strong that he grabbed the rails of his chair, squeezing them; his body shook and for a moment, for a long moment, he wasn't sure that he wouldn't hit her.

He closed his eyes, knowing that he was out of control – knowing that this wasn't him, that he loved his wife, that he would do anything in the world not to hurt her, that he would rather hurt himself than strike her.

And yet the anger was real too; he couldn't deny it. He couldn't deny the rage and wrath, the way his body shook even now. He leaned forward in the chair, breathing slowly through his teeth, gazing at his useless legs.

He was mad at Mack Smith, not her. Not Breanna.

Why was it Mack who would recover? Why the hell not him?

Why the hell not him?

When Zen raised his head, Breanna was staring at him. 'What?' he demanded.

She pressed her lips together, then turned quickly and walked alone down the path.

Just as well, he thought. Just as well.

Aboard the *Abner Read*
0800

Whether she knew anything about computers or not, the Dreamland scientist had the *full* attention of everyone aboard the *Abner Read*, even Captain Gale.

Especially the captain. Storm watched the scientist spreading out her laptops and wires at the side of the Tactical Warfare Center while volunteers hauled down equipment from the Osprey.

'See, it was designed to interface into your general warfare bus,' said Jennifer, bending over to retrieve a screwdriver from the canvas tool bag. 'It's not going to work right out of the gate, because your system is not quite to spec, unfortunately. Looks like they put in some workarounds because of bugs they couldn't decode. But I can hack something together.'

Hack it together. *Yes.*

'And we can control the Werewolf units from here?' asked Lieutenant Mathews.

Drool was practically coming out of his mouth.

'From this station, once it's set up,' said Jennifer. 'I'll have them in the air in a few hours.'

'Where's the pilot?' asked Storm.

'The lead pilot has the stomach flu. I'm his replacement.'

'No offense, miss, but I'd prefer –'

'A man?'

'No,' said Storm. He had women on his crew and was not overly sexist.

Overly. In his opinion.

'So?' asked the Dreamlander.

'I'd prefer someone on my crew, if they can be trained. I understood that the computer does most of the work.'

The scientist had set her jaw and was glaring at him. If anything, she looked even more beautiful than before.

'What I mean is, I need someone who's familiar with the ship, and who can stay on the job if something else goes wrong,' said Storm. 'You're going to be busy making sure our gear is working. I can't afford to lose the systems in the middle of a battle, or just turn the helicopters off.'

'The computer does most of the work flying the aircraft,' said Jennifer.

'Then it should be easy to learn, right? I have someone

trained in, uh, air-type warfare. He's an ex-helicopter pilot himself.'

'I can teach him. If it's an order,' said Jennifer.

Jeez, don't put it like that, thought Storm.

'Very well. I'd appreciate it,' he told her.

Jennifer bent down to get something else out of the bag. 'It'll be a while before I'm ready to do that.'

'Take your time, miss. Take your time,' said Storm.

Diego Garcia
1100

Starship didn't recognize the address, but opened the e-mail anyway.

> LIEUT:
> YOU PROBABLY DON'T REMEMBER ME. I GOT YOUR E-MAIL ADDRESS FROM KICK'S SISTER. I AM THEIR MINISTER. OUR CONVERSATION IN THE KITCHEN THAT DAY HAS STAYED WITH ME. YOU SEEM TO BE A WANDERING SOUL. I HOPE YOU FIND SOLACE. FOR ME, I'VE ALWAYS FOUND IT IN THE 'GOOD BOOK.'
> – REV. GERRY

'*Good Book.*' The minister had put it in quotes.

All the answers, huh? Starship deleted the message. He'd seen what religion could do in Saudi Arabia.

Immediately, he regretted deleting it. The minister was only trying to be helpful. Not even that: just trying to say

328

better what he had stuttered over earlier. He'd been in that position himself plenty of times.

He ought to send the guy a note back, say thanks or something.

Starship turned from the console in the Dreamland Command Trailer's communications area.

'Captain Freah?'

'What's up?'

'I deleted an e-mail by accident. Any way to get it back?'

'Deleted or just read it?'

'Deleted. I wasn't thinking.'

Danny made a face. 'Sorry. The techies have it set up so it doesn't write to disk as the default for security. If you delete, you don't get to write it on the disk. There might be some fancy way around it,' added the captain.

'Don't worry about it. Not worth it,' said Starship, getting up.

Plaza Hotel,
New York City
0900

Which phone was it?

Jed grabbed at all of them in succession – satellite, encrypted, cell phone, hot line, hotel phone . . .

He didn't have a hot line. It was a dream.

Except that a phone really was ringing.

329

Jed pushed out from under the covers and grabbed for the phone at the side of the bed. 'Jed Barclay.'

'Jed, session vote is set for ten A.M.,' said Ambassador Ford. 'We'll have a driver in the lobby in five minutes. Room service is on the way up with coffee for you. Get over here, OK?'

'Yes, sir.'

Jed put the phone down and lay back on the bed for a minute. The Plaza was far and away the fanciest hotel he had ever stayed in. The headboard was upholstered, for crying out loud. And room service . . .

There was a knock on the door. Jed jumped out of bed and walked over – he was wearing sweats and an old T-shirt – then remembered that he had to give a tip. 'Just a minute,' he said, and scrambled over for his wallet on the antique dresser. But when he pulled open the door, the man was gone; there was a full pot of coffee on a table at the side. This wasn't a plastic carafe either – it was a silver pot.

He pulled on some clothes, shaved quickly, then went down to the lobby. The driver hadn't arrived yet. Jed took out his personal cell phone and called his mom in Kansas.

'You're not going to believe where I am,' he told her as soon as she picked up the phone.

'New York,' she told him. 'I saw you last night.'

'You did?'

'At a press conference. You could use a haircut, Jed.'

'Really?'

'At least straighten it out a little.'

'No, I mean you saw me on TV?'

'The Secretary of State did most of the talking. He's a bit full of himself, that one. But you got a few words in about the ship. And Dreamland.'

'I didn't say anything about Dreamland,' said Jed.

'Your father wanted to tape it, but by the time he found a tape you were gone. There was a girl who's going to the national spelling bee from Lincoln.'

'I'm like in a real fancy hotel here,' said Jed.

'Good for you, honey. Did they have silk sheets?'

'I'm not sure,' said Jed.

'You did pull down the covers, right?'

'Well, yeah. I just don't know what silk feels like.'

'You would if you slept on it.'

'Maybe it was,' said Jed.

'Who paid for you to stay there? Not the government.'

'No, Ambassador Ford set it all up.'

'You aren't being paid by lobbyists, are you, Jed? On a junket? You don't want to get in with those lobbyists.'

'No. They're just friends, I think.' Ford had made the arrangements. Jed had no idea who was actually paying, just that it wasn't him.

A tall man in a suit walked into the lobby. He saw Jed and walked over, flashing State Department credentials.

'Gotta go, Ma.'

'Have a good day, honey. And get a haircut!'

'I will.'

The Secretary of State looked as if he hadn't had any sleep; it was likely that he hadn't. He'd gone back to Ford's penthouse on the East Side, planning to work the phones as long as necessary. Ford, who probably had gotten as little sleep as the Secretary, was just about flying. According to the ambassador, the French had come around; there would be abstentions, but the measure was going to pass and not be vetoed. It was an important day for the U.S. and the world.

An overstatement, he knew, but his enthusiasm and conviction were contagious. Jed followed them into the Security Council chamber, holding his laptop bag and some newspapers in one arm and a full cup of coffee in the other. The room seemed almost familiar today, and certainly friendlier. Jed sat, propping the bag by his chair and unfolding the newspapers onto his lap. He hadn't had a chance to read them yet.

He nearly dropped his coffee when he glanced at the cover of the Sunday *Daily News*.

It was his cobbled picture of the tanker on fire.

VII

Friends and Enemies

Aboard the *Wisconsin*,
over the Gulf of Aden
1900

The submarine had barely moved since the last patrol, but now that night was falling, Delaford predicted it would come up to periscope depth, take a look around, then proceed.

And sure enough, as the Megafortress circled to the north to get a better look at the British ship that had come through the gulf earlier in the day, the Libyan sub began nudging upward.

'Here we go, Colonel,' said Delaford, monitoring it with the Piranha.

'Good. Zen, you hear that?'

'Flighthawk leader,' said Zen, acknowledging.

Dog was about to hook into the *Abner Read* when the Dreamland communications channel buzzed with an incoming Eyes Only message. Dog gave his verbal password, then tapped the keypad at the right side of the screen, clearing the transmission in. Major Catsman's face came on the screen.

'Colonel, the UN has just authorized the pursuit of pirates in territorial waters in the Gulf of Aden.'

Good, thought Dog.

And bad.

'Thank you, Major. I'll talk to Captain Gale.'

Aboard the *Abner Read*,
Gulf of Aden
1905

'Go ahead,' the Dreamland techie told Storm. 'It's a channel on your com system. You're always connected now.'

Storm looked down and pressed the button on the box on his belt. 'Captain Gale.'

'The UN is approving the resolution allowing us to attack in territorial waters,' Dog told him. 'We should get the official word in a few hours. I thought you'd like a heads-up.'

A peace offering? Between that and sending the world's most beautiful woman to his ship, Bastian might yet prove human.

'Good. We'll move in and get this bastard,' said Storm.

'No. Too soon.'

'Why do you have to disagree with everything I say, Bastian?'

'I don't disagree with everything you say. Just things that need to be disagreed with.'

'Explain yourself,' said Storm tightly.

'If we attack now, we just get the submarine, and the patrol boat,' continued Dog. 'You want their base. Nothing's changed – except that in a few hours we'll be able to do something about them, once and for all.'

'We have some places we think are likely candidates,' said Storm. 'We can hit them one by one, after we take out the sub.'

'Or we can follow it to *the* candidate,' said Dog. 'And, as an extra bonus, if we wait, we can do it right. By tomorrow night we can have two Megafortresses, each with two Flighthawks. And more important, rested crews. We can bring my Whiplash people up during the day, and they can spearhead the land attack, along with your shipboard tactical teams.'

'The SITT people are good to go now,' said Storm, using the abbreviation for the specially trained teams of sailors who specialized in boarding ships and dealing with difficult situations on land. The letters stood for Shipboard Integrated Tactical Team. 'But I don't have enough of them. I'm bringing in Marines.'

'All the better.'

Storm looked down at the deck. Once again Bastian was right. Attacking now might be bold, but it was also likely to be rash. Wait twenty-four hours, and they'd have more firepower. More important, they'd have a coherent plan, rather than reacting ad hoc.

Of course. That was the decision he would have made himself once he'd thought it out. He was resisting only because it was *Bastian* who'd suggested it.

'Be ready to act if something changes,' Storm told him.

'I always am.'

Jennifer watched Storm as he ended the conversation with Dog. His whole manner had changed as soon as he started talking with the colonel. She had seen the type before: fine, even supportive, when dealing with subordinates who didn't threaten them by questioning their decisions; but come on too strong, and they reacted like an elephant protecting its place in the herd.

She picked up a headset and plugged into the circuit. 'Dog?'

'Hey, Jen.'

'We're set to try connecting into the Megafortress's radar system. But I'm worried that we'll throw you off if something goes wrong here.'

'So what do we do?'

'It might be best to run it when *Wisconsin* is coming off patrol. We can isolate it to that system, then bring it up. Worst case then, we just blind one aircraft.'

'Means you're going to have to wait another four or five hours there.'

'There's plenty to do. I still have the Werewolves to get ready. I'm training a new pilot.'

'You are?'

'Storm wants one of his crew handling them.'

'I warned you. How's Danny?'

'He's fine. The Marines that have been chopped to Xray Pop are the same ones who were at Khamis Mushait, so he's having a good time.'

'Oh?'

If she didn't know Danny was married, she would say he had a serious crush on Lieutenant Klacker, aka Dancer. But this wasn't the place for gossip.

'All right,' said Dog when she didn't answer. 'We'll contact you when we're ready. Take care.'

338

'Love you.'

As always, he hesitated before responding. 'Me too.'

New York
1100

Under any other circumstances the UN session would have been a highlight of Jed's life. It certainly was a success: The council voted to authorize the use of force against 'international outlaw pirates' in the Gulf of Aden, 'wherever they may be found.' A coalition team was authorized to stop the pirates before more civilians were harmed.

'Coalition' was a face-saving way for the others to admit that the U.S. was going to bail them out again.

But Jed didn't feel all that triumphant as the American delegation left the chamber and headed for the press conference. In fact, he felt exactly the opposite. As Ford and the others moved quickly down the hall, he found himself alone with Secretary of State Hartman.

'The picture,' Jed told him.

'Which one?' asked Hartman. He nodded at someone ahead, and Jed said nothing until they were alone again.

'The one on the cover of the Sunday *News*.'

'I'm not sure I saw it.'

'This one,' said Jed, pulling out the newspaper.

The Secretary of State stopped. 'That wasn't in the presentation.'

'It was just – as I put it together, I made it.'

'Ah, don't worry about forgetting it. The presentation

was fine without it. You can't do any better than we did today, Jed. Don't worry. We got the vote. We got it. This is the way things should go – persuasion and consensus. I know you're more a force guy, but this is the future. Coalitions. You'll look back on this and be proud.'

'No, I mean the photo shouldn't have been part of the presentation. Or printed.'

'Was it classified, Jed?' Once sleek, Hartman's face was now a series of puffy lines drawn close together.

'No. I put it together from two different pictures. It's not a real picture.'

'What? You put it together?'

Two delegates were walking down the hall. The Secretary nodded at them, then gestured for Jed to step to the side with him. Jed felt as if he were shrinking as the others passed through the hall.

'What happened?' asked Hartman. The lines had formed massive blots at the sides of his face.

'I was just fooling around. I don't know how it could have gotten on the disk I gave Jake. I must've left it in the folder of the jpgs that were part of the presentation. When I dumped the folder onto the disk, it must've come with the others. It was just a number; I didn't have a thumbnail or anything.'

'You have the original?'

'There is no original. I just fiddled with the shot of the tanker.'

'Fiddled? Give me your laptop.'

'I can't.'

'What do you mean you can't?'

'It's against security procedures. I –'

'*Jed.*' The Secretary held out his hand.

'OK,' said Jed. 'Yeah. You're a cabinet officer. Right.' He handed it over.

'You should say nothing about this until I tell you what to say. Go back to D.C. Talk to no one. Go. Now.'

'Yes, sir.'

Since it was Sunday, the traffic to LaGuardia Airport was relatively light. The car whisked over the Triburough Bridge, bounding over the metal work plates so roughly that Jed was jostled against the door. As they passed from the bridge to the Grand Central Parkway, he glanced at the elevated tracks above the road; a set of red subway cars were just arriving. He felt envious of the people who'd be getting aboard – whatever their day held, it was bound to be better than his.

Not that he had set out to deceive anyone. On the contrary. But obviously, inadvertently, he had. And in a big way – a big, potentially embarrassing and scandalous way.

Jed saw the picture on the front page of the newspaper at a stand as he walked inside the airport. At first he quickened his pace; then he went back and bought a copy. He bought the *Daily News* and another local paper as well, *Long Island Newsday*.

He found a spot in the terminal to sit and read through the story in both papers. *Newsday,* a more sedate tabloid than the *Daily News,* didn't have a picture at all. The *News* story was more sensational, but if it weren't for the photo, it would have been accurate.

A big *if,* admittedly.

The caption to the picture said merely that the attack was the work of pirates in the Gulf of Aden. The ship was not identified, nor was the attack dated.

Well, there *had* been attacks on ships, and at least two had been sunk that Jed knew of. Another had exploded and killed men aboard the *Abner Read.* So it wasn't *that* wrong.

Except for the fact that it was completely made up.

Jed looked at the picture. Between his fiddling and the newspaper's reproduction, it was barely possible to tell that it *was* a ship. There was no way of getting any identifiable details from it, no name or even enough of a silhouette to ID it with.

'Pretty wild, huh? Pirates on the high seas in 1997?'

Jed looked up. A man had sat down next to him and was pointing at the newspaper. He appeared to be in his forties.

'Yeah,' said Jed.

'You think that really goes on?'

'They wouldn't make it up, would they?'

'The government does that all the time. But I guess they couldn't make up pictures, right?'

'No,' said Jed, his voice hoarse. 'No, they couldn't.'

Gulf of Aden
2200

Fatigue hounded Ali's every step as he climbed down the ladder of the submarine. He'd had terrible dreams when he tried to sleep, dreams that kept him awake: Abu Qaed as a babe sucking at his mother's breast; Abu Qaed following him down a street as a young man in Cairo; Abu Qaed with him in Mecca.

The dreams all ended the same way – his son faded into a milky oblivion, and Ali lay wide awake for the rest of the night, sweating profusely.

To sleep once and for all, to lie in oblivion – that would be his paradise. To join his son, his cousin Mabrukah, countless others – that would be reward beyond all measure.

'Captain!' shouted the Libyan commander who had brought the submarine to the base. He told Ali in Arabic that he was honored to be a soldier of God.

'As are we all,' said Ali.

The commander began showing Ali around the submarine, a Project 641 ship known as a 'Foxtrot' in the NATO reporting system. The craft's basic design was dated; the type had first joined the Russian fleet at the very end of the 1950s, though this particular submarine had slipped into the ocean in 1966. Just a few inches shy of three hundred feet, the sub displaced 2,475 tons once submerged; she could dive to at least 985 feet and make about fifteen knots while submerged. She could run submerged for as many as five days, though her range was extremely limited beneath the water – at two knots, she could go perhaps three hundred miles before her batteries gave out completely. Her range on the surface, however, was an impressive twenty thousand miles, a good distance for a diesel-powered submarine. The craft also had snorkeling gear, which allowed it to run its engines while submerged; the captain referred to it as a 'low observable' mode.

The captain showed Ali to the sonar room, boasting that the submarine had been updated with a full range of Russian equipment, including gear found in much newer boats. The batteries were the same as those used in the improved version of the class, the Project 641B, and a variety of techniques were employed to decrease its sound, from an improved propeller system to the sound-deadening material that covered nearly every visible surface.

Ali paused at the steering station of the submarine. To the uninitiated, which included him, the control area was a jumble of boxes and controls, wheels, levers, and dials seemingly arranged in an incoherent jumble. But that was nothing compared to the jungle of wheels nearby that controlled the valves for the high pressure air and trim manifolds. These controls were necessary for stabilizing the submarine, allowing it to dive or surface. The blue and red valve handles looked like intertwined spider nests.

'The small size of our crew gave us some difficulty on the voyage,' said the captain. 'If we could have two dozen more men to train –'

'How many men do you have?'

'We made the sail with thirty-eight. It was very difficult at times. Ordinarily, seventy-eight men take the craft into battle. We can do with a few less, but –'

'If you made it all that way with only thirty-eight men, you will be able to do the same here. Besides, there is no time to train them. By this time tomorrow you will be under way. The cruise will not require a relief crew, I assure you.'

'We would value action,' said the captain finally.

'You will have plenty. An aircraft carrier is making its way down from the Suez Canal. It will be in the Gulf of Aden at dawn the day after tomorrow.'

They moved to the chart table, where the Libyan captain brought out a chart of the gulf area. The maps were not very good – surely another sign that Allah had guided the man here.

'I will get you another set before we sail,' Ali assured him. 'But for now, these will do – we will sail to the eastern end of the gulf as swiftly as possible. It is several hundred miles.' He pointed to 'Abd al Kūrī, a small island roughly seventy miles east of the tip of Somalia. Allah had given him a plan overnight – in compensation for the dreams, perhaps. They would strike where the carrier least expected it: at the end of the passage through the gulf. The other ships would lure the carrier to an attack, allowing the submarine to close in with its torpedoes. *Sharia* would launch its missiles at the same time – the *Ark Royal* would be overwhelmed.

'I have spies all along both coasts, and among the traffic in the gulf,' Ali told the submarine captain. 'They will give us his location without trouble. We will then make an attack.'

He described the three-tiered attack he had mapped out in general terms, giving the submarine commander enough information so he would know his duty, but not enough to scuttle the missions of the other ships if he was captured. The *Sharia*, fueled and disguised as a benign pile of junk ready for the salvagers' blowtorches, would put out to sea at dusk on its slow trek eastward. The rest of the fleet would slip out a few hours afterward. The entire flotilla would be gone within thirty-six hours.

'It is mostly a matter of timing,' added Ali. 'Once things begin, it follows the clock. There will be no need for communications. And no possibility of it. But we will succeed.'

'God willing,' said the captain.

'I have no doubt that he is willing.'

'Nor do I.' The captain looked at the chart. 'We will be sailing more than five hundred miles.'

'It will be somewhat more,' said Ali.

'We will have to go on the surface during the night to accomplish this. It is a risk we must take now,' said the captain.

Ali folded his arms, studying the captain's face. His assessments were correct, and he seemed aggressive. His passage here, however, had demonstrated caution in the extreme.

Which was the true man?

The answer could be seen in the gaze at a chart or the knitting of a brow. Ali would have to trust that the man who spoke of God's will was the truer – or that God would take a hand when necessary.

'There is an American force in the waters. They are a serious concern, far more than the British,' said Ali. He showed the submarine captain where Satan's Tail

346

normally patrolled. 'He cannot go into the coastal waters,' said Ali. 'As long as you stay close to the coast, he cannot attack you. He may follow, though. We will use that to our advantage if it happens.'

Ali outlined his plan. Tomorrow afternoon a pair of patrol boats would head a few miles to the west and then cut directly north across the gulf toward Yemen. The submarine would sail at dusk, followed by two other patrol boats that would shadow him. A few hours later a second group of patrol boats would go across the gulf, with the *Sharia* following roughly the same route the submarine did. Ali would follow in the large amphibian ship's path.

Most likely the Americans would attack the first group of patrol boats as they headed toward Yemen or soon afterward. If this happened, the submarine would have clear sailing. The next possibility was that those boats and the submarine would be missed; the second wave of patrol craft would draw the Americans' attention. The third possibility was that the Americans would detect the submarine and follow it.

'Their sensors are not very good in the shallow water,' boasted the submarine captain. 'I have sailed right past American ships in the Mediterranean many times.'

'This is not the Mediterranean, and you have not dealt with this ship and its commander before,' said Ali. 'Do not be overconfident. Satan's Tail is a ship like no other you have ever seen. The other day one of my vessels fired eight Exocet missiles at it, and it survived.'

'We will do better if we come up against it.'

'No. You must stay near the coast. Keep in the shadow of the Karkaar Mountains. Do not give them a reason to come for you.'

'If they attack me?'

'If they attack you and you have no other choice, then you may engage. But your first mission is to get away.' Ali looked down at the chart. 'I will get them if they interfere. I will find a way.'

'Let me show you the rest of the boat,' said the Libyan.

They went through the forward spaces. Some of the equipment had been updated; even the older gear was clean and freshly painted, a sign of discipline that pleased Ali, for to him it meant not simply that the captain paid attention to details, but that the crew paid attention to the captain. This was another of the lessons he saw from the Italians, in going from ship to ship in their fleet – one could measure the crew by the captain, and vice versa.

The tour continued to the forward torpedo room, where the large tube openings protruded from the wall like the stubby teats of a goat. There were six firing tubes, three to a side.

'Only six torpedoes?' asked Ali.

'I was told you would supply more,' said the captain.

'I do not have Russian torpedoes. Nor anything large enough for these tubes.'

The submarine used a standard Russian design, twenty-one inches, or 533mm, in diameter. The torpedoes that Ali had were Italian A244s – a very versatile weapon, as its adaptation to his boats and tactics had shown, but at 12.75 inches, a much smaller and lighter torpedo.

'Perhaps we can modify the tubes,' suggested the captain. 'The Russians have done so.'

He is optimistic by nature, thought Ali. That would be useful in battle.

'There isn't time for that,' said Ali. 'Six will have to suffice.'

Alexandria,
near Washington, D.C.
1500

Jed took the Metro from the airport and walked the five blocks from the Metro, stopping first to grab the *Washington Post* – no picture on the front or inside the newspaper, where the story played at the top of the international section.

Standing at the register waiting to pay, he glanced sideways toward the coolers at the six-packs of beer.

'Maybe later,' he said out loud. He wasn't much of a drinker.

'Later?' asked the clerk.

'Just the paper,' said Jed. He took his change and walked the five blocks home. His mood swung from anger at himself to depressed disbelief.

How could he have been so stupid?

Why the *hell* had he made the picture in the first place? He was an assistant to the National Security Advisor of the *United States,* not a member of the *Harvard Lampoon.*

Damn, I'm a jerk, he told himself. I deserve to get booted across the Potomac.

And I will be. Probably by the President himself.

The answering machine was blinking at him when he got in: twelve calls.

That wasn't a record, but it was close for a Sunday. He hadn't turned on his phones since he'd left the UN; he did now, and saw that each had nearly as many calls.

Jed put them down on his bed and stood over them.

I'm either going to deal with this, he thought, or I'm not.

I am going to deal with this.

His house phone rang and he jumped, but made no effort to get it.

Man, what are my parents going to say? And Colonel Bastian? And Zen? What is my cousin Zen going to say?

He's going to say I'm a jackass.

Whoever called hung up without leaving a message.

Zen would sit there in his wheelchair, shake his head. Then he'd mutter something like, 'Little Jed, Little Jed, Little Jed.'

Then he took me out to shoot some hoops . . .

It really had happened that way, when Jed got in trouble as a senior in high school, caught smoking a marijuana cigarette in the school bathroom – only his second time ever smoking dope, and of course he got caught. He'd thought that was the end of the world.

It was, then. Zen's appearance in his uniform, fresh from the Gulf War – God, he was a sight, standing in the door. Standing . . .

What would Zen say now?

He'd say get off your ass *and deal with it. If I can deal*

with being in the f-in' wheelchair, you can deal with this,
asshole.

Jed picked up the sat phone and started checking his
messages.

Aboard the *Wisconsin*,
Gulf of Aden
2400

'There's a mooring area for abandoned ships at the
western end of the little inlet there,' said Dog, talking to
the crew of Megafortress *Delta One* as he prepared to
hand off the patrol to the other crew. 'The submarine is
across the arm of the bay, in this area here. It looks like
a manmade cave, with just enough clearance for a small
vessel to get in. According to what we've been able to
dig up at Dreamland, the Italians found it in 1940 or 1941
and began modifying it for use as a submarine pen.
Eventually it was abandoned. The submarine is there
along with two patrol boats. Piranha is right here, about
a hundred feet from the mouth of the cave. At least one
patrol boat is sitting with these civilian boats in this area,
and one of the moored ships isn't a wreck. We'll have
fresh satellite intelligence in a few hours, but from old
snaps, we think the headquarters area is over here, below
the cliffs.'

Dog added that there was a legitimate port nearer to
Karin, a few miles away; at least one patrol craft was
hiding there as well.

'More than likely there are ships and patrol craft hidden in different spots all along the coast,' he added. 'But I don't want to send a Flighthawk over, on the chance it'll tip them off. We'll wait until we're ready to deal with whatever is going on. Your job tonight is to stay far enough away that they can't see you, but close enough so you can react if something happens. No overflights, no combat if at all possible.'

Dog continued, passing along the frequencies that were being used by the *Abner Read* and the other ships, emergency landing fields, and the other necessary minutiae of a successful mission.

Zen swept the Flighthawk toward the coast as Dog finished up his brief with the crew of the *Delta One*. The Flighthawk pilot aboard *Delta One*, Captain Eric 'Guitarman' Mulvus, had seen action as an Army helicopter pilot in Panama and the Gulf War, left the regular Army, somehow managed to get into the Air Force Reserve, hopscotched into an ROTC program, and emerged as an F-16 pilot. Clearly a finagler, Guitarman's real claim to fame was lead guitarist in a pickup band known as the Dream Makers. He was a decent Flighthawk pilot, though this was his first mission in a combat zone.

Zen slid down to fifteen hundred feet, gliding along the coastline. While they were giving the submarine base a wide swath and avoiding any chance of tipping the pirates off, Dog had decided there was nothing wrong with surveying the coastline well to the east as they went off duty. Starting about fifty miles from the cave where the sub was hidden, the Flighthawk would survey the coastline to the Indian Ocean with its infrared video camera. Even if they didn't spot anything, the survey would form a baseline for future operations; the computer would review the recorded images and flag what had changed.

Zen settled onto a path about a quarter of a mile north of the coast. During the sixteenth century, Somalia was a flashpoint for Christian and Islamic cultures. Islam dominated the cities and areas on the coast where Zen flew, and Christians dominated the interior. The severe terrain kept relations between the two religions manageable, isolating the communities and weakening the appetite for conquest. Still, there had been many fights over the centuries; domination by one group or the other had not halted the flow of blood, nor, to be fair, did the sharing of a common religion prevent murder or depredation.

Somalia had been divided in two during the nineteenth century, with the British dominating the northern coast and Italy the eastern, including the tip of the Horn of Africa. In the early days of World War II, Italy had seized British Somaliland; in 1941 the British took it and the rest back. The country's history after the war was partly cruel and partly confused, with the UN Security Council placing Italy in charge of the southern portion and Britain retaining the north, against the wishes of both the people and the UN. Unification, revolution, alliance with the Russian communists, chaos, hunger, and disaster had been the lot of the people ever since. The UN's effort to fight starvation in the early 1990s had ended in disaster for the U.S. when an Army unit tried to arrest followers of a warlord; the bungled politics surrounding the affair was one of many issues that had helped President Martindale win election. But the incident also convinced the UN to pull out, making ordinary Somalians victims once more.

That's always the way it is, thought Zen. The little guy takes it in the ear.

His father used to say that all the time. *That's why you don't want to be a little guy.*

Zen hoped that wasn't the real lesson to be drawn, though sometimes it was hard to argue against.

The Flighthawk chugged along, not caring a whit for history or injustice. A large vessel sat in the water off the left wing. The infrared image seemed a little off as Zen passed. It took him a moment to realize that the ship's image had been fairly uniform; there were no hot spots, which you'd expect if the engines were running.

'*Wisconsin,* this is Flighthawk leader,' said Zen. 'Looks like I found that converted oiler we saw the other night. It's dead in the water. I'm going to take a close-up look at it.'

'Roger that, Flighthawk leader. Something up?'

'Not sure.'

The ship seemed dead cold, the only heat the lingering warmth of the sun. And it was high in the water.

'Maybe we didn't save it after all,' said Zen after a second pass. 'Maybe they had already taken it, got the fuel off, then brought it here. I think we ought to have somebody check it out.'

'Agreed,' said Dog. 'I'll dial it into Storm. Stand by.'

Danny stared at the hologram, which showed the likely location of the pirate camp near a village on the coast and just below a sharp cliff. A sequence of satellite photos had been used to form the basic layout, focusing on three old buildings across from a mooring where there had been occasional activity over the past several weeks. The old ships in the harbor gave the pirates good hiding places and made it difficult to flush them out if they managed to take positions there. While none were visible from the photos, the *Abner Read* would begin the engagement by pummeling the old hulks and neutralizing the possibility. The ship would wait for the submarine to come out of the cave; the shallow water as well as a breakwater and two old wrecks near the entrance prevented an easy torpedo shot.

The ground team would prevent escape by land and secure whatever the pirates had onshore. The old village had been largely abandoned and could be isolated by capturing a small bridge at the southern end accessible from the water; with that out of the way, the main force could concentrate on the buildings directly across from the mooring. The Marines and Danny Freah's Whiplash team would land at the top of the cliff and rappel down from two different points to press home the attack. The troops could be deposited as the Werewolves blazed in from the oceanside. Between the high-pitched whine of the robot helos' rotors and the *Abner Read*'s exploding shells, the Osprey's approach would be difficult to hear.

'They most likely have at least a token watch in this area up here,' said Danny, pointing to a ridge just behind the point of the cliff. 'We have to find out before we attack. We can send a Flighthawk over shortly before the attack and look at the infrared camera. That'll show us where everything is. We can have it orbit during the operation, showing us what's going on.'

'We need at least a token force to come in off the shore to the west,' said Dancer. 'Otherwise they can just filter down here and get away. And just for good measure, we should put people on this side of the village to the east as well. We're looking at three heavily armed teams, lots of firepower, support from those robot helos. If there are two hundred pirates in there –'

'I doubt there are two hundred,' said Danny. 'Not even a hundred.'

'We still need more people,' said the Marine lieutenant. Danny found himself admiring her professional skepticism. Too often junior officers simply parroted what their superiors drew up.

And she was good-looking when she was skeptical.

'We can always use more people,' said Danny. 'But the technology will let us leverage what we have.'

'I'll take two boots on the ground over a silicon chip any day,' said Dancer.

'We can use the SITT teams onshore,' said Storm. 'In a pinch we can make a shore party from some of the people on *Shark Boat One*. They should be able to handle the western escape route. The Shark Boat can be operated with a minimal crew and still provide fire support.'

They worked the changes into the computer driving the holographic display. The elements snapped in: a dozen men down each side of the cliff, with a team at the top of the cliff to keep them secure; two fire teams on the shore below, a Flighthawk for reconnaissance, the Werewolves for pinpoint fire support, the Shark Boat to provide support and cut off any retreat, the *Abner Read* to methodically wipe out the wrecks and any other defenses that turned up.

It looked like it would work. But it was a complicated plan, and Danny would have much preferred to rehearse it a few dozen times before the main event, especially given the fact that his men and the Marines had never worked together before.

'What are you thinking, Captain?' asked Dancer.

'I'm thinking I'd like a chance to work with you guys before we do this, just to make sure we're all on the same page,' he said.

'I wouldn't mind that,' answered Dancer. 'But I don't think we can tell the pirates to hold in place for six months.'

'I'll settle for three days.' Danny turned to Jennifer Gleason, who was standing at the side of the room, working on one of the computing units. 'The Werewolves will be operational in time, right, Jen?'

'Oh, yeah,' she told him, in a voice that clearly indicated she was not happy. 'I have some tests to run, and then we'll finish training our pilot.'

'You're not flying them yourself?'

'Captain, if you want to discuss tasking, I'll be available following our planning session,' said Storm.

'Captain Gale, there's an urgent communication from the

357

Dreamland aircraft *Wisconsin* for you, sir,' a sailor said.

They turned toward one of the screens at the front of the room, where Dog's helmeted head appeared.

'Storm, this is Bastian. We have a ship dead in the water that looks as if it's been abandoned. It's the oiler we spotted the night of the battle. We think you should send somebody to check it out.'

Danny watched Storm scowl. The Navy captain went to the holographic display without saying anything.

'Hey, Colonel,' said Danny.

'Danny.'

'Where exactly is it?' snapped Storm.

Jennifer glanced at the hologram, then tapped something on her laptop. A black box appeared near the coast about fifty miles west of the pirates' camp; it blinked yellow for a few seconds, then turned red. It was about a hundred miles east of them, in territorial waters.

'That's it,' she said.

'I'll send one of the Shark Boats,' said Storm. 'OK, Bastian. Good work.'

'Jen, we're ready for that diagnostic series,' said Dog without acknowledging Storm's comments.

'Coming up,' she said, pulling a seat over. 'But the fact that I was able to add that information to the display means we're going to come through with a hundred percent. The Megafortress sensor data is now available on the *Abner Read*'s network.'

'Let's run the tests anyway.'

'Ready whenever you are.'

'I have an idea,' Danny told Storm. 'What if Sergeant

Rockland and I take some of the Marines and your SITT unit out in the Osprey and run an operation to board the ship? It's not exactly a dress rehearsal, but we'll be able to work together for a little, see if we're going to have any major problems. It would at least let us get our feet wet together before the main event.'

'I like that idea,' said Dancer.

'So do I,' said Storm. 'Good idea, Captain.'

'What do you think, Colonel?' asked Danny, turning to the screen.

'Sounds good to me, but it's not my show.'

'That's right,' said Storm. 'I call the shots.'

Dog cleared his throat. 'And *Delta One* is the aircraft that will be on patrol. You'll have to alert them. I'm turning you over to the copilot, Jen; I've got some things to take care of here.'

Washington, D.C.
1650

'I can't believe you did that,' said Freeman over the scrambled line.

'I know it was stupid, sir. It was idiotic and childish and I have no defense. I should not have made the image.'

'You shouldn't have given your laptop to the Secretary of State,' said Freeman.

'He kind of demanded it,' said Jed, surprised that Freeman was focusing on that. 'I made sure the drive was totally wiped before I left for New York. I always run the shredder program. You know, in case something screws up and it gets, um, like lost. The only stuff on there was the presentation.'

'You should not have handed over your laptop.'

'He was pretty adamant. I guess you could say he was ticked.'

'Jed, when you get that laptop back – if you get it back – anything could be on it. Anything. You'd have no proof of anything.'

'Well, yeah, but –'

'Look, you're a bright kid. You know technology and you know a lot about how countries can use it, and you deal with the people at Dreamland and the other military pretty well. General Clearwater down at CentCom was asking about you just the other day. But you have to understand, son – this is *Washington*. You cannot trust anybody. Do you understand?'

Including you? thought Jed, but he kept his mouth shut.

'As for the picture,' continued Freeman, 'as for the picture . . .'

'I know, I know.'

Neither of them spoke for a moment.

'Should I write up my resignation?' Jed asked finally. 'Should I, like, make a statement about what happened or something?'

'That would be the worst thing to do,' snapped Freeman. 'Especially with the Senate hearings coming up. They'll subpoena you for sure.'

'But if I just said what happened, maybe said it now before the hearings –'

'It'll call attention to it, people will question the Security Council decision, the vote may be reversed – frankly, at this point, I'm not sure anyone would believe that it *was* innocent.'

'It was.'

'I don't want you to talk to anyone,' said Freeman. 'Let's do this – you're on vacation right now, until further notice. OK? Vacation? Which means, talk to no one. No one. Be in my office tomorrow morning at seven. We'll figure out what we have to do.'

'Should I – I mean, I have to tell the President, right?'

Freeman didn't answer.

'I should tell the President, right?' said Jed.

'Talk to no one, until you talk to me. Be in my office. Seven sharp. Get some sleep, Jed,' he added, softening his tone. 'Get some sleep, all right?'

'Yes, sir.'

'You're not going to do anything rash, right, Jed? This isn't – it's not *that* bad.'

'What would I do?'

'Just be in my office. Relax, don't talk to anyone, and be in my office. We'll work it out. Seven A.M. You understand?'

'Yes. I'll be there.'

Boston steadied himself at the side of the ramp at the rear of the Dreamland-modified Osprey, waiting for the go-ahead.

'Figure the water's going to be warm?' he asked.

'As warm as Lake Michigan in July,' answered Danny.

'That's what I was afraid of,' said Boston.

A tone sounded in their headsets. The jumpmaster took a step forward and pushed out the uninflated raft package. Boston and the Marine who was going out with him followed, stepping off into the water.

The Osprey lifted upward as the rear panel began to close. Danny went back and joined the team waiting to rappel to the deck of the oiler. As he reached the door where the rappelling lines had been prepared, Danny saw a Werewolf whip toward the side of the ship. The two gunships were providing cover as the team descended to the open deck a few yards from the bow.

'Marines – let's make your mothers proud,' said Dancer.

Make your mothers proud? Women certainly brought a different perspective to operations, thought Danny as he waited for his turn to rappel down to the deck.

It came quickly. They weren't as high over the ship as he thought, and he hit the deck about a half second early, stumbling but then catching his balance. The ship rolled ever so slightly to his right, and Danny trotted after the others who were racing toward the superstructure.

The Marines had radios, but couldn't tie into the Dreamland discrete-burst system. Danny and Boston got around this by using Marine headsets to talk with the Marines and relay messages through their Dreamland system back to the Osprey and the *Abner Read*. The ship could monitor everything that was going on through the video and infrared cameras in the Osprey. Danny could even give Storm a ground-level view by punching the switch at the bottom of his smart helmet.

Make that a ship-level view.

Dancer had told Danny that the Marines had practiced ship boarding 'once or twice,' but it looked to him like they did it every day. They had already swarmed the deck area and were now taking over the superstructure, a rectangular collection of spaces that rose about four stories over the main deck. The men said very little, using grunts more than words. The earpiece Danny had been given was impossible to wear comfortably beneath his smart helmet, and he finally had to take it off, wedging it at the back in a position that was only marginally better. He couldn't hear much of what was being said.

A pair of muffled explosions announced that the team tasked to take over the bridge had just done their thing, crashing in with the aid of a small amount of explosives and flash-bangs. Danny turned around to make sure the rest of the team had gotten on safely, then ran along the side of the ship, leaning against the rail, his MP-5 ready, its crosshair a dot in his visor.

Something blared in his headset. He pulled the Marine unit out, and after fiddling with it a few minutes, realized it had malfunctioned. He pulled the smart helmet back on and stood tensely near the rail as the rest of the team went about its business. Finally, a Marine came nearby and Danny gestured for him to stay close so he could communicate with the rest of the team. He pushed the helmet back on his head, an awkward compromise.

'Dancer has a communication for you, sir,' said the Marine, holding out his headset.

'Bridge is secure,' said Dancer. 'No one here. No wonder they didn't answer the radio – it's gone. Blood all over the place,' she added before he could acknowledge.

'Remember the booby-traps,' Danny reminded the others. 'Go slow, go slow.'

The first rushes of adrenaline fading, the boarding party moved through the ship methodically.

'Looks pretty boring up there,' said Boston on the Dreamland circuit.

'Not as boring as down there,' Danny replied, pulling the helmet down.

'I figure I want it boring. Say, they ought to see if they can get a more powerful motor,' added Boston. 'This little putt-putt barely goes two knots.'

'You thinking of doing some waterskiing?'

'I had a mind to it, Cap. Maybe I'll lasso one of the Werewolves and let it pull me around.'

Danny moved around to the stern, looking at the darkened coast in the distance. They'd be there tomorrow.

He worked to focus on the job at hand, walking with his new communications aide toward the stern of the ship.

Two young Marines had taken posts there. They were both very young – nineteen, if that – kids trying to act nonchalant on what was probably the closest they'd come to real action in their brief military careers.

He nodded to them, saw their tight smiles. He began seeking out the rest of the team, intending to make personal contact with as many as possible. It wasn't important tonight, but it would seem like a luxury tomorrow. He wanted the people working with him to know who he was, to remember they could count on him – and to do what he needed them to do when people were shooting at them.

Danny worked his way all the way around the ship and up to the bow before Dancer called in from below.

'We found some of the crew,' she told him. 'Down in the engineering space. They're all dead, Skipper. Blood everywhere. Been dead a while. Smells like hell down here.'

'All right. Take some pictures, see if you can find the log, take pictures of its entries, then let's saddle up. Nothing more for us to do here.'

Alexandria,
near Washington, D.C.
2315

So why did the photo only appear in the *Daily News*?

And why was it no longer on their Web page?

Jed got up from his desk, rubbing his eyes as he walked

to the kitchen. He'd been surfing the net for the last four or five hours. The picture had all but disappeared – if you didn't count the million or so print versions that featured it on the front page.

He reached into the refrigerator and took out a large bottle of Nestlé's strawberry milk. He took a slug and went back to the computer, deciding to write his letter of resignation. He sat down, called up the word processor, then stared at the blank screen for a few minutes. When nothing inspired him, he moused down to the browser and got a weather site from his favorites' tab.

RAIN, TOMORROW. HEAVY AT TIMES.

It figured.

His sat phone rang, and he picked it up without thinking.

'Jed, this is Colonel Bastian. I wonder if you can get me some data on a ship . . . I also need better maps of the coastal area. One weird thing we're looking for is something from 1940 or 1941 that might help. See, the Italians started to build a base in British Somaliland around the end of 1940 –'

'Um, I'm kind of on, uh, like on a leave thing,' Jed said. 'I shouldn't even have answered the phone.'

'Vacation?'

'It's hard to explain. I'm kind of on . . . leave.'

'What do you mean "leave"?'

Oh, hell, thought Jed. 'I screwed something up. So, I'm kind of on ice.'

'Like what?'

'I'm not supposed to talk about it, and I really can't.

366

You or the people at Dreamland Command can call over to the White House and get the military liaison's office. They'll help out.'

'Are you in *real* trouble?'

'Yeah.'

Dog didn't say anything. 'You want some advice?'

'I do, but – I know I can trust you, Colonel, but things are so screwed up right now.'

'I don't know what kind of trouble you're in, and I don't want you to tell me, not if it'll make things worse. But in Washington it can be really hard to know who's on your side and who isn't. If you're really in trouble – and I mean *real* trouble – you find a lawyer. All right?'

'Yeah. That's probably good advice.'

'Look, can you help me? I don't have time to spend trying to run this stuff down.'

Jed sighed. 'What exactly is it that you need?'

Diego Garcia
0800

Starship told himself he was just going into the chapel because he was bored. Inside, the minister was wrapping up a sermon about David in the lion's den. Starship took a seat and listened. The minister wasn't a particularly good speaker, and the sermon itself wasn't much better.

Starship rose with the rest of the congregation, joining in a hymn, eyes wandering. When he was a teenager and used to go to church with the family on Sundays, he'd spent a lot of services this way, checking out the women nearby. There were only two in the sparse crowd, and neither would have earned higher than a four on his old scale of one to ten.

As he stood there, he realized everyone else had a hymnal. Belatedly, he reached for one and began thumbing through it. But before he could find the song it was over.

Everyone started walking out. Starship put the book down and waited for the others to pass, then shambled out behind them, bemused – church, it seemed to him, hadn't changed all that much in the few years since he'd stopped going regularly, or semiregularly.

'Welcome to our congregation,' said the minister in a vaguely Australian accent. He had stationed himself near the door.

'Uh, thanks. Nice sermon,' said Starship.

'You only heard the tail end.'

'Yeah, that's true.'

'It wasn't really that good, was it?' said the minister.

His honesty surprised Starship, who wasn't sure how to respond. He shrugged, then started to walk away, but something in the minister's face made him want to say something – anything – to let the poor guy know he didn't think he was a failure. 'I got a question. Is it true that Muslims and Jews use the Bible too?'

'What Christians call the Old Testament. Absolutely,' said the minister. 'Is that your question?'

'Yeah.'

'Come back and pray with us again.'

'Thanks,' said Starship, making his escape.

'We will open Operation Bloodthirst at 2350 with the Flighthawk overflight of the base area,' said Storm. He gestured to the hologram, where a simulation of the operation had begun to play. 'We analyze the video feeds, then get a go/no go on the operation. Assuming a green light, *Shark Boat One* moves forward at 2410 and puts the first shore party into the insertion raft. The party splits up, one watching the small bridge to the village and the other moving farther east along the coast as a backstop to prevent anyone from escaping. Bombardment begins from the *Abner Read*. The Werewolves appear at 2415. The Osprey approaches from the south. Werewolves attack. Second shore team comes off the Shark Boat. *Shark Boat One* moves offshore and monitors the situation. Osprey disgorges the combined teams of Marines and Whiplash troopers.'

Danny watched as the captain continued the briefing. Storm relished the spotlight; there was no doubt about that. *He* was the kind of guy who should be a congressman.

I'm not going to run for Congress, Danny realized. It doesn't fit with who I am. And that means it's *not* my duty, no matter what other people say.

He glanced across the room at Dancer, noticing her intent gaze as Storm moved to the exfiltration.

I'm not sure exactly who I am, but I'm not a congressman.

'*Shark Boat Two* stays in this area to the east, watching for additional boats and mopping up anything that manages to get by the *Abner Read* and *Boat One*,' continued Storm. 'Are we all on board?'

One by one the different commanders checked in. Dog, who was participating by video back in the Dreamland Command trailer, grunted. The colonel seemed more tired than Danny remembered seeing him, worn down by the long missions.

That'll be me in what, ten years?

Unlikely. Oh, he might make lieutenant colonel – given his record, he ought to do so easily. But then what? The general idea would be to stick around and make full bird colonel, then go for general. But that wasn't as easy as it seemed. There was a real numbers squeeze on, and there were going to be less and less slots available at the higher ranks, especially after the Martindale administration, which was generally considered pro-military. Even now, getting the star on your shoulder could be tricky for someone who wasn't a pilot. It wasn't a written thing, and there were plenty of exceptions – *plenty* – but if you wanted to go to the top in the Air Force, it helped a lot to be part of the mafia.

Dog would argue that. Danny knew plenty of guys who would argue that. And hell, his record could make him a general right now, assuming he kept his nose clean and more or less played by the rules.

But did he want to be a general? Talk about being a politician.

So what would he do?

'Captain?' said Storm, looking at him.

'I think it's going to work,' said Danny.

Diego Garcia
1630

'Is Ms O'Day there?'

'Excuse me, what?'

'This is Colonel Tecumseh Bastian,' Dog told the man who had answered the phone. 'Is Ms O'Day there?'

'Do you know what time it is?'

'I'm afraid it's very early,' said Dog. 'Unfortunately, a good friend of hers is in trouble, and I have only a limited time to talk to her about it.'

'Hold on.'

Dog hadn't spoken to Deborah O'Day since she left the administration. The former National Security Advisor was now a college professor in Maine. Contrary to what he had told the man who answered the phone, Dog did know what time it was there – five-thirty A.M. – but it seemed more tactful to feign ignorance.

'Colonel Bastian, Auld Lang Syne.'

'Ms O'Day. How are you?'

'Well, I'm OK, Dog. I'm guessing you're not. What's wrong?'

'A friend of ours is in some sort of trouble. Something serious enough for him not to want to talk about it.'

'Who?'

'Jed Barclay.'

'Jed Barclay. Jed?'

'He's still at the NSC.'

'Oh, I know where Jed is. He's doing very well. I keep track of all my boys – even you, Tecumseh. I remember the first time I brought him into a meeting with the President at the White House. God, what an awful tie he wore.' She laughed. 'As I remember, Dog, you didn't have a particularly high opinion of him.'

'Well, he kind of grows on you. And maybe I was wrong. You might give him a call. I happen to know he's in his apartment.'

'Same number?'

'I'm just guessing, but I'd say yes.'

'I'll talk to him.'

'I appreciate that.'

'How are you, Dog? How's Martindale treating you?'

'Fine.'

'Be careful of him, Tecumseh.'

'I will.' Dog had a different opinion of the President than O'Day did, but this wasn't the time or place to discuss it.

'I'm sorry about the memorial service. I couldn't have made it through. He was a great, great man.' Her voice choked up. 'I loved him.'

'We all miss the general,' said Dog. Neither of them had to mention Brad Elliott by name. Ms O'Day had not attended the service, even though the two had been very close prior to his death.

'I'll watch out for Jed.'

'So will I.'

'Auld Lang Syne,' said O'Day.

'Auld Lang Syne.'

From the point of view of the Dreamland flight crews, the mission was straightforward. They'd get to the area around 2300. Zen, aboard the *Wisconsin*, would handle the Flighthawk flyover of the pirate area and cover the landing. One of the two Flighthawks would be 'parked' in an orbit above the battlefield, providing real-time visuals for the ground team commander, Danny Freah. The other would provide fire support. *Baker-Baker* would patrol farther north, watching for ships that might launch an attack from the Yemen side of the Gulf. Each Megafortress would have a Piranha operator aboard: Delaford in *Baker-Baker* and Ensign English in *Wisconsin*. The Megafortress closest to the probe would control it; at the start of mission that would be English. Once the submarine was destroyed, the probe could be recovered, either by Danny Freah and the Whiplash team or *Shark Boat One*. The Megafortress weapons bays would carry Harpoon missiles exclusively. The Ethiopians had been quiet since losing their planes, and between the Flighthawks and the air defenses aboard the *Abner Read,* they would have plenty of cover.

'I'd put Scorpion AMRAAM-pluses in as well,' said Mack, interrupting Zen as he discussed the capabilities of the other air forces in the region.

'Yeah.' Zen rolled his eyes. Everyone involved in the mission – and a lot of people who weren't – had gathered for the brief, so they'd had to hold it in the common room

373

in the administration building. 'As I was saying, Yemen has been putting its aircraft on alert and turning its radar systems on and off, but they don't seem like they're interested in doing more than that. Did I mention that the Flighthawks aboard *Wisconsin* will be *Hawk One* and *Hawk Two*?'

'I wouldn't take Yemen too lightly,' said Mack.

Zen ignored him.

'*Hawk One* and *Two* are mine. Starship, flying in *Baker-Baker Two*, will have *Hawk Three* and *Hawk Four*.'

'The MiGs are pretty capable,' said Mack.

'Yemen does have MiG-29s,' said Zen. 'The radar operators will be on the alert for that – as they have *every* mission.'

'Pays to be alert,' said Mack.

'And we will watch them carefully,' said Zen. 'Because of the length of the mission, we've arranged for a tanker to accompany us. We'll run the usual routine. We'll tank, gas up, head out. Tanker will come up for a second top-off after the mission concludes, or obviously if we need it earlier. *Baker-Baker Two* –'

'When are we going to get real names for the Megafortresses?' said Mack. '*Baker-Baker Two* sounds like a racehorse or something.'

'We'll get new names when you start walking again,' snapped Zen.

There was a hush in the room, and Zen realized he'd gone too far. But he was damned if he was going to apologize. Mack was quiet for the rest of the brief.

'All right,' said Dog when they were done. 'Let's clear the seas of these scum.'

'I can handle the two Flighthawks, no sweat,' said Starship, coming over to Zen as the meeting broke up.

'Do it like it's a simulation,' Zen told him, gathering his papers.

'No, it's a little different,' said the lieutenant. 'It's like – it's different. A simulation, I mean it looks the same, but it's not. You can't really feel it.'

'Don't get philosophical on me,' said Zen, though he thought he knew what he meant. There *was* a difference, as hard as it was to put into words. 'Just fly.'

'I will.'

'When are you going to give it up?' said Mack behind him.

Zen ignored him, snapping his bag closed. He started to wheel away, but Mack – with what must have been a superhuman effort for him – managed to cut in front of the door and block his way.

'When are you going to stop?' said Mack.

'Stop what, Mack?' asked Zen.

'Stop riding me. As soon as I say one thing –'

'You make stupid comments, Mack. It's pretty much all you ever do.'

'Because I'm in a wheelchair.'

'No. That's about the only good thing that's ever happened to you.'

'You're an asshole.'

'Excuse me, I have a mission to run,' Zen told him. 'Why don't you get off your ass and do something valuable?'

Starship put his hand on the back of Zen's wheelchair. 'Say, Zen?'

Zen brushed his hand away. There were about a half-dozen other people still in the room, standing back uncomfortably.

'I'd walk if I could,' said Mack. 'I'm not faking it.'

'I gotta go,' said Zen, trying to squeeze by.

'Why the hell are you riding my case?' demanded Mack.

'Because you can walk, asshole.' Zen spun back into the room so he could face him. 'Get your butt out of that chair and walk.'

'The hell with you.'

'Walk!'

'You think I'm faking this?'

'It's all in your stinking ass mind. The doctors all told you – you bruised your spinal column. Nothing more. It's better now. You can walk.'

'Like hell I can.'

'Come on, you wimp.'

Mack reared back as if to punch him.

'Go ahead,' said Zen. 'Hit me.'

'I oughta, you bastard. You blame me for making you a cripple.'

'You bet your ass I do, chickenshit. Hit me.'

'Screw yourself.' Mack started to turn his chair to go through the door.

Zen pushed forward and grabbed the wheel. 'Hit me, you coward. Go ahead – hit me.'

Mack spun around and took a swing. Though surprised, Zen ducked it easily.

'That the best you can do?'

'If you weren't a cripple I'd beat the crap out of you.'

'Try it. I ain't a cripple. I ain't a fucking cripple at all. My legs don't work but I ain't no goddamn cripple. Not like you. I could crawl over there and strangle you if I wanted.'

Zen saw Mack's glare tighten. He pushed his chair backward just in time as Mack threw a roundhouse – and missed, falling from the wheelchair face first on the ground.

'Lie there like the coward wimp you are,' said Zen.

Mack bolted upright with a scream, launching himself on Zen so ferociously that Zen just barely kept the wheelchair upright, darting backward under the weight of Mack's blows. Strengthened by more than two years of regular, strenuous workouts, Zen's upper body was more than a match for Mack's, but even so, he had a hard time fending off Mack's blows, and the chair backed all the way to the wall, slamming against it with a teeth-jarring smash. Mack flailed and punched as Zen grabbed for a handhold. Only as Mack's fury began to exhaust itself did Zen manage to hold him upright and off him.

'You're standing, asshole. You're standing,' Zen told him.

Mack looked down at his legs. He was standing, though in fact Zen was holding most of his weight. Slowly, Zen pushed him further upright. He let go with his right hand, then, looking at Mack, he let go with his left.

Tears streamed down Mack's face. He took a step – unsteady, trembling, but it was a real step.

'You're still a fucking asshole, Mack,' said Zen, turning

and rolling from the room, leaving Mack Smith standing on his own two feet for the first time in more than a month.

VIII

Bloodthirst

**Alexandria,
near Washington, D.C.
10 November 1997
0600**

Jed was just about to leave for the office when the phone rang. He grabbed it, thinking it might be Freeman.

'Barclay.'

'Well, Jed, how are you?'

'Ms O'Day?'

'How's Washington treating you?'

'It's treating me fine,' Jed told her. They hadn't spoken in nearly a year. 'How are you?'

'I was talking with a friend of ours, and decided to give you a call. I've been meaning to say hello for a long time.'

Deborah O'Day had been Jed's first boss. He had started with her as little more than an intern; she'd encouraged him and given him more responsibility. While they hadn't worked together for long, he had learned a great deal. By the time she left office with the last administration, he had become the de facto link with Dreamland and Whiplash, one of the main reasons Freeman and President Martindale had kept him on.

Jed guessed that Colonel Bastian had asked her to call.

A week before, even just a few days ago, he might have told her everything that had happened. But now he was wary: He was belatedly starting to understand that he couldn't trust *anyone* in Washington, not even friends.

'I'd like to talk,' he told her. 'But I'm kind of on my way to a meeting.'

Neither statement was a lie; they just left a lot out.

'Are you in trouble, Jed?'

'Not really. No.'

Now *that* was a lie.

'I want you to know that if trouble does come up,' she told him, 'we can find friends who will help you. Legal friends. Don't let yourself be pressured.'

'I won't.'

'And don't take the fall for anyone.'

'I wouldn't do that.'

She didn't say anything for a moment. Jed remembered watching her in her office some days, sitting and frowning at the desktop, considering what she wanted to say. He imagined she was doing that now.

'All right, Jed. Let me give you my number, just in case. You can call it whenever you need help.'

'I appreciate that.'

'You talked to Dreamland, and to Xray Pop,' said Freeman as soon as Jed entered his office a few minutes before seven. 'Why?'

Primed to be fired, the question actually caught him off guard.

'Colonel Bastian asked for some stuff, and I – I just

figured it made more sense to straighten it out for them on my own. Otherwise the whole thing, I mean, I didn't want to make it more complicated than it was.'

'Sit down, Jed.' Freeman sighed. 'Let me ask you one question before we continue.'

Here it comes, thought Jed. 'OK.'

'Do you believe in President Martindale?'

'Well, sure.'

Believe in him? He *agreed* with his positions, or most of them at least, but *believe in him?* What did that mean, exactly?

'Look, Mr Freeman, I didn't do it on purpose, but I understand it's huge,' said Jed. 'I'm ready to resign. It's OK. You don't have to let me down easy.'

'Resigning now would not be a good idea, Jed. It'll only make things much more complicated. It won't help the President, and it certainly won't help you. Senator Finegold will crucify you if she has the chance.'

Surprised – definitely relieved, but mostly surprised – Jed nodded.

'The photo hasn't appeared anywhere else, has it?' asked Freeman.

'No, sir. I was kind of wondering about that.'

'The press will move on, and this will be forgotten.'

'What if it's not?' asked Jed.

'Then we'll deal with that then. The Secretary of State still has your laptop?'

'Yes.'

Freeman frowned. 'Jeff Hartman is very ambitious, Jed. Don't forget that. He's a member of this administration – but he's also very ambitious.'

'What does that have to do with my laptop?'

'Hopefully, nothing.'

'What should I tell the President?'

'You should tell him nothing.'

Jed frowned, and Freeman repeated, *'Nothing.'*

'Wouldn't it be better –'

'Nothing.'

'But he's the President.'

'Do you trust me, Jed?'

No, thought Jed. *I don't trust anyone. Not even myself.* But he nodded. 'Yes, sir.'

'Good. Tell you what. Let's get some coffee and head over to the Pentagon. I'd like to hear what Captain Gale is planning before it happens. You can tell me what Colonel Bastian told you on the way.'

Aboard the *Abner Read*
2300

Danny Freah's stomach fluttered as the Dreamland Osprey dipped a few yards from the deck of the *Abner Read*. Weighed down by the troops in her belly, the nose of the craft dipped forward and her tail pitched sharply left, an unexpected burst of wind trying to wrestle control of the craft from the pilot. The waves snapped at the wheels of the aircraft, and the fantail of the littoral warship loomed in the window.

Danny saw Dancer's face across the cabin as the aircraft leaned hard to its right. The red hue of the interior lights softened her frown; he saw how beautiful she was under the Marine BDUs.

If I die, this is the last thing I'm going to see, he thought. *Beauty.*

The Osprey lurched backward, buffeted by another burst of wind. The tail pushed downward and the aircraft shot right. Danny grabbed for the strap near his head, pitching against one of the Marines. The aircraft sank again, but it was a more subtle, controlled maneuver, a steadying; the Osprey seemed to hiccup in the air and then hopped forward, finally stable.

'Whoa,' said one of the Marines next to him.

Whoa is right, thought Danny.

Storm saw the Osprey dip dangerously close to the waves then jerk back upright, as if the aircraft had paused to take a sip of water.

Months and years of work hung in the air for a moment, stuttering there on the fragile metal wings of the aircraft. He folded his fingers into a fist and punched the air.

'Go!' he yelled from the flying bridge at the side of the superstructure atop the *Abner Read*. 'Go!'

The aircraft stumbled again. This was a real weakness of the mission plan: They had to rely on a single aircraft to transport the assault team. That couldn't be helped – there was only one Osprey available.

Storm's stomach turned as the plane faltered. *I've put too much into this to fail now,* he thought. *Go.*

It moved sideways for a moment longer, then lurched forward, more in control. Storm lowered his night optical device and took one last long breath of the night air. If Operation Bloodthirst succeeded – *when* Operation Bloodthirst succeeded – the future of Combined Action Groups based around littoral warships like the *Abner Read* would be assured. As would his own career.

And if the operation failed, so would he. There'd be no admiralship, no hope of advance beyond captain. He'd be relieved in a heartbeat, given some obscure job counting toilet seats on the Great Lakes. Everything he'd worked for was now on the line.

On the hangar deck below, the Werewolf UAVs were pulled forward on their skids, ready for launch. The aircraft were equipped with Hellfire missiles and extra cannon pods; they looked like the beasts of the Apocalypse, ready for blood. The crews made a few last second adjustments to the weapons loads, then moved back to the hangar area as the rotors began to spin. The loud whirl made an eerie sound in the night, more a growl than a buzz; the Werewolves picked up their tails and leapt into the air, more sure-footed than the heavily loaded Osprey had been.

A half dozen of them flying with each Combined Action Group would more than fulfill the need for airborne defenses. The first thing he would do when this was over was get with Balboa and tell him the Werewolves *had* to be a Navy program. As long as this mission went well, Balboa would be easy to convince.

As long as this mission went well.

'Good takeoff, Ensign,' said Storm, lauding the officer he'd assigned to fly the robot aircraft.

'Thank you, sir, but, uh, Miss Gleason handled the takeoff.'

'Why? I directed you to. I don't want her in the Tactical Warfare Center at all unless absolutely necessary. I don't want any of the techies there while we're in combat. They're civilians.'

'Yes, sir,' mumbled the ensign.

'Give me Miss Gleason.'

'Stand by, Cap.'

'I've been in combat more than anyone on your crew,' said Jennifer Gleason, coming on the line so quickly that Storm realized she must have been listening.

Clearly there was something in the water at that damn Air Force base that made these people so disagreeable, thought Storm.

'I'm not going to argue with you, Miss Gleason.'

'*Ms* Gleason.'

'*Ms* Gleason, yes. I'm not going to argue. Combat spaces are off-limits during –'

'If something goes wrong, do you want it fixed right away, or do you want to waste ten or fifteen minutes finding me before it gets attended to?'

And it didn't help that they were always right.

'Very well, Ms Gleason,' said Storm. 'Stay out of the way.'

'With pleasure.'

Gulf of Aden
2300

His son cried for him. Ali struggled from the bed, the

blankets weighing him down. As he walked in the direc-
tion of the room, the hallway lengthened. His son's cries
intensified and he tried to walk faster, still stumbling
against sleep. One of the blankets had wrapped itself
around his midsection and tripped him as he tried to
hurry; he fell against the wall and the house gave way.

I have to reach my son, he thought.

And then he woke up.

Someone was standing over his bed. For a moment, a
terrible moment, he thought it was Abu.

'The Saudi sent me,' said the man. Ali's guards were
standing behind him.

'All right,' said Ali. He rolled over and put his feet on
the floor, legs trembling from the dream.

'You asked to be woken, Captain,' said one of the men.

'Yes,' said Ali. 'Leave us.'

'I have this,' said the messenger. He took a small card
from his pocket. A set of numbers were written on the
back. Ali led the man to the chart table at the side and
took a ruler, using the figures to measure in centimeters
from Mecca the location of the aircraft carrier.

It had come ahead of schedule. It was already in the
gulf.

They would have to leave now if they were to get out
to the Indian Ocean before it did. It might even be too
late.

The submarine could leave instantly. Some of the boats
as well.

The Yemenis had been told to fly their planes to
confuse the carrier's air cover as soon as it reached the

gulf. That perhaps would buy him some time, but not much.

Nor could the Yemenis be truly counted on. But this was what God willed.

'There is also this,' said the messenger. He pulled open his shirt. For a split second Ali thought that the man was wearing an explosive belt and had been sent by his enemies to kill him. His breath caught, and he cursed God for robbing him of the duty to avenge his son and wife.

In the next moment Ali felt ashamed for his blasphemy.

But the man was as he claimed. He took a small video from the belt, handing it to Ali. The captain took the camera off the shelf and put the cartridge inside. He pulled open the viewer at the side of the camera.

'Ali Qaed Abu Al-Harthi, may the Lord God and the Prophet Muhammad be with you,' said Osama bin Laden. 'Your blow will be the first in a long battle against the unbelievers. The Holy will rise with you and trample the infidel in the final battle. I commend you to him who sees and knows all, whose hand guides the heavens, whose wisdom illuminates the tiniest snail.'

The screen flickered and then went blank. Ali took the tape from the camera and put it into his pocket. He walked to the door.

'Help me wake the others,' he told his guards. 'We must leave right away.'

Aboard the *Wisconsin,*
over the Gulf of Aden
2310

The computer beeped, announcing that the refuel was complete. Zen took the stick, rolling *Hawk One* out from under the big black aircraft. He rode it down a moment, flying ahead of the *Wisconsin* to a preplanned course ahead of the mothership.

'*Two,*' he told the computer, and the view in his screen changed; he saw the Megafortress's tail, as if he were in *Hawk Two,* about a mile and a half behind the mothership. The verbal command was all the computer required to change positions with him, giving him direct control of *Hawk Two* while taking the stick in *Hawk One.*

He pushed *Hawk Two* in for the refuel, guided by a set of cues in the middle of his view screen. He locked in, then, as the fuel began to flow, turned *Hawk Two* over to the computer again, jumping into the cockpit of *Hawk One.*

'How are you doing, *Hawk Three*?' he asked Starship over the Dreamland radio circuit.

'Looking good,' said the other pilot. 'Quiet up here.'

'Well, don't fall asleep.'

'Commander Delaford keeps poking me to keep me awake,' said Starship. His voice suddenly became serious. 'You got a Bible, Major?'

Zen couldn't have been more surprised if Starship had come in and asked for – well, he didn't know. 'A Bible?'

'Is that too weird a question?'

'It's not weird, it's just – no offense, Starship, but you never struck me as the Bible type.'

'I'm not. I just – I wanted to read it. You know what I mean.'

The only thing Zen could remember Starship reading, outside of tech manuals, was along the lines of *Penthouse* – though generally with less words.

'Maybe you should check out the Navy chaplain when we get back to Diego Garcia. Or, you know, one of the British ministry types. They have a couple.'

'Yeah. I'll probably do that.' Starship paused a second, then added, 'You believe in God?'

'Uh-huh.'

'I think I do.'

'Good,' said Zen.

'You blame him for losing your legs?'

'I didn't lose them,' Zen snapped. 'No, I know what you mean. Probably. Sometimes I do. Yeah.'

Sometimes. Though more often he blamed Mack.

Mack mostly.

Which wasn't fair either.

How many times had he told himself that, and yet he still blamed him, didn't he? He still – did he want revenge? He remembered the screaming match, the fight that had finally gotten the asshole to walk.

Jackass.

Zen did still want revenge. Or rather, he wanted something, anything – he wanted . . .

He wanted what he could never have. And everytime he thought he could make peace with it, everytime he came up to – not accepting it, but at least willing or able to live with it – to let it sleep – it came back and bit him.

He didn't want revenge. Seeing Mack in the wheelchair hadn't felt good at all. And the proof of the damn thing was that he'd helped the idiot walk again.

The lucky SOB.

Zen was still mad, just not as mad as he had been. Or not mad in the same way. Because he couldn't blame Mack Smith, much as he wanted to. And blaming God – well, you didn't blame God. That wasn't the way it worked. If you blamed God, if you thought God did it, well then logically the next thought, the next question was: Why? If God did it, he must have had a reason.

So maybe it was God and there was a purpose, or maybe it wasn't – one way or the other, getting angry with him didn't mean zip. It left you back at square one, having to deal with it.

Which was what he did. Again and again and again.

But he didn't blame Mack anymore. Not in the same way.

'I didn't mean to pry,' said Starship.

'This isn't a good place for this kind of discussion,' said Zen.

'I'm going to get a Bible, I think, and read it,' said Starship. 'I haven't read it really.'

'Go for it,' said Zen. 'Let's get to work, OK?'

'Yes, sir.'

'Zen – the submarine is moving!' said Ensign English, breaking into the circuit.

White House Situation Room
1515

Jed paced the length of the outer conference room, waiting as the duty officers and a technician tried to clear the foul-up preventing them from tying into the Dreamland network. The secure connection had been designed to display whatever was on the main screen at Dreamland Command, but there was a glitch in the software and hardware units that did the encryption, and the screen was completely blank. The President and Freeman were en route to North Carolina, and Jed was to provide updates every fifteen minutes.

'The submarine is moving,' said Major Catsman over the speakerphone. They'd dedicated a phone line as a backup until the glitch was solved.

'Here we go,' said the technician.

A sitrep map of the northern African coast popped onto the main screen.

'No audio,' said the technician. 'That'll take another minute. I have to reboot the backup system so I can clear it.'

'Yeah, it's all right,' said Jed.

'Admiral Balboa!' said the officer who'd been sitting at the control station, jumping to his feet as Balboa and the Secretary of State walked into the room, along with two aides and the head of the CIA.

'Hello, Jed,' said Secretary of State Hartman.

'Mr Secretary, Admiral.'

'Jed.' Balboa's pronunciation of his name made it sound almost like a curse.

Jed wondered why Balboa wasn't at the Pentagon. He

guessed it had something to do with Hartman, who wasn't particularly welcome there.

Then again, the same might be said of Balboa here. Jed couldn't remember the Secretary of State ever being friendly with the admiral.

'You have an image from the Gulf of Aden operation?' asked the Secretary of State.

'It's actually a plot of the area synthesized from different sensor views, like radar and infrared,' Jed explained. 'It's usually called a sitrep or a "situational representation." The computer imposes it on a satellite photo as its base image. In theory it's what God would see if he were looking down at the earth. But of course we're only seeing what the sensors can pick up. It's in long-range view now, with the forces represented by bars and dots.'

'Which one of those dots is the *Abner Read*?' Balboa asked.

'That would be the rectangle to the right,' said the lieutenant.

He might have added that it was the rectangle with the abbreviation ABNR RD under it.

'That's the target area?' asked Balboa.

'That's the village near it. It's empty, according to the infrared. These are the buildings they think the pirates are using,' said Jed. 'There are two docks, two patrol craft twenty yards from shore, some other smaller boats all in this cluster here. Only some are probably used by the pirates. There are some defenses along the ridge, and there has to be some sort of entrance to the submarine area from the land, though we haven't found it yet. *They* haven't found it yet,' added Jed, correcting himself. 'The submarine is moving. We can't see it yet on this screen but the Piranha probe is tracking it. It's roughly here. They'll update the view at some point once they get all the sensors on line properly. They have some problems because of the connection with Xray Pop, which wasn't designed specifically to interface with the Dreamland system.'

'What kind of problems?' said Balboa.

'I don't have all the technical details,' said Jed. 'But part of the problem is probably the encryption system and the bandwidth the *Abner Read* uses. It's apparently more, um, limited, than that used by Dreamland.'

Balboa frowned. 'Inferior?'

Probably, thought Jed, but he didn't say it.

'Worried?' Hartman asked.

'No, sir.' Jed shifted on his feet awkwardly.

'Jed, we've got the sound,' the technician told him. 'You can select the circuits.'

'Thanks,' said Jed. He turned off the speakerphone and pulled the headset on.

'This is going to go well tonight?' said Hartman. He tried to smile, but his tone was less than optimistic.

Everybody in the room looked at Jed.

'I don't know,' said Jed. 'They'll do their best.'

Aboard the *Wisconsin*
2330

Zen slid the Flighthawk toward the coastline, letting his speed drop below 300 knots. The infrared viewer painted the craggy cliffs different shades of green and black, a placid mottle. But as he approached the camp, a jagged set of sticks appeared in a black triangle on the left – a lookout post with three rifles positioned to fire. The men who belonged to the rifles weren't nearby, nor was anyone in a similar post about a quarter mile on.

Two figures were moving down the cliff a few hundred yards away. Two patrol boats were idling their engines near the shore, and a third had started out of the harbor. The submarine wasn't visible on the IR scan as Zen passed.

'Positions are open, Whiplash leader,' Zen told Danny. 'I've handed over the GPS data on the emplacements they have.'

'Roger that,' Danny replied. 'We're go. Bloodthirst Command, commence firing. Ground teams are ten minutes from touching down.'

Zen took *Hawk One* higher to avoid any stray incoming shells from the *Abner Read*. Then he settled the aircraft into an orbit over the camp so it could provide real-time images to the landing team and turned it over to the computer. Back in *Hawk Two*, he took a run to the east, making sure the teams securing the village area didn't need any assistance.

Aboard the *Abner Read*
2335

The shudder of the gun rattled Storm's teeth as the 155mm shells left the ship, beginning the bombardment of the hulks in the harbor eight miles away.

The shake relaxed him completely: It was all in play now, the attack under way. Storm put his hand over his ear, filtering out the sounds around him as he listened to the action on the Dreamland Command channel. The landing area was clear; the Osprey on its way in; the submarine was moving. Thanks to the connections made by the Dreamland wizards, his Weapons people had pinpoint locations for the patrol craft at the base.

'Ready, Cap,' said Eyes.

'Target the surface craft moving from the base. We'll take them first.'

'*Craft One* is targeted,' reported Weapons. '*Craft Two* is targeted.'

'Fire Harpoons,' said Storm.

The missiles tore away from the destroyer, popping upward from their vertical launcher. Storm saw them appear in the holographic display; their targets bore tiny initials, literally marked for death.

'Let's get these bastards,' he said. He punched the communications unit at his belt. 'All hands – all personnel involved in Operation Bloodthirst – hostilities are now under way. I promise you, we will revenge the deaths of our comrades who fell in action on November 6, 1997. Each one of their deaths will be avenged tenfold.'

Gulf of Aden
2338

The first shell landed on the sunken trawler nearest to the shore just as Ali got down to the dockside. Water and shrapnel sprayed only a few feet away. A second shell exploded, this one on another hulk farther out in the harbor. The loud boom emptied the air of the noise around him. Ali felt as if he had been lifted physically away from the earth, pulled into a place above what was happening. The connection between the present and his thought was severed momentarily, and he felt as if he were independent not simply from his body, but from everything around him.

The Americans are attacking.

Satan's Tail must be offshore.

I will strangle them with my bare hands.

Another explosion, this one on the nearby wreck close to shore, shook him back to reality.

'Quickly!' he shouted. 'The Americans are attacking us! We will not lay down for them! Quickly.'

As he reached into his pocket for the phone to pass the orders along, another volley from the American guns landed, this time on the land nearby. Dust and dirt flew everywhere; he just barely managed to touch the quick-dial sequence that would signal that he was under an all-out attack. He looked at the phone, not sure if the call went through.

Send all the hell you can, he thought. There was no need to say it, however; the fact that the number was dialed and that he did not answer when called back would be enough.

Ali steadied his fingers to make a second call, alerting his crews farther west. A fresh shell burst near the shoreline, shaking the ground so severely that he dropped the phone. As he bent to grab it, another shell landed directly behind him, and the force of the explosion pushed him down the embankment toward the water. He managed to grab a large stone pillar to stop his fall.

He spit the dirt and rocks from his mouth. He'd lost the phone somewhere along the way and had to scramble back up the hill for it. Another shell landed below, near the water. Ali sensed it before he heard the explosion, and in that small space of time realized he'd been lifted upward by the force. He started to scream, but before a sound could come from his mouth, the world turned black.

Aboard Dreamland
Osprey, approaching northern Somalia
2340

Danny saw the obliterated guard posts as the feed from the Flighthawk played on the visor screen of his smart helmet. Several figures were coming from the caves near the water; another dozen were moving from the village buildings just to the east. But the top of the cliff was unprotected and he zoomed in to it, focusing on landing zone one and then two.

'*Abner Read,* be advised we are inbound to LZ. Do not shell the cliff,' said the pilot over the Dreamland circuit. 'Repeat. We're inbound and will arrive in sixty seconds.'

Someone on the *Abner Read* acknowledged. The shelling of the wrecked ships in the harbor continued; the Navy gunnery experts had predicted it would take a little more than twelve minutes to obliterate them all. As incredible as it seemed, the awesome torrent of shells made it seem like they might do it even quicker. The Werewolves had been unable to keep up with the Osprey and the accelerated schedule;

they were running behind him by about ten minutes. He'd make the landings without them.

'Team One is up!' shouted Geraldo 'Blow' Hernandez, who was acting as jumpmaster, supervising the exit of the aircraft via the ropes. 'Team One is up!'

The Marines and three of Danny's men moved toward the door as the Osprey revved into hover mode, its tilt-wing swinging around as the craft arced to the disembarkation point. Danny's men were used to the jolt of weightlessness that this induced, but the Marines weren't, and even the men who had been with them on the mission the night before jerked against their straps and each other.

'Go! Go! Hit the ropes, let's go, let's go, let's go!' yelled Boston.

'Do it, men!' yelled Dancer. 'Make your mamas proud!'

Danny watched her grab a rope and go down with the rest of the team. They'd given up trying to use the Marine systems with the smart helmets and Dreamland circuit; instead, Danny had given her a backup short-range radio-only headset so she could talk directly to him. His people had been split up to work with different knots of Marines.

'Team Two coming up! Team Two coming up!' yelled Boston.

Danny moved with the rest of them. The Osprey swung around to get into position. One of the chain guns beneath the front of the aircraft began to rotate, spitting bullets at the lip of the crag. Danny thought they were probably shooting at ghosts, but there wasn't time to question the pilots – he put his gloved hands onto the rope, pulled his feet into place, and fast-roped down.

The Osprey stuttered backward as he descended, shuddering under the weight of bullets it was firing. But he got on the ground solidly, pushing to the left as the rest of the team came out.

'Incoming!' yelled someone as Danny jumped from the aircraft. Something flashed thirty yards ahead; it was a rocket-launched grenade fired nearly point-blank, but fortunately without much of an aim. Running forward, Danny peppered the area where it had come from with his MP5 before sliding down to one knee. There was no answering fire.

He swiveled his head back and forth as he took stock of the situation. More gunfire erupted to his right; three members of his team, all Marines, were engaged with someone at the very edge of the cliff.

'Grenade!' someone yelled.

It could have been a warning or a suggestion; in any event, nothing exploded. Two muzzles flashed from the direction of the sea to Danny's extreme left; more terrorists coming up to the defense. The gunfire was answered by someone behind him.

Men were still coming off the Osprey, easy targets.

'Get the machine guns up!' yelled Danny. 'Get the bastards on the cliff down! Go!'

More pirates came up the cliff and began to fire, bullets blazing everywhere. Something exploded behind him; as he turned to look, he saw the right wing of the Osprey break apart, struck by a mortar shell that had the incredibly bad luck to land on the engine housing and detonate. The aircraft veered sideways, spun forward, then sailed toward the water.

'Son of a bitch!' yelled Boston into his open mike.

Danny threw one of his grenades toward the cliff where he'd seen the muzzle flashes. Someone else had the same idea, and their grenade exploded first, followed quickly by Danny's. Jumping to his feet, Danny ran forward, emptying the MP5 before diving flat on the ground, next to a Marine. He slapped a new magazine into his weapon and fired a few rounds. There was no return fire, but just to be sure, he threw another grenade.

'Come on, Marine, come on!' he yelled, jumping to his feet after it exploded. As Danny took a step, a fresh burst of automatic rifle fire stoked up from the right and he threw himself back down. He didn't fire back; he had people in that direction and in the scramble now couldn't be positive who was where. He tried crawling forward but the ground began percolating with gunfire.

'Let's get that machine gun over here!' Danny yelled at the Marine he'd just left. The man lay a few feet behind him, still hugging the ground. 'Yo, Marine, come on,' said Danny pushing back toward him. He grabbed for the man's shoulder; it came without resistance. It was only then that he realized the man had been killed.

Aboard the *Wisconsin*
2350

Zen stared at the Osprey as it flew over the cliff, unsure exactly what was going on for a moment. Then he realized that the wing and engine had broken off and the aircraft was going down. The left rotor tried valiantly to hold the doomed MV-22 upright, but within a second or so the fuselage sagged to the right. The Osprey veered backward and then into a wide arc, slinging down toward the water. A fireball erupted from the aircraft, spitting in the direction of the terrorist village, as if the Osprey had spit at its enemy, a final insult before diving into the grave.

The screen flared as the rest of the MV-22 caught fire. It hit the water a moment later, debris, fire, and steam erupting as if from a volcano. Zen had already started to bring *Hawk Two* over the area; he pressed the throttle against its stop, trying to accelerate.

'We have a downed aircraft,' he said. 'Osprey. Bad. No chance of survivors.'

'Acknowledged,' said Dog.

'I'm bringing *Hawk Two* overhead and then will provide fire support for the landing team,' said Zen. 'Where the hell are those Werewolves?'

'Werewolves are still three minutes out,' said Dog. 'They're doing their best, Zen.'

'They're going to have to do better.'

Aboard the *Abner Read*
2351

Storm stood over the newly installed Werewolf console in the Tactical Warfare Center. 'Let's move it, let's move it,' he told Ensign Young.

'I'm doing the best I can, sir.'

Best wasn't good enough, Storm realized.

'Dreamland,' he said, turning to Jennifer Gleason. 'Can you do anything with this or not?'

'Damn straight, if you let me,' she told him.

'Well do it. Go. Go, do it.'

She moved toward the console. The ensign hesitated, glancing back at Storm, then quickly jumped up.

'Werewolf Control Computer, override established programming, authorization JenJen4356,' said Jennifer, pulling on the headset.

She got a tone and instructions on the main screen:

> OVERRIDE.
> DESIGNATE NEW ORDERS.
> W1 & W2 WILL CONTINUE ON PRESENT COURSE
> UNTIL NEW ORDERS ENTERED.

'Auto designate mode, full pilot command, disregard safety protocols, authorization JenJen4356. Disregard tactical encyclopedia, authorization JenJen4356.'

As soon as the computer acknowledged, Jennifer punched the function key to designate targets. The computer didn't beep for some reason, failing to accept the command.

'Free-form mode,' she told the computer. 'Sitrep on main screen,' she added, asking for a bird's-eye view of the aircraft and the battlefield.

The sitrep failed to come up.

All right, she told herself, you're not thinking clearly

because your adrenaline is blasting. Take a deep breath and go back to the beginning.

She took two breaths, neither as deep and slow as she wanted, then called for the sitrep again. Again the image failed to come up. She was sure she'd done it right; there must be a glitch in the connection with the Dreamland circuit.

There wasn't any time to figure out where the problem was; the Werewolves were almost at their target and would begin firing on their own as soon as they arrived.

'Manual Command,' she said. 'Complete override. Authorization JenJen4356.'

MANUAL COMMAND.

'Trial mode. W1 is lead.'

TRIAL MODE. W1 IS LEAD.

'Good computer,' she said.

UNKNOWN COMMAND.

Jennifer reached to the pad of function keys on the left-hand side of the console, hitting key 3 for a video image. It was dark and the image was blurry, but she could see enough to make out the approaching cliffside.

'Werewolf to Whiplash commander, what's the important target?' Jennifer asked.

'The buildings,' said Storm.

'I'm not asking you, I want Danny . . . Danny – Whiplash commander, where do you want the Werewolves?'

The reply came back garbled.

'Jen, they're pinned down on the ridge by mortar fire from below,' said Dog over the Dreamland circuit. 'Zen is en route.'

'I'm there – give me the location. There's a glitch in the

system and I can't get the data through you directly. I don't have time to figure it out, but I can gun it manually.'

'McNamara will guide you in. I'm not even going to ask what's going on over there,' added Dog.

'Talk to you later,' she said. 'Kevin?'

'This is McNamara,' said Dog's copilot. 'Jen?'

'I have the Werewolves. Give me a rough idea where that mortar is so I can erase it.'

'Stand by.'

Northern Somalia,
on the ground
2355

Danny took the Marine's machine gun. The plastic box that contained the belt of 5.56mm slugs remained full; the Marine had two more boxes at his belt. A mortar round landed nearby; Danny grabbed the boxes and dragged the gun with him as he looked for better cover.

'Captain Freah, this is Werewolf.'

'Jennifer?'

'I'm going to take out the mortars. They're firing from down near the beach.'

'Go for it,' said Danny, skidding into a shallow gully. He could just barely hear the roar of the Werewolves somewhere below, launching their rockets at the pirates on the beach.

He flipped the smart helmet's screen into a sitrep mode, which should have shown him the location of his men.

But the screen was blank; either something aboard the *Wisconsin* or in his unit had gone offline.

'Yo, Boston, where are you?' Danny asked over the short-range team radio channel.

'We're about twenty meters from the lip of the canyon,' said the sergeant. 'There's a set of spider holes or maybe tunnels behind some of the rocks to the left. That's where the ragheads are coming from. We've been trying to get some grenades down it but we haven't made it. And they have a pretty good line of fire.'

'Do you have a good location?'

'I can get pretty damn close.'

'All right. Stand by.'

Danny switched into the Dreamland circuit. 'Jen? I have a hole that needs to be filled. If we use the laser designator to mark it out, can you hit it with the Hellfires after you get the mortars?'

'Do it.'

'Boston, move back and lase it. I'll get the Werewolves in.'

'Working on it, Cap.'

'Whiplash leader, this is Werewolf. Tell your people to duck.'

There was a roar below as one of the Werewolves began chewing up the beach area with its chain guns. Then the ridge exploded with a barrage of Hellfires raining down on the spot Boston had designated with the laser. The AGM-114C was not the optimum weapon for the attack against the foxholes, but the roughly eighteen pounds worth of explosives in its nose did a more than adequate landscaping job anyway, permanently rearranging the geography of the cliffside.

'Boston, you OK?' Danny asked as the smoke cleared.

'Oh yeah, we're cool. We're moving up.'

'Pretty Boy, you on the line?' asked Danny, trying to sort out where everyone was now that the biggest threat had been dealt with.

'I'm your left flank, Cap,' Sergeant Jack Floyd replied. 'We're moving to the ridge.'

'Bison?'

The sergeant didn't answer. He would have been one of the last men out of the Osprey.

'Everybody, take the ridge,' Danny yelled. He cradled the M249 under his arm and began running for it himself.

Aboard the *Abner Read*
2351

Jennifer pulled *Werewolf One* to the west, glancing quickly at the window in the lower left-hand corner of the screen, which showed the aircraft's vital signs. Everything was in the green.

'Werewolf, keep to the south,' said Zen. 'I'm taking a run at the patrol boat off to the east. Remember, they're still shelling the hulks in the harbor.'

'Negative, Flighthawk leader,' said Eyes, cutting in. 'We're targeting the patrol craft with Harpoons.'

'Roger that, I see them inbound. This boat isn't targeted.'

'We don't have it.'

'Watch where I go and you will.'

'Standing by.'

As Jennifer cleared out from below the cliff, she saw a group of shadows down by the water. She pushed the stick in their direction but was moving too fast to get a shot without the computer's automated targeting system, which she'd had to take offline to gain control. She tried to flip *Werewolf Two* out of its automated trail mode but couldn't manage it quickly enough to get a shot with that aircraft either.

And it was a good thing. She saw that the men were moving toward the shore, not away from it. It was the second landing party coming in to try and cut off retreat. She took a deep breath and went back to work.

Storm turned toward the holographic display as the words cut through the cacophony around him:

'Submarine is out of the pen – moving at twelve or fifteen knots to the east, to get away from the break-waters and barriers,' said Eyes.

Don't let the bastards get away. Don't let the bastards get away!

'Weapons, target the submarine,' he said.

'We don't have it on the targeting system. The sound is being obscured by the channel and the battle,' Eyes interrupted. 'We have the location from the Dreamland people and we're keeping track.'

'What's the status of the bombardment?' Storm asked.

'Another few minutes.'

'As soon as it's complete, move east with the

submarine so he doesn't get away,' said Storm. 'I want that son of a bitch.'

Aboard *Baker-Baker Two*
2359

Starship found it difficult to concentrate with the chatter on the Dreamland circuit, but he didn't want to completely turn it off. They were flying just outside the territorial limits of Yemen. The usual assortment of ground radars were working, but at the moment they had the skies to themselves.

Flipping back and forth between two aircraft wasn't as easy as Zen made it seem. Starship found it too easy to confuse which one he was in, since there were no visual cues on the main screen. Granted, part of the problem was that he was flying at night, and there were pretty much no visual cues period, just distant lights and the looming shadow of the Megafortress. But it couldn't take all that much to program in a line indicating which flight you were looking at, a color-coded bar or number at the top of the screen, say.

'*Hawk Three*, this is *Baker-Baker Two*,' said Breanna. 'We have a flight from the *Ark Royal* coming south. The Brits are running a bit ahead of schedule.'

Starship glanced at the sitrep map. The aircraft carrier was at the very far end of the screen, as were two Harrier aircraft flying patrol nearby. The Harriers were versatile aircraft, though not much of a match for front-line fighters or the tiny Flighthawks, which were invisible to their radar except at very close range.

'We've advised them an operation is in progress,' Breanna added. 'Their course will take them through the center of the gulf, as we were briefed. Closest point of contact with the operation should be about seventy nautical miles in an hour or so. I'm advising the rest of the task force.'

'Roger that,' said Starship.

He leaned back in his seat. Commander Delaford was working the Piranha controls next to him. He was in his own world, literally miles away.

'I have two MiGs, coming off Aden,' said Spiderman, referring to an airfield in southern Yemen. 'They may be interested in the *Ark Royal*.'

'Let them know,' said Breanna.

'Doing so.'

The two MiGs were identified as MiG-29UBs, an export model of the front-line Russian lightweight fighter. They were about two hundred miles away from *Baker-Baker Two*.

'Another pair right behind them,' added Spiderman.

'Must be putting on quite a show for the British,' said Starship, turning *Hawk Three* back toward the Megafortress.

'*Hawk Three*, be advised that first flight of MiGs is changing course,' said Spiderman a minute later. 'I may be paranoid, but they look like they're on a direct vector toward the assault area. And they're *moving*.'

White House Situation Room
1600

Jed folded his arms tightly against his chest, staring at the sitrep screen from the *Wisconsin*. It showed the assault team on the ground, moving down the slopes – the positions of the Whiplash team members were marked with green triangles – as well as the locations of the aircraft and ships involved in the operation, all superimposed on a satellite photo of the area. The downed Osprey was marked by the computer with a black rectangle.

'Damn it, what the hell is going on down there?' said Balboa.

'The Osprey was struck from the ground,' said Jed.

'I meant that rhetorically,' said Balboa. 'Storm should have asked for more support. He's a good officer, but he goes off half-cocked.'

Jed stared at the screen, trying very hard not to point out that this was a textbook example of the pot calling the kettle black.

'It sounds confused there,' said the Secretary of State.

'Yes, sir. It is a bit,' said Jed.

'This isn't going as well as I'd hoped,' muttered Hartman.

'It's not over yet,' said Jed, unsure what else to say.

Danny reached the cliffside just as Boston went down. A pair of automatic rifles popped below, but he couldn't see where the enemy was. A Werewolf screamed along the beach area to the right but didn't fire.

Danny saw a knot of soldiers working their way down above the beach area. He knew the hulking shadow in the middle was Boston, but the friend-or-foe identifier system wasn't placing an upside triangle on the screen to indicate Friend, as it should have.

'Whiplash team, this is Whiplash commander,' he said. 'I have a malfunction with the friend-or-foe identifier. It may be common to everyone. Use extreme caution.'

'Hey, Cap, think I have the same problem,' said Boston, ' 'cause I'm looking back up at you and can't see your triangle.'

'Our set's working,' said Sergeant Liu. 'We'll use caution, however. We have some of the pirates pinned down.'

As Danny ended his transmission, gunfire stoked up from his direction. He craned his neck upward but couldn't see anything.

'Werewolves, this is Whiplash leader,' said Danny. 'We're having trouble with the friend-or-foe.'

'I heard,' said Jennifer. 'There's no time to sort it out now. Use the laser designator for targets and I'll have the Werewolves attack only at designated targets.'

'Good,' said Danny. '*Wisconsin*?'

'Yeah, we're copying,' said Dog. 'We see your team going down the face of the cliff. There's some sort of glitch in the programming. My bet is the interface with Xray Pop.'

'Good guess,' said Jennifer.

'Heads up!' yelled Boston.

Almost simultaneously a series of explosions rocked the base of the cliff. Danny fell on his butt and began sliding down the hillside, knocking into one of the Marines. An AK47 began firing directly below, quickly answered by M16s and M4s. By the time Danny got to his knees the gunfire had stopped.

'Couple of caves there, Cap,' said Boston. 'Mo-fo's are holed up in them.'

Mo-fo was Boston's abbreviation for a none-too-polite street term.

'Can you lase the cave?' Danny asked.

'Yeah, I'm going to try.'

'Jen?'

'On it, Whiplash.'

As the Werewolves spun out from over the ocean, one of the ships in the water began firing at it. The arc of gunfire provided just enough light for Danny to see the black streak of a Harpoon missile as it approached. Or at least he thought he saw it – in the next moment the space where the ship had been flashed white and the ocean erupted. The Werewolves, meanwhile, stuttered in the air as their cannons sprayed lead on the caves. Danny got up, grabbing hold of the Marine nearby and tugging him along; within a few seconds they had found a path and were able to clamber down to a ledge where three other members of the team were huddled.

Something flashed to the left.

Mortar, thought Danny. Before he had time to react, two of the Marines had begun firing in that direction and a third had used the grenade launcher on his rifle to obliterate the terrorist.

A second Harpoon struck another ship in the water, this one farther from shore. There was a flash but no secondary explosion.

'Jen, pull the Werewolves out,' said Danny. 'Let's take stock.'

'Clear sailing, Cap,' said Boston ten or fifteen yards below.

'Don't get too cocky,' said Danny.

'Hey, cocky's my middle name. Just ask the girls.'

As if in answer, a machine gun began chewing up the rocks in Boston's general vicinity. Once more the Marines near Danny answered with a combination of rifle fire and grenades; the weapon fell silent.

'Team One? Dancer, what are you doing?' Danny asked as the pandemonium subsided.

'We're at the edge of the village,' answered Sergeant Liu. 'Lieutenant Dancer is preparing a team to begin a sweep.'

'All right. Dancer, are you on the circuit?'

There was no reply.

'She can't hear you, Cap. Another malfunction, I think. I'll pass the word along.'

'Listen, tell her we're moving ahead the way we drew it up.'

'Gotcha,' said Liu.

415

By now the rest of the team was moving in the direction of the caves and shoreline. The landing party from the Shark Boat had engaged a small force at the base of the cliff and was exchanging fire. Danny sent Pretty Boy and two of his Marines in that direction, telling them to try and get into a position where they could either use grenades to attack the pirates or lase them for the Werewolves. He and the others went down the hillside to join with Boston and the Marines, who were clearing the caves.

'Back!' yelled Boston as he tossed a grenade inside one of the openings. The team ducked down as the weapon exploded, then immediately rose again and peppered the opening with gunfire. Despite the heavy onslaught, at least one of the pirates managed to survive long enough to fire back when the party started inside the cave. The earth itself seemed to erupt as the Americans returned fire, nearly everyone emptying their mags on the black hole.

'Discipline! Discipline!' yelled someone as the gunfire died down.

Good advice, thought Danny, though it had about as much effect as yelling stop at a runaway train.

'I'm OK,' said Boston, who apparently had been hit by the gunfire, fortunately in his boron vest. 'Two grenades on the next one,' he added, apparently talking to one of the Marines, not Danny. 'One deep, one shallow.'

'And then a second wave,' said Danny. 'These bastards have nine lives.'

'Mo-fo's always do, Cap.'

The *Abner Read* was capable of launching torpedoes from either its vertical-launch tubes as missiles or its below-waterline tubes near the middle of the ship. The vertical-launched torpedoes had a somewhat longer range, adding approximately six miles to the seven that the torpedo alone could run. While the submarine was within range, the targeting system on the *Abner Read* had trouble picking it out. Storm waited impatiently as the *Abner Read* heaved around, paralleling the submarine and waiting for it to clear into an easier targeting area.

'We have the target,' said Eyes, relaying the message from Weapons to Storm, who was still on the bridge with Peanut and the bridge crew.

'Fire.'

Two missiles popped from the vertical launching pods on the forward deck, their rocket motors igniting them and steering them unsteadily in the direction of the submarine. Launching torpedoes like this had always seemed to Storm an unnatural and awkward act, more so because the erupting rockets always appeared to lurch in the air, moving unsteadily as if the torpedo they propelled in the canister was literally a fish out of water. The ASROC system, however, had been perfected over several decades, and the idea of launching torpedoes from missile pods was little more than an extension of firing them from aircraft – an art perfected in World War II. Lengthening their effective range made excellent sense, allowing a surface ship to strike a submarine before it became vulnerable itself.

The *Abner Read*'s designers had planned for her to carry the latest weapons, and had accordingly designed both the vertical-launching system and torpedo tubes – along with their associated targeting and control systems – for the MK-50 and MK-54 torpedo. The MK-50 in particular was an excellent torpedo. Relatively slim at 12.75 inches in diameter, the torpedo – in its upgraded version – could avoid countermeasures, operate entirely on its own once fired, and strike virtually any ship or submarine operating in the world. The MK-54 was a lighter version of the MK-50, equipped with a more limited guidance system, in essence a poor man's version of the very expensive MK-50 tuned to operate in shallow water.

Unfortunately, neither weapon was aboard the *Abner Read*. The MK-54 – which probably would have been a good choice here – was still in development and not yet available. And the cost of the MK-50 had limited the Navy's purchases. Because it was in short supply, the powers-that-be had rationed it among the Navy ships and aircraft capable of carrying it. The *Abner Read* had not made the cut. Instead, its tubes were filled with old standbys, the MK-46.

When they were first deployed in 1966, the MK-46 torpedoes were at least arguably the best of their class: lightweight, versatile killers with about a hundred pounds of explosives in their teeth. Thirty years and several upgrades later, they were problematic weapons in areas where the shallow water, other nearby contacts, and a system admittedly designed for different weapons, multiplied the confusion factor exponentially.

One of the torpedoes failed completely after it entered the water; the reason wasn't clear. The other, however, made a beeline for the sub. Traveling at 45 knots, the torpedo needed nearly eight minutes to get to its target. By the fourth minute it became clear that it had lost its way; by the fifth, it had veered off course toward the shoreline. The operator couldn't tell what it was tracking, and Storm didn't particularly care.

He gave the order for the ship to close in on the submarine, which was running in snorkel mode almost exactly due east about three-quarters of a mile from the coast.

'Captain, that's going to take us out of the designated patrol area,' said Peanut.

'Are you questioning my orders?' barked Storm.

'No, sir.'

'Then do it. Eyes!'

'Cap?'

'Target the submarine.'

'Weapons is working on it.'

'Active sonar. Find the bastards.'

'Yes, sir,' said Eyes.

The room fell silent for a moment. 'Submarine is targeted,' Eyes said finally.

'Launch!'

The weapons bolted from the launcher.

'Patrol craft coming out from the east,' reported Eyes. 'Two miles.'

'Where'd he come from?' asked Storm.

'Just popped in there.'

Storm barked out orders that the ship be sunk. Within seconds the *Abner Read* reverberated with the steady thud of the 155mm Advanced Gun System. It took a dozen shots to strike the pirate craft, but only two to sink it.

'*Torpedoes in the water!*' warned the computer.

'Evasive action,' Storm said. 'Use the Prairebot.'

'We're down to two, Cap,' said Peanut.

'Now or never.'

'Prairebot.'

The order was passed and *Abner Read*'s forward torpedo tubes opened, expelling the devices. They swam about a quarter of a mile and began emitting their bubble fog. The two torpedoes were completely baffled, and circled back in the direction from which they'd been fired.

Storm glanced at the hologram. He could only find one of his torpedoes tracking the submarine.

'Weapons, how are we doing on that submarine?' he asked.

'Torpedo three missed, sir. Another malfunction. Four is running true.'

'Fire torpedoes five and six.'

'That will empty the vertical launching system,' said Peanut.

'I can count.'

'Target acquired, target locked,' said Weapons.

'Fire, damn it! I want the sharks picking over his bones before daybreak.'

'Firing ASROC torpedoes.'

'We better hit the damn thing this time,' muttered Storm as the rockets whipped away from the ship.

* * *

While the two Werewolves were performing well, real-life combat was proving harder on resources than the test range. *Werewolf Two* was not only out of Hellfires, but down to its last hundred rounds of bullets, and borderline on fuel. Jennifer plotted a course for it to fly back to the *Abner Read* to reload and refuel; if the crews moved quickly enough, she could keep at least one aircraft over the battle area. She had to dial into the aircraft maintenance channel to talk to the mate there, but couldn't find the preset, and ended up resorting to the common intercom channel. Someone acknowledged anyway, and she told the computer to bring the Werewolf back to the deck of the ship, safing the weapons just in case it became rambunctious.

'What are you doing with that aircraft?' demanded Storm.

'There's a knot of pirates hiding in that building there by the water,' Jennifer told him.

'No, the other one, heading toward us.'

'I need to refuel and rearm.'

'We can't recover it now. We're in the middle of a battle.'

Jennifer twisted toward him ferociously. 'What the hell do you want me to do with it? Crash it into the shoreline?'

Storm's face went white. She thought for a moment that he would take a swing at her. But instead he turned, and she heard him ordering someone to prepare to recover the aircraft.

Ali's son called to him from the pool, yelling to his father for help. They'd gone to visit his cousin Abdul, and the boy was playing in the back while the adults debated the obligations a man had to God and his family. Ali's cousin had just claimed that the family must come first – blasphemy, or close to it, Ali argued, for wasn't that the point of the story of Abraham?

His son's cries shook him; there was something in his voice that he had never heard before, a kind of immediate terror that pulled Ali to action. The father sprang to help the son, bolting over the wall at the back of the yard.

The pool was only a few yards away, yet with every step Ali took it moved no closer. He saw his son Abu go under. Ali ran faster, faster, ran with all his might, yet got no closer to saving him, no closer to pulling him out.

Lightning split the sky. Something pushed Ali's head into the dirt. He felt himself flying into the water, flying into the pool.

This isn't happening, he thought. This is a dream, one of the dreams.

I would never have withstood God's test. I would not have killed my son for the Lord's sake, even though I should have. I am not worthy to be a follower of the Prophet.

The ground shook. Ali swallowed a mouthful of saltwater and grit. He began to choke uncontrollably.

Somewhere in the middle of the fit he realized that he was lying at the edge of the water, his body twisted and his rifle in his hand.

A dark shadow filled the water in front of him.

Satan's Tail.

I will be avenged. I cannot achieve my mission, but I will be avenged on Satan. Let me strangle the bastard demon with my bare hands and take him to hell with me.

He pushed down, rising from the water. There were two, three, more of his men nearby.

'The ship – the American ship is out there,' he said, pointing. 'I am going aboard and fighting them hand-to-hand.'

He started into the water. Two or three of his men followed and pulled him back.

'Let me go!' he yelled. 'Let me go!'

'Captain, it's not Satan's Tail. It's one of their smaller ships,' said Saed. 'We've shot down one of their planes. They've sent a boat to look for survivors.'

In his fury, Ali had a hard time understanding the words. Finally, he understood what his lieutenant was trying to say.

'Our patrol craft have gotten out, all but two,' said Saed. He held up a satellite phone. 'The submarine is gone. I've passed the order to the *Sharia* to attack the aircraft carrier. They will not fail.'

'Tell them instead to attack Satan's Tail,' Ali told him.

'But –'

'Do it. Then gather every man you can find and get them into fishing boats. Quickly!' he yelled. 'We have only a little time.'

* * *

Danny selected full magnification in the visor, looking at the rocks.

'Yeah, it's definitely booby-trapped,' he told Boston, who'd first pointed it out. 'Question is, why would they bother?'

'Worth finding out, don't you think?' asked the sergeant.

'All right, we'll come back.' He turned to one of the Marines nearby and told him to watch the cave entrance. 'It's booby-trapped, so stay back, and keep everybody else back,' added Danny.

'Captain, the lieutenant wants to talk to you,' said Liu. 'I'm giving her my helmet.'

'All right.'

'Captain?'

'Yeah, Dancer, go ahead.'

'We think we've found the headquarters in Building Two here. I'm getting the demolition team to look at it now, with one of your men. You want to come and see?'

The buildings were about two hundred yards to the east.

'I'll be along in a few minutes, once we're sure we have this side of the camp secured. Have you heard from the Shark Boat on the Osprey rescue?'

'Negative. My whole communication system is gone,' she said. 'Even the Marine unit.'

'I'll get back to you.'

'My best guess is they used it to store weapons and ammo, Cap,' said Boston. 'Couple of boxes of ammo for AK47s on the ground there. Might've grabbed them when we were coming.'

'All right. Take your team and hook up with the Navy shore party moving in from the west off the Shark Boat,'

Danny told him. 'I'm going to go with Pretty Boy and see what Dancer has.'

'She's hot,' said Boston. 'For a Marine.'

'I'll forget you said that, Sergeant,' snapped Danny.

Aboard the *Wisconsin*
0015

As the situation on shore settled down, Zen turned his attention to the water and the spot where the Osprey had crashed, about a half mile west from the mooring area. He crisscrossed as slowly as possible overhead, hoping the infrared sensors would pick up something in the water he could direct the Shark Boat's crews to. The Navy craft had sent two small inflatable boats to the area; Zen could talk to them by communicating with the ship's commander via one of the portable Dreamland communication systems. He took a first pass at three thousand feet, circling back and dropping lower, working the Flighthawk down through two thousand. He activated the C^3 search-and-rescue mode, directing the Flighthawk's computer to look for men in the water. The computer began beeping immediately, drawing a box about three hundred yards from the northernmost boat.

Zen vectored the rescuers toward them and pushed the Flighthawk even lower, edging down close to five hundred feet. His airspeed bled off and he got a stall warning, C^3 getting nervous.

'*Boat Two* has recovered one body,' reported the Shark

Boat captain after he passed along the coordinates. 'Pretty mangled.'

'Flighthawk leader.'

Dog looked at the radar plot from *Baker-Baker Two* showing the two flights of Yemen MiGs. The aircraft had been flying on the same course for nearly five minutes; there seemed no doubt they were flying toward the assault area.

'*Baker-Baker Two*, this is *Wisconsin*. Bree, intercept those MiGs. I don't want them in the assault area.'

'And if they don't turn back?'

'Direct them to. If they arm their weapons, engage and shoot them down.'

'*Baker-Baker*. Will do.'

'You don't think that's too aggressive, Colonel?' asked the copilot.

'I've already lost an aircraft and its crew,' replied Dog. 'I don't intend on losing any others.'

Northern Somalia,
on the ground
0021

Dead bodies lay on both sides of the wooden planks on the rock-strewn coastline. More than three dozen pirates had been killed, many by the bombardment. Several corpses were missing large parts of their anatomy. A head had landed on the rocks, eyes open, face contorted with pain, as if the man were emerging from hell below.

Danny stared at it, not unnerved exactly, but arrested by the grotesqueness of war and death. The man was his enemy, and surely would have killed him without remorse. Yet Danny felt a stab of pity for him. The absurd futility captured by the man's death stare reached through the body armor Danny wore, reached past the tough shell he donned to do his job. The Air Force captain had seen much brutality in the past few years – he'd been in Bosnia and the former Yugoslavia before joining Whiplash, and had come to know the many ways a corpse could be mangled. But each time he faced death again, there was something fresh, something unexpected, something still capable of eliciting pity and even sorrow.

He reminded himself what his job was and plunged on, following the Marine private across the wooden planks that formed a narrow and crude boardwalk to the main area of the compound. There were more bodies here, including two that belonged to Americans. Danny saw the young man who'd been ahead of him stop, then pitch forward to his hands and knees.

Danny gave him a moment, then leaned down close to his ear.

'Take a second,' he told the young Marine. 'But then you have to move on. For yourself. You can't do anything for them now. We'll grieve later.'

'Yes, sir,' said the Marine, voice choked with tears.

Danny rose and walked alone toward the corner of a nearby building, where another member of the team crouched with an M249 machine gun. Calling the structure a building was optimistic; it was more a hovel that leaned against the side of the hill.

'Down here, Danny,' said Dancer.

He spotted her near the largest of the buildings, on the side overlooking one of the docks. He made his way down quickly.

'We have no more resistance, or at least they've stopped firing,' she said. 'There are two speedboats, some other small open boats tied up in the water on that side there. The *Abner Read* has taken care of the hulks. There doesn't seem to be anyone in them.' She turned and pointed to the boats in the water. 'This building looks like a command post. There's radio equipment and other gear inside. We didn't see any booby traps.'

'It's clean,' Liu said behind her.

'All right,' said Danny. 'Next objective is the cave where the submarine was, beyond that dock and the breakwater there. Piranha reports no vessels inside, but there may be people.'

'I'd like a chance to help in the search for our people on the Osprey,' said Dancer. 'I think we should do that first.'

'I think we can assist the search while we're looking for an entrance to the pen,' Danny told her. 'We need to get the divers in before we take on the cave. The Shark Boat too. I don't want to start an assault, or a possible assault, until we have all the possible entrances covered anyway. I'll check on what the possibilities are while you take charge of the search. Why don't you take Sergeant Liu and two of your Marines with you?'

'Thank you, I will,' said Dancer. 'And I'm holding on to your sergeant's hat. Does this thing get baseball games?'

'Only Yankee games.'

'Those are the only ones I watch.'

'Hey, Captain! I got people! Up here in the second tier of hovels.'

Dancer and a Marine trailed Danny as he trotted up the hill and then climbed a short set of rock steps to Boston. The sergeant was holding his M4 on a pair of frail-looking women. One was middle-aged, the other in her early twenties. They wore heavy black clothes with veils drawn over their faces.

'I have a couple of civilians,' Danny said over the Dreamland Command circuit. 'I need the Arabic translator.'

'He's on the line,' said Major Catsman.

As Danny started to ask for the words 'We mean no harm,' the younger woman jumped up.

'Grenade!' yelled Boston.

Without thinking, Danny threw himself at the woman. Boston tried to grab the grenade, which flew up into the air. Twisting back, Danny saw it hover a few inches above his head, an old Russian-style weapon.

He also saw very clearly that its pin had been pulled.

Aboard *Baker-Baker Two*
0025

Starship took *Hawk Three* down to 25,000 feet, running head-on at the first element of MiG-29s. The aircraft were moving fairly quickly, around 600 knots. They were fifty miles away from his nose; the combined speeds of the aircraft meant they'd run through each other's windshields in a little more than three minutes if nothing changed.

Hawk Four paralleled *Three* by two and a half miles. Starship took control of the plane directly and started a slight turn farther east. 'Intercept doublet pattern Zen-Two,' he told the computer, naming a preset tactical maneuver that Zen used so often it had been named after him. While the contingencies of the encounter could immensely complicate what happened, the outline of the plan was simple: *Hawk Three* would engage the flight nearly head-on, attacking the lead plane, which was running a bit farther west and higher than the second MiG. *Hawk Four* would angle in from the east, aiming for a tail attack on the second MiG as it broke and ran or moved to help its mate.

'Real' pilots probably wouldn't have chosen the attack – for one thing, they'd be flying aircraft with missiles capable of engaging the enemy at long range – but the plan took advantage of the Flighthawk's strengths. The computer was much better at making close-quarter rear-end attacks than it was at any other angle; in fact, it was probably as good as Starship was, so letting C^3 take the plane and follow that attack plan gave it a high chance of success. The small profile of the aircraft meant that neither plane would be detected by the MiGs' radar until practically the moment that Starship began firing. He'd not only be able to begin the engagement on his terms, but probably fire and be beyond the enemy fighter before it even knew he was there.

If he missed and both Yemen aircraft went after *Hawk Three* – the aggressive and logical action – Starship could easily turn and continue to concentrate on his original target, even if the enemy's wingmate maneuvered to get on his tail. That's what he wanted it to do, since it would give *Hawk Four* an easier and more predictable target. And if both planes turned to run away, they would be sitting ducks, at least until their afterburners helped them regain momentum.

Ironically, the strongest answer to Zen-Two was to split and take each Flighthawk head-on – then go for afterburners and cruise home at a couple of times the speed of sound. While it was unlikely to yield a kill for the MiGs, it also presented the Flighthawks with the least amount of tango time – and the higher the tango time for the Flighthawks, the higher the tomb time for the opponents.

One of Kick's favorite sayings.

Kick's not here, Starship thought. Time to let him rest.

'*Hawk Three*? What's your situation?' asked Breanna.

'Lining up for an intercept. Weapons are ready.'

'Roger that,' said Breanna. He heard her switch over to the frequency the Yemen pilots were using and broadcast a prerecorded warning in Arabic that they were approaching a U.S. aircraft and were to turn back.

'No acknowledgment,' said Spiderman after a few seconds.

'All channels,' said Breanna.

The warning was repeated, again without an acknowledgment. Just for good measure, Spiderman repeated it in English.

'They certainly know we're here,' said Telly, the airborne radar warning operator. 'Their fuzz busters are probably hotter than a toaster in a boardinghouse.'

'Intercept in zero-two minutes,' said Starship. 'What's your call, Captain?'

'They're activating weapons radars!' said Spiderman. 'Trying to lock on us!'

'*Hawk Three* and *Four,* engage enemy aircraft,' said Breanna.

'Roger that,' said Starship, leaning closer to the screen.

Northern Somalia,
on the ground
0023

The woman's grenade floated in the air ten inches from Danny's head. As he started to cringe, his body bracing for the shock, an ebony-shaded hand appeared from nowhere, grabbing the grenade and in the same motion throwing it out toward the sea.

A blackness filled his eyes in the next second. He became blind.

Then he was falling, crashing against the rocks, pulling the woman who'd tried to kill them against the ground.

The grenade exploded somewhere below. Danny rolled and pushed upright, his only thought for his pistol, loose in his holster. He gripped the woman unsteadily, then managed to throw her to the left, away from his gun. She continued to struggle, grabbing something from her body. Three shots rang out and she fell back, then tumbled down the hill.

Danny rolled to his feet. 'Thanks, Boston,' he said.

'The lieutenant grabbed the grenade and threw it,' said

Boston. He pointed to Dancer. 'She shot the bitch too.'

'She had another grenade in her dress there,' said Dancer, motioning with the gun. Her voice had a tinge of regret. 'Fortunately she couldn't pull the pin. Crazy.'

'You better search this one,' Danny said, pointing to the older woman on the side. She'd either fainted or been knocked unconscious. 'Let's make sure we're secure here before you go anywhere else,' he told Dancer. 'And thanks.'

'My pleasure, Captain.'

Aboard *Baker-Baker Two*
0023

The thing Starship couldn't figure was: Why make it so easy for us?

Why attack at all? We're just going to shoot you down.

The lead MiG did not see the Flighthawk, either on radar or visually, until the computer turned Starship's firing cue yellow. By then it was too late for the MiG to do much of anything. Undecided about whether to fight or flee, the Yemen pilot attempted to do both, launching an all-aspect R-73 heat-seeker at the Flighthawk and trying to tuck hard on his right wing and roll away.

The R-73 – known to NATO as an AA-11 Archer – was an excellent weapon, able to accelerate to Mach 2.5 and guided by an extraordinarily sensitive infrared seeker in its nose. But even the best infrared seeker – and the R-73 certainly was in the running for consideration – had trouble picking out a relatively small target like the

Flighthawk head-on, especially in an encounter where seconds loomed like hours. Starship flicked left as the enemy started to turn, only vaguely aware of the air-to-air weapon's flash. His cue turned red; he counted 'one-two' to himself and then fired, sliding the nose of the Flighthawk down slightly to keep the stream of bullets on the MiG's wings. By the time the R-73 missile flew past the Flighthawk, the MiG that launched it had burst into a U-shaped ring of red flames.

Starship pulled off abruptly, afraid the explosion would spray debris in the U/MF-3's path. He cleared without getting hit, and corrected slightly north to line up an intercept on the second group of aircraft, some thirty miles away.

He wanted to execute the same plan, but *Hawk Four* was having trouble with the MiG it was assigned to nail. The Yemen pilot turned toward the Flighthawk's path before *Hawk Four* was in range to fire, and the computer changed its attack pattern. It managed a few shots as the two planes passed, the MiG heading farther west. By the time *Hawk Four* came around and got on the Yemeni plane's tail, it had launched a pair of R-27R radar missiles – not at the Flighthawk, but at the Megafortress guiding her.

Starship blocked out the sounds of the crew responding in his headset, taking control of *Hawk Four* himself to press the attack. Anticipating that the MiG would try to run home, he cut back north, slamming the throttle – and sure enough, the MiG swept back, accelerating so fast that even though he'd expected it, Starship nearly missed the shot.

Nearly wasn't good enough for the MiG driver, though – Starship punched two dozen slugs through the rear engine housing, crippling the aircraft as surely as a knife slicing a horse's knee tendons. The pilot bailed a few seconds later.

Starship turned back north, trying to get into position to take the run on the second element of Yemen aircraft. But *Hawk Three* was now too far ahead to pull the same maneuver; he had to settle for what they called Train Attack One – one ship in a deep trail, reacting to whatever was left after the lead aircraft made its attack. He jumped into *Hawk Three* just as the computer closed in for the kill; he got a red in the target screen and pressed the trigger. The computer was too optimistic – his bullets trailed downward, and the MiG jinked hard to Starship's right. This element of aircraft was flying parallel, and Starship flew through without another shot. He banked to get behind the flight, turning as sharply as he could, the small plane recording more than eight g's on her air frame.

Flown by the computer, *Hawk Four* lined up for a head-on shot at the easternmost MiG, which hadn't changed course. Starship let the computer hold onto the Flighthawk and angled toward the other plane, which had begun to dive to the west.

'*Hawk Three*, we're going to take those MiGs out with missiles,' said Breanna. 'We have another group of four MiGs taking off from Yemen. Meet them.'

'*Hawk Four* is engaging,' said Starship.

'Pull off,' said Breanna.

'Roger that,' he said reluctantly, overriding the computer.

Breanna waited until Spiderman got a lock on the second aircraft to give the order to fire. The AMRAAM-pluses clunked off the launcher, whipping forward from beneath the Megafortress's belly.

'Close it up,' she told her copilot.

'They're locking – launching the Alamos.'

'ECMs.'

'Jesus, Captain, they're scrambling their whole air force,' said Telly. 'I have that group of four MiG-29s, and now two MiG-21s, four MiG-21s coming out of the north. They're going for broke.'

'So are we.'

Starship had his pick of targets – four MiG-29s and six MiG-21s had joined the playing field. The MiG-29s were more serious threats to the Megafortress, and closer besides – he set the two Flighthawks up for a run at their front quarters from the east. This time the attack was a no-brainer, with the enemy planes spread out at easy intervals. Despite the two earlier encounters, they were unaware of the Flighthawks and took no evasive man-euvers as Starship approached.

The cockpit of one of the MiGs materialized in the center of his firing screen, the image complete with the bobbing head of the pilot. Starship hesitated – it seemed inhumane for some reason to target the man flying the plane rather than the metal itself – but then squeezed the trigger. The rain of lead flowed across the aircraft for perhaps two whole seconds, twice as long as the Flighthawk's cannon needed to obliterate the Russian-built machine.

A second aircraft appeared almost immediately. Starting to ride the adrenaline high of the encounter,

Starship fired even though the gear showed he didn't have a shot. He scolded himself and turned right, just in time to witness the computer's first score of the night with *Hawk Four* – a screaming attack from above that tore off the right wing of one of the MiGs.

As Starship hunted for his own target, he got a warning from the radar warning receiver – one of the MiGs had managed to turn and was on his tail. He pulled the MiG with him in a dive and then a tuck to the right, weaving back to the left and then pulling up with a twist to the left. The MiG hung with the smaller plane, very close to its tail but not quite lined up for a shot. Sweat rode down Starship's back as he ducked left then right, then left again. The Flighthawk flicked in the sky, changing course so sharply that a live pilot would have been knocked senseless by the heavy g's. Finally the MiG shot past. Starship waited a second for his wings to steady, then zeroed out his opponent with a steady burst.

As the plane exploded, a second fighter came into view; Starship immediately turned to close for an attack. But he'd lost so much airspeed already that he got a stall warning – it was a wonder, between his maneuvers and the effect of the cannon, that he wasn't moving backward. Feeling cocky, he slammed his wing down and circled in the direction he figured the MiG would take. The Flighthawk moved sideways and down, more brick than anything approaching a controllable aircraft. Part of it was luck, but Starship managed to put the Flighthawk on the tail of the MiG and begin firing. He was too flatfooted to get more than a few bullets into the other aircraft, and when the MiG pulled away, he had to let it go.

He turned to check the sitrep screen to reorient himself when he got a warning buzzer from C^3 – he was low on fuel.

Very low – ten minutes.

'MiG-21s are moving to engage us,' Spiderman told him. 'Eight of them. They're five minutes from missile range.'

'I need to gas up,' Starship said. 'Both planes.'

'This isn't a good time,' Breanna told him.

'It's a lousy time,' said Starship. 'But I'm almost bone dry.'

'We're being tracked by a surface radar,' added Spiderman. 'SAMs – we're spiked! They're firing!'

Aboard the *Abner Read*
0030

'Hit on Sonar Contact One!' said Weapons, relaying the news that one of their torpedoes had struck the Libyan submarine.

'It's about time,' said Storm. 'Eyes – status of that submarine?'

'Still trying to determine, sir.'

'Weapons – torpedoes five and six?'

'En route and true.'

Hallelujah, thought Storm.

'The submarine is dead in the water,' said Eyes.

'Time to impact on torpedo five is three minutes,' said Peanut. 'Six is right behind.'

'Stay on him.'

'I'm trying, Storm,' said the executive officer. Storm detected some of his pique at being bypassed creeping into his voice but didn't comment on it; he'd take care of the man later on, reward him for his patience.

He'd reward all the crew members – best damn crew in the Navy, bar none.

Storm turned his attention to the rest of the battle. All of the vessels coming from the targeted base area had been struck, but there were other ships in the vicinity, which he guessed must be part of the pirate fleet. They would have to neutralize as many as they could.

His move against the submarine had taken him in the direction of three ships identified as small patrol boats by the Megafortress; these were heading out from the coastline to his west about eight miles away. *Shark Boat Two* had engaged a similar-sized craft three miles beyond them. Storm decided that since the *Abner Read* was already headed in that direction and the land objective had been secured, they would cut off the three patrol craft and stand by to render assistance to the Shark Boat. He told Bastian to remain over at the pirate camp, supporting the landing team and *Shark Boat One*.

The rules of engagement required the ships to positively identify any craft not at the landing site as a pirate before opening fire, unless they were fired on first or represented an immediate threat. Storm had communications issue a warning to the three patrol craft, telling them that they were interfering with a UN-sponsored operation and were to return to their ports.

'No answer,' said the communications officer.

'Peanut, target the patrol craft identified as Surface Contacts Fourteen, Fifteen, and Sixteen.'

Peanut issued the command. As it was being passed along, Eyes reported that the Libyan submarine had opened its torpedo tubes.

'Weapons, what's the status of the torpedoes?' said Storm.

'Five is sixty seconds away.'

'Torpedoes in the water!' warned the computerized threat indicator.

The twenty-one-inch torpedoes carried by the enemy submarine were heavier and deadlier than those Storm's ship had launched and in theory had a longer range – as much as fifty kilometers. As the crew began to respond, Eyes reported that torpedo five had detonated prematurely, too far from the submarine to damage it.

Storm stifled a curse, struggling to control his anger. He would get the bastard – he would get *all* of the bastards – but to do that he had to remain calm.

But remaining calm was not his strong suit.

'Dreamland EB-52 *Wisconsin* to CAG Tactical Command,' said Bastian over the Dreamland circuit. 'The other Megafortress is engaging fighters from Yemen. We'd like to go to their assistance.'

'We need you to stand by,' said Eyes. 'All of our forces are engaged with the enemy.'

'They're under heavy attack.'

'I know what they're doing,' said Storm, butting in. 'They've shot down half the Yemen Air Force. They don't need any help. Do you have Harpoons left?'

'Affirmative,' said Dog.

'Eyes, give them a target.'

'That amphibious ship they saw the other day is about thirty miles north of us. It has another craft alongside it, possibly as a tug.'

'Sink the bastard,' cut in Storm.

'Your orders covering engagement prohibit me from doing that,' replied the colonel coldly. 'They've been in international waters since before the start of the engagement. And besides, I can't get close enough for a visual without leaving this area.'

How could the Air Force flyboy remain so stinking calm when he had just lost several men?

'Damn it, Bastian – find a way to engage him. Your people in the other Megafortress don't seem to be having any problem.'

'They were threatened and had to defend themselves.'

'A good plan for you. We're going after the submarine.'

'*Wisconsin* out.' The feed snapped clean.

'What's going on with those torpedoes that were launched at us?' said Storm.

'Two are still tracking, Captain.'

The voices came in rapid succession as the different elements of the battle were processed.

'Bingo! We have another strike on the submarine!' said Weapons.

'One of the Libyan torpedoes has self-detonated.'

'We have the patrol craft zeroed in.'

'Second Libyan torpedo is going off course. We're in the clear.'

Suddenly, one of the sonar operators shouted so loud his voice echoed in the space:

'I have sounds of a submarine breaking up!'

'Put them over the loudspeaker,' said Storm. 'Crew, we have sunk the Tango sub. We have routed the pirates from their base. We are in the process of breaking the terrorists' backs.'

The crew began to cheer. This is what revenge sounds like, Storm thought.

The celebration was interrupted by a new warning, this one from the Dreamland EB-52 over the battle area.

'Missiles in the air – four – eight Styx missiles! Launched in the direction of the *Abner Read*.'

Aboard the *Wisconsin*
0040

Dog had just told Zen to take *Hawk Two* toward the amphibious ship when the barrage of missiles sprang from it.

'Multiple launches,' reported Dish. 'They're all Styx missiles. We're confirmed on that.'

'I have three of the missiles in view,' said Zen.

'Can you take them out?' asked Dog.

'Not all of them,' said Zen.

'Dish – can you ID guidance or the missile types?'

'Working on it, Colonel. S1 and S2 have MS-2A seekers – radar, capable of home on jam. Active. Others are similar – may be a P-22 in there as well. That would default to an infrared if jammed. Guess here is that they had a location or at least an approximate location based on the *Abner Read*'s radar and fired.'

'I have S5 and S6,' said Zen, singling out two of the missiles Dish had ID'd as having heat-seeking heads.

'McNamara, target the two closest to *Abner Read* with Scorpions,' Dog said. 'Once the air-to-air missiles are off, we'll sink the ship with the rest of our Harpoons.'

'Working on it, Colonel. Going to need you to come to a new course.'

'Lay it in.'

'I'm engaging,' said Zen.

Dog swung the aircraft into a better position for McNamara, shortening the distance the AMRAAM-pluses would need to take to intercept the missiles. No matter how it was guided, the Russian-made Styx was at its heart a flying bomb, a set of wings and an engine that could take its 480-kilogram warhead just over the speed of sound. In its most recent version, it could travel about fifty-four nautical miles.

'Opening bomb bay doors,' said Dog as he swung into position. The aircraft shuddered as she opened her belly to the elements, exposing the antiair missile on her revolving dispenser.

'Locked on S3,' said the copilot.

'Fire.'

'Firing. Locked on S4.'

'Fire.'

The missiles clunked off the rack, their sleek bodies accelerating rapidly. The standard AMRAAM could top Mach 4; the AMRAAM-plus Scorpion, a Dreamland special, went a hair faster but carried a heavier warhead, which, as on the standard version, sat just forward of the middle of the missile.

'*Baker-Baker*, this is *Wisconsin* – I'm afraid we have our hands full for the moment,' he told Breanna, not wanting to let her think he'd forgotten about her. 'We're engaging Styx missiles.'

'We have it under control, Daddy.'

He *hated* her calling him Daddy.

'*Wisconsin*, I need you to come west with me,' said Zen.

'Missiles are away,' said McNamara. 'Tracking.'

'Button up,' Dog told him. 'And hang on.'

Zen pushed *Hawk Three* into a dive at the course the computer plotted for the Styx missile. In some ways, the ship-to-ship projectile was an easy target – it flew in a predictable path and couldn't defend itself. On the other hand, it was fast enough that he had only one real shot at it; if he missed, he'd never be able to turn and get another shot.

The computer showed the course perfectly. Zen was moving exactly onto his mark. There was only one problem – the missile wasn't there.

Zen slid the throttle back, cutting down his speed. According to the sitrep plot at the bottom right of his visor, the Styx missile should be right in front of him. But neither the synthesized radar view nor the low-light video showed it.

Confused, he tucked the Flighthawk into a bank. The computer had *Hawk Two* – the control screen showed that it was nearly ready to fire. Realizing that he was unlikely to do any better than the computer in the encounter, Zen stayed with *Hawk One.*

'Strike on S3,' reported McNamara, watching the AMRAAM-plus.

'Hey, Dish, they're foxing us somehow, confusing the radar with false returns,' said Zen. 'I just chased a non-existent missile.'

'Working on it – sorry, we haven't seen these ECMs before. More missiles in the air!'

Zen selected his infrared feed and saw two missiles within striking distance; he went for the closer one, putting several cannon shells into the rear and sending it spinning out of control. He glanced briefly at the radar and saw three other missiles there – all phony.

'They're still tricking us,' he told Dish.

'Yeah,' said the radar operator. 'I'm trying to narrow down the units that have the counter-ECMs. Whatever they're using is good – maybe Indian modifications or something new out of Russia.'

'Better alert the *Abner Read* to the false signals.'

'Already have.'

Northern Somalia
0045

The vessel loomed ahead, more a shadow on the water than a ship.

'Come,' Ali told the others who had joined him. 'Commend yourselves to God, and follow.'

445

He stripped off his shirt and pants and slipped into the water, his only weapon the knife at his belt. Six others followed him, the best swimmers of his small force.

And then more – another dozen, eighteen, all of the men who had survived.

But after a few strokes, Ali faltered; the water was too cold and his arms too old to reach his destination.

Let me die if it is your will, he told his Lord.

Water swelled into his nose. He felt himself going down and thought of his son.

And then he was there, his hand touching the side of the ship – it felt like hard rubber, as if the entire craft were sheathed in a diver's suit. Ali didn't know where to put his hands. He had found his way to the flank of the enemy's craft, propelled entirely by God's will.

Allah had delivered this vessel so he could strike the *Ark Royal*. He wanted the devil's own sword wielded in the name of justice.

No one was topside. The ship was about as long as his own patrol boats, sitting low in the water on two knife-shaped arms. The deck held a small cannon forward of a sloped and angled wheelhouse, the broad fantail at the rear dominated by two long rectangular boxes.

A hand grasped him. The others had arrived.

'Wait until we are all aboard,' said Ali. 'God has brought us and will provide. We are in his hands and fight a holy war.'

Danny walked down to the water, heart pounding heavily, afraid the grenade meant for him had killed or wounded the Marine hunched on the ground ahead. But the man wasn't hurt, at least not physically – he was throwing up. Danny knelt beside him and recognized the young man he'd been with earlier.

'I saw a head,' mumbled the kid. 'Oh, God.' The Marine leaned over and puked again.

Danny gripped the jacket of the bulletproof vest. After a few more heaves the Marine straightened, and Danny helped him to his feet.

'I'm OK, sir. I'm OK.'

'I know you are, guy. It sucks.'

The Marine looked at him for a second. 'Does it get easier?'

Danny thought back to the first man he'd seen die – or rather, the first one he'd realized was a man, not a faceless enemy in the distance. He'd puked too.

In one sense, it did get easier – he didn't throw up anymore. But in all the important ways, it didn't get easier at all.

'You'll get through it, kid. You're doing your job.'

'Thank you, sir,' snapped the Marine, a bit of his strength returning.

Danny rapped his arm gently with his fist, then went to check on the others.

The gun at the front of the enemy ship began to fire. The deck shook with it, and the boat started to roll.

The dark hatchway to the interior lay a few feet ahead. Ali could see the men moving inside, two of them – devil men with horns and spikes at their heads.

The knife burned hot in his hand.

447

'For the Glory of God!' he yelled, plunging into the darkness.

'Have Sergeant Liu take charge of securing any documents and equipment from the headquarters building,' Danny told Dancer over the team circuit. 'We ought to try to evacuate it out to the Shark Boat as soon as we can, just in case the natives get restless. We'll use the Navy SITT teams to conduct searches of the other buildings. They're trained for that stuff. But I want them to go slow. There's no sense tripping over more booby traps in the dark.'

'Agreed, Captain.'

Something flashed in the sky overhead. A loud clap of thunder followed. There were two more bursts in rapid succession.

'Missiles,' Danny told the Marine lieutenant. 'Being intercepted. Big ones.'

'Cap, Werewolf is trying to get ahold of you on the Dreamland circuit,' said Boston. 'The most beautiful woman in the world wants to sing in your ear.'

'Boston, you would joke on the doorstep of hell,' said Danny.

'Aw, been there, done that, Captain.'

Danny clicked into the line. 'Whiplash leader.'

'Danny, I have to pull *Werewolf Two* back to refuel. It's going to be at least twenty minutes before I get back to you. *Werewolf One* is being refueled but it may take a while to get back in the air.'

He could hear a lot of voices behind her on the ship, rushed, calm, nearly hysterical – the adrenaline-soaked sounds of battle.

'It's OK, Jen. We're secure here. What's your situation?'

'We've sunk the submarine, but we've been targeted by missiles. Gonna be a few minutes before it sorts out and I can land to refuel – have to go.'

'Go.'

Dancer had climbed down the cliffside and was standing before him with one of her Marines – the one who had just emptied the contents of his stomach on the beach.

'Danny, I'm going to take Luke here and check on the search of the Osprey wreckage as we'd planned. I think it's better to leave Liu and the others to help Boston sort out the situation in the hovel and then bring the papers or whatever's in the headquarters' stash down.'

'You sure you're OK?'

'Hey, we're Marines,' said Dancer. 'Come on, Luke.'

The Marine had to scramble to keep up with the five-seven lieutenant as she strode toward the dock where the small boats were tied up.

'Just that old woman up here, Cap,' said Boston. 'As far as the sensors can tell, no mines anywhere. And no more booby traps.'

'All right. Sergeant Liu is organizing a team to take material out of the headquarters. If you're secure up there and there's manpower available, go down and help out. I'm going to see if I can find some sort of boat we can use to get the material out to the Shark Boat.'

A fresh set of explosions in the distance shook the ground.

'Sounds like we're not the only ones having a party tonight,' said Boston.

Starship turned *Hawk Three* toward the lead MiG then jumped back into *Hawk Four*. He whirled the airplane toward the southeast, hunting for *Baker-Baker Two*.

'I have an idea, Bree,' he said. 'I'll hold them off with *Three* long enough to get a couple hundred pounds of juice into *Four*, then go back and finish them off.'

'I don't know if we can complete a refuel under fire,' said Breanna.

'I think it's worth a try,' said Starship. 'It's better than just running away and losing both U/MFs.'

'Agreed,' she snapped back. 'Let's try.'

Starship lined up *Hawk Four*, then told the computer to take the aircraft in for the refuel. The computer balked – its safety protocols would not allow it to refuel while the Megafortress was being targeted by the enemy. Both he and Breanna had to authorize the override. The extra step took only a few seconds, but by the time he got back into *Hawk Three*, the computer had missed its shot. Rather than breaking and going for the other aircraft in the pack – a human's natural choice, since there were no less than four targets within spitting distance – C^3 had stubbornly stayed on the lead MiG. It led it to the very edge of the connection range with *Baker-Baker Two*. The computer backed off and banked around, taking itself out of the fight even though it had been ordered to stay with the other plane.

It was the first tactical flaw Starship had found in the

programming. It disappointed him somehow, as if the computer should have known better.

He'd figure out how to use it in the next exercise to try and beat Zen, something no one had ever done.

Kick would have loved that. He was always talking about beating the master.

Starship pushed the memory of his friend away as he took control of the Flighthawk. The sky before him was studded with fighters. The MiGs stoked their engines, trying to close on the Megafortress – apparently they were all carrying short-range heat-seekers and needed to get up close to take a shot. He pulled to a half mile of the nearest aircraft and lit his cannon, tearing a long, jagged line through the fuselage and back into the tail plane. He kept moving forward, barely letting up on the trigger before finding his second target, another MiG-21. Before he could fire, a missile sprang from beneath the enemy's wing. Cursing, Starship waited for the target cue to blink then go solid red.

'You better not hit me, you son of a bitch,' he said, dialing the enemy into oblivion.

'Break right, you have to turn right!' Spiderman yelled to Breanna.

'We need to stay straight for the refuel.'

'Bree! There's a MiG closing from your left and two heat-seekers coming from behind.'

'Flares and Stinger,' said Breanna calmly.

The decoys shot out from the Megafortress as the air-to-air missiles sped toward it. The cascade of flares were too inviting a target for the antiquated missiles to ignore –

451

both tucked downward, exploding more than a mile away.

Which left the MiG-29 that somehow managed to elude everything else in the sky and was drawing a bead on their left flank.

'He's taking a cannon run,' said Spiderman.

'Starship, how's your fuel?'

'Two more minutes.'

'We don't have two minutes,' said Breanna as the first slug from the MiG's 30mm cannon began crashing into the fuselage.

'Computer, my control, *Hawk Four*,' said Starship, and in a breath he was falling past the Megafortress. He tilted his wing slightly to the left, feeling his way, not seeing, blind in the dark night. Flashes of red sped overhead. He lifted himself and there was the enemy, dead-on in the middle of his screen.

'Now!' he yelled, and the black triangle hurling itself toward him turned golden orange. Starship flew through it, shuddering as debris rained in every direction. He climbed then circled back, looking for the Megafortress. As he turned he was jerked backward, away from his small plane. Disoriented, he blinked – then saw the flames coming from the top of *Baker-Baker Two* in the screen.

'Radar is offline,' Spiderman told Breanna.

'Least of our problems.'

'Thirty percent in engine two. We may lose her.'

'Fire control.'

'Fire control. Sounding warning.'

A klaxon began to sound in the aircraft. 'Everybody, make sure your oxygen is on,' shouted Breanna over the automated warning.

The Megafortress had a system that flooded vulnerable areas of the aircraft to extinguish fires. It worked by denying the flames oxygen – which of course meant it would kill the crew as well.

'Do it,' she told the copilot.

Starship put *Hawk Four* into a preset trail maneuver, pulled on his oxygen mask, then undid his restraints to check on Delaford.

'You really have to be tied in tight,' Starship told him, snapping and then snugging the restraints on his ejection seat.

'Thanks,' said Delaford. 'We're not going out, are we?'

'Nah, not today,' said Starship. He turned, then flew against the side of the seat as the Megafortress rolled hard on her right side.

The lights began to blink, indicating that the fire-suppression system had been activated. He pulled himself upright and slid in behind his controls as the Megafortress pitched forward. He tumbled against the bulkhead over the panel hard enough to rebound backward into the seat, and he lay there dazed for a moment, temporarily stunned.

Get your gear back on, dude. You're coming undone. Mask is out and where the hell is your helmet?

'Screw yourself, Kick.'

You undid your mask. You can't breathe right.

'Screw it.'

453

Come on.

Something or someone seemed to take hold of the mask and center it on his face. Starship had his helmet and cinched it – when had he put it on?

He fumbled with the restraint buckle on the left side of his seat; when it finally cinched, he went to connect the right and found it already closed. The aircraft pushed back, leveling off – then shot back down, its nose pitched nearly perpendicular to the earth.

Breanna scrambled to compensate as engine four went offline. The radar housing had been smashed all to hell, there were holes in the wing, and at least some of the control surfaces were no longer attached to the aircraft.

'Hang with me, Spiderman,' she yelled.

'I'm hanging.'

'We have engine one and engine three, that's all we need,' she told him.

'Oh, yeah,' he said, though he didn't sound convinced.

'I have the stick, I have the stick,' she told him. 'We have to stay calm and straight.'

Not necessarily in that order either. Breanna managed to keep the aircraft from falling into a spin, but still had to struggle to quell the roller-coaster movements up and down, the plane riding the momentum toward the ocean. Each plunge got a little shallower and more controllable, and she finally managed to get the aircraft level. Pushing her shoulders back, she took a deep breath in celebration – then went back to work.

'First thing I want you to do,' she told Spiderman, 'is get

us a course to an airfield. See what the distance is to that place in India that the Ospreys used. That's probably our best bet at this point. I'll take stock of the damage. At some point we'll see if we can bring engine four back online. Starship?'

'Sorry, Bree.'

'Wasn't your fault – that MiG ducked our AMRAAM somehow. But I think next time, we may test the old saying about discretion being the better part of valor.'

Breanna checked with the rest of the crew; no one had been hurt. The MiGs, meanwhile, had returned to Yemen – those that hadn't been shot down. By their count, they had gunned down seven.

'Eight – *Hawk Three* got one more before it ran out of fuel. It did the honorable thing and blew itself up when it went dry,' said Starship, reviewing the computer file.

'*Ark Royal* is asking if we need assistance,' said Spiderman.

'Unless they want to add another four or five thousand feet to their landing deck, tell them thanks but no thanks,' said Breanna.

Aboard the *Abner Read*
0045

According to the Dreamland people, four surface-to-surface missiles were coming at them. The problem was, the screens in the defensive weapons section said there were thirty.

Even the *Abner Read*'s gun control system couldn't take them all out.

'Target the first wave,' said Storm.

'You're going to have to trust what *Wisconsin* tells you,' said Jennifer Gleason, standing up from her station. 'They can use the infrared sensors and you can manually override the system to target the missiles one by one.'

'You're damn sassy for a scientist.'

'And for someone who's smart, you can be a real asshole.'

Overcome with anger, Storm nearly grabbed her.

'You know I'm right,' she added.

She was, wasn't she?

'Do it!' Storm said. 'Do what Gleason says. Get the Dreamland people to ID each missile as it's incoming, and manually take it out. Eyes? Weapons? Peanut?'

'Aye, Captain, we're on it.'

'I was wrong,' he said. 'And she's right.'

Northern Somalia
0050

God guided his hand and the enemy devil fell to the deck, blood gurgling from his mouth. Ali spun around, following the other man, who was running through the hatch to the left. The man tripped and Ali leaped over him, running forward – there were two other men nearby, one with a gun at his belt. Ali slashed at him, striking so hard that his knife lodged deep in the man's midsection. They fell together, crumpling against a table.

The space filled with Ali's men. Ali saw a sidearm and grabbed for it; the man began to fight back, and his companion came to his aid. But God was on the side of the true believers – Ali felt his strength moving in his arms, and he wrestled the pistol from the holster. Before he could use it, however, the man fell back, limp; the blood he'd lost had robbed him of fight.

'Captain! The bridge is this way!' shouted one of his men.

Ali jumped up. There were now so many of his men aboard that he had trouble squeezing onto the bridge.

Two Americans lay at the side, one with his neck twisted at a grotesque angle. Ali stepped forward and shot him once in the head, even though he was clearly dead. He used two bullets on the other man, whose body continued to jerk for several long seconds after the final shot.

The ship's captain stood near the wheel, pinned by four of Ali's men.

'You – show me the boat,' said Ali, using his very limited English.

'I will die first.'

Ali raised the pistol to the man's head.

'The boat.'

The man spit at him. Ali pulled the trigger. The bullet sped through the man's skull and lodged in the glass of the bridge behind him.

'Throw them overboard. Quickly, search the rest of the ship,' said Ali. 'Find the weapons lockers.'

Ali scanned the bridge. The basic controls were here. Moving the Shark Boat would not be difficult. But the displays and sensors and, most important, the weapons would take considerable amount of study. Even with his experience, Ali doubted he could master them.

But God would help, surely. He had given them the boat.

'Captain, we have the boat,' said Saed, taking him by the elbow.

Ali was surprised to find his lieutenant here.

'I had not realized you were here.'

'Until the end. There are fifteen of us, and yourself.'

'Take the helm. Where is Habib?'

'Outside.'

'Someone find Habib,' said Ali. 'We need his computer skills.'

The runabout tied to the dock looked like a late-1950s eighteen-foot Thompson, crafted from wood and open to the air. A pair of large Johnson engines sat at the stern. A thick coat of varnish covered the pockmarked decking and wooden ribs at the side of the open craft.

Danny got in, steadying himself on the gunwale as the boat rocked back and forth. There was no question the craft had been used by the pirates – there were two AK47s and an ammo locker under the seat bench on the port side, and mountings for a grenade launcher bolted just below the port window.

The controls consisted of a large wheel and a throttle assembly that could be ganged to engage and work the motors together. There didn't seem to be an ignition key; the only thing close was a simple push-button to the right of the wheel, mounted on a plastic plate that had been carefully fitted to the wooden dashboard.

Danny leaned on the button but nothing happened. He started to go back and check the engines, then saw a thick wire running along the decking up toward the dashboard.

458

Thinking there had to be a key or some sort of ignition system, he got to his knee and craned his neck under the old panel. One strand of wire was separated, with the two ends stripped and formed into hooks. He slipped them together, then got up and tried again. The engines coughed, but didn't catch.

A small gauge on the dash indicated that there was a full tank of fuel. Danny guessed that he needed to choke the engines somehow, but he couldn't find a switch or mechanism to do so. There was nothing obvious on the engine housings either; metal wire ran to them, but he couldn't quite see where they connected. He went back and tried again; the motors coughed but still didn't catch. The boat rocked unsteadily beneath him. He jerked his hand out against the dashboard, grabbing a decorative knob in the middle. A swell of the waves pushed him back, and as he tried to maintain his balance by holding onto the dash, the knob came out. He'd found the choke.

It took two more tries to get the motors started. Once they came to life, the boat heaved forward. The line tugged taut; Danny backed off the power to idle, went back and cut the line. His performance wasn't going to win him any honors in seamanship, but at least he had the craft working. There were a pair of lights on the bow; he found the switches and saw the thin beams play over the water as he moved away from the dock, getting a feel for the boat.

'Hey, Dancer, this is Whiplash leader. Where are you?'

'About five hundred yards from shore,' said the Marine lieutenant. 'Roughly due north of the second landing. Very shallow here, maybe twenty feet deep.

We're working with a boat from *Shark Boat One*.'

'I see you. I'm in a runabout or something. I want to use it to bring whatever we take from the pirate command post out to the Shark Boat. I'm heading toward you.'

Danny throttled slowly toward the wreckage area. The windscreen of the boat folded forward, and he managed to lean out and work the beam down so he could sweep the water. Debris covered the surface.

'Looks like we don't have any survivors,' said Dancer, maneuvering her boat toward his. 'I'm sorry.'

'Yeah.'

'Two of the Navy men are certified as divers, and there's diving equipment back on the Shark Boat,' she told him. 'So if you want to start a recovery –'

'That's going to have to wait until we check on the cave where the sub is,' Danny told her. 'Maybe they can dive in from the ocean side after our guys secure the land entrances. The Shark Boat can support them. I want to check back in with the *Abner Read* and see what their situation is.'

One of *Shark Boat One*'s little boats came alongside and told Dancer that they were having trouble raising their ship on the radio. Danny went into the Dreamland circuit and tried to connect via the *Abner Read*, but also couldn't get them.

'*Abner Read* is under fire,' Major Catsman said from Dreamland Command. 'The ECM systems aboard the ship and the Megafortresses are degrading the radio communications. Going to be a few minutes, Danny.'

'Maybe I ought to just take a spin out there,' Danny told Dancer. 'I have to talk to the captain myself, and it might be quicker face-to-face.'

'Ship seems to be moving,' said the Marine in Dancer's boat. He pointed out to the horizon.

'I hope they're not planning on leaving us here,' said Dancer.

'He's moving pretty fast. Maybe there's another pirate boat out there,' said Dancer.

Danny clicked his viewer into the sitrep screen, then into the infrared view supplied by *Hawk Two*, which was still orbiting overhead. Neither screen showed a threat. The Shark Boat had taken a turn in the water and was now heading directly north.

'Colonel Bastian, this is Whiplash leader.'

'Go ahead, Danny,' said Dog from the Megafortress.

'Can you contact the Shark Boat offshore?'

'Stand by. We're countering a barrage of antiship missiles.'

'If you could give me the surface radar operator, I want to know about possible threats off the beachhead here.'

'There are no threats. Dish will get on the line with you in a second.'

'I think I want to go talk to their captain right now,' Danny told Dancer. 'And I want a couple of Marines with me.'

'This is a passive infrared receiving system. It shows heat sources in front of the ship,' said Habib. 'This is an active radar, which is very limited, not much more powerful than ours. This screen, though, this gets inputs from some other source. I can't tell whether it's aboard this ship or not.'

Ali studied the suite of screens. If he was reading the legends correctly – which might not be the case – the

461

external radar had a seventy-mile radius. Rather than putting this vessel in the center of the plot, it seemed to position it far off to the side. It seemed to him that the Americans had found some way to transmit radar information from another source – Satan's Tail, he guessed. This would explain why they had never seen radar signals from the small patrol craft themselves.

'This looks like a radar plot too, but I don't see how that can be,' added Habib, pointing to a large screen near the center of the console. 'It has different modes, but what they mean is not clear.'

'This is our ship,' said Ali, pointing to a set of blue letters at the lower left of the screen. 'That – that at the center – is the source of the information. Flip back to the first screen you started with.'

Habib did so. It was some sort of scale.

'The buttons below the screen change the scale; the ones at the right, they have something to do with the detection modes,' said Ali. 'Go to the longest plot – the small scale. There!' He pointed to the top of the screen. 'That is the *Ark Royal*. That's our target.'

It wasn't clear from the screen what the distance was, but Ali guessed it was less than eighty miles.

'Helm, come five degrees to port,' he told Saed. 'And then get as much from the engines as you can. Habib, you have done a good job. Now determine how to use the weapons systems.' He put his hand on his sailor's shoulder. 'God is with us. He will help you see.'

IX

The Glory of God

Aboard the *Abner Read*
11 November 1997
0052

Jennifer cringed as the *Abner Read*'s Phalanx antimissile system began firing. The fact that the cannon was shooting meant that the missiles they had launched at the Styx had missed, despite *Wisconsin*'s help.

'Strike!' said the defensive systems operator over the shared communication channel. The gun swirled and began firing again; it stopped abruptly, the operator realizing belatedly that the system had fired at a shadow. 'We're losing track of the inputs!' the sailor said.

'Do your best,' said Storm calmly. 'Fire at whatever you have.'

'I can help,' said Jennifer, placing *Werewolf Two* in a hover where the aircraft was, about five miles west of the *Abner Read*. 'The Werewolf's infrared sensors will show the missile.'

'I can't safe it down to let you in,' said the systems officer.

'No, I'll use *Wolf One*,' she said, already punching into the controls for the aircraft, which had just been secured for refueling when the missile attack began. 'Clear the deck! Clear the deck!'

Someone shouted at her over the radio, but she couldn't tell whether it was an acknowledgment or a warning. 'Clear the deck!' she repeated. 'I'm launching!'

'Do what she says,' snapped Eyes. He bent down next to her. 'I trust you, but what the hell are you doing?'

'I can hover just above the ship and use the sensors to help sort the missiles,' Jennifer explained. The Phalanx guns rattled; she revved the counterrotating blades above the Werewolf's body to life.

'The guns will shoot you down.'

'No, not if I stay right above the superstructure. As far as they're concerned, the Werewolf is part of the radio mast.'

She had to override the computer to take off, since the aircraft had hardly any fuel left. It rose off the deck slowly, buffeted by the wind.

'I need my laptop open where I can see it,' she told Eyes. 'I'm going to put the aircraft plot there and look at the radar on the main screen. Come on! Get it!'

Eyes pulled the laptop, which was already open, around so she could see it.

'Hold it for me,' she said, her fingers crashing on the keyboard. 'Just hold it.'

'All right.'

'Your contact M3 – it's real,' said Jennifer, her head swiveling back and forth from the screens. 'M4 – shit, no, M5! M5 is real. M5!'

'Missiles in the air!'

'M3 and M5.'

The ship's guns rattled so harshly that the ship seemed to sink low in the waves. An explosion shook the *Abner Read* – there were shouts and screams.

'M8! M8!' yelled Jennifer.

'Got it!'

'M19!'

The rattle intensified, then stopped. In the silent moment, the ship rose at the bow and Jennifer felt herself thrown forward against the console. As she rebounded to the deck, she heard the warhead explode toward the rear of the ship.

Aboard the *Wisconsin*
0058

'One of the missiles struck the *Abner Read*,' said Dish.

Dog didn't reply. He had just heard from Breanna that everyone aboard *Baker-Baker Two* was fine. Though heavily damaged, she thought the aircraft would make it to India.

It was a good distance away. But Saudi Arabia, the most logical place to land, was out of bounds, and as Breanna had argued, if the plane could make it as far as Kuwait, it would make it to India as well.

Of course, by that logic, if it stayed in the air another ten seconds, it would fly for the rest of the week. She'd volunteered to try Diego Garcia, but he ruled that out.

Dog hooked into Dreamland Command and told them he wanted to arrange a landing in India. Major Catsman switched him over to Jed Barclay, who was at the White

House. Jed's face came up on the screen, a little pastier than normal.

'Jed, we need an emergency landing in India.'

'I heard, Colonel. The request has already been made and approved.'

'Thanks.'

'Good luck.'

Someone behind Jed started to say something, but Jed cut the connection.

Washington, D.C.
10 November
1658

'Bastian – get over to Captain Gale's ship,' said Balboa. 'Render all necessary assistance to him . . . Bastian? Bastian?'

'Why isn't he answering?' asked the Secretary of State.

'I killed the connection,' said Jed.

Balboa exploded. 'What the hell did you do that for? What the hell are you doing?'

'We're not here to run the mission for them,' said Jed. 'I'm strictly observing and facilitating.'

'You are just an aide,' snapped Balboa. 'You carry my orders out.'

'I'm the assistant National Security Advisor for Technology,' said Jed. 'And I am responsible for interfacing with Dreamland.'

'This isn't a Dreamland mission. Get them back,' said Balboa.

'Get them back, son,' said Hartman.

Jed stood up. 'No.'

Balboa turned to the lieutenant. 'Get them back.'

'Sir, I'm sorry, but for security purposes Mr Barclay has to authorize the connection. The computer checks his voice pattern as well as his passwords. If he doesn't do it himself, it doesn't happen.'

Secretary Hartman took hold of Jed's arm. 'Come on now, Jed, be a good boy and do as you're told.'

'Get bent,' said Jed, starting out of the room.

Hartman grabbed him by the shirt outside in the corridor.

'Jed, you and I both know that you want to do as I say,' Hartman said. 'Now just calm down. You can't afford another screwup.'

You can say that again, thought Jed, twisting away.

Diego Garcia
0400

Mack Smith stepped back from the communications console in the Dreamland Command trailer, walking a few steps toward the center conference area and then walking back. Now that he could walk – and he could, though his muscles were stiff and sore and his back ached and his neck seemed ridiculously stiff – now that he could walk he wanted to be out there where the action was, not sitting here in the stinking trailer trying to figure out what was going on from the radio and the lousy sitrep display.

If he were out there, he'd be coordinating the aircraft

better. They needed an aircraft coordinator in the *Abner Read,* directing the Megafortresses and the Flighthawks, and everything else, for that matter.

If they had, they probably wouldn't have lost the Osprey.

What he really wanted to do was be at the stick of an F-22, taking the MiGs down, two at a time.

Give Starship some points, though – the kid had nailed half the Yemen Air Force. Of course, he hadn't seen the MiG that nearly tore the Megafortress in two. That's what came from having Zen teach these kids how to fly.

Not that he had anything against Zen. He owed him a lot.

Did he, though? What had Zen done except be a jerk?

Well, he owed him that, then.

Mack sat down at the console. The *Abner Read* had been struck by a missile.

'Damn it,' he said. 'I ought to be there. I could have shot those damn things down.'

Aboard the *Abner Read*
0102

The first report was not good. The missile had hit the hangar area, igniting the fuel there.

The next report was worse. A secondary explosion had ripped through part of the hull. They were taking on water and had to close down one of the sections below, even though there were men inside.

Most likely the men were dead, but there was no way to know.

The *Abner Read* listed toward starboard two or three degrees, and her bow had started to lift. Storm saw from the damage control graphic on the bridge hologram that a hatch to the compartment remained open. He pushed the sleeves of his shirt up, picturing the sailors there, then moved forward to the weapons bay. He punched the code, but rather than the petty officer he expected to pick up, he found himself talking to a young sailor, Tommy Hall. He knew Hall a little better than the seaman would have wished – two days before they sailed, the boatswain's mate second class had been brought before him for discipline.

'Tommy, I need you to go to the engineering shop and find the emergency response team,' Storm told him. 'They're out of communication. Direct them to dog the hatch there, son. If they are not in sight, you have to do it yourself. You need to secure it, and you need to do it right now.'

'Sir, there's water on the deck here, a foot of water.'

Storm realized the situation was worse than he'd thought.

'Yes, I understand,' he said calmly. 'Go and dog the hatch while it can still be closed.'

'I'm going to try, sir.'

'No, son, you're going to do it. I know you're going to do it, because I'm counting on you. You're going to close that hatch and you're going to save our ship.'

There was no answer. Storm felt the ship lurch; the list was getting worse.

A firefighting team reported that they were tackling a fire behind the main exhaust. The lights flickered, but came back on strong.

Storm looked at the hologram. If they didn't close off

the compartment, the fuel ballast tanks and main diesel generator would be flooded. The damage done by the missile and the secondary explosion made it impossible to seal those compartments directly.

If he were the sailor, would he close the hatch, knowing his friends were inside? Even if he were sure they were dead? Even if he knew his own life depended on it?

Storm resisted the temptation to run down himself and secure the hatch. His place was here, and besides, he knew he'd never make it in time.

Jennifer helped the corpsman carry the injured petty officer out of Tac into a small space used as an electrical shop. The corpsman checked the bandage she had used to stanch the bleeding from the man's neck.

'You did a good job, miss,' said the corpsman, getting up.

'He'll live?'

'I don't know,' said the sailor honestly. 'If we abandon ship, I just don't know.'

'Are we abandoning ship?'

The man winced. 'We've been hit pretty bad, and we're taking on water. But it's the captain's decision.'

The voice was weak and punctuated by sobs.

'I heard screaming,' it said.

'Did you secure the hatch?'

'Yes, sir.'

'Good work, Tommy. Secure the door to the compartment. Tighten it down, and come up here to the bridge.'

'But –'

'I need you up here right away,' added Storm. 'Can you get up here?'

'I'll try, sir.'

'No, son, you come up here now because I need you, and because you're going to help save our ship. You're going to come here and save some lives.'

'Yes, sir, I am,' said the young man, just firmly enough to convince Storm that he would.

He glanced at the hologram, but already sensed that the ship had stopped settling. They were going to make it – but there was a hell of a lot of work to do.

Aboard the *Wisconsin*
0102

Zen took *Hawk One* toward the Shark Boat, running at the craft from the east. There were two smaller craft tracking behind it – pirates chasing it off, or at least that was what it looked like.

'English, look at this screen and tell me what you see,' said Zen, authorizing the feed from the Flighthawk's infrared.

'Well, if I didn't know any better,' the ensign replied, 'I'd say it was a Shark Boat running away from a battle. But that's impossible.'

'Why?'

'For one thing, even if they had no weapons aboard, the Shark Boat could just turn around and run over them,' said Ensign English. 'Besides, there is no way that anyone working for Storm is going to run away from battle. The crews on those Shark Boats were handpicked, especially the captains. They'll fight to the bitter end.'

'*Wisconsin,* this is Flighthawk leader. I have a strange situation I want to sort out. Can you reach the Shark Boat?'

'Negative,' said Dog. 'Danny is going out to talk to him.'

'Where is Danny?'

'Stand by.'

The line clicked twice, and Danny Freah's voice exploded in Zen's ear.

'Something's going on with that Shark Boat,' he said. 'He's going out into the open water – I think he's running from us.'

'I'll take a pass and put some shots across his bow.'

'Hold on,' said Dog. 'The control buoy for Piranha was hit in the gun battle. We're going to have to drop another buoy or we'll lose it. Danny – can you wait five minutes, or is time critical?'

'Five minutes,' repeated Danny. 'That's OK. Yeah, all right, we need the submarine pen checked out, and the probe should go in ahead of the divers.'

'All right. Give us five minutes,' said Dog.

'Flighthawk leader,' said Zen, agreeing.

Gulf of Aden
0105

'Two of our boats are following us, Commander,' said Saed. 'Should we stop for them?'

Ali stared into the blackness before him. The *Ark Royal* was roughly sixty miles away.

Habib had made a wondrous discovery – according to the computer, there were two American missiles aboard the ship, Harpoon missiles. Ali had not worked with the missiles himself; the Italian Navy's standard antiship missile was the Otomat, a more limited weapon. The Otomat's accuracy and effective range were affected by the radar capabilities, which limited its over-the-horizon range to roughly twenty-five miles. Ali was not sure what the range of the Harpoons would be, or whether the ship's low profile meant the reach of its radar wasn't as good.

It was all academic at the moment – Habib had not yet figured out how to use the weapon.

Better to simply take the ship into the side of the aircraft carrier and be done with it, Ali thought. Surely that was what God intended – the British would not fire on an American vessel. He would run close to it, launch the torpedoes from the forward hull tubes – those, at least, had a standard NATO command interface – and then ram the British ship, commending his soul to God.

Sixty miles – given their present speed as well as the aircraft carrier's toward them. It would be over in a half hour, perhaps less.

And then he would join his son Abu, finally at rest. Was it a sin to think of his son when God's sword was in his hand?

'Commander, should we stop for our men?'

'It serves no purpose,' said Ali. 'Keep on the present course, as fast as you can possibly go.'

* * *

They were gaining on the Shark Boat, but very slowly. Danny's fuel gauge showed he was below a quarter tank; it was very possible he would run out of fuel before they reached it.

'Colonel, if the pirates hijacked the Shark Boat, we should just blow it out of the water,' said Danny.

'I don't disagree,' said Dog over the Dreamland frequency. 'But we're out of Harpoons. We have no more weapons aboard.'

'What about the *Abner Read*?'

'I have to check their status, but it wasn't good a few minutes ago. They're fighting to save their ship.'

'I have bullets,' said Zen. 'I'll turn them into Swiss cheese if I have to.'

'Slow them down, so we can get a boarding party on,' said Danny. 'We'll retake the ship.'

'I think that's going to be too risky, Danny,' said Dog.

'If you shoot up the ship, our people on it will die. There were five men aboard when the search parties left to search the area where the Osprey went down.'

'I don't know if it makes sense to risk your lives to save people who already might be dead,' said Dog.

Aboard the *Abner Read*
0110

When Jennifer made her way back to the Werewolf station, she found that *Werewolf One* had been taken down by the explosion. But *Two* remained in its orbit to the west, still circling in the holding pattern she'd given it. Roughly twenty

476

minutes of fuel sat in its tanks, but there was no way it was going to get back down to the wrecked deck of the *Abner Read*. In the meantime, the datalink into the Dreamland circuit was offline; she isolated the problem and decided she could fix it – maybe – with a simple reboot of the computer controlling the communications link.

She pulled on a headset and listened, waiting for a chance to ask Storm about it.

The captain sounded as calm as ever – more so, actually. The men responded quickly, and she realized that they thought they were going to make it.

How much of the credit for that belonged to Storm? Some, at least. His calm demeanor as well as his orders had helped steady them during the worst crisis.

'Captain, I have two questions,' she said finally.

'Yes?'

Jennifer briefly explained the situation. 'We've temporarily lost the connection to the Dreamland system, but I think I can get it back simply by rebooting and doing a new initialization. There's a slight risk that it'll wipe out everything, including your radio.'

'How slight?'

'Two percent.'

'Do it. Next question?'

'*Werewolf Two* is nearly out of fuel. If it would be useful to survey the ship, I can fly it overhead and try and get the infrared directly. Otherwise, I should try and land where it can be recovered later.'

'Can you land it on the Shark Boat covering the operations?' Storm asked.

'Possibly. It depends on whether I can get the connection to the *Wisconsin*'s radar back or not. I have a pretty limited viewer aboard the helo itself.'

'Captain, *Shark Boat One* is the boat we're having trouble reaching,' said Eyes.

Before Storm could answer, someone else broke onto the line, talking about damage to the ship, and Storm began talking to him. Jennifer went ahead with her reboot; rather than bothering with a full diagnostic, she tried plugging into Danny ashore.

'Whiplash leader, this is Werewolf. What's your status?'

'We're ten or fifteen miles from shore, pursuing the Shark Boat,' said Danny, booming into her headset loud and clear. 'What's going there?'

'We've been heavily damaged, but we're still afloat,' she said. 'Are you saying *Shark Boat One* has been taken by the pirates?'

'We're not sure, but it looks that way.'

'I can get the Werewolf there,' she said. She hit the feed – she had voice communications, but no visuals on the Dreamland channel. The missile must have partially damaged the satellite antennas, which had been placed in the hangar area. 'I've lost the sitrep plot but I can follow the standard headings and interpret the GPS data.'

'Could you buzz the ship and take a look at what's going on?' he asked.

'Yes. Give me your GPS reading so I know where I'm going.'

'Stand by.'

Aboard the *Wisconsin*
0118

Zen checked on *Hawk Two* flying over the beach area in a preprogrammed mode, then went back to *Hawk One*, edging in the direction of *Shark Boat One* as the control buoy left *Wisconsin*'s bomb bay.

'In the water,' said Ensign English over the interphone. 'We're good to go.'

'Zen, let's take a look at that Shark Boat.'

'Flighthawk leader.'

Zen pushed *Hawk One* northwestward; he was roughly seven minutes from an intercept.

'Flighthawk leader, this is Werewolf.'

'Go ahead, Werewolf.'

'I'm headed toward the Shark Boat.'

Zen smiled. 'Race ya.'

Gulf of Aden
0120

Danny could see the low fantail of the ship three hundred yards away. They were finally closing in on them.

Dog was right; risking the lives of the others to take the ship didn't make sense.

Still, he was *boarding* that ship.

He flipped the visor into the infrared scan from the Flighthawk, but the aircraft was too far to give him a useful image.

'What do you think, Danny?' asked Dancer over the team communication circuit.

'When the Flighthawk gets here, we see if we can figure out who's where on board. Then maybe we have the Flighthawk get their attention. We hop on. I don't think there's many people there – I can't see anyone on the rear deck.'

'The rear deck would be pretty wet,' said Dancer. 'Going to be very slippery, even with no one shooting at us. Why do you think they haven't turned to fight?'

'I'm guessing they think we're on their side,' said Danny. 'But maybe they can't see us. Shit.'

'Shit?'

'Hang on.' Danny clicked back into the Dreamland frequency. 'Jen – is the Shark Boat still getting signals from the *Abner Read*?'

'I don't know.'

'Well, check. And have them cut if it is.'

'Will do – look, I'm about ten minutes from you.'

'We'll be here.'

Ali looked at the screen. It seemed too good to be true – the target box squared and locked on the aircraft carrier.

The screen blanked, then came back.

It had to be the target.

'You're sure it's the aircraft carrier?' he asked Habib.

'I think so, Commander.'

What did he have to lose?

The element of surprise. The *Ark Royal* showed no

sign that it knew they were there. Ali knew from experience that the Shark Boat could probably avoid radar detection until the very last minute.

If he was interpreting what he saw properly, the *Ark Royal* had two aircraft aloft. They were flying north of the aircraft carrier near Yemen. They would probably spot him and respond if he fired the Harpoons. The British had only two escorts with her; Ali knew one would be primarily for air defense and the other antisubmarine warfare. More than likely, the Shark Boat would be a match for both in a surface encounter – but only if she were manned by a crew familiar with her weapons.

The American weapons would not miss. It was worth the risk.

There was another aircraft twenty miles to the east, close to the coast, and other icons they couldn't make out. But it was irrelevant – he had to act now. God willed it.

'Fire,' he told Habib.

As his lieutenant reached for the button, the screen went blank again.

Zen slid the Flighthawk down toward the waves, riding the aircraft through two thousand feet, coming down to five hundred. The two speedboats were a hundred yards behind the Shark Boat; all three vessels were doing close to 52 knots.

The radar aboard the Shark Boat had not been activated. It had a limited antiaircraft capability – two banks of heat-seeking missiles that were essentially seagoing versions of the shoulder-launched Stinger were mounted in the superstructure fore and aft. As long as the radar was off and he got in without warning, he would be out of range before the system was activated.

What he would do on the second pass remained to be seen.

'Hold on, Danny, here we go,' Zen said, starting his run.

'*Ark Royal* hasn't picked them up, as far as I can tell,' said Dish. 'Hasn't picked us up, for that matter.'

'Let's talk to them,' said Dog.

McNamara raised the British ship on the radio. The seaman on the *Ark Royal* was confused as to who they were.

'This is EB-52 *Wisconsin*,' Dog explained. 'Part of Xray Pop Combined Action Group.'

'Are you the aircraft that was attacked by the Yemen planes?'

'Negative,' said Dog. 'We're pursuing an American craft that may have been taken over by pirates.'

'Pirates?'

There was a pause. A new voice came on the radio.

'This is Captain Joyce. To whom have I the pleasure of speaking?'

'Lieutenant Colonel Tecumseh Bastian, U.S. Air Force. There's an American vessel approaching you that we believe may have been hijacked by terrorists.' He checked the screen and read the coordinates.

'Impossible,' said the captain. 'I'm looking at the radar now. There's no ship there.'

'You're going to have to believe me. If the Shark Boat

has been hijacked, it's going to be very hostile. It may attempt to attack you.'

'A dark day for him if he tries.'

They were forty yards, maybe thirty, from the ship. Danny had slung one of the AK47s over his shoulder, and stuffed some extra magazines in his vest. He pulled himself up over the windscreen, steadying himself so he could jump onto the bow.

Suddenly he lurched forward, the boat slowing.

'Damn, we blew the engine,' said the sailor at the wheel. 'Damn.'

No matter what Habib tried, he couldn't get the screen from the external source back on the display. Ali looked up and recognized the shadow as it leapt above the bow: It was one of the tiny aircraft that had buzzed them the other day in the gulf.

Satan's Tail had survived the attack somehow. He went to the side of the bridge, looking into the darkness.

If God willed it, he would prefer, greatly prefer, battling the American.

But only if God willed it.

'Can you get the screen back?' he asked Habib.

'I can't seem to.'

'The missiles should have a direct mode,' Ali told him. 'A fail-safe.'

'It would require the radar, if it works at all.'

'They must already know we're here. Turn it on.'

* * *

Zen banked back toward the Shark Boat. There were people at the bow. As he approached, red lights began to flicker.

Automatic rifle fire, he realized after he passed.

'I'd say they're definitely hostile,' Zen told the others. 'Even for the Navy.'

'I can see the target, but the computer won't allow me to lock,' said Habib, continuing to work on the problem.

'This line shows where it will lock,' said Ali, guessing by comparing it to what he remembered – not from the Italian missile systems, but from some of the battle simulations. 'This shows where the target will detect us. Clever.'

'Five more miles, then, before we can launch.'

'Yes. Fire when you are able,' said Ali.

'The station controls other weapons,' added Habib, switching the panel into something entirely different. 'There's an air defense module.'

'Use it.'

Danny slammed his head against the dashboard of the speedboat. The Shark Boat was already pulling away.

'Werewolf inbound,' said one of the Marines in the boat.

Danny turned around. The heavy whomp of the twin-bladed aircraft resonated against the wood of the ship.

'Werewolf, I have a problem here,' said Danny.

'What's up?'

'I – Is your navigation gear back?'

'Negative, but I can see you with the infrared.'

'I want you to pick me up and drop me on the rear deck of the Shark Boat.'

Jennifer didn't answer.

'Jen?'

'I don't know if I can, Whiplash.'

'Sure you can. Hover overhead and I'll grab the skid. Hurry, we're only a couple hundred yards away.'

'Danny –'

'Come a little to your left,' he said, moving out toward the stern.

'What are you doing?' Eyes asked Jennifer, looking over her shoulder.

'We're taking back the Shark Boat,' she said, punching the code to override the safety protocol so the Werewolf would get close enough to Danny for him to grab it.

'I don't remember giving that order. Storm has to approve all action.'

Jennifer looked up at him. 'Does everyone who serves under him need orders to do the obvious?'

Eyes took a deep breath, then turned away.

Danny hadn't counted on the wash from the Werewolf's propellers. The gust pushed him down and to the side of the boat. He swung his hands madly, finally grabbing one of the skids. He thought it was too late, felt himself sailing to his right and braced himself for an unwelcome bath. But then he realized he'd managed to grab the skid of the helo.

'I hope this works,' he said to himself.

'I hope so too,' said Dancer, hearing him over the communications channel. 'We'll be right behind you.'

* * *

The Shark Boat had a 25mm cannon on its forward deck, a devastating weapon against the two small boats, and Zen zeroed his sights into it as he made his run head-on to the bow. The gun began to fire as Zen came in, filling the air in front of him with titanium. Zen bore down, moving just fast enough to avoid the slugs. His stream of bullets blew out the gun housing just as the system began to catch up to the Flighthawk.

He took a quick shot at the sloped bridge of the Shark Boat as he passed, then started to bank, aiming to sweep around and rake the deck. But as he did, the Flighthawk yelped – the Shark Boat had launched surface-to-air missiles.

Zen dished flares and hung on, too low and slow to outrun the SAMs. He pushed the Flighthawk hard right; one of the missiles sailed past the aircraft.

Another exploded beneath his right wing.

As the deck slowly inched in his direction, the pain in Danny's shoulders became unbearable. He felt his grip slipping.

'Hang on,' he said. 'Hang on.'

'I am,' said Dancer.

He hadn't been talking to her – or anyone – but her voice encouraged him, and there was the Shark Boat, right below him.

'Jen, I need to get down.'

'I can't get too much lower.'

He let go. The first thing he felt was relief in his shoulder. Then he hit the deck hard enough to rattle his teeth.

* * *

Ali looked at the screen.

'Another mile,' he told Habib. 'God will bring us victory.'

The Flighthawk spun in midair, going through two inverts before Zen could regain control.

Besides the other damage, the explosion had jammed the control surfaces of the wing, making it difficult to control. The weapons system was offline, as the aircraft was limited to its infrared camera.

'Danny, I'm going to get the other Flighthawk,' Zen said. 'It's going to take a bit.'

Danny didn't answer. Zen explained the situation to Dog; they'd have to double back toward the coast to get into range to take control of *Hawk Two*.

'I think I can put *Hawk One* into a wide orbit over the camp area and continue feeding infrared down. It's useless otherwise,' added Zen.

'All right. We're changing course.'

'What's going on with the *Ark Royal*?'

'I'm not sure they believe us,' said Dog. 'They have two Harriers and a helicopter in the air.'

'Is that enough to stop the Shark Boat?' Zen asked.

'It's never worked in the simulations,' said Ensign English. 'If they figure out how to fire the Harpoons, that carrier's going down. And I'll only give them even odds against the torpedoes.'

Danny saw a red oblong in front of him – the doorway to the ship's interior.

He pushed forward, trying to stand and grab his MP5 at

487

the same time. He made it nearly to the opening before he lost his balance completely and fell to the left, sliding down and landing on his back. A shadow, two shadows, loomed out of the space. The shadows had pipes in their hands.

Pirates with guns.

Danny pressed the trigger on his submachine gun. The first shadow jumped back, pulled off the side of the Shark Boat by some mysterious force. The second whirled on him, and turned from shadow to man: Danny's bullets severed his neck.

Jennifer pulled the Werewolf across the low-slung super-structure. Green lights blinked at her – muzzle flashes. She picked the aircraft's tail up and pressed the trigger to fire.

Nothing happened. She'd forgotten she was out of bullets.

'Son of a bitch,' she said.

The gunfire continued.

'Yeah – well, you can all go to hell,' she said, pushing the joystick to send the aircraft into the crowd of men firing at her.

The helicopter plowed into the forward section of the ship, exploding in a burst of flames. Ali turned away as shrapnel shattered the windscreen and the bulkhead of the bridge crumpled.

'Fire the Harpoon now!' he told Habib.

His lieutenant didn't answer. Ali turned and found him on the deck, eyes gaping to heaven.

'God wills that I do it myself,' said Ali. 'It is an honor.'

* * *

Danny threw himself inside.

A body lay on the deck, the man he'd killed.

Someone charged from the compartment ahead of him, firing a rifle. Danny shot back, even as the bullets hit his carbon-boron vest and smacked him back against the bulkhead.

Gunfire exploded around him. He lowered his rifle, then realized the cue in his helmet's visor indicated he was out of bullets.

He dropped the MP5 and swung up the AK47 he'd brought from the boat. After the submachine gun, the Russian weapon felt awkward and unbalanced. But its bullets put down the two men who had been firing at him. As they fell, Danny dropped to one knee and reloaded the MP5.

Something tapped him on the head. Danny looked up to find a terrorist holding a shotgun at his visor, grinning.

The man reared back to fire – then flew backward.

'I'm sure your armor's good,' said Dancer behind him. 'But I thought it better not to find out if it was *that* good.'

Abu wavered on the bicycle. He looked back at his father doubtfully.

'You can do it,' Ali told him. They were living in Naples, and it was a windless, perfect day. He held the boy gently. 'You can. Go.'

The seven-year-old hesitated, but then started to pedal.

'Go,' said Ali.

Quivering, Abu pedaled, his pushes becoming stronger and stronger.

Ali removed his hand and watched his son ride the bicycle

on his own. Abu glanced back. His confusion turned into a smile.

The happiest day of my life.

Ali pushed the memory away, pushed everything away. The cursor was locked on the aircraft. He pressed the button, then pressed the function key to lock the second missile.

The dashboard exploded. He pressed the button to fire anyway. Someone yelled, and he heard his son calling to him, singing his name, welcoming him with great joy to Paradise.

'I'm coming, Abu,' he said, rising from the console. 'I am here. The glory of God is everlasting.'

And then he slumped to the floor, killed by a bullet to the brain.

'Harpoon is away,' Dish told Dog.

'Zen, can you get it?' said Dog.

'I'm not close enough.'

'All right. Hang with me,' said Dog, throwing the Megafortress into a hard turn back to the north. The big aircraft groaned as somewhere over eight g's pounded her body. Dog felt the bladders in his pressure suit pressing at him; the world narrowed against the sides of his head, black unconsciousness threatening as gravity tried to extract her pound of flesh.

The Harpoon flew a bit over 500 miles an hour. The Megafortress could do close to 600, and he had several thousand feet of altitude he could use to his advantage. But the aircraft carrier was only ten miles away.

'I need an intercept angle on that Harpoon,' Dog told McNamara. 'And we need it real fast.'

'Working on it, Colonel.'

The course plugged into his screen. Dog compensated – he needed to get ahead of the missile and use the Stinger air mines.

'Get on the horn to the Brits and tell them not to shoot us down,' said Dog. 'They might miss the Harpoon, but we're a hell of a lot bigger target.'

The bodies lay where they fell – fifteen terrorists and five American sailors. The ship was theirs.

Danny pulled his helmet off and looked around the bridge. Blood was everywhere. What drove people to be so crazy?

'Tired, Captain?' asked Dancer.

'A little,' Danny admitted.

'That was something you did with that helicopter.'

'Stupid, huh?'

'Yeah. But we couldn't have gotten on the ship if those men had made it onto the deck. You took them out just in time. We owe you a beer.'

'Yeah, well, I owe you two. That shotgun would have penetrated the visor.'

'I intend on collecting,' said Dancer. She smiled at him. 'Let's see about getting this thing back. Dad said I was supposed to be home before midnight, and he's got a hell of a temper.'

Dog could see the *Ark Royal* in his windscreen as he pushed the stick of the Megafortress forward.

'Antiaircraft system is coming up,' said McNamara.

'Tell them we're friendly.'

'I keep telling them that.'

'They're still not locked on the Harpoon,' said Dish, disgusted.

'Stinger,' Dog told McNamara.

'Stinger ready. Seeking.'

Dog pushed the Megafortress down. To strike the Harpoon he had to get almost right in front of it and pull up abruptly. The missile skimmed along the ocean only a few feet above the waves; Dog basically had to walk his air mines right in front of it.

The ocean loomed in front of the windscreen. The altimeter in the heads-up display tumbled lower and lower – nine hundred feet, eight hundred, six hundred, five hundred . . .

Even in a small aircraft, pulling up from a power dive at precisely the right spot at very low altitude was not as easy as it looked. It pitted two different forces – gravity and aerodynamic lift – against each other. Often gravity won. In fact, gravity never really lost; engineers and pilots just figured out a way to hold it at arm's length.

Four hundred feet, three hundred . . .

The Megafortress screamed a proximity warning.

'Got it! Locked!' shouted McNamara.

'Fire,' said Dog calmly, pulling back on the stick.

The nose of the Megafortress scraped the waves and the rear of the aircraft rumbled – though whether from the sound of the tail smacking against the water or the air mines exploding in the face of the Harpoon missile, who could say? The B-52's toughness was legendary, and the *Wisconsin* added to the legend that day, pulling herself through the air like a pogo stick as the 215 pounds of explosives in the Harpoon detonated. Dog was so busy trying to hold the plane in the air that he didn't realize at first that the *Ark Royal* had begun firing her Goalkeeper antiaircraft weapon at them.

'ECMs,' he said, banking away.

Though adopted from the American Phalanx system, the British implementation fortunately was not yet as deadly as its cousin. The Megafortress managed to escape without serious harm.

'They're apologizing profusely,' said McNamara as the Megafortress cleared the cloud of bullets. 'They claim they didn't see us.'

'Tell them we'll send them the repair bill,' said Zen from the Flighthawk deck. 'And if they care to say thank-you for saving their butts, I know a base that would greatly appreciate a lifetime supply of British ale.'

X

Conspiracy Theories

White House
11 November 1997
1000

It wasn't hard for Jed to see the President – he and the entire cabinet wanted a briefing on the gulf situation. The trick was to talk to him alone.

Jed could feel Balboa and Hartman staring at him during the whole briefing. He expected them to mention that he had pulled the plug on them, but they didn't. The Secretary of State seemed subdued, and while Balboa blustered as usual, it was more about the combined group concept and how the Navy had shown the way once again. Jed knew that wasn't exactly true – but he did think the idea of the littoral warfare craft working together with cutting-edge technology, whether from Dreamland or somewhere else, was a good one, and had been validated by the mission.

The pirate operation that had supported terrorists in the Gulf of Aden had been smashed completely. The funds to overthrow the government in Eritrea and wreak more havoc in Somalia were gone, at least temporarily. Ethiopia had been chastised. Yemen declared that the air force had mutinied and 'appropriate steps' would be taken. The response was about the only comic relief the situation provided.

Unfortunately, as Hartman pointed out, a large number of people in the Horn of Africa were starving and weren't likely to get aid anytime soon. The UN didn't want to get involved; without them, organizations such as the Red Cross and UNICEF were also reluctant. No one in the room could blame them, not after what had happened in Mogadishu a few years before.

'The choices are never good choices in places like these,' said Freeman, but even he couldn't make a case for mounting a major relief effort in the Horn of Africa, especially not with the situation in China and Korea still incredibly tense.

'We'll have to deal with it, sooner or later,' said Martindale finally. 'I want a plan, at least.'

'We'll draw up something,' said Hartman.

Jed didn't say much as the discussion turned to India and Pakistan, the next exploding hot spot. He felt tired, ready for a vacation – a long one. Very long.

And he was about to get one.

'I wonder if I could talk to you, Mr President,' he said as the others started to leave the cabinet room.

'As a matter of fact, I'd like to talk to you, young Jed,' said Martindale. 'In my study.'

Freeman gave Jed a warning glance, but Jed ignored it. He'd made up his mind, and for better or worse, he was going to do the right thing.

That was all you could do in the end – the right thing as you saw it. Then face the consequences.

'So is it true that you told Balboa to get bent?' said the President as he sank into his leather chair.

'Um . . .'

Martindale laughed. 'I didn't think you had it in you, Jed. You surprise me every day.'

'I wrote a letter, sir.'

Jed reached into his jacket pocket and pulled out his resignation. Martindale smiled at the envelope but didn't open it. Instead he reached into his desk and took out a copy of the Sunday *Daily News.*

'Tell me about this photo,' said the President. 'It looks like a real work of art.'

'It is,' said Jed, and he explained what had happened.

'You don't know the entire story, I imagine,' said Martindale when Jed finished. 'You know how the photo came to be on the disk – it was in your folder with the others – but I'll bet you're wondering why just the *Daily News* printed it.'

'I am.'

'Ambassador Ford would like very much to be the Secretary of State.'

'I don't get it.'

'You gave the disk to one of Ford's assistants. He printed it out, and noticed the photo that hadn't been part of the presentation. He took it to the ambassador, who decided to give his friends at the *News* an exclusive. A favor that he can call in later.'

'Really?'

'That's his version. And I don't lie – about that.' Martindale folded his arms. 'Why were Hartman and

Balboa together in the Situation Room yesterday?'

'I was wondering that myself.'

'Admiral Balboa and the majority in the Senate are best friends. Which doesn't make them my enemy.' Martindale smiled. 'But I suppose it doesn't make them my friends, does it?'

'But Secretary Hartman?'

'Depending on whose story you believe, he's trying to keep tabs on the enemy or he's cultivating the other side because he wants to position himself for a primary.'

'Which is it?'

'I'm not sure, Jed. Both, probably. This is Washington. I suspect that the story line Mr Hartman was hoping for was that we played by the rules and actually achieved something important. A storyline I can't argue with. Especially since it worked. In this case, anyway.'

Martindale reached to his desk and took out a cigarette lighter. Jed watched as he burned the letter. 'I really can't afford to lose you, son.'

'But –'

'Ambassador Ford made it clear to his friends at the *News* that the picture was classified and that giving it out was a mistake.'

'That's not the truth.'

'Actually, it *is* the truth, it's just not the whole truth,' said Martindale. 'If you can't live with it, then yes, you can resign. And if you want to go public and tell everyone what you did, I can't stop you and I won't. But I wish you wouldn't. I don't think you should. I don't think it was particularly smart of you to fiddle around with those photos, but . . . Well, let's say we all make mistakes.' Martindale smiled, brushing the two curls of gray hair from his forehead. 'I wish yours were the sort of mistakes I made when I was your age, let me tell you.'

Jed thought that was supposed to be a compliment, but wasn't quite sure.

'Take a couple of days off, Jed, you deserve them.'

'Yes, sir.'

'And never, ever turn your laptop over to anyone,' said the President. He reached beneath the desk and pulled it up. 'Never. Not even the President. Not in Washington.'

Aboard the *Abner Read*,
Gulf of Aden
12 November 1997
0800

Storm made it out to the deck as the Osprey approached. The tug had tied up next to them, but the *Abner Read* was in no danger of sinking. Six brave men had died in the section of the ship that flooded after the missile hit; at least one gave his life so the others aboard could live.

Jennifer Gleason stood near the landing area, waiting for the Osprey to land.

'I have to say, I misjudged you,' Storm told her. 'You did a hell of a job for us. Sure you don't have any Navy blood in you?'

She flicked her short hair with her hand. 'Afraid not.'

Storm suddenly felt awkward and tongue-tied. He grabbed her hand. 'I hope to see you again.'

She shrugged. 'Maybe. Good luck.'

And then she was gone.

Diego Garcia
1200

'I think that's it for now,' said Dog, wrapping up the post-mission brief. 'We'll stand down for the next twenty-four hours, take a little breather, relax. One thing I have to mention – there are a number of difficult situations in Asia. We may not be going directly home.'

He looked around the small conference table in the Command trailer. He'd expected disappointment – but all he saw was fatigue.

'All right, then, I think that wraps it up,' he told them.

'Wait, Colonel, I had one thing I wanted to discuss.'

'What is it, Mack?'

'Naming the Megafortresses. You put me in charge of that, remember?'

'This is not the time to play the name game,' said Zen.

'I have an idea that I think everyone will agree with,' said Mack. 'Even Zen.'

'Right,' muttered Zen, just loud enough for everyone to hear.

Dog looked at Mack. He was glad the pilot could walk again – but still, he wished Mack didn't always have to be *Mack*.

'So? Want to hear it?' asked Mack.

'Come on, I'm starving,' said Breanna.

'Medal of Honor winners,' said Mack. 'We name the airplanes after Air Force Medal of Honor winners.'

Dog looked around the room. The other officers were speechless. It was an historic moment.

'I think it's a great idea Mack,' said Dog. 'There's only one problem.'

'What's that?'

'You thought of it.'

'I still don't get it.'

Everyone else started to laugh.

'Dismissed,' said Dog.

Starship found his way back to the chapel after lunch. The minister wasn't there, but the door was unlocked. He took a step inside. A Bible sat on a chair a few feet away.

Was it wrong to steal a Bible?

Starship hesitated, then took the book.

'Listen, I owe you an apology. You were right and I got mad at you. For getting on Mack's case. I was being a jerk. You were right,' Zen told Breanna, pushing the wheelchair along the path. 'I got way out of line.'

'I don't know,' said Bree. 'Everybody's saying how you made him walk again.'

'No, you were right. He didn't walk because of me. He would have walked sooner or later.'

'Maybe he needed a kick in the butt from you to get going.'

503

'Oh, he needs a kick in the butt. Definitely. But I was out of line. I've always been mad at him – it was when I got mad at you that I realized I was out of control.'

Should he tell her that he had almost hit her? He wanted to – but he couldn't. It was too terrible.

'I know it sucks,' she said, coming over. Her fingers on his neck tickled his whole body – or what still worked on his body.

Yeah, he thought. It sucks. Every day. That's the way it is.

That night, Zen lay in bed for more than an hour after Breanna had fallen asleep. A wind whipped up and a light rain tapped at the window; whether it was the sounds or the memory of the mission the day before or just too much coffee that afternoon, he couldn't sleep. He got up and made his way over to the Dreamland Command trailer, hoping to find a card game. But the Whiplash troopers had only just returned from Africa, and the only person there was Sergeant Liu. Things were so slow, he was practicing his tae kwon do while standing watch.

Liu let Zen use the computer tie-in to check his e-mail.

As it happened, he had only one item. It was from Dr Martha Geraldo, a psychiatrist who had led the Nerve Center project, an experiment that used brain waves to help control aircraft. Zen had been one of the subjects – and almost gone insane from the drugs and experimental procedures.

ZEN:
   I KNOW SOMEONE WHO'S WORKING ON A PROJECT

AT A RESEARCH HOSPITAL IN NEW YORK. IT INVOLVES
NERVE CELL REGENERATION. IT'S VERY – IT'S OUT ON
THE EDGE. BUT WHAT THEY THINK THEY COULD DO, OR
WHAT THEY WANT TO DO EVENTUALLY, IS REGENERATE
SPINAL CORDS. MAKE PEOPLE WALK AGAIN. THEY NEED
A CANDIDATE.

Zen wheeled back from the display.

When he leaned back to write a response, his fingers
trembled so badly that he had to stop twice, though all
he wrote was a simple sentence:

WHAT'S THE PHONE NUMBER?